A DAZZLING NEW WOMAN WRITER HAS
WRITTEN A HILARIOUSLY SEXY NOVEL . . .
"DELIGHTFUL, ROLLICKING, EROTIC!"
—*United Press International*

"A screaming-meemie of a randy, comic novel . . . a
marathon of stand-up wisecracking and bright and
varied comic darts . . . a cannonade of manic moments in
the sexual Armageddon of Eva Hathaway (alias Fanny
May Tingle, best-selling composer of hymns-for-all-
occasions) as she endures the Voice of Mother; the
high-handedness of God; the deadliness of Boston; advice
from her pals (Manhattan originals); marriage to
computer tycoon Martin; and pure rampaging *lust*—in her
losing battle to pry body (with soul attached) from the
virtuoso paws of a stunning tenor." —*Kirkus Reviews*

THE SECRET LIFE
OF EVA HATHAWAY

"A WITTY AND WICKED NOVEL THAT'S LIKE A
BREATH OF FRESH AIR . . . Eva plunges into the
1980s, poking fun at propriety, relationships, marriage,
neurotic Jewish men, uptight WASPs, children and just
about everything else." —*Richmond Times-Dispatch*

"FANTASTIC . . . A RACY ROMP BY A
MULTI-TALENTED AUTHOR who revels in puns and
luxuriates in sensuous sex scenes . . . has fun
manipulating her colorful cast of characters . . . and
keeps the reader laughing from beginning to end."
—*Cleveland Plain Dealer*

(For more bravos, cheers and whistles, please turn page . . .)

The
Secret Life of
Eva
Hathaway

Janice Weber

A SIGNET BOOK

NEW AMERICAN LIBRARY

To J.C.S.

PUBLISHER'S NOTE

This novel is a work of fiction. Names, characters, places, and incidents either are the product of the author's imagination or are used fictitiously, and any resemblance to actual persons, living or dead, events, or locales is entirely coincidental.

NAL BOOKS ARE AVAILABLE AT QUANTITY DISCOUNTS WHEN USED TO PROMOTE PRODUCTS OR SERVICES. FOR INFORMATION PLEASE WRITE TO PREMIUM MARKETING DIVISION, NEW AMERICAN LIBRARY, 1633 BROADWAY, NEW YORK, NEW YORK 10019.

This is an authorized reprint of a hardcover edition published in the United States of America by Donald I. Fine, Inc., and in Canada by Fitzhenry & Whiteside, Ltd.

SIGNET TRADEMARK REG. U.S. PAT. OFF. AND FOREIGN COUNTRIES
REGISTERED TRADEMARK—MARCA REGISTRADA
HECHO EN CHICAGO, U.S.A.

SIGNET, SIGNET CLASSIC, MENTOR, ONYX, PLUME, MERIDIAN AND NAL BOOKS are published by New American Library, 1633 Broadway, New York, New York 10019

First Signet Printing, November, 1986

1 2 3 4 5 6 7 8 9

PRINTED IN THE UNITED STATES OF AMERICA

1

I LOVE MY HUSBAND. The man married me when he didn't even have to. Then he set me up in a huge house to domesticate the kinks out of my system while he ran his computer company. In four years of marriage he's only raised his voice once, and that was when I pulled his ears in front of Most Distinguished Herr Hans Baumann, the president of a European computer company. But that was Martin's own fault. You see, every time he says "You don't understand," I don't care where we are or whom we're with, I yank his ears. It's a stupid expression and I'm trying to get Martin to stop using it.

Martin is a fine husband and a gentleman. He keeps himself reasonably clean and sober and he doesn't become belligerent over Veal Parmigiana four nights in a row. He will accompany me to church on Christmas and Easter. If I'm comatose when he rolls into bed, he will only try for, say, half a minute to wake me up. He is generous with his money and extremely tolerant of my friends, all of whom are male and most of whom have already asked me to marry them. Martin works tremendously hard and he's a computer genius, one of the most respected men in his field. I suppose he'll be a millionaire by the time he hits forty.

Now I am quite sure that, deep down, Martin loves me more than he does his computers. He might spend twenty hours per day with them, but they can't match socks and I know for a fact that I look much better in black than they do. I'm not complaining: in no way would I want Martin around twenty hours per day. It's just that the house gets pregnantly silent many an afternoon. Pregnantly silent! *A Freudian slip!* my mother would pounce in glee, *That proves it, Eva, time for children! Four to six, quick, before the eggs wither!* Hell, while we're at it let's chuck my mother-in-law into this baleful doomsday. *My only son!* Will Martin be the last to bear the Weaver name? (She hasn't yet forgiven me for remaining a Hathaway. Apparently "Eva Weaver" sounds euphonious and dignified to her.) I'm not about to go into a long discourse about children here. Some women are born with maternal instincts, others evolve them over a twenty-year period, like wrinkles, and others sprout them on the delivery table. Me, I don't like children unless they're nephews or nieces. Besides, everyone knows that women have children when they're either bored with marriage and/or annoyed with their husbands and wish to shock them into adulthood. I wouldn't do this to Martin. He has enough on his mind without learning how to change diapers. Something tells me he would never quite get the hang of it anyhow.

Although I do not commute to an office as my husband does, I do earn a living. I write hymns. No one believes what a remunerative career this is, but let me assure you, every church in the country needs fifty-two offertories and fifty-two choral anthems per year, to say nothing of special occasion deals for Missionary Week and Baptism Sunday and Lent. My biggest seller, *Child My Love,* was composed for Mother's Day and I've already bought Chuck, that's my mother, two fur coats with the royalties. The secret of my success is that I write easy tunes that sound not only grandiose but, if the occasion demands, stupendous, so that even a crew of four old maids and one bullhorn can't louse things up. Believe me, choir directors devour my anthems like manna from heaven. I can crank out one a week if I'm inspired. But I don't do it for money. Obviously I don't do it for fame since I use a pseudonym, Fanny May Tingle. I think she was a Puritan. No, I do it because that's my talent. It's been that way since I was thirteen. *Correction,* **my accountant would** interject, *sixteen.*

I met Martin through my accountant. Once a year for maybe five years, it was the biggest coincidence, I mean, he always had an appointment right smack after mine. He without fail would look at me so oddly that I finally called Jerry and asked who he was.

"That is Martin Weaver," Jerry told me.

"Why does he always look as if he's being audited?" I asked.

"My clients are rarely audited, and if they were, they would have nothing to worry about."

"That's good," I said. "You did some spectacular loopholing yesterday."

"What is the purpose of this call," Jerry interrupted, suddenly and speciously professional.

"Can I afford a BMW this year?"

"Ho ho," he chuckled, "guess who's selling a Bavaria."

"That guy with the glasses? Martin? How many miles? How much? Are you setting me up, mister?"

"Never," Jerry swore. "Here's his number."

I didn't fall for that one, no way. "He can call me if he's interested," I said. "Bye-bye."

It was getting on towards Easter and I had been working on an organ medley with a guy from Saint Barnabus downtown. He couldn't play worth shit. Soon he was phoning every hour begging me to leave more and more notes out, whining that his fingers were "too short." I deleted as much as possible until barely a melody was left but he still kept bugging me. Now he wanted everything slower. The phone rang again. This was the final straw. "Jesus Christ, Arnold," I snapped into the phone, "I've cut you down to two fingers and one toe!"

"Hello?" inquired an uncertain voice. "Is this Eva Hathaway?"

"Hold on," I snapped. I cleared my throat, then counted to five. "Helloooo?"

"Eva, this is Martin Weaver," the voice said. "I hope I haven't disturbed you."

"Not at all. I understand you have a car for sale."

"Yes, I do."

Funny, I hadn't heard anyone say "yes" in a long time. Always "yeah" or "yep" or "yo." I smiled; couth becomes a man. "What color is it?"

"Silver."

"I'll buy it." People who say "yes" usually take care of their possessions.

"Wouldn't you prefer a test drive?" Martin asked.

"Hey, come on," I said. "You want to sell me your car or take me out to dinner?" I never say things like that to men. I don't know what came over me. I guess I wanted to go out to dinner with Martin.

"I'd like to do both," he said. "Are you free Friday?"

"Nope, I've got an organ rehearsal with a monumental cretin."

"I see . . ." A pause. "All right. Then we'll arrange something when I return from Japan."

"What's in Japan?" I asked, furious with that flimflam Arnold.

"Spare parts for computers," Martin said. "Excuse me a moment." He clicked off and shortly returned. "May I call you again, Eva? I've got a long distance call here."

"Fine," I said. "Take good care of my car." I hung up and walked to my window overlooking Central Park. I was tired, tired of winter.

Martin did a terrible thing the year we were dating. He moved back to Boston. I don't care if every computer company in the world has its headquarters up there, it's a ludicrous town full of foul-mouthed delinquents and crypto-eggheads and jackasses who hate the New York Yankees. The trolleys never work and the place closes down at 10:00 P.M., Saturdays included. The blacks, whites, Puerto Ricans, Cubans, Irish, Indians, Greeks, Armenians, Italians, Portuguese, and students all hate each other. So what else is new. But in Boston each of these adversaries owns a car and drives accordingly. Two hundred years ago, a street was barely wide enough for Paul Revere and one horse; the same space now contains three cars, two drunks, and one meter maid in perpetual combat. And I detest Newbury Street. It's supposed to be Ralph Waldo Emerson's version of Fifth Avenue. It's a mess of faggoty barber shops and umbrella stores.

Martin didn't notice any of this, of course, because when he wasn't busy working he was down visiting me in New York. After six months he just gave me his BMW. As I had suspected, it was pristine but for one small dent on the front hood where he had clipped a low-flying crow at eighty-five miles an hour. "I have to pay for this car, Martin," I had insisted. "I can afford it, you know." Martin would hear nothing of it. He did, however, finagle me into driving to Boston the next weekend. Told you he was a sharp guy.

From the beginning, whether skiing or sailing or just walking, Martin looked out for me. He opened doors and neatly shut them again. He recognized good wine and knew which fork to use with oysters. Hey. the man had an innate class. He was also used to money, lots of it; I could tell that from his sheets and the way he ordered appetizers. Against the howls of my self-destructive streak I continued to see him for almost a year. *Bring him home,* my mother Chuck railed constantly. *I should meet the man.* Pfuiii! And wreck everything? The woman had to be joking. "Maybe next month," I told her from one February until the next. In the meantime I had two platinum records and put 20,000 miles on the Bavaria, most of them at illegal speeds on Connecticut highways.

One evening at Lutèce, Martin formally asked for my hand in marriage. There was no point in delaying the inevitable, so we ended up at the justice of the peace in Lenox, Massachusetts, one very cold winter afternoon four days later. Neither of us had ever married before so we weren't particularly nervous or excited; we envisioned marriage vows as something like the Boy Scout pledge, but with a girl. I wanted the ceremony performed on a hillside as the sun set magnificently over the Berkshires, so off we went, Martin and myself in my Bavaria, the justice following in his pickup truck and two off-duty state troopers tailgating as witnesses. Martin had promised them each a fifth of bourbon.

The justice had apparently drunk his fifth already and rammed into a snowdrift halfway up the hill, stalling our nuptial procession in midstream. "Well, I guess this is it," Martin said. "Everybody out."

"What, we're getting married here in the middle of someone's driveway?" I exclaimed. "No way." I was beginning to think maybe I should have invited Chuck.

Directly behind us one of the state troopers had spun his wheels and T-boned into a birch tree. Now we could go neither forward nor backward. There was nothing else to do as we waited for a tow but get married. Everyone piled into a ditch, out of the wind, swearing at the branches snapping in our faces.

"You want the long or the short version?" the justice of the peace asked, his nose tumescing by the minute.

"Short," barked one of the troopers. "It's open season and we could all be shot."

"Dearlybelovedwearegatheredheretogethertojoin—"

"Martin Weaver," said Martin, pointing to a handwritten entry, "right there."

"MartinWeaves," sneezed the justice, "andElsaHath—"

"Eva Hathaway." Martin corrected, getting annoyed. "Over there, the next line."

"In ho-o-oo-o-lo-li-ly m-m-matri—"

The justice's teeth were chattering so fiercely I thought he would bite his tongue off. One of the troopers handed him a flask. The justice kept reading as he drank, holding his Bible high overhead, squinting in the dim sunset. "Do you Martin take Eva to be your wife, for better or worse, for richer, poor, in sickness and in health, till death do you part?"

"I do," Martin croaked in a strange, hoarse voice. I think he was getting nervous.

The justice took a long swig. "Do you Eva take Martin to be your lawful wedded husband, in sickness and healthy. better and worse, in rich, poorness, death do you apart."

"I'll try," I said. I hate making false promises.

The justice's nose had turned a hideous blue, like one of those contraptions on a clown's face. One was tempted to squeeze it and see if it honked. "Does any man here contest this marriage if so speak now or hold your peace forever, till death do you part." Not even a pause. This guy was determined to marry us, no matter what.

A siren and a flashing red light began mewling slowly up the dirt road. Time was growing short. "I now pronounce you man and wife," the justice gasped, relievedly clawing his way out of the ditch towards the warm, bullet-proof squad car. "You may kiss the bride," he shouted over his shoulder.

Martin leaned over to kiss me. His mustache was encased in ice and threatened to cut my upper lip.

"Hey, where's my ring?" I said indignantly. "You forgot my ring, pal," I yelled at the justice. Damn him, he had really screwed this up.

"Shh, darling, we'll do that ourselves," Martin said, trying to soothe me. The red flashers burst rhythmically over his face and he looked enormously happy. We were alone in the ditch. "My beautiful wife," he murmured.

"Hey, you two," one of the troopers called, "help tow this wreck out of the bushes."

We scrambled up to the squad car and began shoving for a solid half hour. By the time we were done it was pitch black and I had forgotten to take pictures.

First thing back at the motel I grabbed the telephone. No one would believe we had gotten married except Chuck. She nearly screamed with triumph when I broke the news, hey, it was a real squeaker but she had actually married off all her daughters before they hit thirty. My father didn't offer much verbal commentary besides "You're kidding, Eva." He had used the same tone of voice when I once told him I was joining the army. Martin's parents were even less effusive. Mr. Weaver kept sputtering "I don't believe it" and my mother-in-law didn't say a word. We thought she had fainted at such unspeakable catastrophe: I had shattered a seven-generation chain of Radcliffe-Harvard unions. Nor were my brothers and sisters thrilled. They didn't think Martin could handle me.

Finally I put down the phone. "Am I missing something or am I paranoid?" I asked my husband.

Martin didn't hear me. He was struggling to light a fire in our bridal suite. I was about to point out that those green logs would no sooner ignite than would the snow outside but I did not want to become a nagging wife before this marriage was even legally consummated. So I let Martin fizzle himself down to two matches before I began shredding the telephone book and handing him a few pages.

A total absence of hymens induced a mellow, understated wedding night. In fact it already seemed like our tenth anniversary. I do recall, however, a mortal terror racing through me just as the last of the Yellow Pages flickered out and Martin became a bulky shadow: this man was counting on remaining my husband for life. *Now you did it,* some inner voice, probably Chuck's, scoffed.

Martin sneezed. "We did it, baby." he whispered. Perhaps he had overheard the voice.

"We did it, all right," I answered. "And I'm glad." Soon we were asleep.

2

I HAVE ALWAYS preferred men. I mean, chemically speaking, ladies do nothing for me. Of course I love my sisters and my mother. I admire Mother Teresa types. But I have never had girlfriends. Let's face it, I have other things on my mind besides lipstick and movie stars. I also detest shopping for clothes. We've already been through children. I don't know how to play bridge and as far as I'm concerned, if you've got a sheet over the window and a cushion on the floor, a room is interior decorated.

I guess I was a tomboy. I do recall spending a large portion of my childhood in trees, alone, poised amid the birds and bees. Nights I'd either read or watch the Yankees. They were hot stuff in those days, believe me. In the lull periods I would beat up my brothers. Actually the point I'm trying to make is that I am accustomed to solitude. I am not one of those types who will wake up one midlife morning screaming, "Oh my God! I'm all alone!" Hey, that's the deal, that's always been the deal, like rain on vacations.

Now many people enter into matrimony hoping against hope that the other guy is going to plug all the leaks and somehow make life watertight. Such persons have obviously not spent their formative years in trees observing the glazed, pouting faces of their relatives below. I, on the other hand, married with my eyes open. No one was going to convince me that Martin would now take an interest in hymnals or ratatouille. Come on, with him it's computers, period. At least the man was tied up with something productive. He created his company long before he met me and I would be a fool to butt in.

In fact one of the reasons we get along so well is that Martin doesn't butt in where he doesn't belong, either. I'm talking about my friends Richard and Lionel, who call and visit just as they did before I was married. I don't sleep with them anymore, but they bring news and salami from New York and we can talk for hours about pasta, choirs, and other items of only niddering interest to Martin, who would come home from work, have dinner with us, then retire to the den with his briefcase. Unless he needed pencils or something, Martin would leave us alone for the evening; he knows we arty types are all bark and no bite.

The only people my visitors seem to bother are my neighbors and my mother. I guess they'd bother my mother-in-law, Ruth, too, but she doesn't know about them. The last couple of times Richard came to Boston, for instance, Martin was in Houston. I took special pains to introduce Richard to whomever was staring accusingly at us. You should have seen the look on my neighbor Harry's face when I said, "Richard's keeping me company until Martin gets back." That's another reason I hate Boston. You don't think anyone in Manhattan would respond, "Does your husband know about this?"

My premarital associations make my mother very uneasy also. Chuck keeps bugging me to find girlfriends. Naturally I ignore this futile request along with the several hundred others on her list like Get a permanent, Get pregnant, Get Martin new glasses, etc. etc. *What kind of marriage is this,* she rails piteously, *I never heard of such a thing.* I tell her either my friends come to Boston or I get myself an apartment back in the city. That cools her jets. Incidentally, I think my mother has one hell of a nerve castigating my style when she herself has done little for the past forty years but chisel my father down to one percent of his former manhood. By sheer negative example she has shown her children what constitutes a humane marriage. I could never take the criticism of such a person seriously.

But my mother loves inflating innocuous tiddlywinks

into crises. Look, it's not as if I had gentleman callers every weekend. I'm a married woman now. I hold it down to maybe one visitor every six weeks, when I'm in a rut and really itchy for New York. Martin knows this is my little escape valve. Otherwise he'd be receiving the hot air himself, of course.

I entertained no boyfriends at all the first year we were married. Somehow it seemed improper, as if I had insincerely burned all bridges behind me. Instead I busied myself making martinis and millions of canapés for Martin's business associates, all engineers, all oddballs. They're thirty years out of sync with reality. Any of these guys could have stepped straight out of the original *Invasion of the Body Snatchers*. And they drink and smoke like mad in order to put a little poop into those crew cuts.

What finally got me, I guess, was their dinner conversation. No matter how I tried to start one, it always ended up with bytes and readouts and transistors. Martin, I must confess, did not assist me in these social matters. Eventually I would say less and less during the course of a meal—please, a tableful of hornrimmed glasses would stultify the tongue of a Spanish whore. Then one evening, near our first anniversary, a Mr. Itsuo Tagahashi from Tokyo mistook me for the maid.

"Come to the Ritz," he whispered. "I wait for you there."

"Forget it, buster," I retorted. "The Ritz is a pretentious flophouse." He still thought I was the maid.

Martin ambled into the kitchen as Tagahashi was trying to pinch my ass. Stuck with a trayful of cocktails, I was hardly in a position to retaliate.

"Your friend thinks I'm the maid," I snapped. "Maybe I am." I shoved the tray at Martin and stomped into my office. With quaking fingers I dialed Richard in New York. Instead of a ring I got a nasal robot instructing me to dial again, this time with a "1" before the area code. That's the fubar Boston phone system for you, always slipping these ones and zeroes before numbers for no reason so you get confused and dial Washington by mistake. It's happened to me many times.

"Richard," I gurgled.

"Hi babe," he said. "How's Beantown?"

"Just splendid, great. Can you get up here right away?"

"What, you and Martin having problems?" inquired Richard, not quite masking his delight under a pall of concern.

"I can't talk. Take the shuttle and I'll pick you up." Richard can take off without notice because he runs his own greeting card business. I met him eight years ago at a hymnbook convention in Detroit. Since then he has illustrated all of my sheet music.

"I'll take the last plane," he said. "Have a bit of work up there anyhow."

"Can you bring a few bagels? Poppy seed."

"No problem."

Composure restored, I returned to the living room. There sat Martin, Tagahashi, and two other space invaders all hunched over a dish of peanuts. They looked pathetic, like a bunch of orphaned pups. Ah, if only their mothers could see them now.

Martin leapt to his feet. "Itsuo is very sorry," he apologized by proxy. "Your green cocktail apron confused him."

"Never mind. Happens all the time," I said, forgiving him, and why not: Richard would be arriving in two hours. I floated towards the door. "Sorry I can't stay, gentlemen," I announced serenely as they took their places at the table, "I must fetch someone at the airport."

"Oh?" Martin excused himself, following me to the bathroom. "Is your mother coming up?" I don't wash my face for everyone.

"Nope. Richard is."

"Richard Weintraub?" coughed Martin. "That nerd? What for?"

"Because I asked him," I said, reaching for my makeup case. "He never mistakes me for a maid."

Martin said nothing until I got to the lipstick. "It will be good for you to see him. Would you like a ride to the airport?"

"No, thank you." I lavished Richard's favorite perfume on my neck. "I'll follow the signs. Dessert's in the refrigerator. Don't try to eat it with a fork."

In a superhuman effort to avoid the potholes on the expressway I flew by the Callahan Tunnel exit and got off several miles downstream, near the dockyard, only to find there was no access back onto the expressway. That's another popular Boston road trick, especially in high crime areas. My little silver Bavaria looked excruciatingly alien amid the barren piers. Don't ask how I got out of there without a brick through the windshield. I just kept my foot on the accelerator and headed towards the airplanes.

Aside from a janitor, Richard was the only biped left at the terminal. "Richard, you look wonderful," I said, ignoring my former sweetheart's hairline, or should I say his progressively denuded forehead. Nonetheless, Richard remained a most attractive man. He's the only blond who ever got through to me; I think it was the flaring nostrils.

"You look good, too," he said, not without melancholy. "Marriage must agree with you." An aroma of bagels slowly pervaded my car.

"It's all right," I said, violently overcome with longing for celibacy.

Suddenly a huge orange bomb swung in front, cutting me off. "You fuckinassholeshitbrain," I shouted out the window as we swerved by on the right. "Sorry," I muttered to Richard, "guess I'm a little hyper at seeing you again."

"What a compliment," Richard said, thrashing surreptitiously for his seat belt. He slowly retrieved a few bagels from the floor. "Interesting factories here. What part of town are we in?"

"Beats me," I said. "I took a wrong turn off the expressway." Only in Boston are the exit signs located three hundred feet down the turnoff ramp. Now we were locked into some midtown artery probably sealed off up to the Canadian border.

We got home around one in the morning. Martin and his cohorts were all in the den fiddling with transistors.

"Hello, Richard," said Martin, shaking hands. "Good to see you again." My husband detests Richard but he's a perfect host. It's a family tradition dating back to Plymouth Rock.

"Hi, Mart," Richard responded. " Keeping busy, I

see." Richard has had a psychopathic hatred of computers since he got an electric bill for fifty thousand dollars. He also hates men who succeed in marrying me.

"Come with me, Richard," I said, leading him to the kitchen, "let's have a few of those bagels."

Countless gravy-shellacked dishes shielded the counters from the naked eye. It looked as if Martin & Co. had been fingerpainting with my Beef Stroganoff. Every last glass in the house, each now half full of liquid, sparkled amid the cold yellow noodles. I knew without looking that Martin had neatly replaced the empty casserole in the oven, forgetting to turn the heat off.

I looked ruefully at Richard. "It's his butler's fault."

Richard remained dumb: his whole apartment could easily fit into my kitchen. "I hope you have a dishwasher," he mustered at last. I sat him down with a couple beers and began cleaning up. Filthy kitchens really bother me. I do not consider myself neurotic about this either: we all know Freud coined the phrase "anal compulsive" because he was a slob and wished to legitimize his behavior at the expense of tidy individuals.

"Where'd you get that apron, Eva?" Richard asked.

"Atlanta," I said, pulling open a drawer. "Look, it has a matching cap. Like it?"

Richard came over to the sink. "I like everything you do. Come back to New York with me. You don't belong here."

As he touched my waist my guts flared. God! "Cut it out, Rich," I said. "I'm a putzfrau now."

Richard sat down and drank more beer. "That depresses me."

"So get up and start drying. Assuage your grief with domestic toil."

"Sounds like one of your hymns," Richard said glumly. He took a towel anyhow. "You've got a beautiful place. Martin must be doing very well."

"He works like a dog. I barely see him."

"No wonder you're still married," Richard laughed peevishly.

"I don't completely understand that remark," I lied as

we moved over to the bar. Our drinks mixed, Richard raised his glass for a toast.

"Happy anniversary," he said. "It's Wednesday, isn't it?" I nodded as we clinked glasses. "You two still sleeping together?" Previous lovers are interested in these things.

"Of course," I assured him, neglecting to add that I had interpreted "sleeping" literally. Hey, that's how it goes. I can no longer wait up until three in the morning hoping to sight an erection within the skivvies. The last time Martin came to bed before midnight was when a fire truck smashed into a power station, killing the electricity for ten hours. He couldn't run his programs, he couldn't read by flashlight, he couldn't even find his way to the bathroom. Obviously this was no prelude to connubial bliss. No great loss, I figure. Come on, orgasms are a dime a dozen. If you do them yourself, that is.

"You're quiet all of a sudden," Richard said, watching me.

"Just thinking," I said with a sigh. "So tell me about your latest project."

Richard talked for about half an hour, long enough for Martin & Co. to raid the kitchen again, annihilating every last bagel.

3

OLD MAIDS DIE HARD. Only near my second anniversary did I finally get used to another body in my bed. I also began referring to Martin in public as "my husband" instead of "Mr. Weaver." I started making suppers that could retain their original composition until at least eleven at night. I no longer asked Martin to wash the dishes or desist rolling his dirty socks into tight little balls. Hey, my mother has been bitching at my father to sit up straight every single day for forty years now. He slouches worse than ever.

In all fairness I must say that Martin had learned to put up with an awful lot himself. Richard, for instance. My shoe collection. My cold fingers on his sweetly slumbering testicles. Lionel calling in tears at midnight. My hymns. And much more, I'm sure, had Martin brought such to my attention. But no, he seemed quite content with the way this little risk in a ditch had worked out. For our anniversary he gave me a silver fox coat. He knows I abhor brown.

His company was doing phenomenally well. Martin was spending more and more time on the road, no, in the air, which is why he was always jetlagged. I learned during that year of marriage to let Martin go on these little trips alone. Take it from me, impotence means being stuck in a hotel room waiting for your husband to get out of conference and take you to dinner. I composed two of my best numbers that year while Martin was in Taiwan.

I joined the Boston Y and started swimming again. Simply getting there soon became one of my major pastimes—crap, a brief trolley ride in this town eats up half a day. By the time I would arrive at the pool, my clogged rage was good for an extra forty laps. Eventually I began using the gym and the weight room; sweat seemed more cathartic than chlorine. I'd whip around the track, peer down at the bodies on the basketball courts below, and somehow forget about that miserable trolley ride home. You see, there are substantial numbers of gorgeous men at this and at all Y's. It's about the only place you can let your tongue hang out and not seem lecherous. I have been sightseeing at Y's for years. No one has ever bothered me because I'm very discreet; I've learned from experience that the merest wink can be misinterpreted. Chuck, of course, has always accused me of being a flirt. Wrong. I can look in a man's eyes and immediately know if he's any good in bed. I can't help it if he's doing the same thing to me.

Muscles and sinews notwithstanding, that year I put sex out of my mind entirely. It was no longer necessary or useful. Married women floated chastely above such crudity, like the angels; we were out of the rat race now. Thank God Martin seemed to prefer snuggling nowadays. I think the decimation of our sexual fervor was a natural by-product of living together. Come on, it's awfully hard to become aroused by a man who incessantly balls his dirty socks into tight little globes and whips them under the nightstand. Likewise it must be difficult to ravish a woman who recites hymns in her sleep. Had my husband been more insistent, we might have had problems.

But Martin is an extraordinarily placid man; he did not marry me to quench the insatiable blaze in his loins. It's more like a pilot light. That second year of our marriage I finally figured out why: parental example. His mother and father, Ruth and Edmund Weaver, have a marriage like you see on 1950s television shows: surgically pristine kitchens, the local country club, even separate beds. In his entire life I doubt Martin has ever seen his mother in hair curlers or even a nightgown. The first time I unleashed Chuck on him he was speechless for a week. Actually it was pathetic. He kept suggesting that she had an inner ear—not a drinking—problem.

It must have been odd growing up in a nonviolent environment. I cannot imagine a youth without broken dishes, spinning liquor bottles, shrieks, maledictions, and a mother perpetually sobbing on the couch. Chuck shouldn't have had six kids, that's all. I think the last three were mistakes (I came second). My father still insists that all seven of us were mistakes, but he includes my mother. We children could never figure out why they never divorced. I think my mother didn't want to be stuck with six kids and no scapegoat.

Contrast this with the Weavers: one boy. one girl, one nanny, and a perfect mother. Personally I think Mr. Weaver has had a mistress since Day One but that's only my intuition. He calls his wife "darling" a little too often. I remember our first dinner together. With great punctiliousness the maid served escarole soup as Martin and Mr. Weaver began discussing circuit boards. This went on for forty minutes and three courses and not once did Mrs. Weaver cease beaming at her splendid menfolk. Every time I tried to engage her in a discussion about, say, roast beef, she would answer in monosyllables and return her attention to Pride (Edmund) and Joy (Martin). What could I do but drink and glare at the baboon affiliated with me. Hey, when you eat dinner you talk about general topics of interest to all. Martin received a severe tonguelashing on the way home. His subsequent behavior has improved only marginally because he keeps inviting engineers over to dinner. All of them are divorced. By my second anniversary I was beginning to understand why.

Now I would not want to give the impression that my relationship with Martin was petering out. I prefer to think of it as "stabilizing"—each does his or her business, meets for dinner, talks about it, and goes to bed. It's not as boring as it sounds. Every few days a catastrophe tends to spice up the conversation. Either a plant in Hong Kong would blow up or, for my contribution, someone would slash my tires or try to alter the lyrics to my latest anthem.

Then there was always some foreigner dropping in unexpectedly. Martin loved to bring them home because my martinis and rib roast had become legendary in engineering circles. I don't mind. Some of my greatest tunes have come to me as I've stood mincing onions.

I must say I am a splendid cook. It's all tied up with a death wish—you know, fruits of your labors destroyed before your very eyes, etc. Plus I like to impress upon our frequent visitors that Americans are not as uncouth as they would like to believe. Come on! I have seen many a European boor pass through my dining room. Half of them wouldn't know a butter knife from a cleaver, yet they scoff at paper napkins. Martin tells me they do nothing but eat Cheetos and Twinkies all day long, moaning that they can't get them on the continent. I usually try to slip an ingredient or two that they can't identify, like cranberries, into these imbeciles' dinners. It drives them nuts. Chuck would claim this is my mean streak. Wrong again. It's my Rabelaisian sense of humor, something she would not comprehend.

And that's another reason I hate Boston. No one up here has a sense of humor. Riders curse the bus driver for trying to collect full fare. You try to double-park for thirty seconds and you're either towed or slammed. Taxi drivers strive to deliver you to your destination with a concussion. In three years no one has ever said "Excuse me" while elbowing me out of contention in Filene's Basement. You wink at a guy in Brooks Brothers and he'll report you to the staff. If you value your life, don't ever ask anyone to put out a cigarette in this town. It will be extinguished in your eye and then you'll be robbed. Get the picture? No sense of humor whatever. And it's ten times worse during the winter when no one shovels sidewalks.

I spent a good deal of time in New York that year, what with conventions, publishers, and sopranos all squawking for an Easter anthem with a dozen high C's. Didn't see Martin from Thanksgiving to Christmas. He had something crucial going on in Mexico.

Now that I had given up my apartment in the city I usually stayed with Lionel Boyd, an old childhood friend.

Out of the blue six years ago I ran into him in Zabar's and recognized him at once, thanks to his wild red hair.

"Thread!" I shouted above the din. That's Lionel's nickname because he's so thin.

"Eva Hathaway!" he whooped. "How ARE you, precious?" Obviously Lionel was now gay. One could have predicted this after having seen a youthful Thread in his drum major's outfit. Big deal. It's his mother's fault. She wanted a ballerina.

"What are YOU doing in New York?" Lionel asked, grasping my arm. The swarm of customers was slowly pushing us towards the smoked fish case.

"I live here," I said. "Central Park West."

"You're kidding!" he exulted. "Then we're neighbors!" By now we had drifted past the fish and were being herded towards the wurst. My nose was hallucinating from the overload.

Apparently Lionel (no longer Thread, please) had become a successful Broadway costume designer. Again, it all went back to that drum major's getup. Lionel and I immediately resumed our old friendship; no one understands you like a childhood playmate who has been exposed to your mother on a rainy Saturday afternoon. Lionel's mother, unlike mine, didn't drink when the going got rough. She ate. The long-range results have been the same; that is to say, our fathers have withered like forgotten balloons, our mothers have corrugated with frustration, and we kids still haven't figured out how or why we were conceived. Supposedly this makes for dynamic artistic personalities. Let me tell you something. It makes for homosexuals like Lionel and misanthropic hymnists such as myself. Only by a crazy fluke of nature did all our siblings turn out to be normal fathers and mothers. Lionel and I have pondered this riddle many times and have gotten nowhere.

Of all my friends Lionel had reacted the most bitterly to Martin. "You married that creep?" he screamed. "How could you DO this to me?"

Now I was beginning to get a little tired of people telling me my husband was thick, bland, odd, etc., especially since no one had said boo during the year we were dating. When people get married you're supposed to cloak your chagrin and say congratulations. It's the only polite thing to do, like swallowing tripe.

"What's the problem, Lionel," I smarted. "You've had many opportunities to propose to me and didn't."

"That's not the point! We are NOT marrying types! Especially to accountants!" Lionel hates accountants because they're always cutting his costume budgets.

"Martin is an engineer," I told him coolly. "I think it will be nice living in a big house with a man who wears suits." Frankly I was petrified. Perhaps I should talk Martin into an annulment while he remained in a cooperative honeymoon mood.

"You'll hate Boston," Lionel predicted. "It's full of drunken Irish polydactyls."

I began to cry. On this point Lionel was correct. "Thanks for your support, Thread. You're a real pal."

The doorbell buzzed. "Who's there," Lionel radioed down to the lobby.

"Martin Weaver," my spouse answered. "Would you mind sending Eva down? I've been triple-parked out here for half an hour."

"Sure," Lionel said. He gave me a hanky. "He's been waiting for you all this time out there?"

"Of course, clownbrain," I snapped. "Tow trucks are murder on Bavarias."

Lionel shook his head. "I think you're both nuts," he said. "It might work after all."

4

SHORTLY AFTER OUR third anniversary (which I celebrated by taking myself out to a show; Martin was in Switzerland) it looked as if I might be pregnant. With considerable foreboding I flipped through my appointment book, trying to plot my last menstrual period against the last time Martin and I had made contact. Unfortunately I could recall neither incident. After ten inconclusive days I realized that this potential catastrophe had gotten me rather pleasantly excited: I was thinking of baby names and maternity blouses instead of my career smothering under a mountain of putrid diapers. Finally I called Martin.

"How's my baby." he yawned. I can never figure out time zones, but I always seem to hit him at four in the morning.

"Martin, I think I'm pregnant!"

There was a short silence. "Are you sure about that?" he asked in a strange voice.

"Pretty sure. Why?"

"I don't recall sleeping with you since your last period, that's all," said Martin. "Remember? Just before I went to London?"

"Oh," I mumbled, "was that the time you were trying to go sideways?"

"Yes, dear," he sighed. It had not been a roaring success.

"But I *feel* pregnant," I insisted.

"Well then, go for a test, sweetie. Then we'll know for sure, eh?"

"Okay," I said, feeling pretty foolish. IUDs were ninety-eight percent foolproof.

We talked about Martin's business. His lower intestine had recently revolted and he wanted to come home. "I'll see you Saturday, my love," he promised. "We'll know then, won't we?"

The next day a few driblets of blood poisoned my maternal fantasies. I became very depressed. That whole afternoon I watched soap operas. I tried to get drunk but gave up; come on, booze tastes like shit. I went to the Y, got to the lobby, and turned back: I did not want to sprint around a sweaty track. I took a cab home because I couldn't face the trolly. I tried to compose some Lenten anthems but nothing came. Called Lionel, who didn't answer. Called Chuck, a basic mistake. She told me to take a fertility test while there was still hope. Called Richard. "Talk to me," I said. He obliged but he was 220 miles away. I took one last shot at the liquor cabinet and went to bed.

Not often anymore, but sometimes the whole deal gets through to me. It's not rational, it's gut, and it hurts. I think it has something to do with looking forward over your life, then looking backward, and seeing no distinction between two flat ramshackle roads leading to the same tarpit. At such moments philosophy, that glutinous pablum of spilled milk and sour grapes, doesn't begin to help. I myself prefer to stomp directly to the top. It probably won't get a response but I feel much better than I would after reading Boethius.

"God damn it," I prayed, "what the hell's going on down here? Life! Death! Martin! What a circus! Bah, what do YOU care? You never listen to me anyhow! Get me out of Boston. Amen."

Now that's a model prayer. Pithy yet restrained, devoid of all those ridiculous flowery clichés like "Lead me not into temptation" which are routinely ignored anyhow. Believe me, I have been praying all my life and I know what gets results and what doesn't. Don't pray for the recovery of sick beagles. Don't pray for fifteen pounds of flab to dissolve, don't ask for the heart of a married man, don't ask for vengeance upon an enemy, in fact, don't ask for anything you really want. You won't get it because then you'll stop praying. Look, too many people think God is Santa Claus. These same people usually end up atheists, spurning religion with the humorless fanaticism of disappointed lovers, and why? Because they didn't get what they wanted. It's a big joke. They could ask their parents for Lake Tahoe and get laughed out of the house, but when they pray for it, God is supposed to deliver, or else He doesn't exist. Such puerile behavior indicates an immature perception of God as the Good Guy with the shepherd's hook. Wrong, all wrong. The artist who painted that sappy, misleading portrait should have been executed. It's probably condemned more souls to hell than forty years of television. You don't pray for favors and happy endings: you pray to register bewilderment. I know I slipped in a small item about Boston near the Amen, but that's legit. You've got to keep believing in miracles or the whole thing becomes an exercise in futility.

Something moved downstairs. I shot up in bed, prayers and miracles forgotten, heart pounding, and listened with all my might. I dislike armed robbery, especially when I am home alone. I remained frozen, anaerobic: the noise did not repeat itself. Cars and trucks occasionally thundered by, vibrating my brittle Victorian house. A street gang shuffled past, treating the whole neighborhood to one hundred decibels of musical infamy. It was two in the morning. *Damn you Martin,* I cursed, *where are you when I need you?* I couldn't even remember which hemisphere he was in anymore; these road trips easily coalesced into one huge indeterminate lump between two trips to the airport. Just as my bloodstream reabsorbed that boost of adrenalin the noise came again. Now the mad rapist was down in the kitchen. He would come upstairs and trap me in my own bed, there to end my little life in a cataract of gore. *Damn you, Martin,* I repeated. Hey, how come this never happened when he was home? I reached for the crowbar on my nightstand and waited in ambush, last wills and testaments flitting through my brain. By dawn it was obvious that my killer had failed in his quest. I could have gozzled Martin, shit, I didn't expect him to make breakfast or do laundry or even kiss me anymore, but I did still expect him to protect his wife. It was the least he could do after thirty thousand flawless martinis.

Spawned by my sleepless night, the next day was a waste. I got hooked on a junk romance at nine in the morning and kept reading masochistically on until dinnertime. The phone didn't ring once because I had unplugged it in order to work on a Christmas oratorio, a project rapidly becoming overdue. Writer's block: who the hell wants to write a Christmas oratorio in January just so your dealer can get in on the racks in time for Labor Day choir rehearsals? I finally finished the book, unbelievable drivel about plantations, humidity, black slaves, and white fannies, and took a walk. All the commuters were shoving to get home and hide for the evening. They kept their eyes glued to the sidewalks, on the lookout for substances inimical to the gloss of footwear. People clutched their purses or briefcases as if they contained their very souls. Thank God I've never had to commute anywhere. It must be a drag getting the shit compacted out of you twice a day in the subways, to say nothing of facing a carful of zombies and realizing you look no different.

I bought a pint of ice cream, returned home, and switched on the television, determined to make this day a total washout. Why not? If no one was going to feel sorry for me then I'd do it myself. Wouldn't you know it, another plantation romance came on the tube, one as inane as the book I had blown the day reading but without that ludicrous foam of lust to pep things up. Once again I kept doggedly watching until the eleven o'clock news drove me away. Why must the networks in this town devote the last broadcast to Mildred Y. of Braintree whose basement got flooded with sewage and Felize B. of Revere who got her lottery ticket ripped off in a pizza parlor? I don't need this nonsense after a bad day.

The phone rang. It was Martin. "Hello, my girl," he said. "How did your test come out?"

"Negative," I replied. "When are you coming home, Martin? I'm very lonely."

"Negative? I'm sorry to hear that, baby. Why don't you have one of your friends come up for a few days?"

"Too much trouble," I said wearily. "And someone tried to break in last night. I was frightened half to death."

"Did you call the police?"

"Of course not! That would have given away my position! Then I would have been murdered for sure."

After a silence Martin changed the subject. He always does this when he knows he's wrong. It's a trick he learned from his mother. "How's your oratorio going?"

"Terrible," I muttered. "When are you getting home, Martin? No one takes me out to dinner anymore."

"Poor baby," my husband sympathized, "why don't you come here with me for a few days?"

"Where are you? I lost your itinerary."

"Munich."

"Can't," I wailed. "I have to finish this shit or Orville will start to scream." Orville is my publisher. "Why don't you just come home? Tell everyone you're tired of not seeing your lovely wife anymore."

"I can't come home right away, darling, there's been a little snag. I'll be delayed here for a few days." He sounded fairly bleak himself; all those three A.M. sausage plates were catching up with him. Fifty to one he was constipated, too.

"Oh," I responded listlessly. What the hell did I get married for? This was less fun than a convent for reformed nymphomaniacs. "Martin, we've got to work something out here," I said finally. "This setup reeks."

"I know, my love," Martin agreed. "I'm thinking all the time of possible solutions." That's an engineer for you. Always thinking there's a solution to everything.

The next day my right hand hurt so much I couldn't even hold a pen. Since I had done nothing to injure it besides maybe shoving my dresser in front of the bedroom door, I was forced to conclude that this illness was psychosomatic. Nothing like this had ever happened to me before and it rather upset me: I'm not the type to pull this stunt. It doesn't work anyhow. People cluck and pat your shoulder then five minutes later walk away and watch a football game.

I attempted to write with my left hand but soon gave up, come on, you just can't draw those teensy notes and stems with your bum hand, it takes all day and still everything comes out crooked. So I went to the movies, three of them. The cinemas happened to be within walking distance of each other. Once again, all I saw all day long were couples lunging at whatever mouths, breasts, or erections lay handiest. And the plots! Pure compost, something you'd never guess from the reviews festooning the lobbies of these establishments. That's what I get for going to arty foreign movies near Harvard. I took myself out to eat since I was not yet prepared to confront that Christmas oratorio. The waiter seated me next to three Greeks who kept looking over and winking as if I was Christina Onassis on the prowl for a gigolo. Crap! Hadn't they seen pearls and cashmere before? You dress decently in this town and you're treated like a whore. My hand hurt so badly I could hardly sign the receipt.

I called Richard Weintraub when I got home. After dinner I had seen one more movie, this one from Hollywood, and it was as lousy as the other three, but with no sex this time, only violence. From the title I had thought it was a musical.

"Richard," I blurted, "how's everything?"

"Hey, sweetie," he chirped, "great! I just finished the mechanicals for next year's Christmas cards! They're dynamite! Little angels in a manger! There's another one with Santa riding a pasta machine."

"That covers the atheists," I snapped. "What about your Jewish customers?" It peeved me that Richard had so effortlessly ground out his Christmas assignment when he wasn't even a Gentile.

"Aha! They have a silver menorah embossed on golden stars of David."

"How tacky."

"Only to a WASP, baby," Richard breezed. "How's everything with you?"

I told him about my hand. "And my insomnia's coming back."

"Thinking about me again, eh," Richard joked, shit,

why not joke, his Christmas job was already in the mail; soon his check would be too.

This called for punishment. "Occasionally," I answered cryptically. Actually Richard is tremendous in bed. He goes totally out of control, shouts, bites, the works. The only thing Martin bites is toast.

Richard paused, weighing whether I had just complimented or insulted him. He decided upon the latter, of course: artistic personalities are so predictably negative it makes me laugh. "Don't play games, Eva," he warned.

"Why not, jackass," I retorted, "there's nothing else to do up here." I was about to cry so I hung up. It would be unfair to cry with Richard because he still loves me.

Another two incredibly wretched days dragged by. To pass the time I wrote letters to a dozen acquaintances whose names casually mouldered in my address book. If they didn't write back by Memorial Day I'd erase them. I did go to the Y once, not to exercise, but to plotz in the sauna. On the way out I noticed a poster for a self-defense course and signed up, ha, as if I would actually resist any male interested in raping me. For an entire afternoon I washed windows.

All this time, mind, my Christmas oratorio had been lurking in my brain like a turtle at the bottom of a stagnant pond. At last, for no intelligent reason, an idea surfaced. You figure it out. Maybe it was the ammonia in the window cleaner. Anyhow, that night I sat at the piano and sketched out a great closing chorus, hardly noticing my lame hand. Then, like a tottering domino, an aria slid into my lap. Composing is often like making love: before you even start you've got to be poised on some kind of suicidal brink, ready to fall, or nothing will happen. It's easy to fall but it's not easy to attain that dangerous exhilarating edge. I know composers who drink their way there. Others write reams of drivel in a daily self-flagellating discipline, hoping for inspiration to take pity on their bleeding cerebra. Everyone else does something mildly asocial until nature takes its course. Let's face it, the artistic impulse is something entirely beyond one's control. Anyone who claims to know how notes get on paper is full of shit.

My husband Martin returned to Boston on Friday night

just as I was constructing a magnificent duet between the Star of Bethlehem and the Chief Magus. To tell the truth I was a little aggravated because now I would have to drop my oratorio, fling out the welcome mat and listen to three solid days of corporate static. My rhythm would be shot to hell, all in the name of conjugal cheerleading. *You complain because the man tells you about his job?* Chuck's voice rattled inside me. *Millions of wives would die to be in your shoes.* Not if their husbands came home during the soap operas, dear, I silently replied.

Martin entered the front door about four in the morning. His plane had blown a fuse in Chicago and had been delayed for five hours. "Hello, Eva, my girl," he called softly upstairs as he came to bed.

Since I had been expecting him I had not shoved the dresser in front of the bedroom door. It was a little off to the corner. Martin walked right into it. "Oooowwfshit," he swore, hopping on his good leg into the bathroom. He closed the door before turning on the light. I heard the water running and debated whether or not to tend to his bruises: no. I pretended to be still asleep so that Martin could wake me with dozens of tender little kisses. Many times he has admitted that this is his favorite part of coming home.

Eventually my husband crept into bed. My nose welcomed his sweet familiar formula of skin and sweat; even when I know he's dirty, Martin smells clean. "My baby," he whispered, kissing me on the face. "I'm home."

"Hi, Martin," I said in a gruff unused voice. "How was your trip?"

"Good," he answered. " I'll tell you in the morning." He coiled me into his arms and continued kissing me hospitably. Over the past few months I think my hymen had grown back, like ivy over a haunted turret. It could be most unpleasant shredding it off again.

"Let me get you a sherry," I said, sitting up. "Come on my side of the bed where it's warm."

"No, no, Eva," Martin said, pulling me back, "stay here with me." Nosegays of whiskey bedecked his breath; it must have been a brutal flight.

"I'm glad you're home," I cuddled, wondering who this foreigner might be.

"Ummmm," said Martin, and moved no more.

Until day lightened the windows I thought about the next numbers on my Christmas oratorio. Then I started hazily dreaming of someone kissing me. He moved like Richard Weintraub but he had black wavy hair. I know, I know, my father has black wavy hair. Big deal. So does a cocker spaniel.

Martin slept the entire day resting his intestines, then took me out to dinner although I know the last thing he wanted to do was eat out again. But the last thing I wanted to do was eat home again. We compromised by going to one of Martin's favorite restaurants, one I can't stand, in Brookline, a suburb I can't stand. It's full of *nouveau riche* cheapskates who drive around in titanic brown Cadillacs. When they're not squeezing you off the road they're shoving for the jewelry store or the Florida travel agent. I only go to Brookline to buy ice cream.

Throughout dinner Martin related his recent exploits; he would rather let a steak go cold than interrupt a tale of patents pending. For two hours I listened thoughtfully to him, beating the Christmas oratorio off the center of my brain. By the time dessert rolled around, however, the oratorio had gained the upper hand, hey, Orville expected my melodies made flesh on his desk in six days or else. Those last three glasses of riesling had unleashed the beast.

"What are you thinking about, darling?" asked Martin, noting my silence. "More mousse? Babies?"

"Please," I reprimanded, "my Christmas oratorio." For the millisecond I would swear Martin looked disappointed: he disliked being upstaged by Jesus, Mary, and Joseph.

"I thought you were done with that. What happened?"

"What do you mean, 'what happened?' I got off to a late start, then you came home." In three years of marriage Martin had yet to understand that composing was not a hobby like needlework but a dangerous gift that might eventually drive his wife insane. Engineers, as I have said, do not tread that fragile line between productivity and adamant uselessness.

"What does my coming home have to do with your Christmas oratorio?"

I saw that this conversation had the potential to become irreparably vile and quickly dodged into a wayside flowerbed. It wasn't worth it. Martin had a right to come home like everyone else; I'd work out my own equilibrium problems. "I was so excited to see you that I couldn't concentrate," I lied charitably. I think my husband believed me. God in heaven! Men's egos are so amazingly uncomplex! Sometimes a woman's greatest challenge is to convince herself that men are a challenge!

I extended my charity that night to the bedroom, making love with Martin although I wasn't much aroused. Nature endowed men with lust but nature fortunately compensated women with recessed sexual organs, cripes, if I had to show up with an erection every time Martin did, he would have left me long ago. I am not the type who can shut off the lights and pretend I'm receiving Elvis Presley: Martin Weaver, the computer genius who still can't boil an egg, is taking me. I save my imagination for things that really count, like my hymns. At any rate, Martin did not notice my tepidity. Two routine orgasms arrived on schedule, a mathematician's dream.

Martin disappeared to the office for the next two days, leaving me alone with my overturned oratorio. Through sheer desperation my momentum came back to me; I cranked out two more pieces although my hand started acting up again. All I needed now was one aria for a soprano capable of shattering four high C's in five minutes. You would not believe how many frustrated Aidas end up in Methodist choir lofts.

Nothing came on Friday so I cooked Martin his favorite meal, Stuffed Onions, a revolting clutter of meat, raisins, olives, and hot peppers, his mother's prize recipe. No melodies came to me as I stood in tears coring onions. Nothing came as I made lemon pie either. Nothing came to me as I sat, pen in hand, stupefied at the piano bench for three hours. I couldn't even decide upon a key. It's damn frustrating.

The phone rang around ten, Martin from the office. An accountant had just committed suicide. Since December 31 she had been trying to hunt down a $31.86 imbalance in five million dollars of receipts. On top of this Martin had to fly first thing in the morning to Washington and talk to someone working on the space shuttle. "What about your Stuffed Onions?" I cried.

"You made me Stuffed Onions?" Martin croaked. Now he was really upset. "Keep them on top of the stove," he instructed. "I'll have them when I get home. Don't wait up, darling, it's going to be late."

Nope, I didn't wait up. Martin came home at three and he left at six. His Stuffed Onions remained shriveled on top of the stove.

That day I was to go to the Y for that ridiculous self-defense course. I say ridiculous because no one has yet been able to show me how to outrun a speeding bullet. As I sat at the kitchen table impotently drinking coffee, telegraphing a deaf Prometheus, my eyes wandered longingly towards a new junk romance I had picked up. Hmmmm, I had only to lift that front cover and this day would be bygone history. No! I was not going to collapse just because Martin didn't eat his Stuffed Onions and lemon pie! In one hour this class started; that's about how long the trolley would take to travel two miles. I slapped on some clothes and left.

Class met in a lower gymnasium where they kept the slashed wrestling mats and bent barbells. Four individuals drifted against the walls. Hey, nine A.M. on a Saturday feels like six A.M. on a weekday. Three of them looked like students and one was a man of, say, fifty cruising for a girlfriend. Then another man walked in with a mound of booklets, keychains, boxing gloves, rubber knives, and toy guns. His hair looked as if it had been trimmed with one of the rubber knives. He had buttoned his flannel shirt one button off. We students looked furtively at each other, hoping against hope that this entrant was merely the janitor and not he who would be teaching us how to save our skins.

"Good morning," the fellow said cheerfully, heaving his burden atop an old bench, "I am Paul Fox." Strong voice, direct eyes, oho, he would be all right in bed. I could pick that up loud and clear. I leaned against the wall, checking his body out: six-two, one eighty, hung average. You can tell that from the way they walk. Now he was distributing some forms that we had to sign to prevent our suing him.

I scribbled on mine and handed it back. My hand was not doing well. Instructor Fox contemplated my blouse, a white affair covered with embroidery and mildly diaphanous, depending on the light. Plus I had three buttons open. I looked at him and thought, *I dare you, big boy.* I walked back to my bench against the wall and by God, his eyes were on my ass. It's worth looking at, believe me. I don't run twenty miles a week for the sport of it.

There being only five students in the class, Mr. Paul Fox went around the room reading names off his papers. He stopped in front of me. "Emma?" he asked.

"Eva," I corrected him. "Can't you read?"

"Can't you write?" he retorted and moved on, hey, one point for the rapier wit of P. Fox.

Milton was the old geezer's name. Walter was a law student from Harvard whose nose had left his mother's teat only to find a book. It was obvious why these two felt a need for a course in self-defense. The remaining pair were girls from Northeastern University, I didn't catch their names.

Now Teacher Fox had everyone form a circle on the wrestling mat. Supposedly we would be testing our reflexes by jumping the person next to us and seeing how quickly he or she escaped. I placed myself two to Fox's left so that he could sense me but not see me; I wanted to goad him. Milton jumped me and nearly broke my neck. The oaf didn't know this was only supposed to be a drill. We fell to the floor, rolling and kicking. The guy had a grip like a steel octopus.

"Enough!" shouted Fox. "Up, you two!"

Out of breath, I brushed myself off. "I see why we had to sign that paper, pal," I snapped, rubbing my sore hand.

Fox grinned at me and my blood soared. I stomped over beside Walter; this guy couldn't whip a bookmark.

Now we began practicing kicks, twists, and assorted dives. Walter and I paired off; Milton affixed himself to one of the chicks from Northeastern. Teacher Fox had the other one. Slowly the undercurrents in the room began rising: women and men don't wrestle each other without experiencing a vicarious titter. "All right, switch partners," Fox called eventually. "We'll move on to rape holds."

"Making them or breaking them?" Milton asked, and the whole class laughed, obviously all thinking the same thing. Milton latched on to me for this particular exercise; he had been eyeing my blouse also.

"All ladies lie on the floor, please," Fox commanded, "on your backs."

I lay down, glanced up, and caught Fox looking—gotcha, one point for Hathaway. I swallowed and he watched my throat, oho, whom did he think he was kidding with this Remote Professional bullshit?

"Gentlemen on top, please," Fox called, straddling a bird from Northeastern.

Two hundred pounds of Milton plummeted to my stomach. "Hey!" I shouted, "kneel! I can't breathe!" Milton laboriously raised himself. Let me tell you, if ever a heavyset clod tries to rape you, close your eyes and pretend you're whitewater canoeing.

"Not too successful there, Eva," observed the Remote Professional as Milton remained preeminent.

"Against my instincts," I answered. Milton was told to release me.

"Let me try that," Fox said.

"No thanks," I said, jumping up. "I get it." Another point for Hathaway; not an easy one either.

Now it was time to fend off attacks from the rear. We all rotated partners again and, yep, you guessed it. I felt him standing behind me and my breath snagged, oh God, it had been so long. Instructor Fox slipped his flannel arms around my neck. I felt his chest against my back: there went the game. I turned my head to the side and his grip tightened; now he could feel my breasts trembling. "What would you do if I were to go like this," Fox said.

"I wouldn't do a thing, man," I muttered, and the class hooted uproariously. Jackasses, little did they know. Fox pressed his pants against me and commenced a lecture on rear holds, never relinquishing his hostage. My pulse hit Mars and kept going; I leaned into him, mesmerized by his flesh.

Suddenly I elbowed him in the ribs. It was that or swoon. He let go.

"What, aren't you supposed to catch your opponent by surprise?" I asked, "You've been telling us that all morning."

"True," Fox admitted, clutching his ribs. "True." He looked me directly in the eye and I was a little afraid of him.

Out came the toy guns. "Hold this on me," Fox instructed. I aimed at his heart. "Lower," he said, "you'll do more damage." Suddenly he ripped my hand backward.

I shrieked in pain. "That's my sore hand, damn you," I shouted. "I depend on that hand for a living."

"Surprise your opponent," Fox continued. "Remember that."

I flounced onto a bench, glaring at him. Of course the class resumed, hey, you don't think any of these morons gave a shit if the pen of Fanny May Tingle was stilled forever. They shot at each other for another five minutes until class was over.

Fox came to the bench. "How's your hand," he said, kneeling, taking it. No man had ever knelt for me before; the effect was quite overwhelming.

"It's okay," I answered.

"What *do* you do for a living." Now he was massaging my wrist, agh, keep talking, Eva, keep talking.

"I'm a composer," I said. "Hymns."

Fox's big gray eyes narrowed wryly. "You? Hymns?"

"That's right." You know, some day I'm going to ask what's so damn funny about writing hymns. It aggravates the shit out of me to hear this same You? Hymns? baloney time after time after time.

Everyone had gone home. I was fighting a tremendous

impulse to linger. Withdrawing my hand, I put on my jacket "Thank you," I said. "That feels much better."

We walked upstairs and outside; it was all I could do not to rub up against him like a Persian cat. What could I do, invite the man to take me home with him? He probably had a wife and six kids stashed up in a North End garret.

"Back to your husband," Fox said.

I looked at him, cursing Martin for presenting his wife with such a tremendous diamond ring. Jewelry, bah, this was a two-carat manacle. "My husband is not at home," I told Fox. "Good-bye."

I walked very slowly to the trolley stop and sat down; I can read handwriting on walls. My breath fluttered like a rabbit's, expecting him maybe now, maybe next week, next year: he would come eventually. A marvelous exultant calm stole over me, oho, I had just been jacked into the fast lane, where I belonged, and where I intended to stay as long as possible before guilt or boredom or despair, the worst of the three, overtook me. I wanted that man and to hell with the consequences. Consequences are the crutches of cowards.

I diddled back to that spectacular empty house of mine and in two more days finished my Christmas oratorio. It exuded from my pores because I no longer cared about stuffed onions, I didn't care about Orville's deadlines, I didn't care about the limitations of Baptist larynges. My body was overtaken by an ancient and illicit excitement which I had never expected to feel again *Not with your husband, anyway,* Chuck guffawed. I ignored that twisted taunt and resumed scribbling. So consumed was I that the final number of my oratorio described a fox wandering through Bethlehem looking for a lamb and finding one next to the manger. It was a great piece and it would sell a million copies over the next ten yuletides. "For Paul Fox" I wrote on the top of the page. Had I been more precise I would have written "In anticipation of Fox" or "To the yet untaken Fox"; alas, such sentiments do not befit pious works and Orville is very picky about protocol. Ten to one, wringing all apostolic connotations dry, he'd make me change it to "To Paul" anyhow.

But my cardboard saint had already wrought a minor

miracle. I speak of my hand: it had completely healed. The lad must be thanked. *Eva, you hussy,* Chuck's voice accused, *what a bald excuse.* Ha, that would be the reaction of a woman who in sixty years has never thanked anyone for anything but a double highball.

I shot my masterpiece, hot off the copier, to Orville, then took myself out for a little drink to celebrate. One thing about Boston, you never have to walk more than thirty paces to find yourself a bar. "Cheers," I toasted The Grand Master. Then I drank to myself, then to Fox. I would have drunk to destiny also but the bartender was becoming obnoxious; besides, the first three toasts had more or less covered it.

I will admit to a slight flagging of courage as I picked up the phone: a previous encounter with dynamite had ended in one rather severe explosion. And what if a woman answered? What if Fox didn't remember me? Worse, what if my overcharged imagination had just been emitting a little heat lightning? *What about your husband,* Chuck interrupted sarcastically. *Non sum qualis eram.* I am not what I used to be, and furthermore my husband belonged to an entirely different domesticated existence. He would have nothing to do with this tide in my guts. Instead I thought of life and wrinkles and my mouth, which would go to waste forever because of what had happened in a ditch almost four years ago.

I punched three numbers before my hands started shaking. *Hang up, Eva,* Chuck's voice screeched, *it's suicide.* "Okay, okay," I whined, slamming the receiver down with craven bravado. Now I felt much worse than if I had never tried at all. Why do I listen to that madwoman? I redialed.

His phone rang. My heart bolted like a kangaroo. Saliva? Sludge. I killed it after two rings.

Jesus, how juvenile! I prayed, lurching to the refrigerator for some orange juice. I poured a tumbler of chablis instead and sank onto a kitchen stool. The more I drank the more my body recalled those plaid flannel arms around me; within minutes it had persuaded my brain that one husband, ten thousand lies, and a fortune in antique furniture were small ransom to feel those arms again.

"Hell," I prayed, "if You had wanted me to remain virtuous, You should not have planted him there." I dialed Fox. "Remember," I added as his phone rang, "You are expected to understand and forgive all."

"Hello," Fox answered cheerfully. That's all I needed! An optimist!

"HmmmmmmellOOOO," I croaked, my voice surfing fifty feet above sea level, "Eva Hathaway calling."

I felt him smile. Hey, why not: he knew he was about to get laid. "Miss Hathaway," Fox said, "how are you?" I knew that voice from some great warm lake before I was born; every last instinct rushed out to welcome him home. My brain just stood ashore watching helplessly.

"I'm fine, thank you."

"How's your hand?"

"My hand? That's what I'm calling about."

"Oh! Would you like me to twist it again?"

I lobbed him ten seconds of silence. Overconfident men usually cannot distinguish between an erection and a torpedo. "Not particularly," I said finally.

That didn't faze him one bit. "How's the hymn business?"

Now I smiled; he remembered me, all right. "Fine. I just finished an oratorio."

"Well! Miss Maccabaeus!"

Since when did self-defense instructors know about classical music? The definition of "oratorio" slithered abashedly off my tongue and back down my throat. "That is I."

"That's you." That voice was turning me inside out.

"I owe you a drink, mister."

"You do? What for?"

"You fixed my hand. It doesn't hurt anymore."

He didn't believe me. That's what happens when you tell the truth. "So what are you doing tonight?" he asked.

I gulped three bricks and each lodged in my windpipe. "Nothing between six and eight." Why play hard to get? It's much more fun to attack.

"What happens after eight?"

"I sharpen pencils. You're coming to my place, okay? My car's at the body shop. Some cretin took out my taillight on Storrow Drive. Tried passing on the divider."

Fox chuckled to himself. "Where do you live, gorgeous?"

Gorgeous, eh? What a shithead. "Thirty-two Ash Lane. Don't park between my neighbor's garbage cans or he'll snap your antenna."

"I'll be there in an hour."

"You do that. Bye."

One hour! Christ! I tore through my house throwing shoes under sofas, stuffing the dishwasher, sanitizing bathrooms. I changed the sheets on my bed—yeah, my own bed, come on, let's not kid anyone, I'm just a whore from New Jersey and I believe neither in the ghosts nor the property rights of absent husbands.

The doorbell rang as my hair was still wringing wet. I thought someone had shot me. *No such luck,* cheered Chuck.

"Hello," I said, dazzled by handwriting on the wall, in the flesh. What a beautiful man.

"Howdy." He was smiling. Neglectful of me to forget those big gray bear-trap eyes.

Someone gunned a large engine next door. With infinite care my neighbor Harry piloted his green Cadillac onto the street, braking at the curb. "Dahris!" he shouted, "Don't fahget it's gahbage night!"

Fox turned around just in time for Harry to notice him. "How's it going, Mahtin?" Harry called. "Long time no see!" The Cadillac rolled off.

"Who's Martin?" Fox asked.

"My husband. Come on in." I retreated; if the bastard touched me now I'd scream.

Fox halted two steps into the foyer. "What a house," he whistled, shutting the door; as the knob clicked my blood began to dance erratically. Fox went to the main staircase and inspected the woodwork, running his hand appreciatively along the bannister. He checked out the wallpaper, the chandelier, the walnut wainscoting. Then he saw the stained glass in the entryway. "This is a great place," he said.

"Thanks." I detest talking about houses almost as much as I detest talking about the illustrious children of other people. "How about a drink?" Before Fox could answer I was halfway to the den.

I poured two shots of port as Fox admired the exquisite
mahogany paneling and oriental rugs surrounding him.
Both had impressed me the first time I had seen them, too;
but that was years ago. Across the way I felt his eyes on
my body and my breath began to surface, playing lightly
over my lips as it scurried free.

Handing him a glass, I sat next to him. Off what carcass
had Fox pulled that atrocious argyle sweater? If he lived
with a woman and she let him out of the house with that
thing on, I had no competition. "Cheers," I said. "You
don't have VD, do you?"

He rebounded very quickly but his cheeks stayed red.
"Not yet, sweetheart."

Now for the left hook. "What do you think you're
doing here?"

Fox put his glass down and a wonderful terror rattled
through me. In a flash it was gone; only its incandescent
spectre remained. Fox stood up. To leave? Bah, I wasn't
going to stop him. If he couldn't answer two simple
questions, he had failed anyway.

Fox looked down at me. "Put that glass down," he
said.

The moment I did he yanked me to my feet. Now his
arms were around me: ah, melt, woman. This one was the
sun.

"I'm going to touch you," Fox whispered in my ear,
"with all your clothes off."

"Is that so."

"Shut up! I'm not finished." He ran two fingers along
my throat. "Then I'm going to kiss your breasts. Then I'm
going to eat you alive. Then I'm going to fuck your brains
out."

I suppose that answered my question, although I wish
the fellow had mentioned something about liking me.
Romantic fool, hooted Chuck, *You wouldn't have believed
him anyway.* As I put my arms around his shoulders a poof
of perfumed sweat escaped my collar. "I wish you luck,
champ," I said. "I've got an awful lot of brains."

I walked to the door. Before leaving the den I turned
around; Fox remained in the center of Martin's prized
Bukhara rug fifteen feet away from me. The distance was

unnaturally long; my body yelped like a pup denied its mother's teat. *Cut if off, Eva,* railed Chuck, *NOW.*

"Care to see the upstairs?" I said. Hah! Was a frog's ass watertight?

Those eyes would be my undoing! He caught my hand at the foot of the staircase. "Who are you," he whispered. I felt the pain: he didn't want to get involved with me either.

"You don't want to know, baby," I said, leading him upstairs.

5

NIGHT OF UNBRIDLED passion, bah! It was one colossal disaster from beginning to end. First of all I forgot to remove the crowbar from my bed and Fox lay right on top of it. That's what happens when you give people only one hour's notice to tidy their homes before you arrive.

"Aiii!" Fox shouted, careening to the side.

I thought he had been electrocuted; Martin has always joked about "wiring the bed" so that I wouldn't snore. "What is it?" I gasped, then saw the crowbar. "Oh, that," I said, tossing it to the side, "Never mind." It felt like ice.

"What's a crowbar doing in your bed?"

"Protecting me," I said, "obviously." Agh, this was no time to be discussing hardware. "Come back here," I called, pulling his arm, "before I lose my place." Fox rolled on top of me; I noticed that this recent frosting had fortified his erection. Whichever soap he used flared quickly then capitulated to a much more intense animal odor. Believe me, on Fox lust smells terrifying and wonderful.

His mouth began with my throat; my mouth didn't want to lose his so I bit his hands. Besides, he was going too fast. "Hey, big boy," I whispered, "kiss me some more."

Fox pretended not to have heard. His head descended yet further, give me a break, what did he think my body was, the Indiana Speedway?

I yanked him up by the hair. "Look, buster," I said, "I need at least five more minutes in park."

"No you don't," said Fox. His hand slithered down my belly. "You're soaking." Nevertheless he recommenced kissing me. Hmmm; either he was a man of massive self-control or he had another woman all the time. I didn't want to know. It takes one hundred percent concentration just to outmaneuver a wild new penis: worry about biographical data and your desire will bolt like a hare, believe me.

Just as I had thought, Fox had enormously arousing hands. My intuition rarely errs concerning a man's fundamental sensuality. Come on, you can smell it a mile off, like the ocean. "Don't stop that," I breathed, agh, it had been ages but my blood still remembered to charge south. Fox had better keep his head above my navel or the tide would leave without him.

"Well, let's get it over with," he said abruptly.

"What does that mean?" I asked, not wanting to know that either.

"The first time is always a flop. You know that as well as I do." By flop, of course, he was referring to my end of the stick. Typical.

"Only my patience fails, pal," I sighed. Damn him, conversation has a way of corsetting abandon.

The phone rang. "Ignore it," I said, feeling Fox tense, "it'll stop."

It didn't. "Why don't you go to the kitchen and bring up some orange juice," I advised presently. "We're going to have to start all over again." It was Lionel Boyd. No one else hangs on for thirty rings.

"Persistent, isn't he," Fox said.

"How do you know it's a he?"

"Pick up the phone, Eva," Fox whispered, pronouncing my name as if it induced migraine. He rolled on his back and shut his eyes. I glimpsed the black hair of his chest and a roll of heat swept me.

"Hello, Thread," I sighed, picking up the phone.

"Eva, Jesus Christ! What took you so long? Listen to this! The arranger just quit! *Cloistrophobia* is going to FOLD before it even opens! Remember the Texan I was telling you about? The conductor tore up his music then they had a fight! Gawd! It was AWful! And my costumes! My soul, I've poured my SOUL into those costumes!"

Evidently things were not going well with the new musical.

"You mean those monks' capes and G-strings?"

"Yes! Yes! Yes!" screamed Lionel. He was crying now. Whenever Lionel holds on for thirty rings he's crying.

"It's all right, sweetheart," I soothed. "The composer will come back, believe me." Composers always come back, like gnats.

"No, NO!" shrieked Lionel. "You don't understand! They were lovers, too!"

I frowned; that loused things up completely. "When's the opening?"

"Tuesday. JEEsus! Tuesday! And no music for the greatest showman in Broadway history! I'll die from this, Eva! I'll just DIE!"

"No you won't just die," I mimicked disgustedly. "Don't be ridiculous." Fox snickered to himself; I had to get off the phone. "I'll write you something," I said. "You just need one tune for that black guy?"

"Yes," sobbed Lionel, "you could write it in an hour. Clarence the conductor likes you. He'll take it, I know he will."

"What's the subject again," I asked, "penis envy?" *Cloistrophobia* was a musical comedy upon anything sacred, if I remembered correctly.

"Yes," sniffled Lionel, eyes drying now that I had bailed him out once again. "You remember. It's right after the monks' orgy scene. Pooh is disguised as a nun."

Sneaking around trying to get himself laid, of course. "Look, Lionel, pour yourself a gimlet and go to the steambath. I'll send you something tomorrow." I hung up amid fervid attestations of love.

Fox opened his eyes. "An interesting conversation," he commented, "for someone who claims to write hymns."

"I thought I told you to get some orange juice," I retorted.

Fox came in close. "Not thirsty," he said, twiddling my hair. Then he began again, at the top. Very very smoothly, very deliberately, he was doing it on purpose to drive me crazy. I had to give the guy credit; this took incredible restraint for the first time around.

"Tell me something," I said slowly, "are you showing off or are you impotent?"

He appeared not to know what I was talking about; then again, people are always hypocritically polite with strangers.

Fox ceased exploring and raised his head. "Something's burning."

I sniffed a faraway blackening stew. "Shit!" I cursed, leaping out of bed, "my cassoulet!" I grabbed a peignoir and tore down to the kitchen. Ruined, twelve pounds of goose, pork, and beans; so much for romantic postcoital suppers. As I carried the charred pot to the sink, the phone rang; I yanked it off the wall. "Hello."

"Hi, sweetie," said Richard.

"Hey, can I call you back? I've got a lover waiting for me upstairs."

"Nice try," Richard scoffed uncertainly. "Sure, I'll be in all night."

I brought some orange juice and brandy to bed. Fox reclined against my pillow leisurely reading *The Collected Sermons of Cotton Mather*. "Enjoying my book?" I asked, not in the least interested in sex. That stew had cost me thirty bucks.

"I prefer *Dracula*," said Fox, putting the book down. What the hell was this guy doing here, come on, I had pots to scrub, dance numbers to write, friends to call. Anyone who preferred Dracula to Cotton Mather was a spiritual coward.

Fox eyed me expectantly. "Come here, sexy." he said.

That irritated the shit out of me. "I think you had better go," I said, picking the crowbar from the floor. "I start sharpening pencils at eight o'clock."

Sighing, Fox put aside the blankets. I watched his long legs swing over the side of the bed and suddenly remembered his expertise in the martial arts. On second thought, perhaps I should accommodate him. I gulped; nothing like a good naked body, approaching purposefully as a panther, to take your breath away.

Fox ditched the crowbar, then untied the neck of my robe with fingers unnaturally warm. "Who called," he asked softly, "your husband?"

"Almost."

He shook his head. I don't think he believed one word I had ever told him. Fox continued lazily toying with my ribbons. I couldn't figure him out: there waved an erection two feet long, the floor was cold, I was about to call the police, and none of this changed his speed or his direction. I began to want him again.

Fox sat me on the bed and poured some brandy. "Good for the throat," he explained.

"Who cares about your throat, man? Brandy is for courage." He needed it, believe me; things were deflating fast.

"Actually, my throat is quite valuable," Fox said, swallowing. "I'm a singer."

I slowly put down my glass. "How nice," I said, wishing he hadn't told me. There are only three people alive I would like to strangle and each of them is a singer. "What do you sing? 'Aiii karate'?"

"Operas and oratorios." His erection was returning, pfuii, happens whenever singers talk about themselves.

"Let me guess. You're a tenor." They have less brains than a duck.

"Yep." Fox pushed me under the covers and began at the top for the third time, imperturbably nosing along my throat as one hand reached over and took the phone off the hook. Good move, I liked that.

For Christ's sake, Eva, Chuck broke in, *He's taking you like the Krauts through Belgium.*

Almost at once, obeying The Unseen Commander, ten thousand memories stomped inchoate pleasure to oblivion. *I don't understand,* I prayed. *Out of all the mothers on earth, why did I get this one?* For quite a while I tried to forget about the slaughter of innocents and concentrate on brutish carnality. It was no use. "Hold on," I said finally.

Fox didn't even lift his face from my abdomen. "Ummm?"

"Wait a minute." I pinched his ears for emphasis.

Fox slid up to eye level, his lower lip gleaming in the dim light from the hallway. "Changing your mind, eh?" he said.

"That's right." I brushed his lips, then those huge eyes, with my fingers; my mouth twitched enviously: a damn handsome man.

"Why?"

"I just remembered something."

"Tell me."

How could I lie to eyes like that? What the hell, I'd give it a shot. "I might get pregnant."

Fox shifted weight and his penis plopped gently on top of me. His eyelids fell ever so slightly. "Don't lie to me, Eva," he said. "I can tell." I chortled once and, pursuing the advantage, he planted his mouth on top of mine. His tongue picked a very complex lock, my legs slid open, and ooof! he was inside of me: paradise.

"That is heaven," he whispered.

"That is hell," I amended. The man had no idea what eight inches of trespass had ruined forever. Inch by excruciating slow inch, enjoying the threshold, Fox rocked back and forth; were that blood he drew instead of sweet water, I would be long dead.

You win, I prayed; so much for deathbed confessions.

Fox paused. "I win what?"

"The National Eavesdropper Award." I frowned. "Couldn't you see I was praying?"

"You were? For what?"

Oh, forgiveness, strength, cunning, and one orgasm. "Never mind. Just shut up and keep moving."

"What do you mean? Don't tell me you can't screw and talk at the same time."

Screw? I thought I was doing something a little more edifying than that! My hips described smaller and smaller arcs, then a straight line. "I screw screws, darling," I said, "and I don't talk even then." And I would have been better off tonight had I screwed screws. Already the damage was considerable: one goose shot and I had had to drive a half hour up Route One, a hell of neon hamburgers, to buy it. I was now obligated to compose a heretical burlesque for Lionel. Plus I'd now have to disinvent some lover upstairs for Richard Weintraub's benefit. Pfuii, I should have known this would be a washout. I can't get carried away with strangers unless I'm drunk or they rape me, preferably both. Only Martin can do it cold turkey and that's because the laws of mathematics and ballistics, intelligently applied to a vaginal canal, can wreak unbelievable havoc.

I had to get rid of this guy, pronto. "It's after eight," I said, glancing at the bedstand clock, "I meant it about sharpening pencils."

In reply Fox withdrew completely, rolled out of bed, and began hauling his shorts on. I suppose he thought he was punishing me.

"Do you have any idea how ludicrous you look," I said, come on, you couldn't pull a circus tent over that hard-on. "Where do you think you're going anyway?"

"Home, baby," answered Fox. "I've got a concert tomorrow and you're sapping my energy."

I laughed out loud. "Hoooo! Ex-cuse me!" If that monster was sapped, I'd eat it.

Fox crammed into his pants. I threw him his purple argyle sweater and draped my robe on; if he insisted upon flaunting his body, I'd do the same. In silence I walked him down to the foot of the stairs. "Sing well," I called, veering into the kitchen; maybe I could still salvage that goose. The front door closed and a car roared off. Ah, poor bruised Caruso. No curtain calls tonight.

Really now, what was the fellow so upset about? He didn't seriously think he could just waltz in here and steal my heart away, did he? Sorry, I let that happen once and only once; now the men following would have to work for it. And it's not even work, damn it, it's challenge. Today's male has got to compensate for the drama that the Pill stole from his towering act of passion. Not one in a hundred can cut it. Look at Fox: a little resistance and boom! flat on his face.

I suppose You call that adultery, I prayed, hacking pieces of goose into a wine marinade. It might camouflage the charcoal overtones. *Well, I don't, buddy! A few kisses! Penetration about as erotic as a Pap test! Okay, I'm punished! My goose is wrecked! I've learned my lesson! No more morons from the Y! Crap, I'm only human! Now let me compose Lionel a good tune. Amen.*

My prayers are generally cathartic but in fact I felt a little annoyed. Fox was one fine-looking man and I had hardly gotten my hands on him before he turned to dreck. *That's what happens to naughty roving hands, Eva,* preached Chuck. What would she know about hands? The only time she puts hers anywhere near my father is to shove the garbage at him.

Well. There I sat, back to the bench: home alone, cold sober, undressed, and definitely not sleepy. Time to compose, hell, why not, it beat the sitcoms. I poured myself a huge glass of gamay and went to the piano. Where was I: one ditty for Lionel's transvestite lover. I stared at my pencil for some minutes. That schmuck hadn't even told me where he was singing.

I finally came up with a deviate monk's version of a cakewalk. Instead of cake, of course, he was strutting for the abbot's rear end. It was an inane number but the tune was quite catchy. And Lionel had estimated correctly: it had taken only an hour of my time. They'd love it in New York, believe me, mockery does extraordinarily well at the box office. Obviously Fanny May Tingle would never have composed such a secular work; therefore I signed the piece A. P. Edgewater. It's the name of someone I knew a long time ago.

I donned a sweatsuit and ran down to Copley Plaza; something had to be done with my unburnt energy. No one looked twice at me because in Boston jogging is a noble pursuit practiced by all intellectuals striving singlehandedly to change the evil universe. In fact I passed dozens of unsmiling itchy thumpers such as myself, all vying for the same two feet of turf alongside the road. Between the potholes, the dog turds, the cyclists, the mounted police, the drunken jaywalkers, and the taxicabs, it's a challenging course indeed. I wondered what had driven so many people outside at this absurd and dangerous hour. Then I remembered. The Celtics had blown another series in Philadelphia.

Martin returned later that week, just as I was finishing a New Year's chorus. I picked him up at the airport so we could go out to dinner.

"Hello, darling," Martin kissed, "how's my angel?" He had lost some weight, as usual. On the road Martin forgets to eat.

"I'm fine," I replied, "very fine. How was Houston?"

"Hot."

"Did I pack you enough short-sleeve shirts?"

"Just enough."

"Did you like the hotel?"

"Very nice."

We walked outside to my car. Some sot in a battered Chevy was honking bloody hell because I had blocked him in for maybe thirty seconds. I walked up to his window. "Please don't make so much noise," I told him. "My husband is blind and your horn is upsetting him."

"Handicap pahkin's up front," the man said ill-temperedly, spitting his cigar into the gutter. Anywhere else on earth I would have received an apology.

"What's your license number?" I asked. "The mayor's going to hear about this." I walked slowly to the rear of the Chevy. One rusty Mass. plate battled a platoon of Teddy Kennedy stickers: you're not In in this burg unless you plaster your car's ass with social commentary.

Martin slipped out of the Bavaria. "Eva, what are you doing back there?"

"Get back inside," I shouted angrily, "you're blind as a bat." With a puzzled expression Martin crouched back into the car. His family background precludes him from arguing in public.

"Don't look blind to me, lady," the man called as I stalked back to my car.

"What was that all about?" asked Martin. "Someone you know?"

"Nope." For a good three minutes I deliberately stalled the Bavaria.

Martin observed me silently. "What are you doing, baby?"

"I'm testing something," I told him. " One minute." The Chevy finally blasted its horn. I smiled, stalled a bit more, and pulled away.

Martin had just eaten on the plane, wasn't hungry, so we headed home. About an hour ago it had begun to snow heavily. I edged up the expressway. nodding perfunctorily at Martin's travelogue as I surveyed the wrecks blazing past: whenever it snows in Boston, traffic accelerates fifteen miles per hour, twenty-five if the car has bald tires. "Put your seat belt on, sugar," I finally interrupted. "We're about to go snowmobiling." Martin obeyed; he would rather canoe in a typhoon than ride the expressway. I jetted into the right lane.

"Hans and I are still trying to buy Kraftika," he resumed, "except that bastard Truog is looking for money in Taiwan. He doesn't know that Hans bought fifty thousand shares last week and intends to buy another forty LOOK OUT!" An abandoned car, color black, no lights, no flashers, plotzed pertly fifty yards ahead.

"Jesus Christ!" I shouted, swerving into the next lane, three feet ahead of a tractor trailer. The trailer bore down on my rear, jerking his high beams on and off. "Can you believe that slime?" I yelled, flooring the Bavaria back into the fast lane. Hey, if this gorilla wanted contact he could mash the '70 Impala ahead of me.

"Watch the road, Eva," Martin cautioned me. "Remember that big pot-HOLE! Ah! Darling! You just can NOT cross lanes like that! Please! Visibility is zero!"

"Calm down, Martin, these tires can do anything." They had better, man, for two hundred bucks apiece. We proceeded in white-knuckled silence. Ah, conjugal bliss. Let me tell you something: were Martin not married to me he'd be sitting in that bucket seat laughing this whole episode off. That's because girlfriends can wreck cars but wives cannot. It's very ironic. Were I still only Martin's girlfriend, I'd feel terrible about smashing his car. Now that I'm his wife, it wouldn't bother me a bit.

"There's the exit! Slow down!" yelled Martin suddenly, pointing off to the right. I floored it, successfully cutting off the tractor trailer yet one more time. With a foul, disfigured blare of its horn, the truck shook by. I smiled: few of man's inventions surpass a thoroughbred automobile.

"So that's the exit," I mused. "No wonder I always miss it." Martin bit his lip; he was thinking, "You miss it because you fly by at ninety." I put my hand on his knee. "Don't worry, cutie, I'll get you home in one piece." Martin laughed drily and stared through the windshield. I wondered if he had met a woman in Houston. No way; she would have made him eat three meals a day with her.

"Here we are, vivacious," I announced some time later,

cheerily pulling the car into the garage. We trudged to the front door through snow whipping everywhere. "Martin, you're not mad at me, are you?" I asked, kissing him. "I won't let you inside if you are." Come on, he had no reason to be upset; thanks to me he could jump on the telephone twenty minutes ahead of schedule.

Martin sighed and shook his head. "How can I be mad at you," he said, "you little devil."

We got a fire going in the den; Martin resumed his documentary. He had just bought a company which did nothing but make electrical switches. "So we figured for an initial six we'd save over two hundred K the first year alone," he explained, bending behind the bar. "It's an unbelievable coup. Digitrodes was dealing like mad and we beat them out with a killer stock option. Then Tagahashi arrived three hours too late." Pausing, Martin stood up, a bottle in his hand. "Whew! What happened to all the brandy?"

I had to laugh. Not once in three-plus years has Martin noticed the disappearance of anything but old tee shirts and telephone message slips. Also, he sounded exactly like my father: now I understood why these innocuous comments infuriated my mother.

"It's been absorbed," I answered, "by myself and a friend from the Y. We were celebrating the completion of my Christmas oratorio."

"You finished it," Martin said. "Terrific!" He eked out a last teaspoon. "Don't you usually celebrate with champagne?"

"It was a spur-of-the-moment invitation."

"Where did you meet him? At the Y, you said?"

"How do you know it was a he?"

Martin looked over at me. "I'd call an ambulance if you had a woman over here, darling." My husband handed me the brandy; the motion reminded me of Fox. I scowled.

"He taught my self-defense class," I continued, "and claims to sing also. A very talented individual."

Martin sat beside me on the couch exactly where Fox had been. "Sounds interesting."

"He was, for about ten minutes." This pleased my husband enormously. He did not want a local version of Richard Weintraub languishing about the house.

"Speaking of self-defense, love, I bought you something," he said.

"A gun?" I asked, knowing this was impossible. You shoot a murderer in your own bedroom in Massachusetts and you'll be the guy who goes to jail.

"No," said Martin, "an alarm system. We'll have it put in tomorrow. Then you can sleep at night, eh?"

"You shouldn't have gone to all that trouble, Mart," I said, touched and humbled. He had bought one alarm system but he had investigated ten.

"I want you to be safe and happy," Martin said. "That's very important to me."

"I am safe and happy," I replied, although philosophically speaking I believed in neither of these conditions. Ah, who else on earth would love me as devotedly as this man? Royalties might vanish, fidelity might backfire, but Martin would strive to keep me safe and happy forever. From the moment I set eyes on him I knew it; that's why I married him. "Martin," I said, "do you think opposites attract?"

"If you're a magnet, I suppose."

"But don't you think we're opposites? Completely?"

Martin laughed. "Of course not, darling! We're two peas in a pod!"

I quietly swallowed the rest of my brandy. It burned; that, too, reminded me of Fox.

A few days later Orville my publisher called. He loved the Christmas oratorio, so much in fact that he was going to print two arias separately. I wasn't surprised; that was an A-1 effort from beginning to end and I knew it. Orville gladdened to hear that I had just sent him a wedding chorus; he had been bitching about this deficiency for months now. I'd soon be receiving a nice check; this year's Easter anthem was selling like hotcakes, particularly in the Southwest. That's because Richard Weintraub had designed a cover with a cactus on it.

I dialed Richard to thank him. "Hey, hotdog."

"Eva."

"What's new?"

"Oh God, I'm up to my neck in work."

"Ergo you're up to your neck in money, so don't complain."

"Are you coming to the city?"

"Maybe next week. Lionel's got me on Broadway."

"No! What now? Don't tell me! A musical revue of the crucifixion!"

"No, a parody of the Torah." That shut him up, ah, what would I do without Weintraub and his persecution complex. "I wanted to let you know that your splendid cover has once again shot my work to the top of the hit parade."

"Which one? The globe? The storm?"

"The cactus, dear."

Richard paused. "Why did I draw a cactus?" he asked uncertainly.

"Come on! Because the piece was named *Perpetual Thirst!*" Crap, where was Richard's mind these days?

"Was that the job I had to do in three hours because you were a month late?"

A strange verbal coincidence. Last August indeed I had thought I was a month overdue. "August was a bad month," I said. "And it was a fairly mundane cactus, if you ask me."

"Love that encouragement, Eva." Richard is full of shit. He couldn't produce a thing if I didn't criticize him and he knows it. Watch, he'd never draw a mundane cactus again.

"And I love your cheer," I said. "Good-bye."

The recent snow had become salty gray slop, the favorite of local drivers: now they could take out pedestrians from twenty feet. The most irresistible targets carried shopping bags and/or wore clean coats, therefore I dressed in a ratty old ski parka and my dingiest boots and proceeded to the trolly stop: hadn't been to the Y in days and my muscles were screaming. Sure enough, a cab got me ten steps from my own stoop. I watched him nail an elderly woman half a block away, then slosh through a red light. By the time I reached her she had regained her feet. "Are you all right?"

"Damn that devil," she snapped, continuing on her way. That's the neighborhood version of thank you.

Glancing repeatedly over my shoulder, I approached the T stop, joining a crowd of sixty irate, slush-soaked citizens all pawing the ground, preparing to stampede the next trolley, whenever that might be. Obviously none had appeared in the last fifty minutes. Mutters of "Damn fuckin' T," "This shit transit system," and so forth issued from all lips. To make matters worse, a car did appear—rambling in the opposite direction. The crowd nearly rioted. "Holy Mothah o' God," someone shouted, "that's the tenth cah goin' th'othah way! Those fuckin' assholes ah havin' a tea pahty at the tehminal!"

Of course they were having a tea party. It's called the Reverse Guilt Syndrome. If I were a conductor making forty thousand per annum for squeaking down a dilapidated track with nothing to do all day but slam doors, I'd hate my job, too.

A lone trolley did finally appear in the distance. The crowd became one huge foaming mouth. I stepped back: better to wait and survive.

Fifty minutes later, approximately twice the time it would have taken me to walk there, I entered the Y. Due to inclement weather a dozen wastrels occupied the lobby couches pretending to read newspapers and Y bulletins as they dried out their uriniferous overcoats. The stench overwhelmed anyone coming in from the street. I walked by swiftly, leaving one aromatic zone for another. Agh! The cafeteria was trying to sell cabbage and meat loaf again. The locker room would waft aphrodisiacal after this.

I entered the stairwell and nearly knocked over Fox, definitely the last person I cared to see in these clothes. "What are you doing here," I said, yanking off my sodden cap. At once my heart began to spin, then blur, like an airplane propeller. Oh God, he initiated a blind chemical reaction which began in my gut and irradiated through my skin, impelling me to touch him.

"Ho, what have we here?" cried Fox with artificial surprise. "A lily among women!"

"Stay where you are," I said quickly, "or I'll kick you." With these army boots and ten pounds of overalls? Come on.

Fox crinkled his mouth, laughing. I couldn't take my

eyes off his face, damn him. Now my lips were itching. They recalled daubing slowly along those pale cheeks. "I'd have to retaliate with a knee twist, love," answered Fox. "You remember that, of course."

"I remember everything," I assured him. Fox took one step forward; I stood firm but every atom of blood, of brain, tore backward. "What a prick you are," I whispered. "I'm married." Soon I would have to touch him; he stood only a breath away.

"I think you prefer it this way," he said.

Hmmmm. I had heard this phrase once long ago, before I raised my prices. It would not happen again, and definitely not in a dank Y stairwell. Ten years down the tubes had taught me something. Prefer it? Like hell!

"You're very tempting, my boy," I said, slinging my gym bag over my shoulder, gliding away. "But I can resist you," I called softly. "You watch." I leaned through a set of swinging doors.

The moment I got to the locker room I stripped and shot into the showers, teeming the water across my face and back. It didn't help. I slumped against the tiles, clutching my stomach: lust I could withstand indefinitely; this omnivorous longing I could not. He was twin of my blood, my last reprieve, the seventh wave, and I could not abide not having him. *You're too cruel,* I begged. *Why do I live?*

A rotund lesbian with huge breasts waddled into the showers and began soaping herself provocatively, hoping I would notice. She had to be kidding, please, it would take a bloodhound all night just to find the clitoris sandwiched between all that flab. My tears ceased. Whistling, I turned off the water and departed the showers, making sure my lovely suitor saw the Weaver family diamonds on my finger. *Very mean, Eva,* my mother's voice chastised as I slithered into my shorts. Had I resisted the advances of a male, of course, Chuck would be beaming with pride. Fight off a woman and it's a different story.

I did roughly eight miles. That's one hundred revolutions of the track. Fox was not waiting amongst the piss and the cabbage when I departed.

That day a hefty royalty check arrived in the mail with a note praising Richard's new cover designs. Orville also wrote an apology for changing the dedication on my Christmas oratorio: as I had guessed, it was now "To Paul." I didn't care. The dedicatee was not about to know, in any event. I adopted two more orphans in Ecuador with part of the money. That brought my total up to eighteen. I also sent five hundred bucks to the church up the street. I've never been to a service there but the place needs paint and at least three new windows. All I ever see coming out of it are senior citizens and people in wheelchairs. It's the least I could do. The place inspired me to write a hymn called *This Feeble Old Christian*. Three printings in Florida alone.

Even the dogs stay inside on Saint Patrick's Day in Boston. That's because everyone from fireman to priest is hammered as of breakfast. Each ounce of whiskey consumed here today will result in one black eye. Enough fenders will be crushed to keep the body shops booked solid until Independence Day. For three weeks now you could not buy a dram of green paint anywhere; as of tomorrow you will be unable to locate any paint remover for love nor money. Before dawn one third of the population will break its noses on telephone poles, trees, or barroom counters. And, of course, those who have drunk the most will have the farthest to drive home.

Martin and I discovered this by accident the first Saint Pat's Day we were up here. We walked around the block for a pizza and nearly lost our hides to three separate bands of rebels. We did lose the pizza. Since that time, I have noticed, Martin is always out of town on March seventeenth.

He was in Missouri this year interviewing some personnel wizard who had discovered a method of stifling office gossip. Martin was determined to bring this demigod to Boston. Reluctantly I stayed home because I had a deadline coming up. Ah, to see green leaves again! Temporarily sucked dry of the creative impulse, I was skidding along the rim of a mild depression, fighting off the romance paperbacks, running miles and miles simply because it conveyed forward motion, reaming through cookbooks for the most garish recipes imaginable. I missed Fox; with absence he only entrenched himself more firmly under my skin. I wondered how his concert went; however, I did not call him.

My solitude was further grayed by midwinter ennui, Boston style. You know things are bad when three people out of four are wearing ski masks. The climate since Christmas had been merciless, never quite snowing enough to invigorate the sportsmen yet never quite warming enough to make one forget about the oil bills. Twelve straight weeks of insipid snow-shoveling had turned the populace wild, avid for the wispiest excuse to explode. This Saint Patrick's Day would be a real topper.

I spent the morning inside, filing; it preoccupies the soul. Around three I quit and began a Caribbean stew involving beef, coconut, and loads of rum. Early in the game I began to nip, damn it, why did I miss Fox and not my husband? I had not thought much about Martin since he left on this road trip. In fact I usually cease thinking about him the moment he exits the front door. Oof, that sounds heartless, and it's not even correct. I don't stop thinking about Martin; more precisely, I resume thinking about my own affairs. The man has a very subtle way of displacing my existence. All right, I allow him to when he's home; wives, women are stupid like that. They have this genetic desire to please no matter what the personal sacrifice. Sheesh, no wonder my mother's a drunk. My father never went on one road trip in his life.

The doorbell rang. I glanced at the clock: five. Couldn't be UPS; the Girl Scouts had already zapped the block. It was probably the Jehovah's Witnesses again. Once you begin debating with them, they refuse to let go. I should never have told them I believed in God but I didn't want their newspaper.

Feeling bold and a mite arch, I parted the curtain over the glass. It was Fox. I could only stare at him, please, the man was a loon to come here. He just stood there laughing.

"Happy Saint Patrick's Day!" He held a bouquet in one hand and a bottle in the other.

I turned the doorknob, then two sets of keys, then another two switches for Martin's ultrathugproof security system. Had I not imbibed several ladles of rum, I could have shaved thirty seconds off the entire exercise. The keys made one hell of a racket.

"Who's Irish here?" Fox swaggered, trooping inside, not quite sober. I smiled; so he couldn't face me without a little fortification.

I locked the door behind myself. "You surprise me," I said very softly.

"Surprise your opponent!" exclaimed Fox, placing the flowers and the whiskey on a small table. He looked at me for several seconds; those deepset eyes rapidly vaporized ten years of very meticulously forged armor. "I had some unfinished business," he said.

The hell with mating etiquette. I put my arms around his neck and we hit the wall. I lost all my bones. "Did you come here to make love to me," I gulped.

"Yep."

I ran to the kitchen. This stew was taken from the stovetop. I lifted the phone off the hook and was about to grab the bottle of rum when Fox caught up with me and flipped me over his shoulder. His hands slid up my skirt and I became pulp before he even got to the stairway.

Now I do not generally take notice of bodies. Hey, why make an issue of hereditary characteristics. I have had endomorphs, ectomorphs, and every imaginable housing in between and in the end, only a languid tongue and a continent penis matter. Ah, but Fox! His arms, his back, his legs were all wired to the same devastating mechanism and believe me, one never quite forgot about it: too dangerous. I suppose my subconscious always hoped that he would try to kill me.

"What a plantation romance," I gasped, the wind knocked out of my lungs as Fox heaved me onto the bed. My left arm hit the crowbar.

Fox hastily untied his shoes. I was gratified to see that his hands were shaking. "Where's Martin?" he asked.

"Away." Had my husband been under the bed I would have said the same thing; my lips were on fire. I pulled Fox down and wrapped my legs around him. This time he was not getting away until I was finished with him.

He kissed me and my stomach reversed, agh, why had I lost so much time bucking the inevitable? This had been out of my hands from the moment I laid eyes on Fox. Only one mystery remained: if it was inevitable, why should it

"My eyes did nothing," I answered. "Your lust connived with your imagination."

"Then why are you still looking at me like that?"

I contemplated the ceiling. Because I wanted him to take me again. Because I wanted him to leave. Ah, because it was too late. Damn! The moment I married Martin I knew this would happen; no matter who my husband was, I would eventually have gone shopping. Poor Martin. It was nothing personal; he was just the middleman. I was gunning for the Big Guy behind him, of course. Shit, why wasn't I a Buddhist?

"Because I'm a fool," I said finally. Fox's fingers brushed my face and I couldn't bear it. "Do it again."

Around ten he got thirsty so I sent him to the kitchen. "How long have you lived here?" he asked, returning to the bedroom with orange juice and the bottle of whiskey he had left downstairs.

"Five years."

"And where did you live before that?"

"New York."

"Why did you move to Boston?"

"Martin lived here."

One topic rammed aground. Next:

"Do you really compose hymns?"

"Yes."

"Are you any good?"

"I'm the best." Hey, the man told me never to lie to him.

"I believe you." He thought a moment. "What kind of stuff do you write? Maybe I've sung you without knowing it."

Sorry, but Fanny May Tingle still belonged to me. I was never going to cash in all my chips in one night ever again. "My, you're a curious boy."

"Am I asking too many questions?"

"Yes."

"So ask me some."

"There's nothing to ask." Or, rather, there was nothing to answer.

Fox downed some whiskey. "I was born in Brooklyn. My father was very poor. I got a scholarship to Juilliard when I was eighteen."

"Can you still sing?"

"I try."

"So what are you doing in Boston?"

"I got tired of New York."

Whoops, my first glimpse of clay feet. "You're joking."

He poured another. "No, I'm not joking."

"Continue your saga."

"I live in Cambridge; have five students. I want to be an opera singer."

"So what are you doing teaching rape courses?"

"Paying the rent, love. You remember rent? That's for people who don't pay mortgages."

"Or property taxes, or plumbers." Or income tax. Enough pussyfooting around. "I don't believe you don't have a girlfriend."

"I haven't had one in years."

"Why not?"

"Too picky."

Another crash, quite close by, made us both start. "Sounded like glass," Fox said.

"It was only a bottle. On special occasions my neighbor chucks them from the second story into his garbage can." I leaned on my elbow. "So you're picky, eh?"

He saw what I was leading up to. "You're an exception."

Money, brains, talent, looks, charisma—an exception? Try again!

"You're genuinely insane," Fox said. "It's charming." He jumped on top of me. "I don't think I've fucked all your brains out yet."

He left around eight the next morning. Through the fog surrounding my front stoop I could discern a brilliant green stripe bisecting the side of his Bel Air. I looked up and down the block: the green line extended towards both horizons. And who said a gallon of paint didn't go far anymore . . . ?

I had no brains left.

6

EXULTANT, FULL OF a calm dread, I turned to the kitchen and brewed some heavy black coffee. I was totally, ecstatically awake and shivering, alive, ah God! and very happy. Who needed coffee? *Eva, you fool,* clucked the voice of Chuck. I did not reply. Pfuii, I was no fool. I was one of the most omniscient and fearless women on earth at that moment. Fox belonged to me.

I sat by the bay window and looked across the sky. It was going to snow, of course. Whenever the original purchaser of the snowblower was out of town, it snowed. Feeling all, thinking naught, I waited for the first flakes to wet the streets: nothing moved but leaking jalopies, all wrenched out of alignment last night, just like me. I sat immobile for a long time, my brain containing too much static to compose, my eyes too rusty to read pseudohistorical slush, my stomach knotted and full of strong potions.

Fox, darling Fox. Now what? Were I a responsible citizen, I would never contact the man again. Instead, I would always recall a magical Saint Patrick's Day in Boston when I had played blackjack and departed ahead of the house. To varying degrees I had done this before, with Richard, with Lionel, with Orville, with . . . with a lot of them. Why not with Fox? I allowed this lone seductive cold arrow to come within millimeters of my heart, then I leapt away: oho no, I was going to play the hand I had been dealt. This time, though, I was going to be much cagier: once you've been cleaned out, you learn to count your cards.

So get with it, Hathaway, out of the chair. Already I had lost half a morning mooning like an adolescent. Again, my fault: I should never have made love in my own bed. Now my mind would be forever wandering upstairs, searching the silence for Fox instead of composing staunch anthems for wobbly souls. How eagerly history had repeated itself! I had already ignored the cardinal rule of tempestuous fornication: always do it at the other guy's place. Stupid! Had I cabbed home from Cambridge this morning, I would have had two stanzas in the can by now. That's because leaving Ground Zero forges the imagination. Hanging around downstairs with a throbbing, aromatic crotch does quite the opposite.

Obviously I had to remove myself from the premises. I called Orville and asked if any of my pieces were being done in Georgia that weekend.

"There's a performance of *Calvary's Shadow* in Buffalo," Orville suggested.

"Haven't you got anything farther south?"

"*Psalms and Proverbs* in Akron."

"Not that Baptist church again!" I shrieked. "The soprano's a butcher!"

"Her husband is the minister."

I sighed. Lent was my slow season. "Thanks, Orv. Let me know about Easter."

"I could use a christening number, Eva."

"One week." Cripes, babies again. I would sooner write about Lot's wife. I bid Orville adieu, poured another mug of coffee, and resumed my post at the window. The sky looked positively churlish now. Fox had left awfully early; to rehearse, he had said. Rehearse what? Tenors never sang before noon! Their tongues were too tired from kissing themselves in the mirror all night long! Fox was probably breakfasting with some nubile accompanist as I sat here with nothing but longing and dirty sheets. That, too, had happened before and it used to drive me crazy. Whoa, snorted the scarred veteran: I had no claims on this man. I never would. He could eat breakfast, or lunch, or anything with whomever he wanted.

Help, I prayed, *It's coming back.*

Chuck interceded. *You can eat with whomever you like also, idiot.* That did it. I would fly to New York as soon as I finished the laundry.

Whoops, el phone started ringing.

"Chuck! I was just thinking of you."

"That's unusual."

Oh, Christ. I glanced at the clock: nine. She had probably swallowed a screwdriver or two with her doughnut. "How's everything at home?"

"Oh—the same." I didn't ask for details; my father's phone bills were ruinous enough. "What are you doing for Easter?" Chuck asked.

"We're going to the Weavers'."

"Are you going to church beforehand?"

"Don't worry about it, Chuck!" Didn't the perdition of her own soul busy this woman enough? I calmed myself. "We'll be going at some point."

"Where's Martin?"

Good question. "Somewhere south of Chattanooga, I think."

"You're not sure?"

"Naw. He changes all the time. Only his secretary knows for sure."

"And where's his secretary?"

"She's in Boston! Come on! I just talked to her yesterday!"

"I don't know, Eva. It's a strange situation you've got up there. He's with that secretary all the time."

"Of course he's with the secretary all the time! That's his job!" I was beginning to shout. "Martin hates painted fingernails!"

"That's what he tells you, Eva." Chuck sighed. "Is she young? Does she have a husband already? How's her figure?" She paused to swallow another half a screwdriver. "I refuse to worry about this—it's all in the Lord's hands."

I thought I'd better change the subject before she started crying. "So what are you and Robert doing for Easter?"

Chuck summarized the excruciating pressures upon a popular grandmother at holiday time. My father was going to have a great weekend schlepping from tot to tot. "When is Martin getting back?"

"I'm not sure."

Chuck swallowed again. "What's the matter with you today?"

"Nothing. I was up late last night."

Chuck swallowed again. "You don't sound yourself at all."

My mother's sense of smell intensifies with alcohol. I had to be very careful. "I'm fine, really, Chuck, just a little tired."

"Did you take that fertility test I told you about?"

"Nope." This time I heard her pouring. "Well, thanks for calling, Chuck. I've got to run. Take care of yourself." Poor thing. She should stop trying to give up booze for Lent. Every year it makes her more frustrated.

As the washing machine purged my linen, I phoned Martin's office. His secretary Paloma answered. "This is Mrs. Weaver. Would you please leave a message for my husband in case I don't reach him today? I will be in New York until the weekend." I paused. "Is his trip going well?"

"Extremely." Obviously Paloma was not about to reveal any corporate secrets. I wondered briefly if Martin had changed his mind about nail polish: in telephone time alone this woman had a four-to-one edge over me. I thanked her and hung up.

Usually I drive to New York, but I could not tolerate three hours in my Bavaria reliving an evening of misdirected lust. Besides, the Connecticut Turnpike is no longer any fun. Ever since that bridge collapsed near Greenwich the truckers have been operating their vehicles like attack helicopters. I showered Fox off of me, then remade the bed: Martin would soon be sleeping in it. Nuts, I could kick myself. Anyone with moves like that must have fifty women panting after him. I must be miles down the line. Stupid, stupid. I set the alarm system and left.

Lionel met me in the lobby of the theater. He had streaked his red hair green and looked as though he'd slept in the same sweatshirt all week. The smell of opening night clung to his breath. "Eva, baby! I just ADORE that fur! You look elegant!"

"Likewise."

Lionel took my arm. "This show is going to be a s-m-a-s-h, I tell you! I've never had such fabulous dancers in my costumes!" That meant he had slept with half the chorus line.

"How did my number work out?"

" FanTAAAAAAStic! Come on! Rehearsal's just starting." We entered an historic theater in need of fumigation. "Eva, your number is the showstopper! What a great filthy mind you have!"

I had not seen Lionel in such a state since his lover Dirk had abandoned him for a woman. One look at Clarence the conductor and I understood why. "You use the same hairdresser," I said.

"Isn't he exquisite," crooned Lionel.

"Can he conduct?"

"He can do AAAAAAAAANything!"

Clarence silenced the orchestra with a pert rap of his baton. I glanced around the theater: twenty or so shadows, each into this production for a minimum of ten grand, slouched in their seats. Crap, where did Lionel exhume these ghouls?

Act III squealed from the pit, mostly saxophones. It was trash, all trash, glitzy trash. It would be a hit. "What gender are those dancers, Lionel?"

"Both."

"You mean males and females, or bisexuals?"

"Shhhh! Look at those costumes!"

"Stunning." Indeed. This insanely whirling yellow stabbed my tired eyes.

The plot involved a marriage between a bigamist and a gay nun, if I understood it correctly. It was a farce. By the third act, everything was totally screwed up, hence all the dance numbers.

"Here comes your tune, Eva! Hold on to your seat!" Lionel said loudly.

The orchestra suddenly became sultry and very, very naughty. I smiled, remembering what I had written. Even a tone-deaf moron could comprehend the superior hand behind this. *Such talent,* I prayed appreciatively. Out slinked the toast of Broadway, Mr. Pooh Excelsior, a black dancer with the body of Smokey the Bear and the gyrations of Mata Hari. This fellow had no inhibitions whatever; he turned my wholesomely irreverent cakewalk into a one-man orgy. I couldn't help wondering what sort of a mother he had.

"Nice costume," I told Lionel, whose eyes remained pasted to Pooh's behind.

"Nice fucking dance," Lionel breathed. "The way your minds work, you two could be identical twins."

"I beg your pardon?"

"Fantastic!" wheezed a man from the audience when it was over. He looked like a porno king.

"Who's that," I whispered.

"The producer."

The show exploded to a grand finale. I escorted a glazed Lionel to the lobby. "Some monks," I said. "Lionel, you amaze me."

"You got me going, babycakes," he said. "Will you be here for opening night?"

"When's that?"

"Monday."

"I'm not sure." Depended on Fox.

"Not sure! Your own music and you're not sure? My costumes and you're not sure? Doesn't Broadway mean anything to you anymore?"

"Yeah, I like that fruit stand around Seventy-sixth Street."

"You're a real brat."

We went to a French bistro beyond Ninth Avenue for lunch. I still wasn't hungry. Of course Lionel picked up on Fox at once . . . sheesh, the guy intuited faster than a Siamese twin.

"I think Eva's opening up a branch office, isn't she?"

I nearly choked. "What a stupid thing to say."

"Please, lambkin, it's all over your face."

I scowled. Lionel had been reading me like the comics for years. "So tell me what to do," I muttered after a pause.

"Enjoy him, you fool!"

"What about Martin?"

Lionel threw his hands into the air. "Martin's a businessman! Waiter! Another martini, please! *Sec!* Dry!" He lowered his voice. "I told you not to get married."

"Too late now, pal. Got any more great advice?"

"Look, Eva, it was inevitable. You and Martin are totally mismatched. He's a lunatic. Don't feel so depressed. Who IS the lucky fellow?"

"His name's Paul. He teaches karate, sings operas, I met him at the Y, and he's from Brooklyn." I sighed. It didn't sound encouraging. "He's unbelievable in bed."

"I had presumed so," Lionel said sagely. "What does he look like?"

"Six-two, nice body, dark wavy hair, dark eyes, good lips, slow on the draw."

"Has he got any money?"

I blew a quick charge of regret out my nose. "No."

"What do you see in him?"

Versailles and the guillotine, for Christ's sake! "I'm not sure."

"What does he see in you, besides the obvious?"

"A little challenge, I think."

"And you call that romance? You two sound like fucking beef jerky!"

Wrong. We were honey and lightning. I eyed Lionel. "Possibly."

"And you'd better keep it that way, sweetheart, you've got work to do."

"What? Compose hymns and collect money until I die?"

"What more do you want, Eva? You're not looking for husband material, are you?"

"I wasn't looking for anything."

"You were always looking, dear."

I finished my wine. It was pointless to discuss marriage with a faggot libertine. So I turned the tables a bit, inquiring after Lionel's mother. At last report she was off to another fat farm, one where she couldn't sneak in Mars Bars like last time.

"She's fatter than a house," Lionel spat, instantly incensed. That's because he had sent her there for a month, plus air fare to New Mexico. "That woman has ruined my life!"

"But Chuck told me she lost fifty pounds."

"That was before she gained seventy."

"Jesus! How'd she do that so fast?"

Lionel furiously stabbed at a green olive with his tooth-pick, wounded it slightly, and scowled as it scampered under the next table. "She said my show made her nervous."

"She must have learned that excuse from Chuck," I soothed. My deadlines have twice sent Chuck to the sana-torium, my awards once. "Just wait until you win a Tony."

Lionel uttered a sharp cry, like a whiplashed hyena. "No!"

Now people two tables away were looking at us. I leaned over and took his arm. "Lionel," I reprimanded, "you are not responsible for the obesity of your mother."

He shook his green hair despairingly. "Who is, then?"

How could he be so thick? "Your mother's mother." I signaled for another round.

We brooded silently until the drinks arrived. "To *Cloistrophobia*," I toasted.

"To your tune."

"To your boyfriend."

"To yours."

"To your mother."

"To yours." That took care of two Courvoisiers. We split the check and left. It was beginning to snow a little now.

I paused at the corner of Eighth and Forty-fifth. "Lio-nel," I said, "this is no casual affair with this man."

With such proximity to the theater, Lionel's confidence had returned. "Enjoy your little honeymoon, baby." he said. "I hope it doesn't last more than two weeks."

"You shithead."

"Precious, I'm telling you the whole truth and nothing but. Let him in your pants but don't let him anywhere else."

"Why not?"

"Because you'd lose EVerything."

That's what happens to your attitude when you fuck four hundred strange assholes per year. I kissed Lionel good-bye. "Can I sleep at your place tonight?" I asked.

"You've got the key." he said. "When do I meet this Superman?"

"You don't."

I cabbed to Richard Weintraub's apartment on Spring Street. He had bought it ten years ago from the widow of a Chinese mobster.

"Over here, Eva," he called from his drawing table. "What do you think of these?" He waved some mechanicals in the air.

I wended through high piles of laundry and paper towards the far corner of the room. Richard had not vacuumed this apartment in nine years. He was the only child of a Scarsdale dentist's wife. I looked down at his present achievement, a face cleverly superimposed over a foot. "Nice," I said. "It's for your podiatrist, isn't it?"

"He's been bugging me for office stationery."

"Is he going to fix your feet now?" Richard was convinced his feet were giving him backaches.

"My feet will never be fixed," he sighed. "It's hereditary."

"That's the spirit." I made him coffee in one mug and put the chili I had brought in another. This was the last of Richard's clean dishes. When I returned to the living room he sat staring at a blank sheet of paper.

He looked up in surprise. "For me?"

"No, the foot doctor." As he ate I told him about Lionel's musical.

Richard shook his head. "You'll be the scandal of the season."

"Not quite. There's a pseudonym on this one."

"How come? Don't you want to be famous?"

I pursed my lips; never talk to the son of a Jewish mother about the joys of anonymity. "Only rich." That he would appreciate.

We worked for several hours on new covers. Richard wielded a zippier pen today than usual; I needed only to sing him the first stanzas of my new hymns and he devised the perfect covers for them. For the christening number he came up with a nimbus cloud gently rocking a baby sunbeam. That cover, plus the sappiest hymn I had composed in years, would go ten printings, believe me.

"Okay, Richard," I finally asked when he had finished, "who is she?"

His face matched the chili. "Who?"

"The lady behind your magic hand. Stop acting confused."

Richard never confesses to girlfriends unless I drag it out of him. He prefers me to picture him as a soul in exile. 'It's nothing serious," he said.

"Neither were the other eight. Have you proposed to her yet?"

"Eva!" That meant yes. It also meant she had said no.

"So what's her name?"

"Tiffany."

"You're in trouble already, pal."

Richard should stop trying to replace me with expensive frauds. He had yet to understand that nowadays diamond rings and two-hundred-dollar dinners make less of an impact than a singing telegram.

"This one's different," he insisted.

"What? She gives blowjobs?"

Richard waffled his eyebrows but said nothing. I knew damn well that the last tongue to tickle his penis belonged to me. "She's a poetess."

I ask you, what's a poetess doing in a First Avenue singles bar? "Has she written you any poems?"

"Little notes here and there. I think they're good."

"Maybe you should hire her to write you a few birthday verses." Hah, that would cleanse the stables fast. When it comes to his greeting cards, Richard is ruthless.

Richard thought for a moment. "Maybe. I don't know her well enough yet."

I shrugged. Richard's caution will always burn him in the end. Women have no respect for men who play life like a game of chess.

"Don't you want to know what she looks like?"

"Nope." The name was quite enough. "I'm sure you make a stunning couple."

"What's the matter with you today?"

Terminal post-coital agony, that's all. "Sorry, Richard. It's pure jealousy." That would prop his sagging struts for another hour. We had two covers to go. God, what was Fox doing this moment? Thinking of me? I hummed Richard a new hymn about the Sermon on the Mount.

"Why did Orville need an anthem about the Flood?" he asked late in the afternoon. Richard had already drawn me a fish sandwich, a talking donkey, and a profile of Esau.

"They're predicting a bunch of them in Arkansas this winter."

"But you just wrote an offertory about Noah's Ark."

"What's the matter? Don't you like seascapes?"

Richard sighed. He looked at me and I looked away; one should not encourage the glances of hopeless suitors. "Here, I'll sing it again," I said. "Sorry."

"It's a little heavy," Richard said when I'd finished.

"So's a major flood, dildo!" I snapped. The sun was setting and I had been noticing all afternoon how similar Richard's hands were to Fox's. My body was wandering back to bed, but not to sleep. I rubbed my eyes and apologized, blaming fatigue. I would never tell Richard about Fox: my marriage to Martin had already set him back five years.

"You look tired," Richard said, pushing himself away from his desk. "We'll finish this later, eh? How about a drink?"

"Thanks, but I'm going to drop."

"Where are you staying?"

"Lionel's." I had to revise the flood tune first thing in the morning; Lionel had a piano and Richard did not. Lionel also had an extra bedroom.

Richard waved at a cab on Spring Street. "I'm walking," I said.

"In that coat?"

Cripes, what were coats for? "It's insured." Besides, I knew how to defend myself now.

Richard kissed my cheek and delivered his standard farewell. "Are you all right?" He had cadged this habit from his next-to-last girlfriend, Columbine.

"Oh yes." So was the *Titanic*. I walked thirty blocks uptown, but the stretch did not relax in rush-hour bustle. "Hold on, baby," I muttered to myself. "It takes a few days." Ha, fat chance; the kissing alone would tar up my system for weeks. Each passing telephone taunted me. Each passing couple taunted me. Hell, each pair of passing lips taunted me. Where had he picked up that technique?

I'm no fool. Somewhere along the line Fox had had an enormous amount of practice on willing human subjects.

Snow continued to chase the air, catching nothing but ears and collars. It should be two feet deep in Boston by now. I went up to Lionel's apartment, consumed a glass of chianti, took a hot bath, and went to bed. It was not restful to lie on my back. *Nice going,* I prayed. *Now what?* There's not much to verbalize when you know you're only one half a piece of an ever-expanding cosmic jigsaw puzzle. Besides, The Almighty One has been hearing prayers like mine since Adam and Eve and has not once responded. Again I thought of telephoning the other half of the piece. Nope. Too soon.

I remained holed up writing in Lionel's apartment until Good Friday. Orville suggested refuge in Saint Louis or Winston-Salem, but the parrot of inspiration was squawking on my shoulder. In two days I sketched out three anthems, including another christening monster that turned out much better than I would ever have predicted. Obviously my brain was whirring with regurgitated passion: see what I mean about removing yourself from the boudoir? I also wrote a Thanksgiving piece, lightened up the flood number and began an offertory based upon the Rapture. Hot, hot stuff, for crack choirs only. Lionel returned once to pick up a black velvet cape, and disappeared with Clarence, his current lover. They were off to the beauty parlor to streak their hair blue for opening night. Richard called but I couldn't see him; mortal flesh would destroy this creative frenzy. Martin called Friday morning and the gears stopped cold.

"Hello, my girl," said my husband, "How are you?" His voice had risen a quarter tone; he had probably lost five pounds.

"Hi, Martin," I said. "How was your trip?"

"Fine." Martin paused. "May I pick you up at the airport?" That was how my husband begged me to come home.

"I'll try for the noon shuttle."

"What have you been doing down there, darling?"

"Working on hymns." I had not told Martin in any great detail about Lionel's cakewalk. "I had some covers to finish also."

"How are all your friends?"

"Fubar."

Martin showed up at Logan with a bouquet of roses. I think he had not enjoyed returning to an empty house.

"Let's do something this afternoon," he said. He looked awful. I doubted he had seen sunlight in a week.

"What would you like to do?" I asked.

"Something together."

"There are a few Good Friday services you might enjoy."

"I was thinking of something a little more upbeat."

"How about a five-mile run? You still have your cleats, don't you?

"How about a walk in the Arboretum?" The Arboretum is Harvard's contribution to rustic violence. Joggers are raped or knifed there by the dozen and the alumni still think it's the greatest tree zoo in the Northeast.

"Let's try the Jamaica Pond." Martin agreed and we drove off. I was a little worried about my husband. An afternoon off? With me?

Whatever snow had fallen was long gone; not even its puddles remained. We did half a revolution as Martin encapsulated his latest road trip. I listened as hard as I could but after the fourth airport landing my mind burrowed into that Rapture offertory. Eventually Martin lapsed into silence and we strolled along, an odd couple indeed amongst the joggers, the frowsy mums exhibiting their newborn, and the Puerto Ricans eternally casting in the shallow waters for sunfish. My coat and Martin's pinstripe suit received many prolonged stares; people probably thought we were Mafia.

"I've been thinking," Martin said at last, "that we don't spend enough time together."

Very perceptive of the man, now that he had reaped what he had sown. Perhaps Fox had left a sock under the bed. "We probably don't," I agreed, "but what do you suggest?" Please, we had been through this thousands of times. Martin had to go on road trips and I had to stay in one place.

"I'm going to try to stay home more."

That made me smile. When Martin works in Boston and sleeps in our house, I still only see him maybe twenty hours a week. "Why this sudden dissatisfaction with our life-style, cutie? It seems to have worked out fairly well so far." Until three days ago, that is.

"I'm a little worried about you, Eva," Martin said. "Alone all the time with no company, no bridge clubs . . ."

Aha. "You've been·talking to your mother, haven't you?"

Martin didn't reply. I didn't continue. It was obvious that his family would never comprehend females who did not graduate from Radcliffe. Our dismal little walk continued another half hour. Shit, why did I have so little to say to my husband? Delete the usual feminine babble about redecorating, the children, the tennis lessons, and what was left to chat about? How I sat on a bench for five hours wearing down pencil erasers? How my sneakers pounded so rhythmically upon the local gutter? How beautiful I found the whorls of a Spanish onion? How I missed New York? Boring. Deadly. Let's not kid anyone, this marriage depended on road trips for its very survival.

We rounded back to the car. "Want to go out to dinner?" I asked.

"I have a bit of telephoning tonight, darling," Martin said. See what I mean about this nonsensical staying at home? He may as well be in New Guinea. On the way back I bought a newspaper, the Boston *Globe*. Everyone in town calls it the *Globule* or just the *Glob*. Read it once and you'll see why.

The house was considerably messier than when I had left it. I have trouble understanding how Martin can be such a prick about precision when it comes to computers but such a slob when it comes to his own living room. Perhaps I should discuss this with his mother on Easter Sunday. Martin retired wordlessly to the den; I poured myself a drink, opened the *Globule*, and flopped on the couch.

Well, well, what had we here now? Monsieur Paul Fox would be singing in the *Saint John Passion* that evening at the Arlington Street Church. Hmmm. A difficult piece: I wondered if he could cut it. Naw, I didn't want to know. If he shat I would not want to see him anymore.

I peered into the den. Pipe smoke encased Martin's head; his breath would reek in the morning. That did it. "I think I'll go to church," I announced.

"Just a moment, Itsuo," said Martin, smothering the receiver. "Need a lift?"

"No, it's okay. I'll be back around twelve if they don't drag the choruses." I pecked Martin's forehead good-bye. "I thought you threw all those pipes out."

"I found this in the back of my drawer," Martin confessed.

"Was the tobacco in the back of your drawer, too?"

"No, I found that in Chattanooga."

I say, how can you get angry with such a tenacious, clever fellow? He would stay one pipe ahead of me until I shut up about the halitosis. Then he'd quit. "You big jerk."

My fond smile flattened the moment I got into the car. *Jeeeesus,* I prayed, *Look how my hands are shaking.* Already my lungs constricted like terrorized mice. I parked in the lot on Exeter Street and walked towards the Common past thirty or so weekending couples. Most of the women had that "Please give me an orgasm before Monday" smile of desperation. Good luck, ladies. As I passed their front windows, the modish pasta emporia of Newbury Street throbbed with intensely hullabalooing customers; one would never guess that this was the most solemn holiday in Christendom. I don't understand. Nothing moves on Yom Kippur.

The magnificent Arlington Street Church, as most downtown Boston churches, hit its heyday about a century ago. Now maybe thirty spinsters, descendents of the original parishioners, graced the family pews each Sunday, shivering in the cold because heating oil and large sanctuaries tend to cancel each other out. A packed house here must have been awesome; were I a kid surrounded by two thousand somber Brahmins intoning *O God Our Help in Ages Past,* it would have scared the shit out of me. Hah, that's probably why the place was empty now. I walked about twenty rows up and sat in a pewbox marked Whittredge.

The heads of several hundred subdued concertgoers puffed

into the semidarkness ahead of me. No one was talking: Omnipotent Everlasting God saturated these forests of carved mahogany. It was not the same Fellow you heard about on the radio Sunday morning as you drove to get the newspaper. Quiet figures rustled constantly past me as the sanctuary filled with lapsed Christians, most of them down from Beacon Hill. A handsome and regular man, my age, entered the Whittredge box, nodded to me, and sat a foot away. The highbacked pew secreted us from our neighbors; I could have given him a handjob and those worshipping in the Percy box behind us would have suspected nothing. The fellow stole several glances at me. He got only my profile in return.

The orchestra suddenly quieted and the conductor emerged from the vestry. His soloists, picking through lecturns, followed Indian file. One ass in the audience applauded briefly. Ah, there was my far-off delightful Fox; now I remembered what he looked like. Surely I had never slept, never awakened with this tall stranger: my mind denied everything and my cheeks blurted the truth. That's known as sophistication.

The *Saint John Passion* started and at once tears came to my eyes. In my highest poetical ectasy I would never equal the one hundredth particle of genius of Johann Sebastian Bach. As the opening chorus buffeted my soul I looked overhead into the daunting arches and I thought *Oho, You're up there, aren't You now, You're watching me and Fox and we're all going to slug it out again, aren't we?* Once more I knew that God would win; He takes the First Commandment very seriously, come on, why do you think it's first? *So why plant Fox there,* I wailed, *Why distribute the hottest lips to the spiritual recidivists? Crap! They're easier to goad than a drunken Irishman!* Believe me, I tried once to slap the Liege of the Universe. I got slapped back.

Slowly I put a handkerchief under my black veil. The gentleman next to me saw me wiping my eyes and moved two inches closer. "Are you all right?" he whispered. Nice eyes.

I nodded and looked straight ahead. Didn't like his cologne.

The chorale ended and Fox, performing the role of the Evangelist, stepped forward. I held my breath: if he couldn't sing, I might still save myself.

It only took two notes. I was lost.

The *Saint John Passion* ended approximately three hours later as the last chorale, serene and confident of reunion with the slain Christ, floated upward to silence. I closed my eyes: heaven, ah, the ultimate hope. Bach knew it; I knew it. Tomorrow I would not be so sure.

The gentleman beside me was not moving, nor was he contemplating his Savior. In fact he was about to ask me out for a drink. I rose, curtly excused myself, and moved into the aisle. Above the narthex gleamed hundreds of organ pipes, half of them now cracked and the other half containing mice. Shit, why didn't Protestants have a little more respect for the king of instruments? With all the money they saved on rosary beads and bar mitzvahs, you'd think they'd have a little spare cash for maintenance.

Clutching my scarf about my throat, I leaned into the wind whooshing off the Boston Common. The bleak night had swept most pedestrians away.

Around Dartmouth Street I paused and then walked back into the wind. Perhaps I had missed him. I waited in the vestibule only a few minutes. I spotted Fox leaving with the alto soloist, a thick-lipped blond whose talent had not flabbergasted me. As Fox pushed open the tremendous doors he saw me in the shadows and stopped cold. The alto kept walking. I figured we had about thirty seconds before she discovered her mistake.

Fox came over to me and peered through my black veil. I think he was refreshing his memory also. "Hello there, beautiful," he said softly. An original line.

"What an Evangelist," I replied. "Such conviction."

The alto stuck her thick head through the doors. "Paul! There you are!"

I didn't take my eyes from his face. My perfume rushed up to my nostrils, whew, the old throat was cranking out BTUs faster than a cast-iron furnace.

The alto plaited her fingers through Fox's. "Foxy! We'll be the last ones there!"

"This is Karfa Nef," introduced Fox. "Eva Hathaway."

"Lovely singing," I lied. I knew Cajuns with more authentic German accents than this sow.

"Thank you very much," Karla crowed. She must have practiced those five syllables a thousand times to achieve such a perfect blend of cream, sugar, and bullshit. "I just adore that hat."

I stared her down a good seven seconds, then turned to Fox. "Enjoy your party now, Foxy." No one moved.

Fortunately a blather of musicians crashed through the inside doors. Karla caught up with a cellist who had called to her. "I'm right outside, Foxy," she cooed. "Just one moment." I had to smile, please, this little ploy came straight out of the *National Enquirer*.

Fox immediately slipped his hands under my coat onto my waist, spreading his fingers so that they covered a maximum of square inches. My breath halted then flew away in a million tiny gusts. "Where have you been?" he said.

"Don't say you missed me," I said. "I'm touched."

"She's just a friend."

"Of course." You don't take your enemies to bed.

"Come back to my place tonight."

Oh God, I prayed, *Life is so short.* I placed my hands over Fox's; his thumbs nudged the bottoms of my breasts. I slid my fingers far under his cuffs, agh, warm flesh. "No."

"When?"

"I don't know," I croaked. "As soon as possible." I disengaged his hands. "So you really can sing."

He grinned and for a moment I thought that he loved me. "Take off that veil so I can kiss you."

"Not in my church on Good Friday you don't." My fingers again edged up his cuffs. Fox took my right hand and gently bit the cleft between my thumb and first finger; against my will I sighed.

"I'm crazy about you," I whispered. "You won't get away with this."

With a little smacking noise his lips relinquished my hand. "So who's running?" Fox brought my hand down to his belt but halted before hitting his erection; kind of him. "I'll call you tomorrow."

"No."

"You'll call me."

"If worse comes to worst." I left Fox leaning against a plaque commemorating all rectors of the Arlington Street Church since 1804. There had been only eight.

Martin, my husband, heard the Bavaria pull into the driveway and opened the front door for me. It was a few minutes after midnight. "How was the concert?" he asked, slipping off my coat and resetting the alarm system. I removed my hat and we walked to the den for a nightcap.

"Sad." I was not in a talkative mood.

Martin handed me a glass and sat beside me on the couch. "I like that perfume," he said. "What is it?"

"You gave it to me when I still lived in New York. Remember?"

Martin slid his arm behind my shoulder. "I remember how saucy you always were." He loosened the collar of my blouse and nosed familiarly along my neck. I felt nothing at all; then I imagined Fox performing the identical exercise and a pendulum swung into my stomach. *It's all in your mind, you tramp*, castigated Chuck, *You have no right to block out your husband like this.*

I tossed down the remainder of my Benedictine. "I am a very bad wife, Martin," I said quietly. "I'm sorry."

"Don't say that," Martin whispered, pausing. "You're a perfect wife."

The pedestal singed my feet. "Does that mean you're a very bad husband then?" I asked hopefully. Secretaries? Prostitutes? Gaming at the San Diego Hilton, maybe?

"No, it means I'm a perfect husband." He wasn't joking: my husband seriously believed this was a great marriage. Jesus, didn't he have any imagination? What did he think I did with myself all day, think chaste thoughts? Pfuii, maybe he didn't care what I thought as long as I washed his socks and occasionally made Stuffed Onions. Wait a moment: I might be a laundress, I might be a chef and bartender, I might be a walking diamond mine and a poor musician's derangement, but I was not an actress. Surely Martin must have seen my new shadow; everyone else who loved me had noticed in five minutes flat. I probed Martin's eyes, desperately wanting to find suspicion or hatred. Hell, I'd even settle for impatience, anything to provide me with an excuse to spread the manure. I found nothing of the sort. Instead, I saw that no matter what he suspected, Martin would never ask me the ultimate question: he intended to keep me and therefore saw no point in exposing the sordid details of my day-to-day existence. *Ask, ask,* my brain screamed. Martin only smiled softly; no self-respecting WASP would think of interfering in the wars within a spouse's soul. Life was the great, the only, solo flight, sin merely the ballast.

"So what was the name of the perfume?" I asked.

"I don't remember."

One hundred bucks an ounce and he didn't remember. Maybe Paloma had bought it. Martin finished his brandy and took me to bed. He was much friskier than usual but I didn't get anywhere. It felt very strange to be sleeping with my husband.

"My son!" cried Mrs. Weaver, embracing dearest Martin as she would stolen goods returned to her. "Happy Easter!" She quickly scanned my abdomen for progenitive bulges and offered me her cheek. "Hello, Eva."

The maid was taking our coats as Mr. Weaver walked into the foyer. "Well, well," he greeted, "delightful to see you." My father-in-law has always responded to primary colors and black hosiery; he took my arm and led everyone into the living room. I could feel Ruth's eyes burning a hole through the back of my dress and stifled an urge to check for runs in my stockings.

Out came the champagne and macadamias as Martin told his parents the events of the last weeks. Computers from Paragraph One, of course. Were he not safely perched in an antique chair beyond my range, I would have kicked his shins. Come on, this was Easter, not closing time at the Stock Exchange. Martin had delivered only half his epic monologue by the time dinner was announced; to my chagrin his mother expressed disappointment at the interruption.

I immediately grabbed Martin's elbow. "Would you please talk about something else at dinner, damn it," I hissed as we went to the dining room.

Martin looked genuinely surprised. "What else is there to talk about?"

"The weather! Your sister! I don't care!"

"What's the matter with you today?" Martin had been on the phone all morning to Taiwan and had made us late for church, not a recommended course of action on Easter Sunday. We got the worst seats in the house, crammed next to a bag man. The choir sang an awful anthem awfully. Throughout the service Martin had jotted notes to himself on the back of a visitation card. Apparently he now felt deserving of special treatment for his chaperone services.

Stifle it, Eva, cautioned Chuck, *Give his parents a chance to enjoy their child.* I frowned angrily. Chuck was a master of the oblique plaint.

"Where the hell's your sister?" I countered, crap, at least she would talk flesh and blood. She was an eye surgeon.

"Mother, where is Clarissa today?"

"At a convention in Bermuda, dear." Ha, probably screwing her brains out. We took our places at the table. Edmund said grace. I bowed my head: *Give me Fox,* I prayed, *tomorrow.*

The butler served asparagus in a lemon sauce. Spring again and another year had gone by and I missed Fox tremendously. "Where did you get these beautiful asparagus, Ruth?" I asked.

"I sent James to the farmer's market," replied my mother-in-law. "Now, what were you telling us, Martin darling? Did you hire that fellow in Missouri?"

I glared menacingly across the table. Martin wiped his mouth with a linen napkin, stalling for time. "I did," he said. "Hem! Might I have some more asparagus, James?"

"This sauce is just delicious," I said. "Did James get the lemons at the farmer's market, too?"

"No." Ruth returned to her idol. "Were the daffodils up yet in Saint Louis, Martin dear?"

Surrender, Hathaway. I reached for my wine; Martin got the message and resumed his Ozark adventures. Ah well, I suppose if I had an only son as successful as Martin and he married a wench who forgot birthdays all the time, I'd grab him the moment he crossed my threshold also. But I don't think I'd carry on this hero-worship routine; it would wreck the boy's marriage. Thank God Chuck had spared my brothers.

Throughout rack of lamb and new potatoes the saga of Weaver, Inc. continued. Mother sat spellbound as son talked and I drank. I think Mr. Weaver was dozing with his eyes open, a trick he had no doubt picked up over forty years of wedlock. Meanwhile Martin had completely changed personalities. It's criminal what a few moments of maternal adulation do to the male ego. A puffed adder sat across from me now. "And so this morning I finally got Taiwan to ship over the relays," Martin bragged. "It was that or give Wortz to Itsuo."

"You gave Itsuo warts?" I couldn't believe my ears.

"No, darling, you don't understand. Wortz is a German company. W-O-R-T-Z."

I thought for a moment, then pushed back my chair, crossed to Martin's side of the table and yanked his ears. A shocked silence filled the Weaver dining room. "Forgive me, dear," I told Martin, "but you've forgotten our little agreement." I turned to Martin's parents. "Every time Martin says 'You don't understand,' he gets his ears pulled. We're trying to discourage him from using such condescending language."

Mrs. Weaver blinked twice, then signaled for James to bring on the strawberry shortcake. "And did Mr. Itsuo receive Wortz?" She pronounced "Wortz" very carefully.

"His name is Mr. Tagahashi," I interjected, plunging cheerfully into the shortcake. *Bad girl, Eva,* remonstrated Chuck. I merely smiled. Come on, if I were eating at home Chuck would be crying on the couch by now, half the dishes would be smashed, and my father would be taking another of his long walks. The Weavers needed a little steam in their starch, that's all. "Itsuo's just a nickname. I think it means bun pincher."

"Do the Japanese people consume buns?" I had to give Ruth credit, she was one hell of a conversationalist.

"Some of them do," I replied.

Martin was getting annoyed with me. "Espresso, Eva?" he offered. Shit! Why couldn't my husband just come out hurt? Ah! Because The Fellow who had sent me this man was the same louse who had made up those fucking battleship rules of marriage! To play such tricks on unsuspecting humans was worse than entrapment: it was gallingly poor sportsmanship. Let's face it, if I had betrayed Martin, then The Grand Admiral had betrayed me.

Fox took off my clothes, then his own; the man certainly knew his way around bra hooks and panty hose. As always, he took his own sweet time, tormenting me with those slow procrastinating hands. Please, this was no time for a Braille reconnaissance of Eva Hathaway. "Step on it, baby." I whispered.

Fox slipped inside. He hadn't said three words in the entire afternoon. "God," I shuddered, maybe in bliss, or accusation, probably in hopelessness. Fox started to move and my body loped gently away from me, clinging to him: mutiny most sublime. I recalled the cost of such folly and I'll tell you something, I didn't give a damn. I swallowed the ten million memories slowly wriggling, like awakening asps, in my throat, and I crossed the boundary separating the merely physical from that estate which is much wilder and much more beautiful.

Meanwhile holiday activity in the street had begun to pick up: I heard several shouts and some breaking glass, my neighbor Harry backing into his garage door for perhaps the fiftieth time. He insists on leaving it open and his wife Doris insists on closing it. After a few drinks he forgets who did what. Two fire engines shrieked past en route to the bar down the street, where the patrons keep flicking ashes in each other's hair. Dogs howled lugubriously from the ramparts.

I could just make out Fox's profile in the dim bedroom. He smiled at me and my guts winced. "Forgive my curiosity," I said, "but are you married?" Say yes, you bastard.

"No."

"Have you ever been married?"

"No."

I lay still. "That's too bad." *You always collect, don't You?* "Why did you come back here, baby?"

He toyed with my lips. "Your eyes gave you away."

and say "Will you curb that drunken tongue of yours?"
Everyone knew that's what he meant!

Mr. Weaver finally came to my rescue. "How's your
family, Eva?"

"Fine, thank you." Actually they were terrible. My
brother had just lost his job for the fourth time and it
looked like Chuck would have to go back to that sanitar-
ium in Stockbridge. Whatever she wasn't spending on
booze she was blowing on the lottery. My younger sister
was pregnant.

"And how's your work?"

"Oh, coming along. I'm nominated for Hymnist of the
Year again."

Mrs. Weaver leaned over her coffee but not to congratu-
late me. "I understand you were in New York this week."
Damn, this family said less and implied more than a
staring corpse.

"Eva was probably looking at apartments," Martin joked.
He did not want me telling his mother about Lionel Boyd.

"My goodness, you couldn't be thinking of moving
back to New York!" Ruth exclaimed in horror.

"The idea has always appealed to me," I said. "I
should never have given up my apartment on Central
Park."

Martin sighed; he hears this phrase ten times per week.
"Eva does a lot of work in the city," he explained, eyeing
me intently. I obediently sealed my lips, what the hell, the
three of them against one of me? I'd get creamed.

Mr. Weaver placed his hand over mine. "We'll make a
Bostonian of you yet, my dear. Everything in good time."

"Everything," echoed Ruth. The implication was obvious. I felt like running from the table, running miles and
miles back to Manhattan, where I should have stayed in
the first place. I didn't belong with bone china and people
who never shat or fucked. Come on, it had taken me two
years to coax the most anemic, half-audible fart out of
Martin's backside. This Puritan royalty setup was unnatural and I would never get used to it. Notice that the
Weavers made no mention of *my* making New Yorkers out
of *them* in good time.

"What delicious strawberry shortcake," I said.

"This is one of Martin's favorite desserts," his mother announced.

"You never told me that, Flappy." Hey, if I could learn about desserts, Ruth could learn about nicknames. "Flappy" referred to Martin's sexual organs when he was asleep.

Martin blushed. His mother barely skipped a beat. "It comes from a treasured family recipe," she said.

"Just like the stuffed onions?"

Why did a huge silence follow every comment I ever made in this house? It was much more deafening than Chuck's shattering dishware. I did not understand. Here I didn't smoke or throw wild cocaine parties, I offered my husband the utmost hospitality whenever he was in town, I kept discreetly to myself when he was away, and I never nagged the man about anything. I just didn't worship him enough to have his children, that's all. For that my mother-in-law barely tolerated me? Then she was an ass. In Chuck's worst alcoholic stupors she understood me better than this.

Edmund Weaver, diplomat supreme, again sledded into the void. "Martin, I bought a canoe kit last weekend." Father and son plunged into ardent debate concerning balsa, polyurethane, and the original tribe of Massachusetts Indians. Don't ask me how Ruth kept a straight face; her husband had already built eight canoes and they were all out in the greenhouse.

Suddenly a new hymn tune flashed across my mind. It was a march and the choir was singing about how happy they were in heaven. *Jesus,* I prayed, *What brought that on?* Nevertheless I focused my attention on it and was soon floating beyond the damask tablecloth towards Elysium and, beyond that, to another darker world without clothes, with Fox. I saw but did not register the Weavers; my breathing did its usual mount as the body recalled certain skirmishes of recent history. The march faltered but I willed it back to its feet. If I lost it in a wash of Fox it would never resurrect itself; it had come upon me too suddenly.

I noticed Mr. Weaver getting up from his chair and stomped the march into a trench of brain tissue. Ruth was contemplating my face, wondering where I had been. Martin smiled over at me, oblivious of my absence but grateful for my silence. "Come, darling," he said, "Dad's going to show us slides of Austria."

We adjourned to the den. My body was yelping for exercise so I quelled it with a double shot of Calvados from the bar. That reactivated the march. I got snagged on the third stanza. "Say, Ruth," I whispered, nudging my mother-in-law, "do you have a Bible handy?" A linzertorte hovered briefly atop one of her cheeks and flitted away.

"There's the Festspielhaus!" shouted Edmund above the projector.

"Anyone here have a Bible on him?" I repeated, turning back towards the menfolk. Martin sat fixed on the screen as Edmund frenziedly previewed slides in the dim reflection of the projector. I looked around, then flung a small pillow at Martin. It hit him in the face.

"Hey! Got a pocket Testament on you?"

Martin caught his glasses a microsecond before they zipped behind a standing globe. He angrily scooped the pillow off the floor and took aim at me. But he didn't throw it because he knew I would duck and the pillow would then hit a crystal lamp. Plus I was sitting way too close to Ruth. So Martin sat on the pillow instead.

The Weavers meanwhile pretended that their little green pillow had remained immobile on the couch. Ruth asked nonsensical questions like "Isn't that the Goldener Hirsch, darling?" until Edmund drew Martin into a long-winded dialogue about the collapse of the Austrian empire. I clenched my teeth and re-edited the first two stanzas of the march. Let me tell you, I wished to hell Ed would quit Salzburg and move on to Vienna. Richard Weintraub and I had first slept together in Salzburg. If anyone had told me that five years later I would be primly seated on a leather couch watching slides with a husband and two in-laws, I would have laughed sarcastically.

"What is so funny, Eva?" inquired Ruth.

"I think I recognize that hotel." No one asked why I should be laughing at a hotel. Bah, Chuck would have squeezed a full confession out of me in two minutes. I laughed again exactly the same way.

"Eva, darling," Martin disciplined from the rear of the room.

"WhaaAAat?" I nearly shouted at him. Jesus Christ, this tongue-biting was getting on my nerves.

"Come sit here with me."

I tiptoed back to Martin. On the way I caught Edmund's eye and he smiled subtly at me: if he didn't have a mistress, I'd eat the slide projector.

"You're so restless today, my baby," Martin whispered. "What's the matter?"

"I don't like you anymore."

Martin chuckled. Whenever I tell him this he thinks I'm teasing. "Shall we go soon? I've had about enough myself."

"Don't be so mean, Flappy. Let your father finish his slides."

We vegetated on the couch for another fifty-odd minutes. Edmund's pictorial essay ended in Kitzbühl, where he dropped his camera. "Your mother loaded me down with too many packages," he lamented.

"That was great, Dad," Martin complimented, tucking away the file cards upon which he had been scribbling for half an hour. "Your sense of composition has improved tremendously."

"Hasn't it?" Ruth cried proudly. She had been in most of the pictures.

We wound down the afternoon with a light stroll through the Weaver's garden. The crocuses were up and the earth was sprouting little green daffodil tits. Soon, on one of these musky spring nights before the bugs came, I would take Fox to Walden Pond and kiss him to death.

In the car Martin laid his hand on my knee. "Thank you for behaving so well, love." I thought he was kidding, so did not reply. Martin slowly drove twenty blocks as I looked out at the sumptuous homes lining Beacon Street. Each of those homes contained a woman who raised children, bought Persian rugs, and threw big parties for many friends every couple of weekends. It was incredible. "I know my parents are difficult," Martin continued.

"They're all right. They're just so different from Chuck and Robert." I paused. "Particularly your mother."

"She likes you, really, Eva."

"Could have fooled me."

"And my father is crazy about you."

"Of course." I did not elucidate. "And what's this about strawberry shortcake? I ask you all the time for your favorites and you've never said strawberry shortcake."

Martin shrugged. "I only had it for birthdays." That explained it. Martin had not been in Boston for his birthday ever.

The phone rang as we stood on the doorstep fiddling with the locks and counterlocks of the alarm system. My blood jumped: Fox. "Step on it, Martin," I said.

Martin got the front door open, then dropped his key ring. In my haste to get past him I kicked the key ring off the porch. "Damn it," Martin shouted. "Find those keys!" A little mechanical whine behind the front door reminded us that we had exactly ten seconds to deactivate the alarm.

"You find yours, I'll find mine," I shouted back, tearing into my purse. They weren't in my purse. I tried all pockets. No. Meanwhile Martin had disappeared under the porch. He'd locate a skunk before he found those keys.

I dumped the contents of my purse onto the porch floor. Aha! There were my keys wedged in my checkbook. I got to the deactivator switch a millisecond before the sirens and gongs went bananas.

"I got it, Martin," I yelled irascibly. As far as my pulse was concerned, I had just been robbed and pistol-whipped. The telephone ceased to ring; my husband remained on hands and knees in the shrubbery destroying a six-hundred-dollar suit. Feeling the smoke billow behind my eyes, I ran upstairs and changed into some running clothes. My feet would bear the brunt of this, not my husband.

Martin stood brushing leaves off his knees as I stomped by. "See you later," I called.

"Be careful, baby."

I logged about eight miles through the Common and along the Charles River. The paths vermiculated with runners, cyclists, amblers, and, of course, the truly mad on roller skates; thousands of sailboats and kayaks skimmed the river and everywhere everyone was out marketing. The earth reeked of fuck; it drove one mad. I ran very fast for fifteen minutes towards Cambridge, where Fox lived, then doubled back at the Harvard Boat House, locale of the area's most enduring traffic jam. Motorists habitually begin turning left half a block away from this intersection, so the gridlock extends two hundred feet in four directions. Before I reached the BU Bridge I had passed four rear-enders on Memorial Drive. It happens whenever the shorts first replace the sweatpants. I continued towards MIT because I had to exhaust myself.

As the sunlight faded I spotted an empty park bench facing the Charles River and flopped onto it. My knees burned, whoa, time to stop this punishment. For a long while I observed dozens of cuddly sailors drift aimlessly into the paths of oncoming vessels, secure in the assumption that lovers held universal right of way. Two of them neglected to think that they themselves might be crossing the path of two other lovers, whoops, three amours overboard, one remorsefully gazing at a punctured hull instead of his girlfriend. That's what happens when you forget about rudders.

With a sigh I decided not to see Fox anymore. Before he barged in I had led a moderately contented life. Now I couldn't sleep, had no appetite, chewed out my husband for being alive, and I had to change underpants three times a day. Soon I wouldn't be able to write hymns anymore. And for what? A sexual fairy tale! Please, the man had no career, no awe of me whatever, and an ego twice the size of Puccini's. He was unpredictable, overconfident, disgustingly talented, and probably an atheist to boot. In short, he was the total opposite of Martin. That's what attracted me to him in the first place. Whatever that theory was about two halves making a whole, forget it. Anywhere outside of pure mathematics, the fractions don't add—they multiply. Quarter speed was even pushing it in my case. And the sneaking around! The phone calls from "Mr. Smith!" The bogus plane tickets to Albany! No man was worth that. Thus what began between the legs ended two weeks later between the ears. Very proud that I had not allowed history to repeat itself, I stiffly arose from the bench and headed home.

I took a trolley because my arches hurt. What a mistake. The MBTA had a driver-in-training at the wheel and he closed the rear door on a baby carriage that some Cubanos were wedging into the car. The carriage to begin with was a good four inches wider than the doors, a fact which you'd think the Cubanos would notice. Plus they weren't even wheeling kids, they were wheeling toys, skateboards, and a huge cha-cha-spewing radio. The kids perched shrieking in mother's arms. All other passengers quickly escaped through the front exit; believe me, nothing would budge on the Green Line before midnight.

"What happened to you?" asked Martin when I finally dragged in the front door. He was reading his three Sunday papers in the den.

"That fuckin' trolly, that's what," I snapped. Nothing makes you loathe a town more than a worthless transit system. I stripped naked at the foot of the stairs and stomped up. I didn't care who was looking in the windows, I had been hobbling in these clammy stenchola clothes for four miles now.

Martin accompanied me to the top of the stairs. I knew exactly what he was going to do. He was going to calm me down. But before he succeeded I had to get one lick in. "This fuckin' town," I fumed. "I'm moving back to New York."

"The subway doesn't work any better in New York, Eva," Martin reminded me. There had been a big article about this in the *Globule* two weeks ago. I hadn't read it.

"That's not the point," I choked. "I don't expect it to work in New York. I expect it to work here."

Martin put his arms around me. "My little girl," he crowed. "My angry little girl with the cutest buns in the world."

See how he changes the subject? How could I continue raving about trolleys now without sounding ridiculous? Ah, forget it. "How about some Stuffed Onions tonight, big boy?"

"After you take a shower, stinky." I ran into the shower. "Stinky cute buns," Martin called after me.

Martin left early the next morning for California. I would have accompanied him, but I wanted to see the opening of Lionel's bigamy farce on Broadway. It was pretty rude and I didn't hang around for any drunken stage parties, please, you could smell anal lust from the tenth

row. As expected, the cakewalk got the biggest audience
response but then again, audiences don't know shit. Only
the critics could tell them for sure if they had enjoyed
themselves.

I flew back to Boston and planted roses all week. Between thorns I composed a Pentecost aria and an anthem
for Father's Day. Tried to finish that march I had been
concocting since Easter but the third verse still eluded me.
Ruth called once asking what Martin might like for his
birthday. I recommended dancing lessons. Oh yes, I consumed three romance paperbacks. Pure clap.

Lionel called early one morning as I was about to kill
myself. "It's a smAAAAAAsh!" he screamed.

"What time is it?"

"Five-thirty Wednesday morning, dear heart." That meant
Thread & Co. had been partying straight for twenty hours
waiting for the reviews to hit the stands. "Let me read
this! Hold on, Eva! It's TOO much! I can't believe it!"

"Read, jackass."

"Clarence, get out of the light! Here! Wait! Let me see
that! Watch it, will you! That's my copy, damn it! Eva!
Will you three get OUT of the phone booth! Please! Ow!
My hair! Damn you!" Lionel cleared his throat. "Not to
be missed in the final act is Cakewalk, a number which
adds new dimension to the term 'naughty.' It must be seen
to be believed. Mr. A. P. Edgewater, a composer hitherto
unknown to us, should be slapped on the wrists for making
wickedness so delicious."

"What a stupid review," I said. "Which paper was that
from?"

"The *Times*." Should have known. "Wait until you hear
what the *Post* said! My GAAAAwd, we're the toast of
the town! Ready for this one?"

"No."

"Why not? Are you sick or something? Is your boyfriend there with you?"

"You know I hate reviews."

"Eva, you're crazy! I've got a fistful of raves here and
you don't want to hear them?"

"Nope." Come on, I know what I wrote and Richard

told me what he thought of it. What the rest of them think doesn't concern me.

"Jesus Christ, what a party pooper! Clarence! Come here with that cape! I've got to go, baby, I'm furious with you!"

"You are not." Lionel was hammered, period. He'd call in two days, when he woke up, full of apologies and dim memories of a phone booth on Madison Avenue.

"Yes, I am! This is the break of my career! Good-bye!"

Shit, why wasn't I in New York blithely strangling Lionel instead of putrefying here in my bed? I got up, don't ask why, and began chipping away at the third stanza of that fucking march through Paradise. Around ten Chuck called to read me Lionel's review in the *Times*. She and Lionel's mother enjoy a friendly rivalry, you see, and Lionel and I are the racehorses. I advised Chuck not to see the show: she abhors sex. "It's going to be sold out for months," I said. "Plus it's drivel." Chuck refused to believe that I might be right and the critics wrong. What can I tell you? She also subscribes to *TV Guide*. My mother asked about Martin's birthday. I suggested a bottle of scotch.

I flew out to Nashville that weekend to hear an oratorio I had composed eleven years ago, when I was just a kid. Even then I was damn good. As usual the soprano tried to sing louder than the twenty-five people behind her. She succeeded not only in singing louder but half a tone sharper. Afterward she gave a pleased little smile and snuggled into her padded choir bench. Then the minister delivered a sermon entitled "The Joys of Obedience." Over the years I have heard approximately thirty versions of this theme, and once again it left me cold: here I had obediently given up Fox and I felt joyful as ashes. Let's face it, only trained seals and Moslem wives enjoy being obedient. The rest of us prefer to hear "Ain't Misbehavin'."

7

PARADISE MARCH, stanza three, was about to hatch. I felt it as I closed the covers of *Passion's Avalanche*, a banal romance about an ingenue on Swiss holiday. She fell for the tour guide, natch, and in the end his Saint Bernard brought them together in a snowslide. By the third chapter I knew it would end that way but I kept reading in hope of real-life trauma like passport problems or the disappointing sex technique of a Swiss he-man. No way! Even the Saint Bernard fell in love with a villager's Schnauzer! Crap! I flung the book directly into the trash and resolved to read only nonfiction until Memorial Day. For the first twenty years of my life I had gorged on nothing but history and philosophy books. That's what got me started on the junk romances.

Fraught with remote ski cabins, the Matterhorn, and crackling fires, my brain whirred impatiently. It was about to metabolize all these mental chocolates into immortal hymnody, you see. Hey look, it ain't easy triggering the sublime from the ridiculous. Beethoven took long walks in the woods. Hemingway shot elephants. Only people who have never composed think that notes emerge of their own accord. I wrapped myself in a blanket and went to my study. It was about midnight and I would be good for only an hour.

I had been attacking the *Paradise March* from the wrong angle. Instead of forcing the third stanza into a goosestep like the first two, I should have been molding it into a very quiet, ecstatic coda. After all, the whole parade was already in heaven, what more could they shout about? Too much swaggering around and this hymn would only sell in Texas. So I made the last verse a tenor solo while the choir just hummed or chanted "Paradise" at critical harmonious points. The rapidity with which the final verse appeared surprised me. *You couldn't make it this easy all the time, I suppose,* I prayed; tonight I almost felt conversational, like an old fart shooting pool. Near the end, in a final burst of inspiration, I modulated into E major. The whole thing got softer and softer until only the tenor was left with a little paean to immortality. I shut off the lights and went to bed; in the morning I'd touch up the transitional passage and then it would be finished.

I didn't sleep very well; the brain was still twirling although the body had conked out. I fitfully dreamt about that last verse, about my alarm system going off, about Lionel's cakewalk, and of an amorphous encounter with Richard Weintraub. I sprang awake near three-thirty and Fox was in my throat. I missed him fiercely. Listening to the night, I lay still for many moments, feeling warily for the crowbar. Were Martin snuggled up against me, of course, I would not have awakened at all; body heat is nature's best soporific. But my husband was in California again. I turned up the electric blanket, one paltry substitute, and stared at the gray ceiling. Bah, what was the matter with me? Surely I had heard tender voices before. Surely other hands had done what his had. Now I was totally alert. "Fox," I called softly, writhing at quarter speed. What now? Cry? Masturbate? Phone the guy? *You know,* I prayed, *I can't take much more of this.* That little message calmed me considerably, like an irate call to Customer Service. I drifted off again, clutching the crowbar.

First thing next morning I went down to finish *Paradise March.* To my disgust I discovered that the third stanza was not quite the masterpiece it had seemed last night. Also, I was out of music paper. Martin had been using it for his little computer diagrams; the five-line pattern had highly intrigued him. I quickly dressed and went out to the car. Strange: the proud professionals of the Boston sanitation department had not picked up the garbage. Usually the team comes crunching and squeaking by around six A.M. After having emptied your trash cans, they wing them onto your neighbor's stoop. Not your next-door neighbor, mind: the neighbor across the street.

A tremendous clank came from next door. "Hi, Harry," I called. "Looks great." My neighbor was hammering another patch to his garage door. This time his wife Doris had driven through it. I wondered why Harry had not gone to work today. He issues building permits at City Hall; from the look of his cigars you'd think he was more powerful than the mayor. Despite his intimate association with the local contractors, however, Harry knew nil about the construction business. That patch would fall off the instant Doris slammed the garage door shut.

I drove slowly up the street, trying not to wing the scavengers dragging old washing machines, mattresses, and, yes, a Christmas tree out of the refuse heaps. Barely any traffic impeded my way downtown although this should have been rush hour. The sidewalks lay open also. Only when I hit a police blockade on Beacon Street did the evidence finally tally: today was Patriot's Day. Shit! The music store would be closed! In fact, everything would be closed! Patriot's Day is an arcane state holiday when all the banks, schools, and municipal offices in Massachusetts shut down and, once again, the transit system slashes its force by eighty percent. The residents of Lexington and Concord get dressed up in Revolutionary War uniforms and re-enact the shot heard 'round the world. It's supposed to enhance everyone's patriotism but in fact what happens is that five hundred thousand high school students and civil servants pile first into Filene's Basement, then into a wayside bar, then smash towards the Prudential Center to watch the finish of the Boston Marathon.

When these holidays occur only once a year, it's easy to forget abut them, especially if you don't read the *Globule* or watch the news. Now I knew why I had been twice sideswiped on the Y track this week alone: I had stood in the way of some fading greyhound's laurel wreath. I made a quick U-turn at the Christian Science Headquarters and retreated home; today a car would be better off in the

Boston Harbor than anywhere within five miles of that race course. Already a minimum of twenty souls, weighted with folding chairs and lemonade pitchers, huddled at each bus stop. Pfuiii, if they wanted to reach Beacon Street via the MBTA, they should have left last week.

Having affixed his patch to the garage door, Harry stood on the sidewalk admiring his handiwork. "How's yah husband?" he waved. Ever since Richard Weintraub spent that week with me two years ago, Harry asks me this whenever I see him.

"I have no idea," I waved back. That's how I always answer.

Rutting through four back drawers, I finally located a yellowed pad of staff paper. I didn't feel like composing. This was a holiday. Perhaps another injection of caffeine would put me in the mood. I was ready for a nap: navigating one's favorite car downtown is anything but a relaxing experience. I hesitated at the foot of the stairs: either straight to the kitchen, or straight up to bed. *You really are one lazy tramp*, Chuck's voice castigated, *I thought I brought you up better than this*. "Guess what," I replied, hitting the kitchen. "You didn't."

Coffee in hand, I slopped onto the piano bench. Where was I? Yes: rewrite stanza three plus compose transition passage. For twenty minutes I futzed around the keyboard and nothing worked. Then my hand wandered near high C and a little tendril of notes came to my attention. I curled it this way and that and eventually had something that did not sound too contrived. But it could be better. Best to take a nap and return refreshed for a second assault after lunch.

Two naps and two lunches later, I had it. God Almighty, why had these few measures taken me the whole damn day? Once everything was in place it seemed so logical and obvious. *Glad You don't have deadlines*, I commented.

I apologized two hours later when I copied the whole thing over. It was a very fine hymn. Now my hand hurt—from writing, from erasing, from old age, who knows? I tried shaking it up and down but it was pretty stiff. So Fox had not fixed it after all. It figured. To get my mind off quacks and paralysis I took myself out to dinner at a new gourmet restaurant in Dorchester that used to be a Howard Johnson's until its tenth armed robbery. Now you walked in the door past a two-way mirror and a hefty bouncer. I had brought along a book about the Norman Conquest that turned out to be much lighter than the meal; they must have retained the midnight-to-six cook from the HoJo's.

"Excuse me." I looked up. It was the bouncer. "I can't help wondering if your date stood you up."

I thought polyester designer-initial ties had gone out of fashion about the same time as bellbottoms. "No one stood me up." My fingers fondled the heavy paper under them, half turning the page; my diamond ring clamored at the candlelight.

"I hate to see a beautiful woman dining alone."

"I've finished eating."

"Would you care for an after-dinner drink? On the house?"

"After that meal, gladly."

He brought me some unripe cognac and sat down at the table. Terrible eyes; this fellow could not satisfy a woman if presented with a dildo the size of Cuba.

"I'll bet," the bouncer said, "your husband is on a business trip."

"I'll bet," I replied, "your wife is home eating Oreos."

Whoops, time for the direct approach. "My name is Don," he continued, "and I find you incredibly attractive."

Oh, come on! Is that how they did it on the tube now? I stood up. "Forget it," I said. Lies like that aggravated the shit out of me. Maybe ten years ago I was beautiful but I'm not anymore, I know it. The only thing that has improved with time is my wardrobe.

I walked to the maitre d's desk. "Your friend works too hard," I said. "I'd like a check on my table when I get back." Why couldn't this guy have visited me? His eyes had acres more potential. When I returned from the ladies room my check was waiting. Don was not. I paid in clean cash and left.

Once home, I immediately called Martin. To my surprise he answered the phone. "Why, hello, darling," he greeted cheerfully. "How are you?"

"What are you doing there this time of day?"

"I just stepped out of the shower and I'm about to go out to dinner with Knute." That's the West Coast sales manager.

"When are you coming home?"

"In a few days, sweetheart. Are you all right? Why don't you fly out here and we'll take a little tour of wine country."

"We don't need any more wine." Each time Martin goes to California he brings a case back with him. He drinks one half bottle, then forgets about it.

"How's everything at home?"

"They had the Marathon today."

"Right! Who won?"

"How should I know? I was finishing a piece." Why hadn't I married a writer? Martin had about as much empathy for my agony as I had fair Paloma's White-Out. What the hell, I'd try to make him understand. "It took all day."

"I'm sure you outdid yourself."

Easy for him to say. Forget it, subject closed. Two or three notes would never have eluded Martin as they had me for eight hours running. *Will you stop this whining for sympathy,* reprimanded Chuck. *The man understands more than you think.*

I sighed; why milk a dead cow? "I went to that new restaurant on the highway."

"How was it?"

"Terrible. The bouncer tried to pick me up."

Martin laughed gently as he always does. He thinks I imagine these things. "Poor baby."

I waited several moments; he was not going to pursue the topic. "I miss you."

"I miss you too." Before these echoes became too maudlin, Martin began telling me about his trip. As usual he was accomplishing everything he had set out to do.

After ten miles on the exercise bicycle I went to bed. The house creaked and snapped, but I didn't care. "Come on up," I thought. "Keep me company." Hah, that would guarantee it was only the wind.

* * *

Orville called the next morning. I had been voted Hymnist of the Year.

"About time."

"About time, Eva? You've gotten the award twice already!"

"I wasn't talking to you."

"They've increased the prize money a thousand dollars."

"Do me a favor, Orville."

"Yes?"

"Send it to the Arlington Street Church in Boston. Tell them it's for the Organ Cleaning Fund."

"That's very generous of you. They should appreciate that."

"Yeah." They'd probably spend it on one bottle of detergent and three thousand gallons of heating oil. "Hey, I just finished a great march. I want you to get it out for Labor Day." Choirmasters like to start the season with a flourish. It attracts new choirmembers.

"Delighted." We discussed several alluring commissions. Three big churches in New York were doing my Christmas oratorio this year; it seemed to be the hit of the season. Next to the *Messiah,* of course.

I took the morning off to shop for spring clothes: one new pair of shoes beat three psychiatrists. The downtown still lay recuperating from yesterday's bacchanalia. A half dozen inert college students, Marathon leftovers and all from BU, snored metronomically in Copley Square as the spring sun irradiated their complexions. A jockstrap crowned the marble female guarding the portals of the Boston Public Library; eventually a bum knocked it to the sidewalk. His cronies cautiously approached the fallen treasure as they would a wounded copperhead. I walked to Newbury Street, noting that every last car parked on Clarendon had a ticket. Egad, it would serve these diabolical meter maids right if, one day, some MIT researcher found their fluorescent orange summonses to be carcinogenic.

I picked up a few goodies from the shops behind Bonwit's, then, stultified by boutique interiors and their highnosed inhabitants, cut over to the Y.

Instead of hanging around the lobby, bums sprawled in the sunshine on the front steps of the Y nicking all traffic

for quarters and dimes. Things were getting blatant in the
locker room also. Enough! These endless solicitations un-
hinged neither my cash nor my libido. Perhaps Martin
should build me that gym and sauna he'd talked about after
all. But then I couldn't watch the men, you see. It was a
tradeoff: if I wished to observe the thighs on the basketball
courts, I'd have to endure the derelicts in the lobby and the
dykes in the shower. Why was I losing my sense of humor
about these things?

Simple. Because it was spring. Many years ago, in
springtime, I had fallen in love with a bum steer. Even
now, when the earth became heady like this and the flowers burst overnight, when the sun gently warmed my hair,
I remembered and sorely wanted that man back again. *The
man was married*, Chuck cried exasperatedly. *What did
you expect?* Come on! I expected him to leave his wife and
marry me, damn him! My anger disturbed me: I truly
thought I had outgrown this. Last year I had escaped with
just one bad afternoon. Since my marriage, in fact, this
vernal despair had weakened tremendously: how could I
contemplate April suicide when the man I lived with didn't
even remember which month it was? He'd miss the whole
point.

Now Fox resurrected all these shadows. I drummed
around the Y track for forty minutes, detesting him. The
janitors had opened the gym windows and the moist earth
overpowered even the asphalt in the Y parking lot. Another spring! Time was flowing by me and my husband
and my fine house and all those pencils on the piano. I
stopped running and suddenly leaned over the guardrail.
Headphoned athletes shot behind me, fanning my legs.

God! Was I going to lose my shirt twice in one lifetime?
Why must Fox come along just before the shellac har-
dened? *It's perfect timing*, observed Chuck. *Now you can
wreck three lives instead of two.* "Ain't wreckin' nothin',"
I sighed without conviction. Let's face it, Chuck had
raised a coward. That's someone who does the noble thing
but feels shitty about it. I trotted nobly another dozen laps
until it was no use, then walked to the stairwell. *You made
spring*, I prayed, *and You made me*. Not a bad prayer:
resignation, adoration, and confession in one neat sentence.

I went home, took a long bath, and removed a terrifically expensive set of lingerie from my top drawer. Over this I slipped a dotted Swiss dress I had bought just that morning. I took a taxi to Cambridge because I'd rather fork my money over to a working man than to the Traffic Violations Bureau. Cambridge maintains Resident Only parking laws and its own plague of vigilante meter maids will nail you faster than a jackhammer.

Fox resided on a quiet street behind Mass Ave. The majority of his neighbors still wore wire-rimmed eyeglasses and a ponytail, as Ben Franklin and other pure folk had before the capitalists savaged the universe. Even if I agreed with this theory I'd say that ponytails looked ludicrous on forty-year-old men. Come on, the whole bit was a reverse manifestation of Hitler's mustache. The local women remained partial to Indian skirts, boob-drooping tee shirts, and hairy armpits.

Number 49, a large gray house, split into six apartments. Around its massive front porch grew flowers and potted plants of the variety that decayed the moment I removed them from the florist's. A wind chime made of old spoons clinked delicately in the breeze. Above me I heard Fox practicing a Rossini aria that hovered two notes beyond his range. For several moments I leaned against the porch railing listening to him, remembering a picnic on such a day maybe ten Aprils ago; today the earth wore the same cologne, and I had not been this happy since. I checked the card above the doorbell: no roommates for Paul Charles Fox.

The porch door stood open, so I walked upstairs, my heart thumping as the singing grew louder and louder. Really now, the lad would strip gears if he continued to force this Rossini past his throat. I was rescuing him just in time.

I knocked; the singing stopped. His hands undid the latch. *Make me evaporate*, I prayed desperately. *I'll do anything You want from now on.*

The look of shock on Fox's face compensated for this latest rebuff from the Almighty. He wore a tattered tee shirt that read "Disco Sucks" and a pair of tie-string doctor's pants. I doubt he had combed his hair since Good Friday. Thank God I was dressed to kill.

"Why, hello there, darling," I said peppily. "I could hear you straining your voice all the way from Harvard Square." My insides reeled; I had forgotten how the curve of his chin bulldozed my digestive tract.

Fox flushed guiltily: musicians are about as public with their practicing as is a blond with a bottle of peroxide. But he recovered. "And you just happened to be passing by," he said. "What a coincidence."

It was obvious that I would not be invited inside. I did not want to see who had beaten me out this time. "Just thought I'd say hello. I'll be off now, Foxy!" I'd be off, all right. To slit my wrists.

"Not so fast, love." Fox pulled me into his apartment.

I cased the room: much neater than Weintraub's sty. Fox's grandparents had had dour furniture and ghastly rugs. I saw a set of barbells in one corner, an upright piano in the other. I could see no trace of womanhood. "Where's the trap door?"

"Under my bed." Fox clamped his arms around me: good-bye, ribcage. I licked his throat, making contact from shoulder to hip. "I've been expecting you all week."

"Get your hands off me."

"What's the matter? I was just kidding."

"Like hell." The man was infuriating. "Let go."

Fox sprang me loose and plopped into an overstuffed chair, knees far apart. He was barefoot. "I like your dress."

Frowning loudly, I deposited myself upon a bulky green sofa across the way. His grandparents should have left him the little doilies for the top and arms. We sat there staring at each other for enough moments to become crazy with lust.

"When are you doing that Rossini?" I asked finally. Below the window a set of spoons waltzed in the breeze.

"No particular date. Why?"

"Perhaps you might get yourself castrated first," I suggested. We stared at each other some more. My new dress itched like fiberglass. "How's your karate?"

"It's still there."

This would be my last attempt at small talk. "Am I keeping you from something you'd rather be doing?"

"Sit on my lap and I'll tell you."

I went to his chair and straddled him: ten thousand polka dots rained on one erection. He pulled me in by the small of my back and kissed me. I cleaved to his mouth, sinking, surfacing, sinking for good.

"Let's go to bed," Fox said.

"Please, I only dropped by for a friendly chat." That, and a triple bypass.

"Later."

"Open your eyes, moron."

Fox looked very steadily at me. Brittle chips of blue flecked his gray eyes. As his breath hovered irregularly over my face I detected the ghost of a peanut butter sandwich. It beat salami. "Don't call me moron," he said.

"Don't make me jump right into bed with you." A whimper rather than a demand, bah, so much for coolness under fire. I held his eyes a moment, then wavered away. Come on, he could make me jump anywhere he wanted, whenever he wanted. I bent my head to his shoulder, my nose clocking his pulse. Soon I'd have to start chewing on him.

Fox slowly strummed his hands up and down my back. With not too much effort he could throw me across the room. Hmmm, I could think of worse ways to die. My left hand crawled up to his throat, fanned like a peacock's tail, and began slithering down his chest. Two millimeters beneath my palm lay the flesh which had destroyed a decade's ceasefire with The Great Puppeteer. My fingers fondled a vestigial tit-nub and the diaphragm beneath them momentarily halted. I wanted that tee shirt off.

"Come here," sighed Fox, lifting me off the chair. He led me by the hand down a hallway past an autographed glossy of Richard Tucker. We stepped out onto a back porch. Suspended from a neat little clothesline hung the shorts Fox had worn last time I saw him; from a corner birdcage twitted a yellow canary.

"Who's that?"

"Mildred." Fox whistled uxoriously through the slats and Mildred sang her brains out: of course. I leaned over the railing to see pink and white peonies spattering the backyard. With the right breeze they'd flick up to the porch. On the other side of the fence a woman lay sunbathing.

Fox entertained Mildred until she became exhausted. He'd make a great father, but he'd spoil the kid rotten. Look what he did to the canary. Eventually Fox broke away from the birdcage and came to my corner of the porch.

"Where'd you learn that trick?" I asked.

"What trick?"

"The bird routine."

"What bird routine?"

Please, I've used props like Mildred myself and they come in very handy with difficult cases. Floral deliveries work better, though. "Never mind." I refocused my attention upon the peonies.

"Sometimes," Fox said, "I don't understand you."

"You wouldn't." That's what intrigued him. I looked sideways at Fox. He was watching his neighbor sunbathe; this vantage did more for her cleavage than a fistful of foam rubber. We said nothing more but gazed over that balcony like immigrants beholding the Statue of Liberty. Within one minute I was suffocating: silence thickens the blood.

Fox turned his head towards me. I had no idea what he was thinking. Jesus! What if he told me to leave so he could practice Rossini!

"I want you," he said.

Now we were getting somewhere. Downhill, I think. "So take me."

Fox immediately unbuttoned the front of my dress. I pushed his hands away. "Here on the porch? No way." I walked inside to the room with the brass bed. Fox followed me in. "Sorry," I said, "I'm not the outdoor type." Bugs bite, wind chills; I prefer desire to rebound off a ceiling.

"You don't trust me very much, do you?"

"Nope." Should I? I was nothing to him but a handy pocket. I draped my dress across a chair and rolled off my panty hose. I gave him five seconds, then removed my slip. Finally I stopped. "What is this, the inspection station?"

"Keep going."

I dropped my bra, then my panties, onto the chair. Richard Weintraub had bought the set, a birthday present, in Paris. For an instant I pictured Richard toiling over his desk, drawing faces on feet. Richard never ordered me around like this and he still made fine deliveries in bed. I turned to Fox. "What now? Would you like me to bend over?"

He raised his eyebrows a hair, then sat on the bed, patting the place next to him. I sat down. "What's the matter with you?"

The next person to ask me this question would be terminated. "Nothing."

"Do you always act this way?"

"Act how?"

"Hostile and afraid."

I crawled across the covers and sat on a pillow, hugging my knees. "Let me tell you something, Sigmund. A little bit of begging would get you a hell of a lot further than bogus psychoanalysis." I could smell the sweat eroding my perfume and wondered how I would ever get my clothes back on with any shred of dignity. "Besides, I don't believe in relaxing and enjoying myself. I'm a WASP, remember."

Fox pulled my ankles out, stretching me along the mattress. "Such a liar," he murmured, kissing my stomach. "I love you."

Predictable as a traffic light! People say "I love you" to bus drivers who let them off between stops. They say "I love you" to their plastic surgeons for pinning their ears back. They say "I love you" to well-dressed walnuts they would really like to fuck. "Don't lie to me," I said. "It's not necessary."

After a moment, deciding I would not tolerate his denials, Fox slid his hands under my shoulder blades. His breath on my nipples sired enough goosebumps to populate India. My body undulated beneath him like a lamprey. Perhaps the motion would draw him south.

Fox eddied north to kiss me, and I nearly swallowed him. Martin had not kissed me like this in years. To him my breasts had become tiddlywinks, my throat, plumbing.

I know, I know, it takes two: so I confess! I only put Martin's penis in my mouth now to distract him from the *Wall Street Journal*! I call him to bed not to hose down my flaming passion, but to warm my toes! I had brought this all upon myself by deliberately marrying a brother, not a lover. I knew a brother would not plunder me the way a lover would. A brother would give me my freedom and my privacy, and very slowly, over years and years, we would achieve the same fusion of souls that Fox and his piratical predecessor had achieved with one glance. Oh God! I think I had made a huge mistake!

I located the hem of Fox's tee shirt, dragged it up to his armpits, and thrust against his stomach: all blood turned to wine. Fox nibbled the tendons of my neck as one hand loosened the string of his doctor pants. With the soles of my feet I pushed them down his legs then kicked them onto the floor and rolled on top of him, trying to fingerprint his body with my own. Finally I engulfed the critical area.

"You damn sexy woman," Fox muttered. "You drive me crazy."

"Don't you dare come."

"Easy for you to say."

I spat him out before it was too late. Why wreck an afternoon gagging? You've got to have either a rubber esophagus or tonsils ten inches deep.

Fox flipped me onto my back. Jesus, what a tongue! He was even better than last time! The instant I laid eyes on him I knew what that tongue could do; those dark eyes, lazy smile, that easy walk, please, the clues just about slapped me in the face: here was a fellow who knew how to dine well. It's a rare and almost mutant talent, believe me. Seven out of ten men, confronted with a delectable woman, behave like moose at a salt block. Two out of ten can never quite dispel the impression that they're only inches away from an anus. Ah, but the tenth wields a divining rod, not a tongue, and when he's prospecting, watch out. He'll locate wells you didn't even know existed.

"You must have been a lesbian in a former life," I commented.

Fox's eyes and nose surfaced above my pubic hair. "Don't tell me you're gay," he said flatly.

I let him blanch a few moments. Stupid statements deserve stupid answers. "Does it matter, darling?"

"You're gay, aren't you?"

I smote my forehead. "Aii! What gave me away?"

Fox brought his shoulders up to mine but left one finger inside of me. "A total lack of feminine modesty."

"Not the hair above my lip?"

He hesitated. "Are you kidding me or not?"

"What, can't you tell?"

"I can never tell with you."

Ah, I had won this one. "I do recall kissing my mother once or twice," I said.

His finger twitched tentatively back to life. "Is your mother gay?"

Chuck? Come on! "Don't be an ass."

"Gotcha," said Fox. Our mouths touched again and I tasted myself. I don't know what he found so delicious. "I'm going to kiss you all day."

But we didn't have all day. In fact, we had purloined too much time already. I wrapped my legs around his. Each time we started over again it got a little headier, like hard cider; that's because repetition breeds ennui only when you are married.

My body could tell it was about to receive a present and it began to quiver like a child on Christmas Eve. Fox nosed inside of me, looking for China. "I'm going to come," I whispered.

"Not yet."

Whoops. "Sorry."

He almost caught up with me, like a relay runner. I suppose I should have given him a little more warning. "I thought premature ejaculation was a man s problem," Fox panted.

I smiled slowly as a queen: my body commanded his pulse. "Told you I was gay."

He bit the side of my neck for a few minutes, regaining his breath. "Thank you for coming over."

Was that a mild invitation to leave? I rolled out from under him. "You think I do this every day, don't you?"

He observed my pupils. "Maybe."

I slowly turned on my side, away from him. It was sport to Fox, therefore it was sport to me. The bastard.

"Eva." He cupped a hand over my shoulder and rolled me sunny-side up. "I'm sorry."

"Never mind," I exhaled, intoxicated with this strange cowboy who had lured me back to poker. Fox hooked his hands under my arms and lifted me overhead the way a father would his child. Very slowly he lowered me onto his chest and we began an intense review of all past material. The details remained the same, but the pleasure multiplied by ten. In fact, it approached the threshold of pain. Bah, Hathaway, you think too much. Soon I was making noises like a test animal.

"What's the matter?"

"You're inside of me, that's! What! Don't! Stop!"

"Are you coming on me again?"

"Can't you! Tell!"

This time he caught up. Not that it mattered, please, simultaneous orgasms are the spawn of Madison Avenue. "Oh my God," laughed Fox anemically, surrendering with a stupid smile. He collapsed onto the sheet.

With a lascivious little smack I expelled him, then, crouching, popped his penis into my mouth: eggplant sauced with Eva. "Oh ho ho, hold it," Fox rambled. "You're going to—kill—me."

You bet I was, baby. I would never forgive him for plucking my heart like some wayside posy and propping it in his hatband. I drew whatever was left right out of him, not stopping until I thought he had passed out. Now his cock looked like Sonny Liston after thirteen rounds. I retired it to the corner.

We both smoked an imaginary cigarette. Finally Fox turned his head. "Do you have a good marriage?" he said.

"I have a good husband."

"That's not what I asked."

"I had a good marriage until I met you." My stare transpierced the ceiling. *Which is why we met, of course,* I prayed sarcastically. No event in history has repeated itself more often than Eve's taking of the apple. You'd think The Great Orchardist would have tired of this game by now. "Don't fret over it," I said to Fox. "It doesn't concern you." Come on, the guy had had a pleasant afternoon screwing around. He didn't want to hear about Accounts Payable.

"It damn well concerns me."

Rub it in, pal. I looked at Fox and these insane coals in my gut reddened anew. "You don't know anything about me, darling," I said. "It's pure animal magnetism with a few taboos chucked in."

"That's not true."

I paused; such obstinance was tantamount to a confession of love. Impossible. No one fell in love with me. They fell in love with my money, my looks, my talent, my distance, but not with me. Why didn't this fellow quit while he was ahead? He was confusing me. "I have a husband," I explained. A very weak image of Martin flitted across my mind without making the least impression. That's because Martin didn't have a thumb up my vagina and two fingers around the bend.

"Then what are you doing in my bed?"

Paving the road to hell, you idiot! "I . . . I'm not sure."

"You mean I still have some convincing to do?"

"I'm convinced, Foxy. Now you have to make me forget." I pulled him my way. It was amnesia upon impact.

Fox called several hours after I had left him and Mildred to their mutual occupation. "I'm coming over tonight."

"No you're not." Richard Weintraub was flying up to lick his amorous wounds for a day or two. "I've got company."

"Martin?"

"Nope."

Fox paused. "Tell your company you can't make it."

"This is an old friend," I said. "I can't just tell him to walk up and down Broadway until he feels better."

"What's the matter with him?"

"Some JAP gave him the shaft."

"When's he getting there?"

"Uh—tomorrow." I have always been a lousy liar.

"Tomorrow? And you can't see me tonight?"

Nope. Had to work on my distance running. "I've had about enough of you for one day, Foxy-poo."

"Well, I haven't had enough of you!" He hung up.

I took a bottle of port from the cabinet and lay down in the den. My body was a swollen nibbled wreck. I did not want to see Fox, nor anyone, tonight. I didn't feel like seeing Richard tomorrow, either. Look, brakes work best when you're alone in the car. After a time I went to my studio and reviewed *Paradise March*. It had not deteriorated since I had last edited it, good, good. Perhaps I should show the third verse to Fox and have him sing it. Naw, not yet. I still didn't trust him.

I went to the front porch and waited for him, toping occasionally from the bottle of port. The damp evening had leached untold households of their pubescents, who now roamed the neighborhood in search of coitus. Didn't these hoods ever have any homework? Several troops passed the house, hooting and cackling. Hell, they may as well enjoy themselves. Half of them would have cirrhosis by the age of thirty. The other half would be condemned to Bingo every Thursday night until they died.

The moon floated into the sky. Someday I would find myself a dress that soft black and that delicate yellow, and I would wear it only for Fox. His Bel Air, muffler gurgling, chugged down the street, paused, and cranked into reverse. He was not an outstanding parallel parker. I watched him step onto the sidewalk. *Ah God,* I prayed, *Let it last as long as possible.*

"Hey," I called from the shadows as he was about to press the doorbell.

Fox came over to my recliner. I wanted to touch those beautiful thighs. "Port?" I invited, lifting the bottle.

"Have you been drinking that all night?"

"Hardly, darling." Unlike mother, this daughter.

Fox picked up my feet and placed himself beneath them, stroking my calves. "I can't stay away from you," he said after a while.

I said nothing. Too tired.

"What are you thinking?" asked Fox when the moon was about up.

"I'm not thinking, I'm praying."

"Don't tell me I'm not the answer to your prayers."

I didn't reply right away; one prayer's answer is the next

prayer's problem. "You're an atheist, aren't you?" I said, taking a swig.

"Never thought about it one way or the other."

Very bad. That meant he spent all his time thinking about himself. Fox was more of a tenor than I had guessed. "How's the Rossini?"

"Coming."

A Mercedes blistered up the street. Stolen, no doubt; you don't lay patches with a six-hundred-buck set of tires unless you're a drug dealer. I studied Fox's fine nose as he stroked my leg. Thump! Passion rammed reason. I wondered how many more spring nights like this I could withstand in one lifetime. They contradicted every last lesson that daylight had ground into me, and their contradictions were so beguiling, so real, that I never wanted to see daylight again.

"I'm going away tomorrow," said Fox, " for about two weeks."

You stupid ostrich, scoffed Chuck. *Pull your head out of that hole.* "Lucky boy."

"Come with me."

And die of orgasmosis? "Where are you going?"

"Minneapolis. For *Tosca.*"

"So why are you practicing *The Barber of Seville,* moron?"

Fox bit my calf. "I told you not to call me that."

"Answer the question then you can go home."

He climbed onto my chair and kissed me. Hah, his lips were puffy, too. "Rossini's for this summer. And I'm not going home."

Who was I to refuse such a lovely boy on such a night? "I have to sleep."

"Aye-aye, captain," Fox said. "You'll get your beauty sleep." He didn't tell me it would be in two-hour installments.

Richard Weintraub looked terrible. "She was bad news from the start," I soothed. "You don't pick up anything but garbage at Maxwell's Plum."

"But she told me she loved me!"

"Oh come on, Richard!" I shouted exasperatedly. "She

loved all the free rides you gave her to Mamaroneck!''
Richard should have expected this behavior from a female
who wore spike heels, designer jeans, and twenty cheap
gold chains.

I sighed. ''Why didn't you take my advice and find a
nice girl at the synagogue?''

''They don't fuck.''

''Switch synagogues, then.''

Richard stared glumly at his granola. ''I'm tired of
hunting for women.''

''That's your big mistake, baby,'' I said. ''Quit hunting.''

''And then what? The perfect ten drops into my lap?''

''For you, maybe a five.'' It was no use. Richard would
rather screw up his own life than allow God to screw it up
for him, like me. I squeezed his arm. ''Let's go shopping.''

''For what?''

I shrugged. Actually we were going shopping for Martin's birthday present. I first took Richard to Filene's
Basement because he had never been there, but the air,
rank with putrid hotdogs, nauseated him.

''And now for the scenic route to Neiman-Marcus,'' I
announced, cutting through the Combat Zone, Boston's
tawdrier version of New York's tawdry Forty-second Street.
The whores here looked allergic to penises.

''How about one of these dolls,'' I suggested.

''Will you stop it!'' Richard snapped.

''Hey! You said you were tired of hunting!'' The man's
sense of humor was shot completely. That JAP must really
have picked him clean. Richard needed a ride in a swan
boat. I steered him towards the Common.

''You know, I wouldn't mind so much,'' Richard said,
''but Tiffany said that she wanted children. That made me
think she was serious about me.''

''Think back, Richard. Did she say she wanted kids, or
did she say she wanted you to be the father of her kids?''

Richard flung a dandelion into the water. His back
slumped another five degrees convex. ''What's with you
and kids, anyhow?'' I asked. ''You're already immortal.
Look at all those great designs you've made.''

''I'm going bald,'' Richard moaned.

''Come on! Who cares about your head!''

"I'm lonely."

"Wrong. You only think you are. There's a big difference."

Richard stared into the water. I knew exactly what was running through his mind: that I lived with a rich man who gave me a very long leash, that I could have one or twelve children whenever I pleased, and that by dint of having signed a marriage certificate my soul had found peace forever. What fairy bosh infests a bachelor's mind!

We got out of the swan boat and continued silently along a paved path.

"Look out, man!" shouted someone close behind us. I skipped to the side but Richard the Klutz froze. Of course he got knocked down; you can just about ski down the slopes of the Boston Common. A black Atlas on roller skates twirled in place as I picked Weintraub up. "That dude all right?"

"He'll live." Why did the males of this race have such perfect thighs? "You're lucky you didn't knock down an Irishman," I told him.

"Why do ya think I'm wearin' roller skates, sugah?" The thighs glided off.

"That fucker cracked my rib," Richard gasped. I walked him down to the Ritz and kept ordering brandy until the afflicted bone passed out. By then we were hungry and stayed for lunch. Richard talked ceaselessly of the departed Tiffany and life as he thought it should have turned out. What could I do but listen with phony empathetic furrows impressing my face? I was missing Fox; that last round had turned me inside out.

"Look on the bright side, Richard," I said when he had fantasized himself flat. "At least you didn't marry her." I signaled for the check.

"That's what you told me last time."

"That stupid poetess and you? It wouldn't have lasted a week" Obeying a private drumroll, the waiter ceremoniously set a sixty-buck tab on the table. "I keep telling you, Richard," I said, handing the waiter a credit card, "treat 'em well enough and they'll leave."

"Martin treats you well and you don't leave."

Is that so, said Chuck. I rubbed my eyebrows. "That's

because Martin doesn't think he's treating me well." We got up to go. "What's the matter now?" I asked Richard. He was limping exaggeratedly. "Did he bust your hip, too?"

"It's my back," he winced.

"It's your brain! Forget the synagogue! Pick your next girlfriend from the nursing school!"

Richard slung his arm around my shoulder; he liked that joke. The doorman looked us over as we exited and I could read his mind: Yep, they do. "Want to hit Shreve's?" I asked, heading right on Arlington Street.

"What's that?"

"A neutered Tiffany's." Everything they sell in that store you could wear to a funeral. Maybe I'd find a pair of cuff links for Martin's birthday. We passed the Arlington Street Church, where I had first heard Fox sing; perhaps if I ran inside, I might find him again. A crypto-Krishna stood on the front steps hawking peacock feathers and Red Sox pennants. Richard bought the last feather and stuck it in my hair.

"Watch it!" A cab brushed inches away from Richard's elbow.

"I don't believe this," Richard cried, on the verge of tears. "He actually tried to hit me!"

"Stop it," I corrected. "He was going for that guy in the wheelchair." We rolled into Shreve's and received the same smug, omniscient look from the floorwalker as we had from the doorman at the Ritz. I pulled Richard over towards the pendants. It was the nearest counter and we were both a little tottery.

"Chokers," Richard commanded, pulling himself together. The salesgirl checked us out and withdrew the most expensive tray in her case. They looked like dead planarians.

"Have you got anything a little larger," asked Richard.

"Do you mean longer, sir?"

"He means louder," I said. "Something a woman under sixty might wear."

"I'm afraid I don't understand."

"All right! We'll try something else!" Richard said, waving the tray away. We toppled mildly towards the bracelets. "I am interested in a heavy gold band," Richard told the salesman. "Price is no object."

"What's gotten into you?" I giggled. "You've never talked like this in your life." Richard is the only man I know who will tip a waitress $6.98.

"This is how you meet interesting women at Bloomingdale's."

"Where'd you learn that, *Cosmo*, Spanish edition?"

"My rabbi."

Unfortunately, the salesman had overheard everything so we had to move a few counters away, to the earrings. "Show me those pearl clusters," Richard said, pointing. "Try these." He clipped on an earring. It looked ludicrous with the peacock feather in my hair; the earring itself was not half bad. "We'll take them," Richard said.

"Are you kidding?!"

"You bought me lunch," he said, unpocketing his credit cards.

"You're nuts." I put my arms around his neck; Dame Miranda must have severed Richard's brain from his pocketbook. "Tell her to put them back," I whispered in his ear. "And where did you get that big hard-on?"

"Hello, Eva."

There stood my mother-in-law. "Ruth!" I exclaimed. "What are you doing here?"

"I'm shopping for my son's birthday present," she enunciated slowly and clearly. I thought her two-piece suit would get up and walk away.

"So were we," I answered, glancing at the small package in her hand. "I thought you were buying him dancing lessons."

The salesgirl presented Richard with a similarly-wrapped box. "Here you are, sir," she said. "Enjoy them."

"We shall," Richard honked, placing his arm around my shoulder. The gesture was obviously not a new one.

"I'd like you to meet my friend Richard Weintraub," I said to Ruth. She did not extend her hand. "Ruth Weaver, my mother-in-law," I told Richard.

"Martin's mother?" Richard said in a curiously jagged voice, slithering his arm off my shoulder. I could have spit. Fumes of cognac befogged my face. "Martin is a very lucky fellow," declared Richard.

I turned to him, seething. "Why, because Ruth's his mother?" Come on, what an asinine statement! I squeezed Richard's hand to shut him up. Ruth stared at our fingers as if they were interlocking sex organs.

"I'm sure your friend meant something quite different," she said stiffly. "Good day."

"Jesus, she must be sick," I said as Ruth's suit jerked onto Boylston Street. "She didn't even ask about Martin."

"Does she always say 'good day' like that?"

"Like Jane Eyre? Yep." I frowned at Richard. "You can put your arm back around me now."

We cabbed home, worked hard on some hymn covers, then took a nap. Richard woke up first, around seven. I felt someone's mouth on my neck and my insides drooled: Fox. "I think I'll go for a little run," I said, breaking away. "Coming?"

"My ribs are killing me."

I sighed and lifted his shirt. Richard's ribs weren't even black and blue. In fact, they were pale pink and protected by an inch of flab. I bit the flab and quickly rolled off the bed; Richard becomes very cozy when he awakens from naps.

Before tripping into the twilight I told him to take a hot bath then start some dinner. I ran over to the Jamaica Pond; the air smelled of honeysuckle and dead fish. Couples, benignly awaiting the moonrise, half registered me as I bobbed past their park benches. The eyes of single men and women, on the other hand, clenched mine as I padded past: solitude attacks with particular force on a warm spring night. Unable to bear those same desperate faces twice, I veered left at the boat house and ran along the Jamaicaway, an undulating four-lane thoroughfare from which few fenders emerge unblemished. That's because the road is only wide enough for three fenders.

Oh! Fox! I was crazy for him! He lurked behind the trees, in the back seats of cars, just beyond the forsythia by the footpath . . . how would I scrape by until he was back inside me? My insanity increased as the moon idled up the sky. I reversed back to the pond and did another lap; by this time the night had obscured the grim faces of those still seeking companionship. Most of the couples were lying down behind the benches.

A police car, blue lights flashing, was stopped outside my house. "What's up?" I asked my neighbor Harry, who stood chatting with the woman across the street. Between them they owned five German shepherds.

"Someone called in a muhdeh," Harry said.

I dashed inside. Richard, unmurdered, was talking to two officers. "There you are!" he cried, rushing over to me. "She's okay!"

"Of course I'm okay," I said, backing up. I smelled like a forgotten mackerel.

"But you were gone almost an hour!"

I shook my head. "My friend is from New York," I explained to the policemen. "He gets excited when people don't return in ten minutes."

The patrolman with the mustache and blue eyes looked at Richard, then at me. Richard did not cut an imposing figure in a white terry bath wrap. "Your friend really looks out for you," he said. His intonation made me pause: virile but rough, good for one shot then he'd bore me.

"That's what friends are for," I replied, showing them to the door. The older policeman never took his eyes off my legs. "Sorry to trouble you."

"Ah, an alarm system," noticed Junior. "A good thing."

"It helps." I shut the door and looked at Richard. "Weintraub, you are paranoid." I looked out the window. My neighbor Harry was telling the cops everything he knew.

I began a new hymn, *Lookin' Out For Me*, the next morning. Orville had been bugging me for some time for a country/western number that juvenile churchgoers could relate to. This sugary God-loves little-ol'-me trash turned my stomach, crap, when would these naive Evangelicals realize that God didn't worry about anything?

I dropped Richard off at the shuttle and cruised over to the Delta terminal to pick up Martin, who was returning from San Francisco. *There's your husband,* pointed Chuck as Martin emerged into the reception area. *Go welcome him.* I felt like running away.

Martin saw me and his face lit up; guilt whapped my face. "How's my girl," he said, kissing my cheek.

"Hi, Flappy." Martin had gotten a little sun and looked rested. He seemed to have put on a pound or two besides. "How was California?"

"It was great," Martin replied, in excellent spirits. "You have a new dress."

"Where's Paloma?"

"She came back Friday." Very sharp of Martin. He knows he would have had to take the limousine otherwise. The porter followed us with one suitcase and three cases of wine. "And what have you been up to, sweetie?"

"The usual." That flew right by my husband because he suspected nothing. "How was the weather?" Very arthritically, question by question, I reassumed my former identity. I couldn't believe that Martin was scheduled to remain in my house for eight weeks this time; if I remembered correctly, the tribulation of Jesus Christ had lasted only forty days.

We went to the Copley for a drink so that Martin could tell me all about his road trip. I nodded and asked some insightful questions, but by and large I did not pay very strict attention to the words emanating from his mouth. I had heard these same words thousands of times before: Knute, computer, sale, account, Rodotron, blah blah. Shit! It's a huge mistake to assume that your profession is as interesting to your spouse as it is to you. My mother impressed this lesson upon her six children every day of her life: the moment he stepped in the door, my father would receive a blow-by-blow account of Chuck's frustration-ridden day. The more she told him, the more he buried his nose in the newspaper. He's the only man I know who has read the sports page twice through, beginning to end, for forty years.

But I'm smarter than my mother, you see. I know that my husband is not interested in hearing how I daily erase B-flats then C-sharps, then finally settle on C's. Martin doesn't relate to erasing anyhow. Since I contribute so little to our conversations, the least I can do is listen politely to Martin's daily verbal autobiography. Had my father done the same, he could have bought himself a villa in Cannes with what he saved in bar bills.

"By the way, we have a table reserved at Pops a week from Tuesday," Martin mentioned as we drove to his office. "It should be lots of fun."

"Sounds good," I agreed. "Who's coming?"

"Oh—Jason, Paloma."

The president plus wife, one vice-president, one executive secretary. That made four. "Who else?"

"Possibly Itsuo Tagahashi."

"Possibly?" Come on, this whole Pops night was conceived around the advent of Itsuo Tagahashi. I know how Martin's mind works. It's Ruth all over again.

Martin glanced over from the steering wheel. "Come now, darling, he's all right." Martin continued to look at me; the Bavaria drifted starboard.

"Hey! Cut left!" Martin knifed back into his lane, squeezing a cyclist, who shot us the finger.

"Eva!" Martin barked. "Don't screech when I'm driving!" Supposedly these sudden noises are ten times more likely to make him crash into something. I bit my tongue and looked pointedly out my window.

We drove in silence out to Route 128. Then, whistling, Martin slipped his hand inside his coat and pulled out a little box. "I brought back something for my favorite girl," he said, eyes twinkling. You'd never guess that ten minutes ago he had almost killed me.

In spite of myself I had to smile. "What's this for?"

Martin shrugged and continued to drive. Oh God, he knew, I was certain of it. "Because I love you, cutie."

It was a thick, plaited choker of freshwater pearls, hundreds of them. "Oh Martin, it's beautiful," I said. "I'll wear it to Pops." Why did I feel sad, not happy?

Martin smiled to himself. He loves to see me all dressed up.

The night of Pops was also Martin's birthday. Paloma called that afternoon to inform me that she had ordered a huge flaming cake for afterwards at the Budapest. The woman was madly in love with my husband. I could tell by her forced tone.

I didn't need any more interruptions like that, so I shut myself up in the study and began an organ toccata based upon Easter themes, deriving a perverse pleasure from the thought of the organists who would buy the score and then not be able to play it. It was insanely difficult. Why should I be any easier on my fellow humans than The Great Bellows was on me? I had not seen Fox in two weeks and I was perpetually angry with Martin. Chuck had called earlier in the day crying because my father had refused to be her bridge partner the night before; she would now call each of her six children, imbibing one ounce of gin with each telephone call, and remind us of our sire's callousness. I had wasted the entire morning with an architect who was going to construct a greenhouse off the side of the kitchen. My husband wanted to experiment with solar batteries.

Around six o'clock Martin came home. He opened a few more birthday cards that had arrived in the mail. I gave him a black leather jacket that spiced up the gray streaks in his hair.

"Mother came by the office today," Martin said.

"Oh yeah? How's she doing?"

"Fine." Martin exhibited the cuff links that Ruth had bought for his birthday. First class. "She says she saw you in Shreve's."

"I was there with Richard," I said. "We were a little drunk at the time." I laughed. "What'd she tell you, that she saw me with some Jewish prince checking out the ankle bracelets?"

"Something like that." Martin would elucidate no further. Once he had heard it was only Richard, he stopped worrying. No wonder Richard disliked him.

Martin reached for the *Globule*. "We really should be getting ready," I said. Once Martin becomes engrossed in the clashes of fanatics eight thousand miles away, he forgets all about domestic reality. "The show starts in an hour. Is Tagahashi still coming?"

"Oh yes," replied Martin. "He could hardly see straight, he was so excited." I shook my head. Foreigners delight in ridiculing the Yank barbarian, yet the first thing they want to see in America is Disneyland, then the Boston Pops.

We took a shower and it was all I could do to keep my hands off Martin. *Residual lust,* I prayed. *Your first ten lashes.* "You know, Mart," I observed, shooting water off his balls, "I'm awfully fond of that smooth little bottom of yours."

He soaped his armpit. "You're just saying that because it's my birthday."

I raised his penis up on the bristles of my backbrush. Ah, men have such beautiful bodies. "That's right." I bounced it up and down a few times, weighing. One pound? Half a pound? Once when Richard and I were in Salzburg we had knockwurst that looked just like this. They were delicious.

"Hey! That tickles!"

"Come on, Martin! I'm conducting scientific experiments!" I ran my fingers along the insides of his legs. "No cellulite here."

"What's gotten into you," Martin cried, stepping out of the shower. I know he loved it. I followed him to the toilet, where he stood trying to pee. I reached between his legs from behind.

"Here, let me help aim," I said. Urine splashed all over the toilet seat.

"Are you crazy?" Martin yipped. His upbringing sealed his bladder.

"What happened?" I said, looking down. "Are you finished?"

"Eva, leave the bathroom."

"I can't, I have to wash my face."

Martin went into a one-man huddle over the toilet bowl: after five years of marriage he still considered his excretions private business. Come on, man! Bodies were only dust and water! I pinched Martin's buns as I left the bathroom. Another little squirt hit the back of the toilet seat. "You vixen," Martin growled after me.

Naked, we crisscrossed the bedroom, retrieving undershirts and hosiery from wayside drawers. My body aroused Martin about as much as his socks did. *That's just the way you wanted, wasn't it?* reminded Chuck. *No erections, no children.*

"Martin, what do you think about having kids?"

My husband glanced at his watch. He'd better answer this one correctly or Itsuo Tagahashi would have to order the first bottle of champagne at Symphony Hall. "Children?"

"Yeah, you know, the little guys with no teeth."

"That would be terrific, Eva." Martin kept slowly and steadily dressing himself; his family believes in silent example. "What brought this subject up?"

"Your thirty-ninth birthday."

Martin whistled, genuinely surprised. "I'm thirty-nine?"

"You ain't seventeen, baby."

Sniffing danger, Martin warily pulled his trousers on. "I think my father was forty when I was born." Once again he consulted his watch. "Eva, it's getting late."

I paraded around the room a few times more: nothing doing. Martin's new cuff links occupied his full attention. If I ran away with Fox, he would probably degenerate just like this five years down the line, except instead of cuff links it would be canaries. Or other women. Maybe once men became familiar with me, I turned them off. "Hey, Flappy," I said, slipping a dress on, "do I turn you off?"

Martin never stopped combing his hair. "Of course not."

"Do other women turn you on more?"

Now he was polishing his shoes. "What a question! No!" He stood up. "What's gotten into you lately?"

"I told you that spring is a bad time of year."

Martin did not like to be reminded that I had married him on the rebound, so he changed the subject altogether. "Were you really wearing a feather in your hair when Mother ran into you at Shreve's?"

Feather? Mother? I thought we were discussing my emotional scars! Ah, fuck it! "Yep." I put Richard's pearl earrings on. "The biggest, fattest feather in town."

Martin put his arms around me. "My little girl," he mused. "What am I going to do with you?" He mussed my hair and went downstairs.

The company limousine pulled into the driveway before

I had even decided which shoes to wear. "George is here," Martin called.

"You don't say," I muttered, whishing some mascara on. My hair looked like the receiving end of the shot put. I tied a ribbon around the worst cowlicks. Martin called twice more before I grabbed some scarves, perfume, my new necklace, and trotted downstairs.

"Nice," whistled Martin, toying with the alarm system.

I looked like a bag lady. "Thank you, Flapper. Could you help me put this necklace on, please?" It felt thick and wonderful around my neck.

"Well, what do you think of it?" Martin asked.

"There are certain advantages to being Mrs. Weaver."

We boarded the limousine. "George, we're running a little late," Martin said.

Never removing his foot from the accelerator, maneuvering with the perfect blend of *sang-froid* and tunnel vision, George cut downtown and through the huge traffic jam outside Symphony Hall, depositing us on the steps shortly before eight o'clock. "Great driving, George," I said.

"We'll be going to the Budapest afterward," Martin instructed. George nodded and rolled off.

"Gee, Martin, don't you ever thank the man?" I asked as we went inside. "He shot us down here like a croc through the Everglades."

"Darling, I thank George profusely twice a month," Martin said, handing the usher our tickets.

I hooked his arm. "Promise me you're not going to talk business all night," I said as we entered the murmuring auditorium. Squares of sparkling lights tiered the stage like some giant football diagram.

"I'll do my best." Around us hundreds of people laughed, drank, and observed the attire of passing strangers. Just as the lights dimmed we arrived at the table.

Jason Street, vice-president of Weaver, Inc., stood up. "Perfect timing, Martin," he greeted. "And what a beautiful wife." Jason's looks improved with each divorce. That's because he kept marrying hairdressers and gym instructors.

"Ho, Jason." I shot a quick hand to Tagahashi and

Paloma before the music started. Itsuo looked stuffed. So did Paloma's dress.

The Pops cranked up with a big soupy march by Rimsky-Korsakov. Oh God! What a fantastic fucking orchestra! The people in this hall had no idea how spoiled they were. Jason poured two glasses more of champagne, emptying the bottle.

"Cheers," said my husband, clinking my glass.

"Happy birthday, old man," I whispered in his ear.

Once the novelty of classical music had worn off, maybe two minutes after the march had begun, the crowd resumed laughing and chattering, a little more loudly than before, of course, because the orchestra was making so much noise. Not once did some horse miss an opportunity to drop a glass, or pop a cork, or laugh hysterically during the most quiet orchestral interludes. Shit, no wonder the musicians behaved as if Symphony Hall were Three Mile Island.

"Did you hear," Jason said to Martin just before the reprise, "Rodotron's stock just split."

"No! That's incredible!" Martin leaned forward, clearly entranced. "What did they get for it?"

Now Paloma got into the act. It was the only legitimate way to finesse the boss's wife. "Fifty-four a share," she said. "We did very well on that." I wondered why Martin didn't pay more attention to this ripe tomato simmering on the vine. I noticed Itsuo Tagahashi admiring my necklace. Ignoring him, I turned towards the orchestra. They were nitpicking dully through a Debussy/Satie arrangement.

"Wait until Roger hears about this," Jason said. "He'll hit the roof."

I gestured to a waitress for another bottle of champagne. "Now he can buy KTD back from you."

Jason and Paloma looked at me with some astonishment. What the hell did they think my husband talked to me about? Nine-irons?

Tiddling a finger under my chin, Martin made one of his little Eva-only smiles. I felt sorry for Paloma. "KTD is our little tiger," he said. "Haifink will never get it back." How could he trust me so much? My insides cringed with shame.

Paloma bent her ballooning bodice towards Tagahashi, who sat staring at the Pops. Just as she was about to speak, the Debussy ended and the audience clapped insipidly; this French mush evoked less of a response than halitosis. "They are just fabulous," she pronounced.

"They're super," agreed Jason, who had not listened to one note, and who could not distinguish a clarinet from a tuba.

Tagahashi stirred from his ecstasy. "I would like a Boston Pops tee shirt."

Whoops, the applause cut Paloma off again. She had to content herself with a prophetic smile at Tagahashi instead. Now the orchestra was cranking out a bunch of Andrews Sisters arrangements. I thought the musicians would gag.

The waitress plunked down another bottle of champagne. "Thank you," said Jason, leaping upon the cork. "And so," he continued as he poured, "they'll probably be going into microchips with that little weasel Haifink."

"Haifink won't go near them," Martin rejoined. "He's way over his head as it is."

I glanced reproachfully at the birthday boy, who continued to edify his tablemates with a pithy analysis of Haifink's operation. Sparks of light from the stage caught the silver in his hair as he spoke. A youthful glow animated his face. Martin really loved that business of his: it was child, wife, mistress, pet dog, church, and country club all rolled into one. I suppose if I loved Martin in a different way, I would be murderously jealous. Instead, all I felt was relief.

A further round of uninterested clapping turned my attention stagewards: a burly soloist advanced through a herd of pouting baldies towards the podium. He was going to sing. The orchestra looked as if it were plotting to kill him. Pretending the Pops and its conductor did not exist, the soloist inflated his chest and began "O Sole Mio."

Ach! I took a deep breath; my skin singed, feeling Fox's mouth. *Stay where you are,* Chuck cautioned. *It will blow over.* Wrong! If I stayed, it would blow up! "Excuse me," I blurted, taking my purse and arising from the table. Everyone assumed I had a menstrual emergency.

I went right to the telephone. As it rang my heart stepped lively.

"Hello."

So that was what he sounded like. I had almost forgotten. "Is Mildred home?"

"Eh, bambina."

"I can't stand it anymore," I said. "I have to see you." Since Martin had returned two weeks ago I had not communicated with Fox. Something in my genetic makeup prevented me from rolling from his bed to my husband's dinner table.

"I was beginning to lose hope," Fox said. I had also forbidden him to call me.

"Don't say that."

The soloist was holding stubbornly onto a high G as the Pops tried to drown him out. For ten seconds it was anyone's ball game. "What was that ungodly noise?" asked Fox.

"Some tenor just lost his transmission." Fifty to one the orchestra was smiling for the first time that evening. "I miss you incredibly, mister."

"Where are you calling from?"

"Symphony Hall. I'm at a birthday party."

"Whose birthday is it?"

"Martin's." Oop, that slowed traffic like a pterodactyl on Wall Street. For God's sake! I have no control over events that transpired exactly thirty-nine years ago! "We're at a Pops concert with some business associates." I pictured Paloma's frilly bodice hovering ten inches from Martin's nose. The poor woman was doomed.

"Having a good time?"

"Oh, stop being an ass! You know I'm having a miserable time!"

That cheered him way up. "When can I see you?"

Lust slid across my gut. "How's tomorrow?" I stood to cancel the hairdresser, the architect, and five hours towards a missionary anthem.

"I have to teach until noon."

"Where?"

"Kenmore Square."

"I'll be at your place at one." *Dangerous, Eva,* Chuck

warned. I smiled; danger was the ambrosia under Fox's tongue. "I'm going to tear your clothes off."

"I won't be wearing any."

"What a host."

"God, I'm crazy about you." He began chewing on something like carrots or celery. "I am nuts about you." Crunch, crunch. "It's insane."

The crowd was applauding again: I had to return to my obligations. "Don't forget to shave." I hung up and walked back into the auditorium.

Martin pulled my chair out for me. "What you missed," he said, rolling his eyes. I immediately put to rest all that had transpired at the telephone: that was tomorrow; tonight I had a birthday party. In my absence the waitress had brought a bunch of ham sandwiches and another bottle of champagne to the table. Jason and Paloma were pretty well hammered; Martin was getting there. Tagahashi acted precisely the same after one, or ten, glasses of anything. Smitten with intermission wanderlust, concertgoers lurched around us.

As I helped myself to a sandwich, Jason reached under his chair, dredging up a large square box. "Happy birthday, Martin," he said, "from your admiring co-workers." Paloma giggled admiringly. Fifty to one she'd spend the night with Jason and pretend it was Martin.

With a large grin, Martin lifted a softball glove out of the box. They had to be kidding. Martin was less coordinated than a dammit doll.

Tagahashi sprang to life. "You play baseball?"

"We have a softball team," Paloma explained. "They won first place last season." She didn't tell Tagahashi about the three divorces the victory had cost, Jason's included.

"We play every Tuesday night," Jason continued. "Come on, Martin, we need a shortstop." You bet they did. That was almost Divorce Number Four.

"I've never played baseball in my life," said Martin.

"He was a miler until he broke his leg skiing," I told Tagahashi. Actually Martin wasn't even skiing. He was standing still and fell down wrong.

"Miler? What is that?" Tagahashi asked.

"A base runner without bases," shouted Jason. Tagahashi

digested this a moment before laughing along with everyone else.

Someone behind us knocked over a chair. Jesus, this must be Alcoholics Anonymous Recidivists' Night at Pops. The lights went down and the band cranked out three Broadway tunes, transforming even these soupy arrangements into rivers of gold. Just wait until I arranged my cakewalk for this orchestra! I'd start with a big bad solo for that adorable concertmaster. Then I'd hit the trombones. They'd have to hire a sixth percussionist by the time I got cooking.

Martin leaned into my ear. "We'll be hearing a little cakewalk up there soon, won't we, darling?"

I was so dumbfounded I could only stare at him. In five years Martin had taken about as much notice of my hymns as he had of my bowel movements.

"You remembered the title," I said feebly. Tagahashi was staring at me like an oriental state trooper.

"Of course I do," Martin whispered. "You're famous. It's in the papers every day."

"It is? Why didn't you ever tell me?"

"I thought you knew, Eva."

I sighed disgustedly. There was no excuse for this. "Come on, Flaps, you know I don't read the papers."

"Don't you talk with your friend Lionel every other day?"

"I haven't talked to Lionel in weeks!"

"Is that a fact?" Martin asked politely, neutering this small altercation before his tablemates noticed it. "Did he leave the country?"

"Why should he do that? Is he sick? Is Local 802 after him again?" It was becoming difficult to keep my voice porcelain. Thank God the Pops were stomping all over "Oklahoma."

"He and some conductor friend were burning up the sheets at the Hotel Pierre." Martin spoke contemptuously: the Pierre is one of his favorite hotels.

"Clarence? Jesus Christ! I told Lionel a thousand times to stay away from that screaming queen!" That's why I hadn't talked to Lionel in weeks, of course.

Martin winced. He was going to end this conversation

before "Oklahoma" withdrew its cloud cover. "He should have taken your advice, lamb, and spared his boyfriend a night in jail."

Onstage, "Oklahoma" ended with the ubiquitous brass fart. I felt the ham sandwich, now spiced with bile, creeping up my throat.

"What a terrific program," Paloma said, clapping and twisting back in her chair to face us. "This is a special night." She called my husband neither Mr. Weaver nor Martin in front of me. That meant she called him Martin at the office.

"Happy birthday!" Jason shouted. "So Mart, how about the softball team?"

"Jason, when was the last time you had your hearing checked?" I said irritably. Christ! I hate loud men! They screw like apes!

Tagahashi's mouth curved into a Buddha's smile. "I make for my company a baseball team, too."

I looked at Martin. "What were they in jail for?"

Martin pretended not to have heard. "It's a wonderful sport, Itsuo," he said, emptying champagne into everyone's glass but mine. That was an old trick of my father's.

Their faces masks of pure disdain, the Pops torpedoed through a few big-band arrangements to close the show. I smiled in secret admiration: this orchestra shat gardenias. Not even the New York Phil could do that.

For the tenth time that evening, Paloma applauded, turned in her chair, and exclaimed, "They're terrific!"

"They're mercenaries," I snapped. I had not spoken directly to her before. Coloring, Paloma reached for her glass. Were I in her shoes I would have laughed out loud and asked Martin to dance.

Jason popped up from his chair. "That was great" he shouted. Holy God! Where was Fox?

I looked at my watch, then at Martin. "Where to now, birthday boy?" He had two hours before his magic pumpkin exploded.

George was waiting outside with the limousine. Martin helped Paloma in, then Tagahashi, then Jason. "Take them anywhere they want to go, George," he said. "Except Fenway Park." Of the three of them only Tagahashi

thought Martin had romance in mind. He waved good-bye
and winked at me as the limo pulled off.

"Quick thinking, Flappy," I cheered, waving as well.
"You surprise me."

Martin grabbed a cab. "Thirty-two Ash, please."

"What happened to the Budapest?" I asked as we returned home. Poor Paloma was going to have to eat triple
portions of birthday cake. The cabbie swerved to miss a
wheelbarrow someone had left in the road and hit a huge
pothole instead. The motorist behind us hit the wheelbarrow.

Martin looked out the back window and shook his head.
He hates to see machinery abused. "You didn't really
want to go there, did you, darling?" he sighed.

"No, not really." Outside of Peter Bent Brigham—that's
a hospital, not a gay bar—the cabbie ran the light, narrowly missing an ambulance. Unless they nailed stretchers
to the floor, that patient would arrive at the emergency
room with fifty ribs. "Martin," I said, "do you find
Paloma attractive?"

"She's a good-looking girl."

"Would you ever sleep with her?"

"I doubt that very much."

"How come?"

"Because she's a great secretary."

What did that have to do with anything, for Christ's
sake? Orville still sold my hymns, Richard still designed
their covers, and Jerry still did my income tax. We'd all
still be dead in one hundred years. "Oh."

The cab shot by the house. "You missed number thirty-
two," Martin called. The car rammed into reverse and
accelerated. "Stop! Here it is!"

With a crunch the trunk flew open. "Thank you,"
Martin said, paying the man. The cab sped away with the
trunk waving good-bye just like Tagahashi.

As Martin unlocked the door and killed the alarm system, I glanced at the porch furniture: had Fox and I
spooned there under a yellow moon? There was no moon
tonight, only sizzling streetlamps and the faraway pyre of
a steak. I followed my husband into the house, hating him.
"Coffee?" I said.

"That would be wonderful." Martin entered the library.

He would spend the rest of the evening on the phone with Roger Dueser, negotiating for a birthday present.

Martin sat reeling off numbers when I brought him coffee and his birthday dessert. He put his hand over the receiver. "Strawberry shortcake," he said. "Eva!"

I shoveled a giant forkful into his mouth as he was trying to sweeten Dueser's stock options. "I see," said Martin. "Quite right." You'd never suspect his oral cavity contained anything but teeth. "How about four hundred?" Martin continued, opening his mouth.

"Five hundred," I whispered, throwing in a strawberry.

"All right, three-ninety," said Martin. He engorged another handful. "But I want Rodotron." I plowed my finger through the whipped cream and poised it in the air. "Hmmm," Martin thought aloud, lapping my finger just in the nick of time, "that's a bit hard to swallow." He winked at me. I wondered if Dueser sat three thousand miles away with a dame on his lap and a huge crock of chocolate sauce at his elbow.

A few mounds later, Martin had had it with the strawberry shortcake, so I left him to his telephone. Whether my husband knew it or not, we had just made love for the evening. I went to my studio. The moment I closed the door, Fox swirled over me. *Make him go away,* I prayed. In response The Great Painkiller lanced down a bolt of longing that brought tears to my eyes. *Oh God,* I whimpered, leaning against the door, traumatized. *Now what are you going to do, wise ass,* needled Chuck, *stand there whining all night?* I did not reply for several moments. Finally I swallowed everything and went to my desk. I began working on a piece that had been pecking at my brain all day long. It was funeral music.

8

I SNUGGLED INTO my husband's backside. "Martin, wake up."

He cracked an eye, smiled at me, and closed it again. "What time is it?"

"Six o'clock." The sun—and I—had been spitting fire since five. "Guess what we forgot last night?"

Martin did not move; word games are not his forte. "Mmmmmmhuh."

"We left your softball mitt at Symp¹ ony Hall."

I felt him halt, then shallowly awaken. "Tsk." He took a deep breath. "Damn," he said, then rolled on his side. He'd think some more about his mitt later, in the shower.

Seven hours until I saw Fox. The moment light had first warmed the bedroom window, my body had begun its countdown, first laughing awake and now running wild in all directions, scooping alternate fronds of terror and joy from overhanging memory. This was not real life: this was super-life hurtling along that slim track very, very close to the precipice, and nothing today or tomorrow could derail it. Too new. The old, real life, of course, lay smashed in a ditch far behind.

Until Martin's alarm went off, I lay still, attempting to cull four hours of deep sleep from thirty minutes of inertia. That funeral music had stymied me until two; Martin was still in the den, icing his deals, when I had gone to bed. From the way he had slipped between the covers I knew he had not quite gotten what he wanted. He had not kissed me goodnight, either.

"Martin," I said, "would you like to sleep another half hour?"

"No." He took stray aim at the alarm clock. I finally climbed over his shoulder and killed it.

"You almost got Rodotron, didn't you?" I said. That would bring him around.

Yawning, Martin rolled onto his back. "Dueser is being difficult."

"Why?"

"He doesn't like me."

"That's understandable."

Martin said nothing.

"Oh, come on, Flaps! I was just kidding!" Even in jest my husband disapproves of me sympathizing with the adversary. "Why doesn't he like you?" I could think of a thousand reasons.

"I'm too successful." Make that one thousand and one.

I lay still for another moment. "So go out there and kill him!" I shouted, suddenly yanking off the covers.

Martin lay like a plucked hen as the sun yellowed his pale, smooth skin. "What was that all about," he said without amusement.

"That was your pep talk, Flaps." Believe me, I was as surprised as he was.

Martin shuffled into the shower. *What a great wife you are,* said Chuck, *Supportive, sympathetic . . .* "Come on," I interrupted, "his birthday was yesterday." Twinged nevertheless, I followed Martin into the bathroom. Outside a faint churchbell from the Jehovah's Witnesses chimed. My stomach compacted itself into a squash ball and caromed off my intestinal wall: six hours now.

"Are you okay. Martin?" I asked, sitting on the toilet. "Do you have a hangover?"

"No."

"What's the matter, then?"

"Nothing."

"Are you depressed because you're thirty-nine now?"

"No."

"Are you afraid someone stole your softball mitt?"

"No."

"Are you mad that you didn't buy Rodotron?"

"No."

"Are you tired of me?"

"A little."

I urinated pensively. "I see." For once I understood my husband completely.

Martin stepped onto the bathmat. I handed him a towel, sorry to see such superlative equipment destined for nothing but prostate surgery. "What's on your schedule today. commander?" I asked, flushing the toilet.

"Work."

Whew, he was really out of it. Martin padded past me into the bedroom and began bleakly dressing. Maybe he was thinking about how he had shafted Paloma & Co. last night. Hell, maybe he was kicking himself for not having married Paloma. She would have been feeding him important facts and figures last night instead of strawberry short-cake. I put on a kimono and went to make some coffee; my husband obviously did not want me in the bedroom.

He came down shortly. "Eva," he said, knotting his tie, "would you do me a huge favor?"

"Sure." *Before one o'clock,* I prayed.

"Could you get that softball mitt back for me?"

"Sure." From Symphony Hall I'd catch a cab to Cambridge. "Are you coming home for dinner tonight?"

"I expect to."

My faith in that answer had incinerated a herd of steer over the past five years. "I'll check with Paloma," I said, pouring the coffee. "What's the architect coming over for? I thought we were all done with him."

"He wants to show you the new blueprints." Martin was expanding his little greenhouse. The original structure could not contain eleven solar panels, twenty experimental batteries, three telescopes, and an herb garden.

"Why do I have to see the new blueprints?" I asked. "I thought you two had figured everything out."

"Gerald wants to make sure you approve."

"Are you kidding? The old fart wants to look at my legs and talk about sunken bathtubs."

Martin sought sanctuary in the *Globule*. "Eva, that's ridiculous. He's sixty years old."

"Well, I'm not!"

Martin turned to the business pages. With a sigh I peeled a banana. It would have been nice to have maybe three kids at the breakfast table throwing eggs at each other, distracting me from this monolith I had created. *The monolith is permanent,* Chuck instructed. *The children are temporary.* She had found out the hard way, six distractions, one monolith later.

Damn it, why did Martin have to pick today to be a pest? Didn't he realize how good Fox would look after all this pouting? I smelled a trap, care of The Great Bushwhacker. "Come on, Flaps," I said, fingers teasing the *Globule* out of reading range. "Tell me what's the matter." Martin continued reading. "Did I say something in my sleep? Did I forget to wash your favorite shirt? Are you mad at me?"

"No more than usual, my dear." Sipping his coffee, my husband scanned the obituaries. "And stop asking silly questions. You put ideas in my head."

Those ideas, of course, represented the tip of a monstrous iceberg around which Martin had been blithely yachting for some time now. Sooner or later he would ram them. But not today. not if I could help it: I refused to wash up on Fox's stoop clutching a splintered mast named Martin. Much too easy.

I stood up. Today was too hot for dramatics. "Enjoy your day at the office, Flappy," I said. "See you tonight." Ten deaths from now, if Fox was in good form. I went to my study to see if that funeral piece had arisen overnight, like Lazarus. Hah! It had dug its own grave and crawled in. I tore it up. Dirges were not my strong suit; cheerful, fervent, rally-'round-the-Cross-boys tunes were. That was a conundrum only God and the IRS could appreciate.

Martin stuck his head in the door before leaving. "I'm off, baby." he called spritely. "I got a great idea from that book you left on the kitchen table."

Heart Ablaze? Perhaps he was going to torch Rodotron.

For an hour, leaping again and again through a narrow,

flaming hoop of lust, I doodled stupidly on staff paper. I filled two pages with grapes and pears and two pages with very tiny checkerboard designs. As I switched to colored pens and some serious cubism, the doorbell rang.

"Hello there, Eva!"

"Whew, it's bitching hot out here," I said, muzzling the alarm. Mister P. Gerald Noonan, master architect to Boston's most eminent clients, entered the foyer and paused, as always, to admire his handiwork. He and Martin had rebuilt this house stone by stone, or, more precisely, dollar by dollar, back when Martin was flush with gentrification and about ten stock splits. By some miracle the two of them had finished their restorations within a month of our marriage. I think Mrs. Weaver had hinted to her son that it was very foolish to leave his bride alone in a house with twenty Italian carpenters. I think also she was afraid I'd try to displace that brass jail upstairs with my waterbed from New York.

"Care for some iced tea, Percival?" I asked, taking his jacket. Underneath he wore a long-sleeved shirt and an undershirt. Under that he probably wore a girdle.

"Excellent," he answered, following me three paces behind into the kitchen. That way he could check out my ass. As he sat at the table, Percival glanced swiftly around, making sure that I had not desecrated his Mexican tiles with gaudy trivets or tacky copper molds of lobsters.

"I'm in a little rush today," I said, fetching his tea. "So let's get going." I looked expectantly at Percival's briefcase.

He paused, gauging the current. Then he jumped in. "My Lord, you look gorgeous in peacock blue."

What did I do to deserve this? "Not today, Percival," I said, passing a hand over my forehead. "I'm in no mood for games." Damn it, I knew I should have gotten dressed before he came over. Certain men just cannot control themselves in the absence of buttons and zippers. "What's the problem with the greenhouse?"

Percival reluctantly opened his leather portfolio. If he didn't invent some severe bullshit fast he'd be back on the sidewalk in two minutes. "I thought you should see the new plans," he said. "After all, they're not what you originally wanted."

"I originally wanted nothing."

"That's right! Ho, ho!" Percival seemed to find this amusing.

With a disgusted sigh, I grasped the blueprints and studied them briefly. A huge glass parasite blotted one entire wall of my home. They had to be kidding: you could run a watermelon farm inside that monster. "Does Martin intend to open a Jimmy's Harborside South?" I asked, eyeing the clock: four and a half hours. The contents of my lower intestine turned to pudding; I bolted towards the nearest exit.

"Where are you going, my dear girl?"

"I'm not going to mow the lawn."

I returned in a few minutes, this time in running clothes. Pereival had loosened his bowtie and refreshed his iced tea. He was leafing through *Heart Ablaze,* which I had been using as a straightedge. "It gets good around page 179," I said. Percival hastily returned to his blueprints.

"What do you think of our new plans, Eva?" he said.

"Oh, they're terrific!" I had to make another trip to the head. "Look, Percival, why don't you two just put a glass roof on the house?" I stood up. "Now I have to get going."

"You don't like it at all. Gad, you're beautiful when you're angry."

"Will you stop this!" I shouted at him, swatting him with the blueprints. "You're supposed to be an architect!"

"You're the only woman who's ever called me Percival."

"You're the only man who's ever told me his name was Percival! Cripes! Go back to your office and start ordering glass!"

I got Percival's coat from the hall closet as he retrieved his blueprints from the kitchen floor. "Take the book with you," I shouted.

"My God, I love a tiger," Percival said as I pushed him out the door. "You have no idea what you do to me."

"You hopeless idiot," I snapped.

"Ah! No one's ever talked to me like that! You're delightful!"

I slammed the door shut and did a hundred sit-ups. Shit!

Why had Martin foisted his architect on me? If he wanted to get me interested in greenhouses, he should have looked into some on East Sixty-eighth Street! I felt like calling him up and chewing him out. *Let the man work,* Chuck said. *You've already ruined his day.*

I called Chuck instead.

"Hello, mother dear."

"What's the matter? You've had a bad morning."

Chuck was most psychic just before her second drink.

"I've been fighting off a senile architect."

"Architect! What are you and Martin building? A nursery?"

"A twenty-thousand-dollar hobby shop." There was a slight silence as Chuck swallowed. "What are you drinking?"

"Coffee?"

"Coffee and what else?"

"Nothing." That meant vodka.

"What did the doctor say yesterday?" Every year I buy Chuck a physical examination for her anniversary. I'm not sure which event she detests more.

"He said I was under a lot of stress."

Ah, stress, that great twentieth-century idol that had only come into its own when everyone had stopped going to confession. Stress and its twin, fear of failure, had made a lot of charlatans rich. "What kind of stress Chuck?"

"Every kind! Physical, mental, spiritual, economic, marital . . ." Chuck couldn't remember the other fifty-seven varieties. That's because she was on her third coffee-*mit*-nothing.

"And what did he recommend to cure this terrible suffering? Death?"

"That's not very funny, Eva. I'll be gone in a few years anyhow."

I sighed. Since her last child had flown the coop, abandoning my mother to her lawfully wedded husband, this had become one of her favorite themes. "Gone but not forgotten," I agreed. "So what else is new down there?"

My father's ears must have burnt him pitifully for the next ten minutes. I listened patiently, then asked about the nieces and nephews. Chuck began mixing their names up.

When she rewound the tape and began again on my father, I decided it was time to sign off.

"Where's Martin?" Chuck asked suddenly. I immediately thought of Fox. A quick herring of fear flashed up my spine: only three hours now.

"At the office."

"How was his birthday? Did he get my present?"

"Not yet. Did you send one?"

Chuck had to think about that. "I know I sent a card." Two years in a row now she had excoriated the local postmaster, only to find Martin's birthday card in the bottom of her bathing-suit drawer. In September.

"We'll get it, then," I assured her. "Don't worry about it."

"What did you get him?"

"A black leather jacket."

Chuck giggled. "Trying to spice up Reverend Weaver, Eva?"

Things were getting dangerous. Chuck was pulling within points of me now. "Something like that." I pictured Fox in a black leather jacket. Jesus.

"What are you doing this afternoon?"

My breath converted not from gas to liquid, but from gas to solid. Solid rock, one in each lung. I sat on my bed gagging as Chuck sat at her kitchen table drinking. It was a tie. "Eh—I have a few errands to do." I told her about Martin's ill-fated softball mitt. I said I needed some more shoes and pocketbooks. Then I excused myself.

By the time I got outside, the sun had approached its zenith. I marveled that a ball of fire some zillion miles away had the power to burn the back of my neck with no effort whatsoever. This uncanny sneaking up on me from behind gave me the idea for a hymn, *Can't Run from the Son*. It would be another guitar/bongo number aimed at young audiences. Orville would love it. As I passed another jogger, we eyed each other as if we were crazy.

I dialed P. Gerald Noonan the architect when I got back to the house. My head throbbed like a sun-ripened tomato. His secretary said he was in a meeting.

"Tell him this is Mrs. Weaver."

After a few moments, Percival was on the line. "Yes, Ruth! What can I do for you?"

"Hi, Percival."

"Eva! I thought it was your mother-in-law!" Percival had designed Ruth's summer home on the Cape. "Are you a Weaver now?"

"Nope." Ear pinning the phone to my shoulder, I started stripping. "I just had an idea for the house."

"The greenhouse?"

"Forget the greenhouse. I'm talking about a gym in the basement. Air-conditioned. Cold showers."

Percival thought that was a stupendous idea; cold showers were one step removed from sunken bathtubs. He'd talk to Martin about it immediately.

A bit later than planned, I tore into the Symphony Hall box office. In the interim hour I had tried on and rejected twenty dresses before finally finding one that looked attractive, was clean, and came off quickly. "Did someone turn in a softball mitt last night?" I asked the woman at the window. "My husband left it at the Pops concert by mistake."

"Can you describe it for me?" she said.

I made gorilla hands at the bars of her window. "It looks like this but it's big and brown."

She ducked under the counter. I heard some tissue paper crepitating. "Can you tell me the color of the box?" she asked.

"The box? What box? What's the problem? Do you have two softball mitts down there?" I remembered nothing about any box. That's because I had just returned from a phone conversation with a heavy date. "There's a card inside that says 'To our next shortstop,' isn't there, signed Paloma and Jason?"

The woman dredged a huge squat brown box to the counter and opened the window. "I guess this is yours," she said. "But it's against house rules to throw or catch softballs at Pops concerts."

"They were eggs," I said, taking the box. "Thank you very much." The clock behind her read one-fifteen, Jesus Christ! I rushed around the corner just in time to catch a meter maid writing out a parking ticket for the Bavaria.

"Hey, why am I getting a parking ticket?" I protested.

"This space is perfectly legal." I pointed to the sign behind her.

The meter maid peered at the sign, slowly forming the words with her lips, then checked her watch, then her ball-point pen. Then she continued writing. She had already nailed the block and was on a roll. "Sorry, once I've filled in the license number I have to give you the ticket."

"That's really fucked up," I said, popping the softball mitt into the trunk and slamming it. Each fine point of debate was costing me precious minutes.

"You can contest this at City Hall," she said.

"Just write the ticket as swiftly as possible, please," I said, furiously hopping into the driver's seat. "I would appreciate that." They have the parking violations system down to a science in this town: you have to contest your ticket in person, not by mail, on a special date, at a special time assigned only to you and two thousand other motorists. Only the most severely irritated are willing to kill four hours in line at City Hall attempting to deprive Major Flynn of fifteen bucks.

I bolted away from the curb the moment she placed that insidious orange rectangle in my palm. Now that the students had removed themselves and their parents' Hondas for the summer, the downtown speed limits had unofficially returned to fifty miles per hour, sixty where there were bicycle lanes. I made it over to Fox's in record time, hauled into a lot off Mass Ave, and started trotting. It was one-thirty.

He was sitting on his porch reading *Opera News*. When he saw me he put it down and stood up. I broke into a run and sprang into him like a chimp from a coconut tree. He caught me as easily as a pop fly.

"Helloelloelloelloelloello," I said, trailing my mouth across his face, "you beautiful man, you, you robber, you gorgeous disgusting bundle of muscle, sadistic bastard, why didn't you ever call me, you wimp shit, God I love you, two weeks! don't you ever stay away that long again, you worm, you're making me crazy." I clamped my legs around the small of his back, indenting his chest with my breasts.

"Hi," said Fox.

We spent the next two hours raising the temperature of his bedroom from ninety degrees to one hundred and ten. We gussied our noses with more odors than an oven at Thanksgiving. We soaked the bed. We shouted. We chaffed our lips raw and left warm, evaporating ribbons of saliva over every square inch of each other's skin and still we didn't begin to make up for three weeks of neglect. Finally we had to take a break: certain portions of the anatomy were not meant to blister.

So we took a shower. Fox gave me a spare undershirt and we went out to his back porch. He drank beer, I water. Mildred his canary twitted reproachfully when she saw her master. Fox stuck a few fingers in her cage, chirping conversationally until she perked up.

"She doesn't like the heat," he said.

"It's hot up here. No doubt about it." I wondered if he owned a fan.

"Is your house air-conditioned?" Fox asked.

"Very tastefully."

"Then what are we doing here?"

"We're committing adultery as discreetly as possible, my dear."

Fox put a hand on each arm of my deck chair and leaned into my face. "Why did you say that? Do you think you're committing adultery?"

Only when I slept with Martin. "Occasionally."

"What are you going to do about it?"

"Take a stress test."

Fox went to the kitchen for another beer. It helped him ponder these subtle asphyxiations. "Eva, come here," he called from inside.

As I walked into the living room he was sitting at the piano. "I want you to hear something."

He hit a chord and began singing the Rossini. In three weeks it had metamorphosed from a hideous caterpillar into a midrange butterfly. "Hey, that's good," I said. "You've been practicing it, haven't you."

"I've been busting my ass on it!"

"What's that for?"

"A festival in Rome."

"When's that?"

"August."

"When did that happen?"

"I got a letter last week."

"How long will you be in Rome?"

"A month."

Not true! I refused to think about it. "Sing me something else."

Accompanying himself, Fox did an old standard about bodies and souls. He looked at me when he sang. If I had any doubts that he loved me, they disappeared by the second verse; you don't sing like that for the cleaning lady.

"What's that for? Rome too?"

"No, you."

I came up behind he piano bench and put my arms around his neck. "I believe you," I said. "Sing me one more."

He kissed my forearm. "Then we'll go back to bed?"

"If you do a good job."

He pulled out *Salome* and leafed to a recit by Herod. This time he couldn't play and sing at the same time so I pushed him off the bench and flubbed through the piano part myself. He needed to do a lot of work on this. "Hey, that's a B-flat," I pointed. "That's the third time you've sung an A."

"Where?"

I showed him. "And put a little more juice in that umlaut, eh?"

"Let me try again." This time he screwed up some counting. I let it go but I made a face at him. He stopped.

"What's the matter?"

"Look, baby, that's a dotted half. You're singing two quarter notes."

"Oh. Right. Thanks."

Thanks? I would have belted me by now. That's why I never made it as a singer. "One more time."

Fox did the tune again, this time very well. He still needed a little phrasing and diction work, but I'd mention it to him under more formal circumstances. "Not bad, not bad," I said, closing the opera score. "I wouldn't mind paying to hear you sing."

Fox scratched an itch under his blue underpants. "The ultimate compliment."

"It is, but you don't know that yet." I stood up. " Do you have a manager?"

"No."

"How do you expect to become rich and famous, then?"

"Slowly."

What, and have me scrubbing floors and mending socks in the meantime? No way. "You're going to be fifty before you know it."

"What's the problem? If I can sing perfectly when I'm fifty, then I've accomplished what I wanted."

"Is there something wrong with perfection at age thirty-five?" Martin had bought and sold two dozen companies by the time he was thirty-five. The least Fox could do was sing correctly.

"Not at all. I just don't want to bum out too soon."

"Baby, you haven't even lit a match."

Fox didn't like that. He thought it was quite okay to sit in this rambling apartment singing melodies to girlfriends and eating peanut butter sandwiches until word of mouth made him internationally famous. Bah, singers were hopeless. "My voice isn't ready yet," he said.

"I could name you five prima donnas in the ninety-percent bracket whose voices aren't ready yet."

Fox took his beer and walked back into his bedroom.

"What are you doing in there?" I called after a while.

"Waiting for you."

The hell with the future! I wasn't even utilizing the present! Fox stretched across his bed; the sight of those lumpy blue briefs set off a few flares behind my lower gut. He was pretending to be asleep. I sat on the side of his bed and watched his chest move quietly up and down. I didn't care if he remained an unknown pauper for the rest of his life, as long as he spent it with me.

I lay down beside him, slipping an arm across his chest. At once my pulse began to bounce. Following its own radar, my hand moved across his nipples.

"The problem with you," Fox said softly, keeping his eyes shut, "is that you have too much money."

My hand stopped. "The problem," I told him, "is that

I have more money than you." He'd turn into an impotent mushpuddle if he knew exactly how much more. Shit, why did people with no money always think that the possession of money was such an evil? I had earned it fair and square, it was mine, and it was good. Who the hell did he think was going to make him an opera star? Not his fellow musicians, for Christ's sake!

"Did you marry Martin for his money?"

Again, a question only a pauper would have the gall to ask. "Sorry to disappoint you," I replied. "No." *Atta girl!* shouted Chuck, her throat hoarse. I leaned up on my elbow and looked Fox in the face. "I told you, I write hymns for a living. I don't need Martin's money."

"What do you need him for, then?"

Cripes, this guy really knew how to spoil a good party. Why didn't he follow my example and stick to factual questions? You don't start dismantling people before you've even shared a bathroom with them.

"Don't be so hard on the guy," I said. "He's really very nice."

Fox flipped upright. "Nice? He's an asshole! He leaves you alone for two months, then comes home for dinner and there you are! He throws his socks on the floor and you pick them up! Shit!" He flung his beer can into the wastebasket across the room.

"How'd you know about the socks," I said.

"Oh, Jesus! You make me crazy! Do you know what it's like to sit here at night and think of you two?"

"What are you thinking of Martin for? He has nothing to do with us."

"You're kidding yourself, Eva. Seriously kidding yourself."

"You're kidding yourself too, buster, if you think I'm going to drop everything and run away with you. Come on! This entire conversation is ludicrous! Why can't you just pretend I'm a groupie or something?"

Fox reacted as if I had poked him in the Adam's apple. "I love you! Can't you understand that?" He exhaled swiftly and angrily. "Probably not! Too bad! I'm going to have you whether you like it, understand it, or not!"

A gust of fear—or was it just wind off the porch?

—cooled my brow: this man played by an entirely different set of rules than I did, and I was losing. WASPs are
not trained to handle direct assaults. All I could do was
frown vaguely at him.

"Talk," Fox said. The humidity had candied us with
sweat.

About what? Why I picked Martin's sockballs off the
floor? "Why do you love me?" I asked, rolling on my
elbow. "You know it's pissing in the wind."

"How enchantingly put."

"Answer the question. And don't tell me I'm intelligent, rich, sexy, loads of fun to be with, blah, blah. That's
self-evident."

"A modest damsel, aren't you."

"When I'm around modest gentlemen."

Fox closed his eyes for a few moments, wondering
where to begin this poignant and dramatic epic. "It was
love at first sight."

I swatted him with a pillow. "None of this once-upon-a-
time baloney, either! I'm asking you a serious question!"

He swatted me back, harder. "And I'm giving you a
serious answer!" Fox retrieved his pillow and lay his head
on it. "You felt the same way."

"Pfuiii! Don't flatter yourself."

Fox smiled. "Eva, you're such a clown." He rolled on
top of me. "Don't you believe in impulses? Intuition?
Destiny?"

Maybe once, when I was nineteen. I got over that with a
bang. "No."

"Yes, you do." Fox nibbled my neck. "I know you
do."

"Come on," I said, "This is real life, not *La Traviata*."
That cool pink tongue was slowly dissolving the bound-
aries; I pushed it away. "Okay okay." I sighed, "it was
love at first sight." We'd discuss culpability later, when
we had clothes on.

"Tell me about your hymns."

"I take a pencil and write notes on paper." *And make
lots of money,* Chuck said. *Tell him that, too.*

"You don't say much about it, do you."

"Nope."

"Can I see them some time?"

"Sure."

"What are you working on now?"

"I just finished a great march. It's for special occasions like D day. Then I did a cowboy tune for teenagers called *Lookin' Out for Me*. My publisher Orville is big on that hype shit. Lately I've been doing straight instrumentals like organ medleys and trumpet fanfares. Orville wants a couple of generic offertories by July, you know, the kind of thing an Oshkosh choirmaster could throw together in one rehearsal."

"You sound very prolific."

"I have a teeming brain and a lot of spare time." And no children, and no friends, and no husband.

"What do you do all day long?"

"Write hymns and think about you."

Fox kissed me for a very, very long time, his tongue circumnavigating mine as slowly as an astronaut around the *Challenger*. "I want my tee shirt back," he said.

Every time I uncovered that body of his, some demon in my libido started a slow aboriginal dance that did not stop until Fox was inside me. I had never felt like this with any man, not with Martin, not with Martin's predecessor: I had been too young then. It was very sly of The Great Matchmaker to slip me someone like Fox just as I was hitting my sexual prime. The man had an ass more perfect than a McIntosh apple; I couldn't keep my hands off it. Now I understood what Lionel was always squealing about. But it wasn't his ass, or related parts, that turned me to lava; it was what he did inside of me. No matter where I hid my switches, he always found them and leisurely tripped them, looking at my face, smiling coyly to himself. Impulse? Intuition? Destiny? *Try adultery*, Chuck blustered. "I am," I retorted. "It's fantastic."

"Aaagh," Fox interrupted, "you witch."

"What did I do?"

"Your usual," he croaked. By now I knew what that smoky, bovine look meant.

"Hold it," I said. "Come in my mouth." I knew I was taking an awful risk. What the hell, if I started to choke,

I'd grab his tee shirt lying at the foot of the bed. Fox's lips twisted to the left: I had about two more seconds.

Old Faithful delivered right on the money. I nearly lost it once, hey, my throat was accustomed to ice cream and bouillabaisse delivered in dainty spoonfuls. But then I thought about how Fox had turned my life upside down and backward, and brother, I neatly swallowed everything, with gusto.

"I'm helpless," Fox whimpered. "You slay me."

"That's right." My tongue performed an extended encore, shortly after which I looked at his alarm clock and gasped. "Is that the time?" Of course it was the time. "May I use your phone?"

Fox nodded. A rueful smile vexed his lips: he knew the recipient of this message. I went to the kitchen and dialed Martin's direct line. There was no answer. I tried the office.

"Hello, Paloma, this is Mrs. Weaver. Is Martin there?"

"No, I' m sorry," she said. "We tried to reach you all afternoon. He's got to catch a plane to California at seven-thirty."

"Where is he now?"

"He left the office about half an hour ago. He should be home by now."

"I see," I said, remembering something. "Did you have a nice time at the Budapest?"

"Super." The woman was lying through her teeth. She was also going to California in two and a half hours.

"That's good. Well, thanks, I'll shoot home. Good-bye."

Damn it. I returned to Fox's bedroom; he hadn't moved. I sat next to him. "I'm sorry," I said, "I didn't mean to do that."

"What, mix business and pleasure?"

"Ouch." I picked up my dress. It had more wrinkles than a dried fig. "Listen, Martin is going to California tonight. Can you come over?"

Fox turned his head. "How many socks should I bring?"

"Six minimum."

"My, you're getting daring in your old age."

I took a quick shower although no amount of water could wash away that recent raw gleam in my eye. Hold-

ing my hand, Fox walked me to the car. I think he would
have driven home with me, with no socks, had I allowed
him. "Call me," he said.

Running lights, weaving through the lanes like a water
moccasin, I blasted down Memorial Drive. Traffic, sur-
prisingly sparse, moved slowly and apathetically. I wondered what had happened to the usual rush-hour maniacs.
Then I remembered it was Friday: they were all testing
their high-speed tailgating skills on the expressway, en
route to the Cape for the weekend.

Newspapers in hand, Martin opened the front door for
me. "Hi there, Flappy," I said. "I hear you're going to
California." I continued to the kitchen for a drink; if I
stood still he'd want to kiss me. *What a louse,* muttered
Chuck, *You can't even keep up appearances anymore.*

"Where have you been all afternoon, baby?"

"At the Y." *Liar,* Chuck screamed. I clenched my jaw:
my mother had graduated with top honors from the blunt
and most bellicose school of marital warfare. She had no
conception of the verbal subtleties which keep a relationship alive. It was futile to explain to her that I was doing
this for Martin's own protection.

Martin put an arm around my shoulder. "I'm going to
get him, Eva," he said.

I nearly keeled over. "Who?"

"Dueser!"

As my quaking hands poured a spritzer, Martin told me
exactly how he was going to snatch Rodotron. It would
take about a week and started with a nice cruise aboard the
unsuspecting victim's sailboat tomorrow evening in the
San Francisco Bay. Whatever was eating Martin this morning ate him no more; his mood invariably soared when he
knew he had someone by the balls. And he was such a pro
that by the time Dueser signed that contract, Martin would
have him convinced that he had made the deal of the
century. My husband should go into politics someday.

I packed his bags as he took a shower. "Why don't you
come along, darling," Martin said. "This trip is really
going to be fun."

You bet it was. But only if we were on opposite coasts.
"I can't, Martin, I have too much work. Maybe next

time." *That's two lies in two sentences,* observed Chuck. *Hats off.* I felt so guilty I packed Martin some rubbers.

"Eva," he said, rubbing his scalp with a towel as he returned to the bedroom, "I had the strangest conversation with Gerald Noonan this afternoon."

"Percival? What about?"

"Did you tell him you wanted a glass roof on the house?"

"I was only kidding! His blueprints were beyond ridiculous."

"What was the matter with them?" Martin asked defensively.

"Come on, Flappy, that greenhouse was a mile long! Don't tell me you need all that space."

Martin paused. Obviously he had told Percival exactly how much space he needed. "I thought he did rather well."

What the hell was I so steamed up about? This house belonged to Martin and Percival. I only worked here. I threw my hands in the air. "Fine! Do it!"

He'd do it, all right. It was good for the business. "Gerald took particular pains to plan you a nice herb garden," Martin said. "Did you like that?"

"I didn't even see it," I shouted. "I was too busy fighting the guy off! And his name's Percival, not Gerald!"

"Is that what that P stands for," Martin mused, knotting his tie. "He never told me that."

"It was the first thing he told me," I said. The second thing he told me was that I had perfect legs. Bah, drop it. The man was a good architect. The rest didn't matter, as long as he kept his distance. "How are you getting to the airport?"

"George."

Great. That meant I could embark upon some serious imbibition. I snapped Martin's suitcase shut and went to the wine cellar in the basement. There was half a case of great Chardonnay somewhere down here.

"Eva?" Martin called from the top of the stairs.

"What?" I replied sullenly. I don't know why I was so angry with him. After all, he was doing precisely what I wanted him to do: go away.

His footsteps tapped the stair treads. "What are you looking for, cutie?"

"That Chardonnay you brought back last year."

Martin immediately pulled two bottles from an upper quadrant of the rack. "Here you go." He held on to them and turned around. "Eva, you're upset. Do you want me to stay home? I'll cancel this trip if you want me to."

"I do NOT want you to stay home," I blurted. "And you do NOT want to stay home either, so do NOT make such stupid statements."

Martin grinned. "I do NOT think I should give you this wine."

Nice going, said Chuck, *he thinks you're drunk.* "You should know," I retorted.

Martin thought I was addressing him and put the bottles back. "Hey! Give me that wine!" I jumped up and down, trying to reach the top nooks.

Arms folded, Martin leaned against the other wall, watching me. "Let me know if I can help, Bonzo."

"Go to California," I snapped, continuing to jump up and down. Things were truly fubar. I had intended to be extra nice to Martin this afternoon.

The doorbell rang: George the chauffeur. Martin pulled the two bottles of Chardonnay from the rack and went upstairs. "By the way," he said, "your friend Lionel called. He says he's coming to Boston." Martin placed the bottles on the kitchen counter. "I sincerely hope he does his visiting while I'm away."

"Why is that?"

"He's bringing up his new boyfriend."

"Oh."

Martin opened the hall closet. "Where's my umbrella, sweetie?"

"Forget it. It doesn't rain in California."

Martin stopped with his hand on the doorknob. "I'm sorry I'm going away, Eva, really I am. I know it's difficult for you."

I said nothing. I had done enough lying for one day.

Martin hesitated. "Believe it or not," he continued, "I was sitting in the office around two this afternoon when a tremendous desire to sleep with you nearly knocked me out of my chair.''

And then the pink elephants came flying out of the telex machine. ''Is that so.''

''But you weren't home,'' Martin sighed. ''I should have sent George to the Y to pick you up.'' He turned the doorknob. ''I'll remember next time.''

''Have a good trip.'' I walked him to the limousine, where the chauffeur stood sweating for his money in that heavy black uniform. George encased Martin in the back seat and put the gears into reverse. ''Hey! Wait a minute!''

Four tires gently clamped the asphalt. I ran up to Martin's window. ''I got your softball mitt back.''

''That's my girl,'' Martin said. ''I was afraid to ask.'' He kissed my hand. ''Bye, my love. Be good.''

I watched until the limousine had made the bend in the road. Then, before my husband's trail was even cold, I went straight to the telephone. ''Hey Foxy.'' I said, ''I need a babysitter.''

Maybe, when I'm sagging and senile, I might cease to remember that week Fox spent with me. I doubt it, though. Something tells me I'll die remembering the details very clearly: from the start I have been richly punished with sanity and memory. Ah, and don't let me forget desire. That must only deepen with decrepitude.

Fox arrived two hours after I called him. He had taken the T and paid dearly for his mistake: the Red Line broke down between Kendall and Central. It's too bad some nearby MIT researchers couldn't seize this priceless opportunity to measure the effects of darkness, one hundred degrees Fahrenheit, carbon monoxide, body odor, radios, and pickpockets upon the depraved human psyche.

I waited for him on my porch, but I wasn't reading *Opera News*. I was sipping a magnificent Chardonnay and wondering if Fox had smashed his Bel Air on the BU Bridge. The minute I saw him dragging down the street I knew what had happened: passengers emerging from protracted rides on the MBTA all move like freshly branded cattle. I didn't get up, though: I loved to watch Fox walk. Even after two hours in the tubes he had a natural rhythm—a

cross between a hula dancer and a West Point cadet—
which alternately frightened and seduced me. All the man
had to do was put one foot in front of the other, and I was
not myself. *Delightful,* Chuck commented.

He knew where to look on the porch now. "That's a
great transit system," was all he said. "I need a beer."

"There hasn't been any beer in the house since Octo-
ber," I apologized. The occasion was Martin's victory
cookout for the softball team. After half a keg they broke
the deck railing by accident. Martin got angry with Percival
the architect, I got angry with Martin the host, and we
haven't had any parties since. "How about some wine?
Soda?"

Fox had a few huge glasses of ice water tinged with
scotch. "Much better," he said. We went to the living
room and piled into a fat stuffed couch. Fox turned his
head. "Miss me?" he asked.

"Naw." I glanced at his shirt. "What's in your pocket?"

"Socks."

I pulled them out. "Only two socks?" They didn't even
match. "Are you leaving tomorrow?"

"Check the other pockets."

Aha. Six more socks and a telescoping toothbrush.
"What's in the knapsack?"

"Music," he said, "cassettes, letters, metronomes, cough
drops . . ."

"German dictionaries?"

Fox frowned. "Hey, baby! Didn't I bring enough work?"

"Never mind," I said, "I've got some grammar books
upstairs."

"I've been thinking about what you said this afternoon." Stretching his legs, Fox jimmied off his loafers.
The socks on his feet didn't match either.

"What did I say?" Whatever it was, I probably didn't
mean it.

"You were telling me to get off my ass," Fox said.
"I'm going to."

"Oh?" I've known musicians all my life and this is how
it goes: every six to twelve months, when they get tired of
baked beans, they decide to get off their asses. They'll
write two dozen letters to conductors and managers, then

they'll wait several weeks for either no answer at all or a polite letter telling them to get lost. Then they'll feel hurt and dismayed and won't write any more letters for another six months. This goes on until they're about forty years old and then they begin to love baked beans and hate people who eat truffles. "How do you intend to do that, doll?"

"I've been putting off some auditions," Fox said, "but I'm going to take them now." He pinched my lip. "I'm more ready than I thought I was."

"Of course."

"Will you help?"

Let's see. I could buy him a new suit and plane fare to Timbuktu. I could correct his diction and fine-tune his breathing. I could set him up with ten conductors in New York. "Of course." My index finger tickled his bellybutton. "What would you like me to do?"

"Leave Martin."

Curve ball, a big strike. "What made you say that," I said accusingly, pulling my finger from its snood. "Damn it, you really have no self-control at all." *He's just surprising his opponent*, Chuck swaggered. Forget the wine: I headed directly for the scotch on the kitchen counter. "That was the stupidest thing you've ever said to me," I called over my shoulder. "It was unbelievably callous." I slammed the freezer door shut, lost my balance, and scattered a handful of ice cubes all over the floor. "You couldn't wait a day or two, could you?" I shouted. "No, no, you had to blabber it right out like a ten-year-old!" I got down on hands and knees and started retrieving ice cubes, muttering every curse in the book. In this regard Chuck had educated her children thoroughly. My ankle smacked a corner counter and I moved from ecclesiastical to corporeal profanity. "You fucking moron!" My voice was rising precariously.

"Don't call me moron, I told you," Fox said behind me. He had sneaked into the kitchen while I was preoccupied. "And you didn't answer my question."

"It wasn't a question," I shouted, my voice shredding like a paper kite, "it was a statement." Very much like one I had made myself, once upon a time, when I had been very sure of intuition, impulse, and destiny.

Fox picked up a few ice cubes and lobbed them into the sink, where they landed with a splitting crash. Then he just stood there watching me snivel and crawl impotently in circles. Finally I retired under the kitchen table like a wounded pup, half expecting him to come at me with a rolled-up newspaper. Neither of us moved. I wanted him forever.

"Eva," Fox began in that melodious ebony voice, "come over here. I want to talk to you."

Didn't this fellow understand that there were certain things you just don't talk about? What the hell, maybe he was going to apologize. I slowly showed myself, but not waving any white flags. *Who needs white flags?* said Chuck. *You both know who's got all the ammunition.* "Let's talk upstairs, eh?" I sighed. "I'm tired." Whew, it had been a killer day: four fights with three men. And it wasn't over yet. I locked up the house and we went to my bedroom.

Somehow everything was all right once we got under the sheets; mammals derive a supernatural consolation from contact with the bare, soft, warm flesh of their kind. The Great Zookeeper had been nuts to defoliate the gorillas. We just lay there like two cigars for a while, I drifting asleep, Fox cogitating his recent blunders: I could tell that by the way he was breathing.

"Are you awake?" he whispered presently.

"Uh-huh."

"Do you think I was kidding around downstairs?"

"No."

"Then why did you get crazy?"

"Come on, baby! Do you talk about tangos to an amputee?"

Fox sifted through that one. "Not unless I want to dance."

"What makes you think I want to dance?"

"You're not an amputee."

This discussion was getting way too delphic for me. "Say what you mean."

"You know what I mean," Fox said. "You just don't believe me." He turned on the light. "I love you, you little nut! How many times must I tell you that? I want you around when I wake up in the morning, I want to see you in cocktail dresses and ripped-up sweatshirts, I want to be in the next room when you finish a hymn, I want to make love to you slow as molasses after you've had a lousy day, I want you in the box seat at my first *Butterfly* . . .'' Fox put his hands over his eyes, rubbing them as if he had just missed the last train. "I'm not going to let you go, you know that.''

Again that nameless fear drifted over me. "Why not?''

"I need you.''

What for, howled Chuck, *inspiration?* "Don't need me,'' I begged. "Don't need anyone, ever.'' If I failed at everything else, I must teach Fox to paddle his own canoe.

"What are you afraid of, Eva?''

YOU, moron! "Nothing.''

Fox chuckled. "I see I have to teach you a few things.''

"You don't have to teach me anything, pal!'' Shit, what was this, Lover's University? I had already flunked out!

Fox ran a palm along my hip. Bone became cloud: he was beginning to own me, just as he had predicted. "So you don't need anyone, eh?''

Not anymore, pal. "No.''

"Could you do without me?''

Sure, sure, and I could do without ice cream and eyesight. "I could manage.''

"You lie,'' Fox said, damn him.

I turned the light off. "Try me.'' *No Oscars for that one, Eva,* Chuck clucked.

"Wait a minute, we're not done talking yet,'' his voice said from the dark.

"Change the subject.''

Fox paused, selecting from a huge field of armament. "I have a confession to make.'' Herpes? Parole? A Sicilian fiancée? Pain lapidifed my heart: I had no idea what he was going to say to me. But that was typical with Fox.

"I don't intend to be sneaking around like this forever.''

My autonomic functions resurged into operation. "And you call that a confession?'' I felt like breaking out the champagne.

Fox turned the light back on. "Plus I'm a sore loser.

Very." *Great,* yelled Chuck, *he's a sore loser and you're a cheat! This is going to be one hell of a match!*

I had to get a little edge on him. He's not the only sore loser. "Can't lose what you don't have."

"Oh! Meaning you?" He slid two fingers in the ground floor. "Answer me." Now his thumb wandered in.

No fair. Most fair. My mouth didn't answer, but my hips did.

The next day, Saturday, we spent mowing the lawn, trimming rose bushes, and practicing Fox's rape holds in the backyard. I was becoming quite adept at weaseling out of rear clutches; by the end of the week, if these lessons continued, I would be good enough to start attacking people myself. We washed the car and played with Martin's mitt; the team had left a few souvenir softballs behind at their victory cookout. Fox practiced Rossini while I threw a few lamb chops onto a grill. We spent all night messing up the bed again.

Sunday morning, my mother called. She was checking to see if I had gone to church. "Hi, Chuck," I said. "Maybe next week."

"What are you talking about? I called to say happy birthday to Martin."

"Martin's in Silicon Valley."

"What's that? A new Moonie outfit or something?"

"It's in California."

"I knew it! All the crackpots are out there!" Including that guy with the drive-in glass church Chuck sent four hundred bucks to. "Why aren't you with him?"

"It came up at the last minute."

"Is that secretary there?"

"I suppose so." I sighed. Chuck never trusted secretaries. She used to be one herself. "What's on the menu today, Chuck?"

"Nothing."

Always nothing before she shook hands with the preacher on Sunday morning, congratulating him on a fine sermon. "Where's Dad?"

Chuck did not immediately reply. She was relieving her thirst. "Reading the newspaper. You should've seen'm

last night! I could've crowned'm!'' Chuck crowned the
next five minutes relating how my father had lost an
important tennis match. They were playing doubles. Then
he had blown an important bridge game against the same
opponents. They were playing doubles that time, too.
Then he forbade her to have any more martinis after she
began accusing the other team of playing with a marked
deck. ''He's intollable,'' Chuck moaned, ''Just intorrable.''
She was about half an hour away from forgetting his name
completely.

I couldn't really sympathize with her. Since the age of
three I have been advising my mother never to play tennis,
or bridge, or even shell peanuts, with my father. They
have polar theories about how these things should be done.

''Wha zat singing?'' Chuck asked after a pause.

Fox, of course, playing Herod. ''The radio.''

''Can' you tur' some shursh prog'am on?''

''Sure! Sure!'' As if on cue, Fox stopped. ''Are you all
right, Chuck?'' It was unlike her to blow out on a Sunday
morning.

''My poor chilrn 'rall havn problms! Izza stress'z killn
me!''

''Chuck! I told you not to worry about us! We're all
fine!'' Except for my one brother. He was thinking of
marrying this twerp from Idaho. Fox started singing again.

''Whappnd tooth shursh pro'm?''

''Forget the church program, what's going on with you?
Go to bed! You sound smashed! Put Robert on the phone!
I don't like this!''

Chuck politely said she didn't feel well, wished my
sister's husband a happy birthday, and hung up.

Humming, Fox tripped spryly into the kitchen. ''Who
was that?''

''My mother.''

''What's the matter?''

''She's not feeling very well today.'' Neither was I,
now. ''Want to run through the Rossini?''

''Sure.'' He waited for me at the door. ''What's the
matter with your mother?''

''She's getting old.''

''How old is she?''

"Fifty-three. Let's drop it."

"No! I want to know what I'm getting into here."

"She's always been a very unhappy woman."

"Why?"

She married the wrong man, that's why. Then she never divorced him. "How the hell should I know? I'm only an innocent by-product!"

"Do you get along with her?"

"Of course."

"Does she drink?"

I'd be damned if Lucifer was not handing this fellow crib sheets. "Here and there." I looked at Fox's big gray eyes. "And there, and there."

"Doesn't your father do anything about it?"

"Sure! He reads the newspapers and takes out the garbage." I guess that's how you'd describe the strong, silent type.

"Do you get along with him?"

"Of course."

"I'd like to meet your mother some time," Fox said, opening his books. "She's the great clue to figuring you out."

"No she's not."

"Who is, then?"

"Someone you don't know and wouldn't appreciate."

"Going to tell me who it is?"

"Not today." Not tomorrow, either. This secret I'd protect like the Holy Grail. We practiced for an hour or two; his Strauss was improving daily. Fox was a genuine top-drawer talent. All he needed now were a few lucky breaks and one hundred thousand dollars.

"Fine," I said eventually. "Time to do the crossword puzzle." Not that mushbrain rubbish from the *Globule*, either. You know how little respect a newspaper has for the intelligence of its readers when it prints the answers in the same issue.

We sat out on the porch just as my neighbor Harry was chugging his bullfrog-green Cadillac into the driveway. "Hi, Mahtin," he called. "How's it goin?"

Fox bristled. "Forget it," I said, waving, "he hasn't seen Martin in three years."

"Do I look like Martin or something?"

I shrugged. "You both have dark hair and you're both tall." But even from two hundred feet, any idiot could tell this wasn't Martin. I never sat on his lap.

We finished the crossword puzzle along with a bottle of wine, went to bed for a nap, and remained there for twenty hours. I think I gained a kilo in semen alone. Once, around midnight, the phone interrupted: Lionel screaming that I never called him back anymore. I had completely forgotten that he called in the first place.

"Doesn't your husband tell you anything?" Lionel cried. "I told him at least TEN times that I was coming up."

"He remembered that."

"He did, did he? So when am I coming up?"

Next week? Tomorrow? I had no idea. "Friday."

"No, NO, I knew he'd get that ALL screwed up! I told him I wasn't sure."

Amen. "Are you sure now?"

"Of course I am! Why do you think I'm calling? We'll be there Wednesday."

"No way. Lionel."

"What? Don't tell me you're not going to be there! We have ACRES of things to discuss! We're going to open your show in Boston!"

"You're kidding."

"I have never kidded you in my life, my dear girl."

I put my hand over the phone. "How long are you staying here?" I asked Fox. "All week?"

"Try all life."

Shit. He was no help at all. I raked my memory: how long did Martin say he'd be gone? A week? What day did he leave? What day was this anyhow? "You can come on Saturday. Lionel."

"Saturday? I have a party in P-town on Saturday!"

"Hey, you want to see me or you want to get sand in your bunhole? Make up your mind."

"Jesus, you've turned into a SHREW! It's that new boyfriend!"

"That's right," I said coolly. "And he's going to beat you up if you keep me on the phone any more tonight."

"GoodBYE! This friendship is on the ROCKS!"

"See you Saturday. Pillbox."

Fox stopped playing with the crowbar. "Is that the same guy you wrote a dance number for?"

His memory astonished me. "Yes. We go back a long way."

"Did you ever sleep with him?"

"Are you kidding? He's been gay for years."

"You did, didn't you?"

Of course I did. We were trying to determine if Lionel could cut it as a bisexual. "I have no secrets from Lionel," I said. "And I still have a lot from you."

"Oh yeah?" Fox rolled on top of me. "Am I going to find them out one by one, like Chinese water torture?"

"That's right."

Fox began torturing himself. "How many lovers have you had?"

"One." That wasn't a lie, it was a compliment.

"How many morons have you had?"

"Enough."

"Can I take a guess? To the nearest hundred?"

Shit! Musicians above all should know that practice makes perfect! "Don't be ridiculous."

"Three hundred."

"Nope."

"Five hundred? No? More?"

"Of course."

"Wait a minute! Are you counting repeats?"

"No, I'm dividing repeats by morons. It gives a better average." That, plus my right hand, shut him up. We spent the rest of the night dividing one into one.

Fox had to teach a few rape-defense lessons the next morning while I went shopping for beer and bratwurst. I did not like him out of my sight for even three hours: all types of umbilicals began hemorrhaging. *This is nothing*, Chuck said. *Wait until next month.* I refused to think about it the way a smoker refuses to think about lung cancer. At one o'clock I picked him up in Kenmore Square.

"What a class," he wheezed. "There was this two-hundred-pound behemoth trying to sit on my face the entire morning."

"Why didn't you just bite her?" I beat a yellow cab to the light.

"Her pants were too tight." How could he be so jovial when we only had four days left? Ah, because he had distracted himself with people all morning. *No fair,* I prayed. *Why didn't you make me a waitress?*

"Waitress? She was the garbage disposal."

I looked over at Fox. "Eavesdropping again," I said. "What would you like to do this afternoon? Wash the screens? Trim the hedges?"

"Drink beer and fuck you blind."

"Oh." I stepped on the accelerator. We hit a huge traffic jam at Fenway Park. The Sox were attempting to play the Yankees. "Want to go to the game?" I asked.

"Wanna' go home." Ho, he missed me all right. That two-hundred-pound fanny hadn't helped one bit. It just made things worse.

Fox carted in the groceries for me. I followed with his beer. Watching him unload tomatoes and melons from those brown bags filled me with the most agonizing happiness: he should be in my house always, unpacking my groceries, rumpling my sheets, singing in the next room . . . *The classic obsession,* Chuck called. *You should speak to Richard Weintraub about it.* Instead I went to the porch with a huge wedge of watermelon.

"What kind of beer is this?" Fox asked, joining me.

"Pilsner Urquel. How do you like it?"

"It's beautiful. You've got great taste."

Who me? It was the only beer Martin kept in the house; I figured it had to be good. "Thank you."

An easy breeze drifted through the screens. Last night it had squired the humidity out to sea and left it there. "Ah," Fox said, stretching his legs, "it's fantastic to be with you."

I brushed his unshaven face with my finger, wanting those abradant cheeks stuck in all possible crannies. "It is." *That's because it's only for a week,* Chuck elbowed. *You haven't gotten the phone bills, no one's scorched the oatmeal, and you're still on your first bottle of mouthwash.*

"What's the matter?" Fox asked as I watched a huge

mutt defecate robustly near my front fence. Why in hell don't I ever see stray chihuahuas or toy poodles?

"Are you behaving naturally here? I mean, do you blow your nose in towels and forget to put out new toilet paper and stuff like that?"

"No."

That's what I was afraid of. For several minutes we observed the Puerto Ricans playing in the fire hydrants they had uncapped.

"What kind of business does Martin have?" Fox asked.

"He makes computers."

"Why isn't he ever home?"

"He's buying computer parts."

"How come he hasn't called you since I got here?"

"I told you! Because he's out buying computer parts!"

"What? Twenty-four hours a day?"

"Twenty-five."

"Don't you ever call him?"

"Sure." If I remembered to get his number from Paloma during business hours.

Fox directed those big gray eyes at me. "What does he think you do here all by yourself?"

"Write hymns. Read books. Go to the Y." Christ! What a dull life!

"I'd be calling you three times a day."

"That's because you don't trust me."

"No, that's because I'd miss you."

"You're implying that Martin doesn't miss me?"

"I find his behavior a little unusual."

Of course he found it unusual! He didn't live with the man! I know people who, after one year of marriage, didn't think it the least unusual for their spouses to polish off three pumpkin pies in one sitting or watch television seven nights per week. "Martin is an unusual fellow."

"You're an unusual woman."

Come on, I wasn't unusual. I just wanted what every woman alive wanted: a man or two. "Flattery will get you nowhere."

"Will it get me upstairs? Right now?"

We came down for some more watermelon around six that evening. My body kept expecting to eat breakfast because it had been doing nothing all week but get out of bed. That was the least of the confusion, believe me: my mind had totally surrendered to my displaced body. Not one hymn had flitted across it since Fox had removed his socks from his pockets. I had not once thought of lifting weights or reading books or calling Martin: Fox's body had overgrown all of those neat little daily rows like a ferocious chickweed. I wanted him inside me at all times. When he was inside me, I wanted him deeper inside me. When I was sleeping, I wanted to dream he was inside me. I did not want to wake up except to a gently swinging time bomb. Hadn't prayed in ages: it was counterproductive.

We went to a late movie out in Dedham. It was the usual propaganda disguised as entertainment; Fox had wanted to see it. Then we took a long drive around Route 128 because the moon was out and the roads were empty. As the Bavaria shot by Weaver, Inc., I glanced over. Jason's Porsche stood in the parking lot; he was probably on the phone with Martin. Both men were only names to me.

"How fast are you going?"

"One hundred."

"Slow down."

"Oh, come on! The car loves this!" I looked over. "Don't tell me you want to live to a ripe old age." Ah, I had forgotten. Atheists want to live forever.

"Sure do, honey. With you."

I cut down to ninety. "That better?"

"More."

I started crawling at seventy-five. "Okay?"

"Yes." He thought we were doing sixty. That's what's great about a BMW.

The moon had not quite set when we got back home, so we went out for a little run. It was that magical hour when the winos had passed out into the bushes but the *Globule* trucks had not yet hit the streets. The only noise came from our shoes, our lungs, and an occasional burglar alarm. We ran out to the Gardner Museum and around the Fenway. Several rapists looked me over, then looked Fox over, then pretended they were out birdwatching.

I broiled some kebabs as the sun rose. Fox worked on another beer and some rice pilaf. "You mean you know how to cook?'' I asked in surprise. The other men in my life could barely cope with boiling water.

"Please!" Fox said, deftly pouring rice into a pot. "You insult me." I noticed that he did not use measuring cups.

"Who taught you to cook?" Not his mother, certainly.

"I taught myself."

"My goodness! Are you handy with a darning needle, too?"

"Buttons only." He stopped stirring. "Poverty has its advantages, lady."

"Certainly." It made rich women forget all about fur coats, white roses, and dinner at eight. For limited periods of time.

I brought up some more wine from the cellar and we sat out on the deck, stuffing ourselves. "I can smell you," Fox said.

"I've been running for an hour, dear boy."

"That's not what I smell."

My insides began to tickle me again: Fox had tripped some sort of perpetual motion machine between my legs. "Don't tell me you want to retire for the morning."

"Uh-huh."

It just kept getting better. All the man had to do now was put a finger on the ignition and I began to gurgle and chum like a diesel after 50,000 miles.

The phone woke me up. It was Richard Weintraub. " 'Lo."

"Eva? Were you sleeping?"

"I just haven't been talking."

"Martin away again?"

"Of course." I yawned and stretched. "How are you?"

"Hot." Richard would rather sweat than patronize Con Ed. "I saw your show last night." I had sent him two tickets.

"Hey! How'd you like the cakewalk?"

"It's pretty clever, Eva." Believe me, this was a remarkable compliment. Richard is about as extravagant with praise as he is with electrical current.

"Did the audience like it?"

"I would say so." Translation: hit of the show. "That black priest is a real ham."

"Did you see Lionel?"

"See him? You can hardly miss him! His hair is red, white, and blue now."

"Who'd you take with you?"

"My mother."

"What happened to that nursing student?"

"I found out she used to be married to an Arab."

"Before or after you slept with her?"

"After."

"That's too bad." Richard would spend the next three months inspecting his penis hourly. "What else is new?"

"There's a card convention in Boston in December."

"Are you coming up for it?"

"Can I stay at your place?"

"You don't have to ask."

After I'd hung up, Fox said, "Who was that?" His tone of voice reminded me of my father's when he asked Chuck where the corkscrew went.

"Richard Weintraub. He's my illustrator and an old friend. Lives in New York."

"Have you slept with him?"

Please, did it matter which hotels I had checked into years ago? I had checked out, hadn't I? These jealous inquisitions were beginning to aggravate me. *You love them,* Chuck hooted. *You just don't like answering yes all the time.* "Foxy." I began, "I've been around a long time."

"So have I, baby," he answered. "But not that around."

Hey, that was his own fault. "What's the matter with you? Any woman alive would want to get into your pants! Why didn't you ever have any girlfriends?"

"Told you I was picky."

Gee, I was picky too and I had still been able to find plenty of acceptable bunwarmers. *For eight hours apiece,* Chuck counted. *Great, Eva.* "You mean I'm the first woman you've ever spent any time with?"

"You now hold the distance record."

Jesus, that meant I would be the first to break his heart. Such responsibility terrified me. "I don't understand where you perfected your technique," I said.

"What technique?"

I frowned. "Skydiving."

Fox shrugged. "You make me do it." He looked down. See, you made me do it again."

Pfuii, just by lying here? "I'm going to have some breakfast."

"No, you're not. It's Thursday already."

Following a lazy midafternoon breakfast, we went to Cambridge. Fox was running out of socks. I waited outside as he checked his mail and his canary Mildred, guesting with the downstairs neighbors. Watching him return to the car, I seriously thought of driving far away with him that afternoon, never to see Boston again. It made perfect and inevitable sense.

"Hey, a letter from Rome," Fox said, bouncing in. He tore it open. "They want me in two weeks. The local boy got strep throat." He looked out the window at a swami playing the violin in Harvard Square. "I'm not going."

I turned my head. "Of course you're going," I said calmly. "You have to." Oh God! Who said I wasn't an actress! We screamed at each other all the way home. To make matters worse, Martin called the moment we stepped in the door.

"Hi, baby."

"Hi." My brain chopped my tongue into monosyllables. It was impossible to talk to Martin in front of Fox.

"You sound out of breath."

"Am."

When I didn't ask when he was coming home, Martin said, "My flight's due in late tonight."

Fire: my stomach walls had just ignited. "Tonight?"

"We wrapped it up this morning. No use hanging around here! Dueser's ecstatic."

"Great." Now I couldn't talk at all.

"Could you pick me up?"

"Tonight?"

"Yes, darling, at midnight."

"Uh—uh—"

"Are you in the middle of something?"

"Yes."

"Should I get George to pick us up?"

"Yes."

"Okay. I'll let you go. We're going to celebrate! I can hardly wait to see you!"

"Hehhhrgh." I hung up the phone. Fox stood two feet away. "Guess who?"

"He's coming home tonight?"

"Yes."

Fox steered us into the library and poured two brandies. He was quite at home now in the room in which I had first challenged him. For ten minutes, hands warming the brandy, we imitated the walls. "Cheers, love," Fox said. "It's not over yet."

Easy for him to say! He wasn't ninety stories high in an earthquake! My head rumbled ominously. I could not imagine unpacking my own groceries any more. I could not imagine drinking coffee at eight in the morning. In my blackest recesses I could not imagine lying within fifty feet of Martin Weaver. Soon I'd have to do them all. I looked at Fox. "My life is ruined. Do you have any idea what you've done?"

"Hey you. We were made for each other."

We were, by the reckoning of two strong and lawless little hearts. We weren't, by the reckoning of four in-laws, five years, one businessman, and one tattered conscience. God, I was the stupidest ass on earth! I had to marry a nice guy! I put my face in my hands. Such jokes deserved rich laughter, but they usually received only shakes of the head and tearstained palms. *Tell him it's impossible*, said Chuck. *Suggest that he visit you after he's met a nice girl.* "When am I going to see you again?" I muffled through ten fingers.

"Tomorrow," Fox said. "I need another diction lesson."

I raised my eyes. "You trying to kill me?"

"I'm trying to own you, dummy."

That killed me instead. I looked at my watch. "How would you like to spend the next four hours?"

"We have eight hours."

"Not if I have to do the laundry."

"Let's give the washing machine something to think about."

Fox took the MBTA home. He felt it was the only poetical conclusion to a week spent in my presence.

The instant I sat at my desk, a melody popped to mind. It was a seraphic and innocent tune for a children's choir at Christmas. I blazed through three verses before hearing the front door open: my executioner had returned. I sat still as a Sargent portrait following Martin's progress to the study. First he dropped his suitcases onto the marble floor. Then he ripped open some mail. Then he hit the refrigerator and opened a beer. Then he tiptoed upstairs, thinking I was asleep. About two minutes later, after flushing the toilet, he came down again. This time there was no escape.

Martin softly pushed open the door to the study. "Eva?"

"Hi." I put my erasers down but didn't get up. Fox had bound me to the chair.

My husband sat in the leather recliner next to my desk and watched me pencil in a few corrections. Finally I put the paper away and looked at him. I don't think I was smiling. "So you did it," I said.

Something told Martin that this was not a propitious time to recount military history. He just nodded his head, keeping his eyes on me.

"What are you looking at, Flappy?"

"I sometimes forget," he said, "how beautiful you are."

I? Only because I contained several million of Fox's sperm madly whipping their tails upstream. Still I couldn't rise off the chair.

"Would you like a brandy?" Martin asked presently.

"No, thank you." There wasn't any left.

"Thanks for buying beer."

"You're welcome." If he didn't leave the room very soon, I would scream. For ages I kept writing and erasing intently, my mind a vapid lump. Still Martin didn't move. Soon my erasers were giving out. Jesus Christ! So was I! Dashing one onto the rug, I looked ferociously at Martin. I wanted a divorce.

Head leaning against the siderest, arms daintily folded around that bottle of beer, my husband was asleep in his chair. Martin looked very young; as always, dreams sweetened his countenance. Where did he get his serenity? Why would I be forever incapable of that? A torrent of guilt scalded me from head to foot. How could I trash a sleeping man who had done nothing but love me?

"Damn you, Fox," I whispered, my voice shaky as smoke rising off a campfire. *It's not Fox's fault,* Chuck was quick to point out. So whose was it? Mine? No way! I knew Who did this and I knew exactly why: I was becoming too content, too efficient at running my life, and much too secure about where I was headed, like the Weavers. Now that I had married Martin and kept my nose clean for five years, I had a greatly diminished fear of going to hell. That was a huge threat, see: once you stop fearing hell, you tend to stop pursuing heaven. No wonder Mr. Sunflower was irritated. Every time He tossed out a few crumbs, the pigeons didn't take Him seriously anymore.

I left Martin crooked in his chair, turned out all the lights but one, and went upstairs. Without Fox, my bed was my sepulchre. *Keep Martin in that chair,* I prayed, then stopped: I would be better off praying for peace in the Middle East. Sure enough, Martin came creaking up around dawn. One by one, I heard pieces of clothing slither off. Then the bed lurched. I shut my eyes: Martin slid over and touched me.

"Hi, Flappy," I said, pretending to wake up a little. Ten thousand demons drew their talons down my throat and through my abdomen.

Martin held tight and went to sleep.

9

AT SEVEN, after the garbage men had eviscerated the block I disentwined myself from my husband's arms and silently donned a pair of shorts and a tee shirt. I ran up to the corner for some croissants and the *Globule*. I also called Fox.

"Sleep well, Little Boy Blue?"

"No." He was hurting. "You?"

"Hnnnff." Fifteen customers walked into and out of the bakery as we breathed tersely into mouthpieces five miles apart. There was everything and nothing to say. I pictured all six feet of him lying in bed with no clothes on and quickly stuffed a honey bun into my mouth.

"What are you chomping on?"

"Nuffhn." We lapsed into another overcast silence. Soon my dime would run out. I squeezed the last sticky lump past my tonsils. "I miss you."

"How encouraging!"

"Don't be mad."

"Oh! Ho! Me? I've only been lying here all night eating the sheets!"

"Stop it. Martin didn't even come to bed until two hours ago."

"What was he doing? Telephoning Jupiter?"

"He fell asleep in a chair." I didn't like Fox deriding Martin. "Be nice."

The phone clicked ominously; as I deposited another

dime I wondered if it were tapped. "What are you going to do today?" I asked.

"Write fifty letters, sing, and go crazy."

"That sounds interesting."

"It sounds awful, you bitch!"

I burst out laughing. No one but Lionel has ever called me a bitch. "You adorable man." I bit into an almond croissant.

"What's so funny?"

"You, you. You." I replaced the croissant and tried a blueberry muffin. "I love you."

"I know you do." We thought about that for another four bites.

"What are you eating now?"

"A blueberry muffin." I put most of it back and searched the bag. Somewhere near the bottom of this carnage I knew there lay a Banbury tart. "Who's getting all the letters?"

"Opera houses, conductors, the usual shits."

His industry impressed me. "So! You wanna be rich and famous now?"

"You know why."

Ah! There was that damn tart! "Hold on a minute." Seeing a break in the traffic, I hied to the counter and bought a cup of coffee. "Hello?"

"What the hell are you doing there?"

"I'm eating breakfast, darling."

"How can you eat at a time like this? How disgusting!"

I tossed the tart back into the bag. "I've got to keep up my strength."

"You're strong enough! When am I going to see you again?"

I stuck my finger into the coffee. Too hot. "That depends on Martin."

Fox disagreed. "That depends on you, Eva."

Each time he pronounced my name, Fox put another crack into that hollow plaster column known as my marriage. "Next Wednesday?" I suggested. "Lunch?" Martin always ate at the Harvard Club on Wednesdays.

"Let me refresh your memory, sweetheart," Fox answered. "I'm leaving in two weeks and I'm going to be gone for five."

Hold the coronary, Chuck yodeled, *You're the one who told him to go.*

"Oh." What the heck was Martin's schedule this week? I vaguely remembered him saying something about a clowder of Europeans blowing into town. "What's today?"

"June twenty-fifth."

Wait a moment. Was it Europeans or was it Ruth's annual Cape Cod clambake? Shit! Once again the phone coughed its three-minute blackmail. I paid off.

Fox got tired of waiting. "How about this afternoon? My place."

His bed. Larks fluttered through my stomach. "I can't."

He didn't pursue it. "Saturday."

"Lionel's coming over."

"What? That red, white, and blue faggot?"

"Hey! He's my friend."

"And what am I? The garbage man?"

"No, the undertaker." Christ! My life was ruined! "Baby. I can't tell you anything without a calendar."

"Where's your calendar?"

"With Martin's secretary."

We breathed angrily at each other in the short time remaining to us. "Check that calendar, princess, if it's not too much trouble," snarled Fox sweetly. "I'll call you at nine o'clock."

"What will you do in the meantime?"

"Pushups."

We hung up and I scampered home. To my surprise Martin was up, attempting to feed himself. "Where's the coffee, pet?" he asked, scraping around the cabinet containing roasting pans. Uh-oh: when Martin breakfasted in his bathrobe, that meant he was taking the morning off.

"Over there." I pointed to a huge cannister smack in front of him. "From the bakery," I announced, neatly stacking the contents of my little white bag on an antique tray. As I took over the coffee-making, Martin hacked up a melon, forgetting everything the Boy Scouts had taught him.

"Feeling better today?" he said.

Were I in his shoes I would have teed off with something like "You were a real pain in the ass last night."
That's what Chuck had done for years and, believe me,
each and every time it caught the opposition by surprise.
The Weaver Method, on the other hand, eschewed such
crassitude: one merely had to respond to the question
"Feeling better?" with the formulaic "Yes," and the
topic was efficiently dropped forever, as if it had never
occurred.

"Yes. Sorry I was such a pain in the ass." You see the
serpentine beauty of the Weaver Method. It made the other
guy apologize.

"Poor baby." Martin said. "You must have a deadline
coming up."

You bet I did. "I'm way behind," I sighed. "Haven't
written a note all week." I brought the coffee pot to the
table. Again it was a beautiful summer morning. Exactly
one revolution of the earth ago Fox and I had been honey-
mooning out on the deck. I stared intently at the empty
chairs, waiting for some enhanced laser image of Fox to
rise off of them, like Christ off the Shroud of Turin.

"Hey! What happened to the pastries?" Martin was
holding the cannibalized remains of the Banbury tart between two fingers.

"I got a little hungry on the way home." Martin continued to inspect his breakfast piece by piece, looking for an
unnibbled unit. He could have saved himself the trouble.
"So tell me about Dueser," I suggested, attempting to
deflect his attention. The moment I said it I had the
distinct suspicion that Martin had been lifting and setting
down pastries with the intention of getting me to ask about
California. Bah, I never was good at verbal chess.

In a nutshell, Martin and Paloma had given Dueser a
one-week course in economics, sunbathing, and fine dining, at the end of which time Martin was his best buddy
and Paloma was more intimate with Dueser's brain than
was his wife of forty years. Dueser had finally capitulated
after they took him on a day trip to Martin's favorite
vineyards. "All of this thanks to you," Martin said to me.

"What did I do?"

"Remember that book you left on the table? The one with the wench on the cover taking a man's shirt off?"

"Oh! *Heart Ablaze*. Percival took it home to read."

"That's what gave me the idea for Dueser."

"Gee! A three-buck paperback got you a twenty-million-dollar company?"

"That's right," Martin smiled, "and there's a great little bonus."

"What's that?"

"We're going to have an apartment in San Francisco."

"How come?"

"Because I'll have to be out there all summer and most of the fall." *I warned you to stop reading that swill,* Chuck told me. *Now look what happened.* Martin put the tail end of the almond croissant into his mouth. "I'll be damned! Look! Here's an article about us in the *Wall Street Journal!*" He read it out loud. "That says it even better than I did."

It hadn't really registered the second time either; I was concentrating on some other, much more vital, information. "What are you doing this week," I asked Martin, "like this morning? Say around nine o'clock?"

"We're going to celebrate, baby!"

"Wait a minute, I have work to do."

"So do I! So what! Let's drive up to Maine and get some lobsters."

I know how this worked. We blew the day driving up to Maine, returned home when I was too tired to do anything but read trash, but just in time for Martin to start phoning Japan. "No road trips," I said. "Maybe we could go out to lunch instead."

"Aren't you excited about California?"

For Christ's sake! Who cared about California when my labia were the size of blood sausage? "Of course I am! It just hasn't registered yet."

"Would you come out with me on the next trip? We'll find a place then."

The coffee acidulated in my mouth. "When are you going?"

"Next week."

"Can you tell me when exactly?"

Martin paused. "You're intrigued with my schedule all of a sudden, aren't you?"

Whoops, time for some rapid ionization of brain tissue. "Will you stop it! I'm trying to organize a surprise party for your parents! It's their anniversary!" I had no idea when Ruth and Edmund had gotten married.

"It is?" Martin said. "I thought their anniversary was New Year's Day."

Stupid of me. For forty years now Ruth had had an open house on January One. I had thought she was just showing off her Christmas decorations. "That's why it's a surprise, Flappy!" I cried exasperatedly.

"That's very nice of you, Eva," Martin said. "When's the party?"

"When are you home?" One certainly paid heavily for information these days.

At last Martin got his appointment book from his brief-case out in the hall. "Today's Friday . . . I'm here until next weekend."

"A whole week? That's outrageous!"

Martin chuckled then checked his calendar. There was a little space on it next Tuesday night from four to seven. "How about a cocktail party?"

I grabbed his calendar and inspected it. "What's this? Theater? Hans? Tanglewood? Newport?"

"Didn't you promise to take Hans Baumann sightseeing next time he came to the States?"

"Now wait a minute. You told me the guy was never coming back."

"I can't help it if he changed his mind." Martin leafed through his book. "Would you mind taking Dueser around with Hans? He'll be in Boston this week, too."

"Where's Tagahashi? How about five hundred of your best employees, too?"

"Eva," Martin said in a very calm voice, "I told you Hans was coming."

"You most certainly did not." I would have remembered: Hans Baumann was a good-looking man. At least I had thought so until I met Fox.

Martin sighed. ''Well, we'll just have to make the best of it.'' That meant that I would have to take Hans and Dueser on a tour.

''Shit, Martin! This is the worst timing possible! These next two weeks are absolutely jammed! Can't you at least slough Dueser off on Paloma?''

Martin didn't answer. That's because Paloma had already said no. ''I thought you enjoyed doing things like this.''

Once, perhaps, I did, when there was a dearth of live entertainment. Not anymore. *Shut up and do it*, Chuck commanded. *You lucked out on the richer or poorer, now eat the better or worse.* ''We'll see,'' I said. ''I'm not promising anything, though.''

Martin knew he had me licked. ''Thanks, sweetie,'' he said, kissing my hand, ''you're a great help.''

Such a great help, echoed Chuck but with a totally different inflection. I chomped on the last of the blueberry muffin. ''My mother was really out of it last time I talked to her,'' I told Martin. ''I'm a little worried about her.''

Martin's eyes lingered over the stock reports but he finally tore them away. ''That's too bad.'' He did not like to talk about Chuck. Shortly after we were married, Ruth had taken him aside and told him that daughters usually turned out like their mothers. When I countered that sons usually turn out like their mothers too, we had gotten into our first huge argument.

''It might be time for her to take a little vacation in Stockbridge,'' I said. There's a great loony bin for boozers out there.

''Great! You can drop Chuck off while you're showing Hans and Dueser around.''

''Very funny, Martin.'' With grim and impeccable control, I placed my coffee mug in the sink and went upstairs to dress. Martin kept turning pages of the *Globule*, looking for the auctions. I stepped into the shower and stood under the water, turning the soap over and over in my hand, searching for soft black hairs that did not belong to me. Fox had left no footprints in the bathtub, either. Hadn't he used a washcloth? Which of my towels had dried that sweet bottom? Oh God! Had he completely disappeared already? *Fox!* my body suddenly screamed,

Fox! I quietly closed my eyes; he was inside of me again, you see. I could feel him there. I cut the hot water to absolute cold: that pain I could deal with.

"Are you finally clean?" Martin asked as I walked into the bedroom.

I took one look at that playful spark in his eye and stopped dead. "I thought you were reading the newspaper."

"I was, until I thought of you up here in the shower."

I strapped on my watch: Fox would call in five minutes. Plain as the rising sun I knew what was going to happen. *Bad timing,* Chuck clucked without a trace of sympathy. *You really should have tried to compose a little this morning.*

"I really should compose a little this morning," I explained, hastily walking to my dresser. Once I got some underpants on, Martin would back off.

"Don't get dressed, Eva," my husband said, pulling me away from the highboy. "It's been a long time." He cut between my hand and the brass pull of my top drawer. "Plus we're celebrating."

"Celebrating?!" Jesus Christ! Did men always have to celebrate with their pricks? Unfortunately, Martin had seen a few too many bikinis from Dueser's top deck to take no for an answer. I could have kicked myself for not bringing my underwear, plus farmer overalls, into the bathroom with me. *Zut! C'est la vie,* Chuck shrugged, throwing her hands into the air like a French farmer's wife.

Telling myself that I was about to perform a purely clinical physiological function like sneezing, with nothing personal involved, I allowed my husband to lead me to bed. At once the sheets howled at me and my guilt fulminated like Mount Saint Helens. Every black nerve rankled on edge, waiting for the phone to ring. It was more difficult to picture Martin as a Kleenex than I had thought.

Martin has never been a slouchy Romeo. Unlike Fox, though, he did not acquire his technique from thin air and randy sultanas. He developed it with hundreds of women eager to continue eating mashed potatoes at Lutèce. As a result, Martin is something of an amateur gynecologist. "You're a little swollen," he said.

"Jogging in the heat," I said. "It will go down if we leave it alone."

Martin disregarded my suggestion: he had his own swelling to attend to. Tenderly but completely, he entered me and began to stir lazily as a sous-chef with his thousandth béarnaise. I lay there insanely reciting German poetry, pretending I was sitting incorrectly upon a Lippizaner.

"This is fabulous," Martin said. "No one on earth feels like you." He decelerated to one millimeter per hour, knowing what this would do to my powers of resistance.

The phone dirled. "Don't answer that," I quavered at once. "Don't." After five shrieks, it stilled. I imagined what Fox was feeling at the other end and wanted to turn to stone. *Congratulations,* I prayed, and immediately heard Chuck burst into sardonic laughter: she knew as well as I that the Great Toll Collector intended to receive thousands more tokens before letting me by.

Martin was barely moving now. He knew my body so well I would swear his name was tattooed on my brow. With despair I felt a faint rumbling way down in the mines and knew that an orgasm would soon be shuttling up. I desperately switched to another poem and a roughshod palomino—Christ! anything but my husband!—and held on for dear life. It was no use. With one contraction all verses and imaginary steeds vanished. Only Martin remained.

Restricting his movements admirably, he spilled himself. "Eva," Martin said once. That was how we kissed each other now.

I lay there like a stuck pig, wondering what all of Martin's sperm would do when they ran into Fox's. What a mess! Maybe they'd have a microscopic armageddon and destroy my fallopian tubes. *Maybe they'll give you a baby,* Chuck tortured. I winced outright. I had just paid another token.

"Are you okay?" Martin propped himself on an elbow and shooed an elfknot off my forehead.

"Just a little sore," I repeated.

"There's an estate sale in Peterborough," Martin said. "How about going for a ride?"

"Why not?" Maybe we could buy a headstone. "Are you looking for something in particular?"

"Not really. Just some fresh air with my doll."

"Who, me?"

"My voodoo doll." Martin walked into the bathroom.

I let the shower run for a minute then picked up the phone. "Foxy-poo."

"Where were you at nine o'clock?"

"Horseback riding."

"The hell you were! Never mind! I shouldn't even ask! I don't want to know!"

"Will you stop it," I said.

"Gettin' over here today?"

"I have to go to New Hampshire."

"What about tonight? Give Martin a dozen back issues of *Business Week* and he won't even know you're gone."

"You shithead."

Fox shut up. "Sorry." He sighed. "What's the schedule, Eva?"

"Don't call me that."

"What would you prefer? Mrs. Weaver?"

"How about Hey You?"

"How about your real name? When am I going to see you? Eva? Madame? Hortense? How the fuck did I ever get hooked up with you? You're insane!"

I blew my nose. It looked like come. "Forget today and tomorrow. Shoot for Sunday morning." Lionel would cover for me. He was extremely good at that.

"I'll shoot for you."

What for? I was already dead. The shower ceased. "Gotta go."

"I love you. I miss you."

"Go practice umlauts." I hung up the phone and went into the bathroom. "Any hot water left?"

Martin stood wiping steam off his glasses. "You just took a shower, stinky."

"And you got me all stunk up again." I performed a quick hosedown. "Okay. let's get this show on the road."

I lured Martin into a Babelesque discussion of antique furniture as we drove up to Peterborough: otherwise Fox would pounce upon the silences and twist my brain daft. For fifty miles I learned all about the evolution of rocking chairs. Then I fed Martin a question about Pilgrim butter churns which got us out of Massachusetts into New Hampshire. The last twenty miles were devoted to a discussion of chamber pots and what made them so valuable. As always, my husband's encyclopedic knowledge impressed me. "Martin, where did you learn all this?" I finally asked as we got out of the car. "Harvard? Milton?"

He winked at me. "From your favorite source, darling."

I stopped in my tracks. "The Bible?" Maybe there was a furniture section stashed somewhere in Deuteronomy.

"The *Globule*."

"Oh." We had lunch plus wine. With the first sip Fox rippled back to me, so I didn't drink any more: I wanted to forget all about that sweet nightmare and devote this day to Martin. We probably wouldn't be spending twenty straight hours together again until Christmas.

Martin dropped more money at that estate sale than Fox had earned in the last twelve months. We picked up two extremely rare rocking chairs, a set of andirons, some old candlesticks, and four hand-painted flowerboxes for the greenhouse. While I searched for a bathroom, Martin had a long chat with the proprietor, Hayward, an only son who had waited seventy years for his mother to shuffle off. Now he was selling everything and moving to Paris. He wanted to end his days flopping into couches and leaving cigarette burns on tabletops.

Hayward accepted Martin's invitation to dinner and talked incessantly of his deceased mother, a Yankee dowager who sounded exactly like Ruth. While I sat there mechanically twirling pasta around a fork, wondering how many umlauts had pursed Fox's lips that day, Martin invited Hayward to my fictitious cocktail party on Tuesday. Then they got going on hooked rugs and salt cellars. Every ten minutes or so, as another urge to telephone Fox evaginated my guts, I horned into the conversation with some specious question or comment. By the end of the meal Hayward was lapping up these stupid interjections like a famished don.

"Hey, Martin," I said the moment we got back into the Bavaria, "I didn't know we were having a cocktail party on Tuesday."

Martin looked over at me curiously as I cranked the seat far back and prepared to sleep. "The surprise party for my parents, darling. Don't you remember?"

Of course not, you idiot! I was busy dropping tokens in a bottomless pit. "I do now."

"Well, that's great! Now what?"

"I guess we'll have to go ahead with the party."

"Just call the caterers, darling. Don't make any extra work for yourself."

Spoken like a man weaned on butlers. "What if your parents can't come?"

"They'll come." I had forgotten: Ruth would cancel an audience with the queen of England if her son invited her to tea.

Martin decided that this would also be a fine time to celebrate the acquisition of Rodotron. Before I knew it he had filled the house with dozens of husbands and wives, to say nothing of Hans Baumann and Dueser types. *That will teach you to tell those little white lies,* Chuck bloviated. Accepting my fate, I lay back in the darkness and mentally cracked a few cookbooks. "It's about time we started entertaining again," Martin continued, running his hand along my thigh. "You are alone way too much for your own good."

"Flappy, stop telling me what you think is good for me."

"Sorry, baby. You know what's best." I would swear I heard Chuck cackling in the rear seat. I checked behind me: chairs and flower boxes, period. I pretended I was yawning. "Tired?" Martin asked.

"A little."

"Here, we'll put you to sleep." Martin turned the radio on: of course! Mahler Eight! Not even Judas Iscariot needed this many tokens!

"Martin, sweetheart, would you mind switching stations?"

My husband obliged. Now I got the slow movement from the Rachmaninoff Second Symphony. Music, ah, hell, the price of Fox. I shut my eyes and became an electric mass of pure longing. I cursed the inventors of violins and particularly the inventor of that clarinet solo which could tear a heart out fifty years after the composer's own had stopped. Would that my revenge were this sweet!

When the symphony ended, the station shut down for the night. Martin turned the radio off. As if in retaliation, a hymn began rumbling my flat thoughts like knees beneath a heavy blanket. Again, it was a variant of the funeral music I had recently discarded. I don't know why, stubborn as a boomerang, it kept returning: the best time to write funeral music was when you were sure you'd be going to heaven. What the hell, I'd give it some line and see what it snagged in the morning. If it was a bust I could always slip it into an Easter oratorio somewhere down the road.

By a telltale series of swerves and potholes, I knew that Martin had arrived back within the city limits. Rubbing my eyes, I sat up.

"We're almost home, my pet," Martin said. "You'll be in bed in five minutes."

I was unnaturally tired. I would like to sleep for two weeks and wake up only when Fox was on the plane to Rome and Martin was in California.

As we sat at breakfast the next morning, the doorbell rang sharply three times. Someone then banged on the door. "Who could that be?" Martin asked, rising. "Stay there, Eva. I'll get it."

Would I have time to call Fox before Martin returned to the kitchen? Probably not, unless it was the Jehovah's Witnesses on the stoop. Since they habitually attended church services on Sunday morning, the chances of Martin getting sucked into debate in the front hall were slim. I had better remain huddled nonchalantly over the *Times* crossword as if I did not suffer contemporaneously from ulcers, nymphomania, carditis, and acute irremediable lunacy.

"We're HERE!" I heard Lionel scream, " EEEEva!"

Seconds afterward, Lionel burst into the kitchen. Not only had he dyed his hair red, white, and blue, but he had had a star tattooed on each cheek. He wore a gold jumpsuit that accentuated the flagpole aspect of his physique. A thick purple belt cinched his waist; I recognized the fabric from *Cloistrophobia*.

"Good morning," I said, putting my pen down. "Care for a sedative?"

Lionel swept me into his arms. "Babycakes! You look senSAtional! Peacock blue is your color! Pooh! POOH! Come HERE! Where's the water? I'm parched! What an AWful trip! This town is HELL on tourists! I'm NEVer coming back!" Lionel threw open the refrigerator, opted for a beer, and withdrew half a watermelon. "You were always the perfect hostess! Pooh, love! Where ARE you?"

Into the kitchen bounced the star of *Cloistrophobia,* his shocking-pink satin hot pants stretched to the boiling point over that nouveau-fameux bottom. Since I had last seen him onstage, Pooh had gained another ten pounds and looked more than ever like one of those teddy bears you win on the New Jersey Boardwalk. Pooh had painted all of his nails bright red.

"Hi, Pooh," I said. "Did you have a nice trip?"

"Oh, yeaaaahs," Pooh drawled. This one was definitely from south of the border. "Til Lahnell got us lost."

"I did NOT get anyone lost! There are no road signs anywhere in this town! And that expressway! You could drop the Statue of Liberty in those potholes!"

"They're rebuilding it."

Lionel waved his hands disgustedly in the air. "I will NOT drive on that road again as long as I live. Several people tried to KILL us."

Martin walked into the kitchen. He no longer wore his bathrobe but was dressed in navy pants and a plaid sports shirt, all tightly buckled, buttoned, and belted. "Well, I'm off," he said, picking up his coffee.

"Where to?" I asked in surprise. Martin had planned to spend the morning planting ivy and some more rosebushes. We'd go to church next Sunday.

He rolled his eyes at me as our guests began bickering over who should get the outside slice of watermelon. "The car wash, the nursery . . ."

"How about your folks? You can ask them about Tuesday."

"Oh! Great idea! Maybe I'll stay for dinner."

I accompanied Martin to the front door. "Look, Flappy. we'll stay out on the deck. You can come back and read your newspapers all afternoon and won't even know we're here. We'll have some steak for supper then I'll ship them to Buddy's.'' That's a gay bar in Back Bay. It draws more crowds than the Boston Pops on July fourth.

Martin looked doubtfully at me; Lionel's voice alone could saw down a sequoia. "I'll try, my girl," he said. "I was rather looking forward to spending another day all alone with you."

I scratched my head. "With me? Very boring."

Martin licked my nose and left. I immediately spun back to the kitchen. "Well! How long have you two been an item?"

Lionel stopped pinching watermelon seeds at Pooh's pectorals. "Since June fifth."

"'Leven thuhty-fahve ay yem," Pooh chimed in. "Dressin' Room B."

I whidded into a chair. "Look, Lionel, I've got to do some errands this morning. Can I borrow your car while you two read the papers or something?"

"Are you still hanging out with that karate chopper?" Lionel shrieked. "I told you to cut it out two months ago!" He dug into his pockets and tweezed out a ten dollar bill. "You win, Poo-bah."

Pooh tucked the bill into his hot pants. "I tol' Lahnell you'd still be hangin' out with that Foxy."

My mouth dropped open. "You two shits were betting on my private life?"

"Isn't she a stitch and a half?" Lionel said as he carved up some gouda. "We are going to have a GREAT time here, Hershey Bar. Here, sweetheart, take my keys. Who am I to stand in the way of lust on a Sunday morning?"

More chimes from the Jehovah's Witnesses tinkled faintly over the rooftops. They reminded me of the spoons on Fox's porch. "Cover for me, Lionel," I said, "in case Martin comes back."

My accomplice popped a cube of gouda into Pooh's mouth. "I sent you out for some raspberries and cream, sweetheart. Just be back by two, would you? That's when lunch is ready."

I changed, hopped into Lionel's Triumph, and beelined over to Cambridge. Fox was upstairs, vocalizing placidly. How could that bastard sing when I was too deranged to write? I stubbed my finger aggravatedly against his doorbell. "It's the Jehovah's Witnesses," I called upstairs. "Got a moment?"

Fox looked as if he'd been soaking in turpentine all weekend. Shit! Now I had to feel guilty about him, too? *I told you about wrecking three lives instead of two,* Chuck reiterated. *You didn't believe me.* "Hello, Foxy." I said, curling my arms around that haunting body, "you handsome dog."

His lips rippled. "You again."

"So where's my breakfast?"

"You're breathing on him."

We stood there for a few minutes alternately whetting and losing our appetites. I couldn't look him in the face; those big gray eyes would be asking me the perpetual question to which I still had no answer. In the meantime, Fox's hands slowly rubbed my spine: every inch of skin they soothed now would scorch tonight, believe me. *So back up,* prescribed Chuck. Instead I put Fox's hands into my shirt. My mother and I fundamentally disagree on painkillers.

"Are you all right?" I asked. "You look tired."

"I'm okay," he said. "What's going on at your house this week?"

"It's a mess," I muttered. "Martin's got a huge party going on Tuesday night for God knows who and their wives. The in-laws are coming to it so I have to clean the place, too. Then I'm supposed to schlepp some visiting businessmen to the great tourist points. That will kill at least two days."

"We're up to Friday."

"Then Martin's going back to California." Fox waited. I sighed. "With me."

Fox sat in his wide-load green chair without doilies on top. "Why're you going?"

"To find him an apartment." Without going into columns and commas, I explained that Rodotron was a big deal.

"Are you planning to stay out there with him?"

"Are you crazy? I hate California!" Too much sunshine. I sat down on the floor in front of Fox's chair and took his hand. "I'm staying in Boston."

"And how do you think your husband's going to like that?"

He'd miss me two or three nights a month, when his laundry piled up. "He'll survive."

Fox passed a hand over his eyes. "I don't believe that man."

"You don't know him."

"I don't want to know him, either!" Fox carted me backstage and chucked me onto his bed like a spare tire. "I just want his wife."

"You've got her." An hour here, an hour there, freshly bathed, wearing her cleanest clothes, on her best behavior . . . what more could the fellow want?

"For how long?"

"Until two o'clock."

"Well, my goodness! I'd better not waste any time, then!" Fox jerked his shorts off and reached under my skirt.

"Hey! Pull down, not straight out!"

He left my underwear dangling around one knee, my skirt, my blouse, and my shoes on. I think he was annoyed at something.

"That hurts," I said. "Stop it."

"Oh! I'm so sorry! Does this hurt?"

"Of course it does, your cock is bigger than a fire hydrant! What's the matter with you? Ow!"

"Scream some more, you little tart, it gets me excited."

"You're excited enough!"

"I'll stop then." Fox cut his engines.

"No! Damn you!" I buried my fingers in his back. "I hate your guts! You've ruined my life!"

"*I've* ruined *your* life? That's priceless!" Fox gunned it and nearly split me in half. *Just let me die,* I prayed.

"Stop going for the easy solutions," Fox snapped. "And I'm not eavesdropping." Hands cupping my rear end, he obverted my hips and mired himself another two inches. I think he hit my coccyx. "Like that? Nice, isn't it?"

Nice? So was a swim in the Styx! I shut my eyes, gulping for air. Whoops, now he tripped the little switch; I had about ten seconds of independence left. "You . . ." That was as far as I got. My fuse was way shorter than usual.

Dodging and then attacking like a sadistic matador, Fox paraded around my throes until I was drenched. God Almighty, where did he learn these tricks?! I didn't even know half of them! "Come on, Eva," he whispered, "I'm going to make you do it again."

"No you're not!" I shouted. I tried to back up but hit the headboard. Fox kept advancing; this time he undid a few buttons on my blouse and slid those long slender fingers inside. "Aiiiii!" I shrieked.

"Keep screaming, you brat. It only makes me harder." Now he had my blouse entirely undone.

A little resistant mote in my brain turned a corner and I suddenly saw the rest of my life spent with Martin, without Fox. It was fitting, placid, and noble and it was unmitigated daily death. This man, whoever he was, had deracinated me from the only soil I knew, my past; I had no idea where he was taking me. I only knew that if he let go now, I would never put down roots again but would wither away on top of the rich earth. Fox, Fox, the bane, the cure: life. "What do you want from me?" I shouted. "You already have it!"

"Liar," he said. "For that you'll have to come again."

"What for? I just did!"

That really irked him. Fox flipped me on my knees and pushed my face into the pillow. Then he started taking serious advantage of me. I don't know exactly what went where, but I do know that it all arranged to meet at my bellybutton. " Hey! Cut it out, damn you! I am NOT going to come! What are you trying to do, kill me?"

I just got my face shoved into the pillow again. "That's right."

Now why should that stupid comment get me excited. *Because you deserve to die,* said Chuck. Deserve? I burst out laughing. I *wanted* to die! That guaranteed that I would live!

"You think this is funny," panted Fox.

"It's hilarious."

That made him crazy. He hammered me like a railroad tie and I'll be damned if he didn't trip that little switch again. Maybe I had two of them. "Congratulations, you creep," I cried, no, I laughed. "You bought it." Aagh! Morphine!

He pulled my knees out and we crashed down to the mattress. "I bought nothing," said Fox. "I own you."

The hell with women's lib! I was born to be owned!

I wasn't meant to be flattened, though. "Hey, could you move? I'm suffocating down here." Fox rolled off my back. I looked at his face; acquisition had daubed his mouth and cheeks cherry red. The rest of him remained pale white. With my fingertip I outlined his eyes and nose and the contour of those beautiful somnolent lips; this man thought I belonged to him, but in truth he belonged to me. I didn't want anybody else to touch him, to feed him, to sight his first gray hairs, to wring his umlauts, oh no, that was for me. *Goodness*, said Chuck. *You've done it again, haven't you.*

Yep, I had done again what I swore I would never do again: barter body for soul. But it was different this time around, see. I was the married one, Fox the free agent; that meant that he would do all the final lacerating and I would only have to wave a resigned good-bye. And this time around, from the beginning, I had thought of Fox as a brilliant and mysterious bruise, not as a suture binding the various compartments of my life together. And most importantly, this time I would never pray to have him. That's what had cost me the ten years before.

"What are you thinking?" Fox asked.

"I'm wondering if I've got another ten years to spare," I said. I kissed his mouth.

"What are you talking about?"

"Detours along the road to salvation."

Fox opened his eyes. "Why do you have to be home at two o'clock?"

"Lionel's holding the fort with his boyfriend." I sat up. "That's also when my alibi turns to shit." Lionel reacts violently to unpunctuality.

Fox remained nipples skyward. I looked forward to the day when that body would cease bewitching me and I could return to my original husband, sadder but wiser. *Then what*, Chuck scowled, *a month in port before you raise anchor again?*

"The first time I saw you," Fox mused, figuring he

didn't owe me any apologies, "I knew I had to have you. Can you explain that?"

"Sure," I said. "It means you hadn't been laid in months."

"I was laid the night before," Fox corrected, snorting. I swallowed rusty nails and hot tar. "No more stupid interruptions." I lay down.

"I love you," Fox said. "I'm not sure how or why that happened, but it did, and it was the best thing that ever happened to me." The best? Jesus! He was the worst thing that had ever happened to me! I kept swallowing. "You make me feel alive the way no one else does. We belong together. You know exactly what I'm talking about." His hand covered my mouth. "No wounded outbursts, please. Someday you're going to have to stop denying the inevitable."

I pushed his hand away. "We have conflicting opinions of the inevitable."

Fox quickly turned his head. "Why'd you marry Martin, baby?" he said so softly that I knew it was not an accusation. "That's the one thing I don't understand about you. It drives me insane."

"But you've never met Martin," I objected.

"What would be the use? Answer the question, why'd you marry him?"

My resistance was down, plus he asked nicely. *How about you loved him, you stupid moron?* Chuck screamed. "It was time," I warbled miserably.

"Then why can't you leave him?"

Now that one was much easier. "Because he loves me."

"And what about me? I don't love you? You don't love me?" Fox pulled my shoulders close to his. "I don't want to share you with anyone, Eva."

I shut my eyes: familiar words, signposts en route to the shootout. A decade ago I had lost mine: now Fox would lose his. God! So soon? "Why can't you share like everyone else?" I cried, shit! "No one can belong to anyone anyhow!"

"What kind of werewolf philosophy is that?"

"Mine." It was mighty tough to kill a werewolf.

Fox grinned; I shrank from those teeth as if they were daylight. "Am I going to have to teach you everything all over again? I might not live that long."

"Sure you will," I said. "The best always die young."

Later, Fox walked me to Lionel's Triumph and a neat white parking ticket. "What's this for?" I asked.

"You're thirteen inches from the curb."

I stuffed the ticket into Lionel's glove compartment, then popped into the bucket seat. "Where can I find some raspberries and cream around here?"

"Fresh Pond." A woman walked by on the sidewalk with two little blond boys in sailor outfits. They had all been to church and she looked radiant. *So would you*, said Chuck, *if you had the guts*. I looked once at Fox: we would make beautiful babies. Bah. We made better sandcastles. As he shut the door, I noticed that his pallor had returned. That made my skin burn.

Fox sighed. "Not easy," he said.

"What?"

"You. Life."

"You forgot singing."

"That too." He leaned into the window. "Are you thinking?"

"Yes."

"Think faster, then." Fox backed away. My body leapt after him. "And I'm not talking about your hymns."

"Aye-aye, commander." I hit the ignition. "I love you."

"Say it again."

I hooked two fingers behind his belt buckle and hauled him in. "I love you."

"Okay. You can go now." I shifted into first and rolled down the street.

I got home at five after two and went straight to the kitchen. Lionel and Pooh had already started eating. "You're late, sweetie pie," said Lionel, glancing up. "My GAWD, just look at those clothes! What were you two trying to do, eat them off each other? Go up and change! You're lucky your husband isn't home yet, Mrs. Weaver! He'd have your hide!"

Wrong. He'd think I'd been scrapping with a meter maid. I changed and returned to lunch. "So what have you two been up to?" I asked, daggering a pasta shell.

"Not quite what you've been up to," Lionel said accusingly. "And wipe that stupid smirk off your face! You look like a whore!"

Amen, Chuck praised. "You're charming today, Lionel," I said. "When did you say you were going home?"

"Lahnell's all shook up," Pooh explained. "Yo' mothah called fo' you 'n she talked wi' Lathnell instayud."

"What did Chuck have to say for herself?" I asked.

Lionel forked a marinated artichoke heart onto the epicenter of his tongue. "She wanted to know where you and your husband were. I told her church." He looked over. "You owe me for that one, dear heart."

"Did she believe you."

"Of course she believed me! It's Sunday morning, isn't it?"

"How sober was she?" Here Lionel hesitated. "Come on, Thread."

"How should I know? Her pronunciation was a little off."

"How was her hearing?"

"That was okay."

That meant she was between her second and third drink and that she hadn't believed one word Lionel had told her. I frowned. "What else did she say?"

Now it was Lionel's turn to grind teeth. "She said that she and my mother were going to see *Cloistrophobia* this Thursday."

I looked at Pooh. "Are you going to be doing that show?"

"It's in mah contract, honey."

Lionel flung his napkin to the table. "God damn it! Why did they have to pick Thursday, for Chrissake! You're going to make life *hell* for the two of us, Nut Roll!"

Pooh looked at me. "Wha's he tokkin' bout?"

"Don't pay any attention to him. Our mothers haven't reconciled themselves to the monsters they've created, that's all."

"Where's the scotch?" Lionel shrieked. "Agh! My life is ruined!"

"Sit down, you flame," I ordered. "Eat your lunch." Lionel obeyed after he had located the bottle of scotch. He inhaled an ounce, then began to shovel artichokes around his plate, muttering about obesity and the salacious minds of female hymnists.

"So, Pooh," I said, pleasantly eliding paragraphs, "I understand the show's coming to Boston."

"You bet it is, you bitch," Lionel snapped. "And this whole town's going to know about that cakewalk."

"Whoa," I said, "we had a bargain, Mr. Boyd. The cakewalk remains anonymous." Lionel was unnaturally testy today. Chuck must have amplified on her usual Sunday themes before she hung up.

"Eva, you're hopeless! You have no conception of public relations! Do you realize what a great story we've got here? 'Sacred Music Composer Exposed as Porno Lyricist and Mistress of Karate Thug.' Isn't that fanTAStic? Do you have any iDEA what that scoop would be worth to the *National Enquirer?*"

"Yeah? How about this one: 'Drum Major's Mother Balloons to 500 Pounds After Seeing Son's Black Lover in Nun's Habit.'"

"Soun's verra intrestin'," said Pooh.

"Shut up, you illiterate!" shrieked Lionel. "It sounds like SHIT!"

At that moment, the front door slammed. "Okay, boys," I said, "Back to Vanderbilt etiquette. Right now."

My husband strolled into the kitchen. "Hi, Martin," I called, "have you eaten lunch yet, sweetheart?"

Lionel blasted a phony cough into his napkin. I placed a hand on the back of his neck. "Too much partying in Provincetown, Lionel?" I asked ominously, squeezing as hard as possible. "Maybe you should go lie down in the hammock."

"Where are those raspberries I sent you out for this morning?" Lionel said.

I released his neck. "Right behind you."

Lionel got up. "Pooh, clear the table for me, will you please, while I make dessert?" Pooh stood up. Half a ball had slipped out of his pink shorts. I don't think he got it all tucked back in before Martin noticed.

"So, cutie," I postured, executing Pooh with my eyes, "what did you do this morning?"

Martin ceased genteelly inspecting his fingernails. "I bought a few rosebushes. Maybe we could put them in this afternoon."

"Great." Not quite by accident, Lionel banged a copper bowl against the counter. I ignored him. "Did you see your parents?"

"Yes, and they're coming on Tuesday."

"What's Tuesday?" Lionel inquired, deluging the raspberries with kirsch. "A party? Super! Am I invited?"

Martin regretted his words for the first time since I had known him. Gracefully as always, however, he answered the question. "Eva and I are having a little business celebration. If you and Pooh are still in town, you are certainly invited. Now if you would excuse me, I have some reading to do." My husband left before Lionel volunteered to help him plant rosebushes.

"Nice job, Golden Boy." I said as Lionel brought the berries over. "Now that you've crashed the party, you can start cooking for it." Lionel excels at finger food.

"What's Pooh going to do?"

"He and I are going to dynamite the house."

"What? No maids? No caterers? You mean you're still paranoid about people invading your private territory? That's riDICulous! We're supposed to be on vacation!"

"You're on mental vacation."

I permitted my guests a brief sunbath before hitting them with the cookbooks. As my husband adorned the grounds with more rosebushes, we figured out what we were going to serve one hundred conservatively-dressed palates plus Ruth. We farted around with rape holds and self-defense for a while, then I shipped them off to Buddy's. I forbade Lionel to return before two in the morning. That way, Martin would probably be asleep and would not notice them bashing around the hallway changing bedrooms. I myself spent the evening in the study attempting to compose but passing most of my time erasing quarter notes and thinking of how I might best tell Martin that we would be much happier as just friends, not as Mr. and Mrs. Weaver. It was going to be tough; the more time I spent with my husband, the more he seemed to think this arrangement was permanent. After a week in California, through sheer osmosis, he might convince me also.

I decided not to go.

At quarter to five Tuesday night Lionel, Pooh and I were still in the kitchen squeezing savory fillings out of pastry bags. We had been at it all day and were getting fed up with manufacturing thousands of horrid little mouthfuls of food and for what? After three drinks, no one would taste anything anyhow. After four drinks they wouldn't care if they were shoving perfect shrimp sandwiches or football cleats down their throats.

I blatted the last of my chive filling into a miniscule eggplant. "Forget it," I said, "whose idea was it to buy all these stupid little vegetables?"

Pooh looked hurt. "In New Yo'k ever'one lahks it."

"They sure do," reassured Lionel, rubbing his companion's knees affectionately. "Eva, stop your pissing and moaning. We're having fun."

Of course they were having fun! They were together! "Let's see if that champagne is alive," I said. Lionel and Pooh had been testing the rum all afternoon; from time to time I had run a little quality control on the scotch. It would be wise to check on the effervescents.

The cork shot across the table straight into Lionel's masterwork, a gougère pyramid which he had been meticulously constructing for two hours now. The erection was not only decapitated, but douced with champagne to boot. I guess I had had a little more scotch than I thought.

"Eva, damn you!" Lionel shrieked, "I spent HOURS making this puff pastry!" For some reason I couldn't stop laughing. Hey, you should have seen this guy nitpicking over the cheese, the butter, precise driblets of albumen, et cetera, all afternoon. You'd think he was making an atomic bomb.

"Ha ha, I'm so sorry," I choked, "Ha ha, I knew you should have made a quiche."

Uttering anal oaths, Lionel grabbed the bottle, shook it, and blasted me with champagne. Pooh got the backsplash. Then Lionel fell backwards off his chair into the garbage. We had just thrown away a few thousand shrimp shells.

The doorbell rang. "Who's that?" I said, panicking. "I bet it's Ruth!" I belted Lionel with some champagne.

Lionel attempted without much success to pull the shrimp shells from his shirt. "Who bought these VILE things?" he sputtered. "Go answer that door, Pooh! I'm sure it's the florist! You're the only one who's decent!"

"Are you joking," I said, "he's wearing less than a Barbie Doll." Pooh pushed back his chair, wiped his hands on his yellow nylon bikini, and made for the foyer. His penis was definitely not in the flaccid mode. "Let's get out there, Lionel," I said. "If it's an Irish cop, your friend's had it." Lionel raked several more shrimp shells from the blue section of his hairdo and we raced to the front door.

As I had suspected, there stood my mother-in-law on the front step all dressed up in a seersucker business suit. "Hi, Ruth," I greeted, "you're a little early. We were just finishing up in the kitchen." As a little breeze brushed my wet blouse, I felt my nipples pop up like Mexican jumping beans. Shit, I knew I should have worn a bra today. "Please come in."

"Can I get you something to drink, sugar?" offered Lionel. "It's hotter than a WHORE out there! Champagne? How about some rotgut vino? That cheapskate Martin's gone and hidden ALL the good stuff! Right, Lollipop?"

Pooh was busy tucking another loose testicle back into his yellow briefs. "Wheh'r all th' flowahs, princess? You leav'm in yo' van?" He leaned flirtatiously out the front door. I frowned; the guy was asking for the business end of a broomstick.

Ruth didn't move an inch. "May I ask which catering establishment has sent you two gentlemen over here?" Her tone did not imply prospective employment.

"My name is Lionel Boyd," Thread sniffed, "and I am here at the personal invitation of the lady of the house. I am not a servant. Neither is my associate, Mr. Excelsior." Pooh bowed gracefully. "May I ask which florist sent YOU over here? They should switch uniforms. Lime green looks postively GHASTly on you."

"Lionel, this is my mother-in-law," I said. "Behave yourself."

Lionel shrieked. "CRIMiny! YOU're Martin's mother?!" He looked more closely at her face. "OF COURSE you are! Now I understand EVerything!"

I ushered Ruth to the den. "Please excuse my friend. Dr. Boyd has been working too hard," I said under my breath. "He's a very respected psychotherapist. Mothers are his specialty."

"I see," said Ruth. Sbe could not take her eyes off the shrimp shells in Lionel's red, white, and blue hair. They looked familiar but she just couldn't place them.

"What are you two whispering about?" Lionel interrupted. "It's VERY impolite."

Pooh came into the den. All this strutting and tucking had shifted his penis from the left to the right side of his yellow shorts. It had grown another inch. "Ah see no flowah truck, honeycake."

"Pooh, why don't you and Lionel get changed," I said, turning him around, "it's almost show time." I shoved them both out the door. "I should be getting ready myself." In five years I had still not overcome a primordial fear of being alone in the same room as my mother-in-law. I would rather face ten thousand miles in a Morris Minor with Chuck and a bum road map.

"I came a bit early to see the rocking chairs Martin bought on Saturday." Ruth said. "I understand that Hayward Tolland will be coming down from Peterborough."

"That's right." I led Ruth to the dining room. "There they are.

"Oh! They're gorgeous!" She had to be kidding. They were just old chairs for Puritans with no behinds and no girlfriends to sit on their laps. I pointed Ruth to the candlesticks and flowerpots and excused myself. She seemed on the point of saying something confidential to me about Martin; I didn't want to know. "Would you cover the bar for me in case Dr. Boyd doesn't get down in time? Thanks." Ruth would have the time of her life looking for dust under the Persian rugs.

I charged up to the guest bedroom and rapped on the door. "Make it fast, you two," I warned. "The kitchen is a catastrophe."

From inside Lionel's voice cried, "Oh shut UP, Eva!

We've been slaving for two days STRAIGHT on this party! Now we can't even DRESS decently! And where the hell is the HOST of the evening, may I ask? Did he forGET about this?''

"Quit screwing around," I said. "I need you downstairs in five minutes." I cleaned myself up and threw on a set of fire engine-red hostess pajamas that Lionel had bought for me a long time ago somewhere in the Village. I heard the doorbell ring a few times and assumed that Ruth would be rising to the occasion as dowager empress of Weaver, Inc. I just hoped she stayed out of the kitchen.

The phone rang. It was my sister reporting that Chuck was feeling a little under the weather. She had not been a winner in the latest New Jersey lottery.

I called her. "Hi, Chuck," I said. "Having a good day?''

"Uhmph."

"I hear you're not feeling so good. How would you like a visitor? Me?''

"Uhmph."

Jesus, she was way around the bend. I had to get down there fast. "Fine! I'll come down Thursday or Friday and we'll take a little ride, okay? Maybe you should take a few days off in Stockbridge, what do you say?''

Chuck dropped the phone and I couldn't raise her. I called my sister back and told her to swing by, preferably before Robert got home from work. If he sees Chuck passed out on the floor, he doesn't speak to her for months.

Lionel burst into the bedroom. "Help! I've lost a button!''

"Crap! Don't you ever knock?''

"Why should I knock? Nothing you do could surprise me." Lionel preened himself in front of a full-length mirror. "Hey! You're wearing my pajamas!''

"No kidding." I pinned Lionel's frilly white buccaneer shirt together. You couldn't pack another molecule into his black leather pants. "I just talked to Chuck.''

"Lucky you! What did you get? The Sermon on the Mount?''

"I think it was the Martyrdom of Saint John." I stood back. "Is this a pirate costume or something?''

"This is nothing. Wait until you see Pooh!''

"What's he? A mermaid?"

"No, NO. He's my parrot. Pooh! Come HERE!"

Instead of Pooh, Martin walked in the door. He was shocked to see me in the bedroom with another man, Lionel notwithstanding. "Hi Martin," I said. "I was just pinning Lionel's shirt together."

"Let me know when you're done dressing each other." Martin walked out, shutting the door behind him.

"Congratulations," I hissed. "You just gave the poor guy heart failure."

"Me? Wait until he finds out this is the REAL guest bedroom."

I stood very still, contemplating life without Lionel. It could be done.

As usual, he read my thoughts. "I'm sorry, Eva," he said. "Don't look at me like that. I was just joking."

"It's no longer funny," I replied. I continued looking at him like that. Out in the hall, Martin cleared his throat. "Get down to the bar, will you? God knows what that woman is doing downstairs."

I heard Lionel apologize loudly to Martin as he passed him in the hallway. Unknotting his tie, Martin came into the bedroom. "He doesn't want to cause 'any more' trouble? Exactly what does that mean?"

"Ruth will tell you all about it," I said, flushing guiltily. *Covered your ass just in time*, Chuck noted. I put some jewelry on. "Who's here? We should get downstairs."

"Don't worry about it. Mother's taking care of everything."

"She is? What's she doing?"

"Shipping everyone outside with champagne and a handful of cashews." Of course! That was her favorite trick whenever the hollandaise curdled.

"Who's here? Anyone I know?"

Martin adjusted his collar and fresh tie. "Not yet. Come on, darling. Everyone's dying to meet you." Now would be the perfect opportunity to tell Martin I was leaving him: too many business associates were waiting downstairs for him to put up a major fuss. Then Martin extended his arm. "Let's go, gorgeous." All my great swashbuckling plans shriveled like shrink tubing.

An early-bird crowd of twenty, waiting for the alcohol to take effect, meanwhile had gathered at the bar, listening fascinatedly as Lionel explained to them what he did for a living. Thank God Ruth was outside carting the horticulturalists around the rosebushes. One couple had actually seen *Cloistrophobia* and wanted Lionel's autograph. "Oh no, NO, you don't want MY autograph!" he cried. "The star of the show is here! Get HIS!" The doorbell rang. "Enter! Come IN!"

As if on cue, Pooh emerged from the kitchen carrying an enormous platter of teriyaki chicken wings. His outfit would make the Caliph of Baghdad look like Whistler's Mother. I looked at Martin and shook my head.

"Martin!" Jason Street called, striding across the den with four ounces of straight scotch in his glass. "Hello, Eva, don't you look sexy tonight. This is going to be one hell of a celebration. What a bartender!"

"Wait until he starts playing piano," I said.

Martin introduced me to several dozen connubial acquaintances. A few of the husbands might have piqued my curiosity some other day now past me; tonight I didn't even want to hear their first names. The wives, all unbearably well-architected, driveled endlessly about Martin's Victorian house and the presence therein of two Broadway stars pretending they were butlers. Time and time again, Martin ascribed his success to me and made these women feel charming. His graciousness continually surprised and impressed me. *That's because you couldn't do that in a million years,* explained Chuck.

Pooh circulated a horde of shrimp sandwiches as I excused myself to the kitchen. En route I passed Percival Noonan chatting with a buck-toothed redhead.

"Eva, you look ravishing."

"Would you excuse us for a moment? Follow me, Percival, I have something to show you." I led him to the kitchen and pulled an apron from a drawer. "How are you with microwave ovens?"

"Superb, darling! The best!"

I pointed to a huge spanakopitta on the counter. "Prove it." I tied an apron on and put some fire under the cocktail wieners. Out of the blue, as I stood spicing up the chili sauce, I received yet another version of the funeral music that had been intermittently choking me. This time the whole thing was in C minor.

"Eva, should I slice this up? It smells heavenly! Did you make it?"

"Quiet! I'm concentrating!"

"Oh, you little coquette!" Percival located a cake knife and pretended he was whittling condos out of a mansion on Commonwealth Avenue. Soon Pooh swiveled into the kitchen and traded in his empty platter for Percival's neat cubes.

"Things'r loosenin' up out theh," he reported. "Ev'-body's askin' me ta sing."

"You can sing after you pawn off all your micro vegetables," I said. "And what's Lionel up to? He's not talking about his mother, is he?"

"Ah think he's givin' th'ladies some costume advice."

"God damn it! He's the bartender, not Coco Chanel! Get him in here!" I was at a party once before when Lionel started telling people what they should wear. Half of them went home wearing someone else's clothing. But no one at that party was married.

A great cadence for my funeral tune popped into mind. I hummed it a few times, ironing out the rhythm. "What are you singing there, Eva?"

"A dirge." I snapped a little hotdog into my mouth. "Come here, Percival, what do you think of this chili sauce?"

Outside, Lionel started playing piano. I had told him not to do that until everyone had had at least three drinks, at which point his presence at the bar would no longer be desired: from here on, the true lushes would prefer to mix their own.

"Spicy! Excellent!" Percival pronounced. "Another please, Eva?"

I didn't exactly put this hotdog right into Percival's mouth. Instead I twirled it around on the fork, making him lunge for it a little. This was much more fun than simply engulfing, chewing, and swallowing like all those idiots outside.

"Gerald! When did you decide to become a cook?" said a voice at the door.

Ruth, of course. "About ten minutes ago, when I asked him."

"Really, Eva! Mr. Noonan is an architect!"

"Not today, Ruthie," Percival twittered. "Go out and enjoy the guests! We're doing just fine back here."

Ruth backed up as if Percival had hit her lapel with a cocktail wiener. She disappeared through the door.

I turned around. "Percival, are you crazy? You just lost the contract on a chalet in Vail!"

"Who cares? I've never had so much fun in my life!"

For that, he got another hotdog. Now Martin sailed through the door.

"Eva! What are you doing in here? Where are the caterers? People are asking for you. Please, sweetheart, take that apron off and come outside."

"Forget it, Martin," I said, waving a wooden spoon at him. "I've met enough bridge partners for one day." Martin started to protest. "Come on, Flaps! They're all talking about their kids and the PTA now! I don't need that shit!"

Pooh came whipping through the door. "Mo' vegetables, please, sugah." I piled a couple dozen eggplant fetuses on his platter.

"You can sing if you get rid of these," I told him. I hate eggplant.

"Gerald," Martin persisted, "you are our guest, not our butler."

"Rubbish!" Percival cried, opening the microwave. "Perfect! Where's my spatula, Eva?"

"Here, Flappy," I said, pushing a mushroom pâté at Martin. "Try to sell this for me, will you?"

"Eva, you don't understand," Martin protested, "you should be outside with me."

Putting down the wooden spoon, I walked over to Martin. Instead of joining him with our superb guests outside, however, I yanked his ears. "Flappy," I said with discouragement, "you are relapsing into your old habits." Martin stood absolutely still a moment with the pâté. I thought he might put the platter down and spank me. No way, not with Percival there. So Martin left the kitchen. He was furious.

"Gee, can't a girl enjoy her own party anymore?" I frowned. "It's disgusting."

Percival peered over at me. "Did I really see you pull Martin's ears, you vixen?"

"It's our special sign."

"It looked as if it hurt!"

"Keep slicing."

Percival obediently returned to his casseroles. "How old are you, my dear?" he inquired presently. "Wait! You don't have to tell me! I know how women are about their ages!"

"Thirty-four. Why? How old are you?"

"Sixty." Percival kept slicing. "That's a little too old for you, isn't it?"

What was he talking about? Men approaching sixty are like perfect Stilton. "Don't even consider it, Percival. I'm taken."

"I know! You're married!"

A cold hand—Death's or the Other Guy's?—passed over my heart. I said nothing. From the main hall came a ribald round of applause.

"When are you going to have children, Eva?" Percival said, cutting to a parallel track. "I think you'd be a wonderful mother. Two would be perfect. My God! You make me say the most impulsive things! Have I gone crazy? I shouldn't even be talking like this."

Why not? Words were the closest he'd ever get to me. "It's nice." Except for the bit about children.

Then Edmund, my father-in-law, came into the kitchen, three sheets to the wind. He didn't think I knew; like Martin, he misprized the practical side effects of Chuck's infirmity. "Well, well! So here's the real party!"

"Correct," I said. "Want an apron?"

Edmund sat at the table. "Ah, Eva," he began.

"You've been sent in to bring me out," I finished.

"That's right."

"What do you think, Percival? Should we let them starve?"

Percival hesitated. He obviously had not finished his discourse; on the other hand, he had just blown a chalet in

Vail. "We'll take out the last three trays, what do you say." He thought a moment. "But I love to wash dishes."

"I surrender." Removing my apron, I handed a huge cheese board to Edmund; should he drop it, the damage would be minimal. Percival got the cocktail wieners. I took out a glut of pirogies. A blast of cacophony and drunken laughter coincided with our evacuation from the kitchen: Lionel, ten thumbs, plus eighty-eight ivories in the living room. With my right leg I directed Edmund into the bar with the cheese; Percival followed me into the living room. As I passed the front door, a trenchant urge to tear my shoes off and run barefoot to Cambridge seized me. If I did that, of course, I should not bother ever coming home again. I decided to see what Lionel was up to. *Chicken*, muttered Chuck.

The Buccaneer was seated at the piano explaining the plot of *Cloistrophobia* to his mesmerized audience as Pooh pantomimed the best burlesque moments. There stood Martin leaning against the fireplace with Jason and Paloma. Ruth sat three steps off to the right with Hayward Tolland, the used-furniture salesman. I didn't want to go near either of them; in fact I didn't want to go near anybody in the room. Before one of these trespassers noticed me, I'd can the pirogies and go to Cambridge; I didn't belong here. After quietly placing the rolls on a sideboard, I sashayed to the door.

"EEEEEEva! There you are, you naughty thing!"

Sixty pairs of eyes swiveled rearwards. "Anyone care for a cabbage roll?" I said.

Martin immediately came to my side and put his arm around me. His ears were still a little red. "This is my wife Eva," he announced, "in case you haven't noticed her yet."

Everyone thought that was just hilarious. "She's di-VINE," shouted Lionel. "I keep telling her she should have married ME." Everyone thought that was even funnier, except Ruth, of course. Her face was set in stone. I think she knew all about Fox.

Lionel bashed a chord out on the piano, regaining center stage. Every last ruffle on his shirt quivered as he played. "Where WAS I? Pooh! HELP!"

"We wuh jest abou' at mah cakewalk."

"Oh! OH! This will tickle you PINK!"

"I remember this," exclaimed the woman who had seen *Cloistrophobia* in New York. "It's an absolute scream!"

"Who's that asshole?" I asked Martin in an undertone.

"Eva! Shhh! That's Maynard Lory's wife Claire."

Pfuii, I knew Maynard Lory had no class the first time I saw him driving his Ferrari. I don't care if he owned half the Wharf, the man had no respect for first gear. "Don't ever introduce me to her."

Martin reached tautly for a pirogi. So far he had not interested his wife in one bridge partner, one shopping companion, or one thrilled contented mother.

"Donnerwetter! Die hübsche Eva!"

None other than Hans Baumann sucking on a cocktail wiener assailed us. "What brings you back?" I said with a trace of annoyance that Hans would surely misinterpret. Last time he had visited this house, he had cornered me in the pantry while Martin was on the phone, claiming that I had been undressing him with my eyes ever since he had removed his Alpine hat.

"Eva!" disciplined Martin jocularly. That really irritated me. My husband has no idea how many times he's left me to deal with rape and pillage while he yaks long distance. "Hans is looking forward to celebrating July fourth in the States."

"Go to New York," I advised. "They shoot off fireworks in Central Park."

"I vass tinking off Tangellvood."

Tanglewood? Not with me, buddy. It's a zoo out there anyway. The lawn is foul with thousands of crypto-gourmands and their candlesticks pretending they're dining at Windows of the World instead of a mosquito-plagued field. On July fourth every kid with diaper rash in the Berkshires is imported to hear the *1812 Overture* and watch the fireworks over Lake Mackeenac. You can't even hear the music over the wails of infants and the whines of toddlers asking dad when they can go home.

"Tanglewood's sold out," I said, handing Baumann a pirogi. When Fox returned from Rome, I'd take him out to Lenox. We'd bring a blanket and a bottle of great bur-

gundy and lie in the remotest corner of the lawn under a
white moon. The orchestra usually plays Mahler that last
weekend.

Lionel teased the opening bars of my cakewalk from the
piano. "Everyone shut UP!" he yelled. "This is PRICE-
less!"

I looked up at Martin. "Your mother is not going to like
this," I said. "Maybe you should take her for a little spin
around the rosebushes." Martin agreed with me. He walked
over to Ruth and whispered something in her ear. Her eyes
lit up as if he had just announced an impending grand-
child, even one that was half mine. Together they exited
the living room.

"Excuse me," I told Bau, "I've got to check on something." I went immediately upstairs and dialed Fox's number. There was no answer. Shit! I tried again. Nothing.
What are you trying to do, kill the guy? Chuck lashed. *Put
that phone down.* "Who's side are you on, anyway?" I
cried, hanging up. She did have a point: I remembered
getting telephone calls from parties I was not attending.
For a sharp instant, all of that torment I had long ago
buried rose up and scored me for old times' sake. I walked
to the window. Out in the yard I saw my husband prome-
nading arm in arm with my mother-in-law. Martin bent
down and carefully fixed a wayward branch. Then he
lifted a pink bloom to his nose; the gesture was one of a
good and kind man. I sagged against the window frame.
Oh Jesus! Why was I destroying everything I had for one
wild card? Were these people really so *odious* that I couldn't
bear them anymore? *I can tell you who's odious,* Chuck
volunteered. "Shut up," I whispered.

I arrived downstairs just as Lionel and Pooh were taking
their bows to abnormally energetic applause. It wasn't just
the cakewalk; after four drinks nothing is sacred and everything is hilarious, particularly sex. "I hope I haven't
spoiled the show," teased Lionel like a deflowered debu-
tante. "Thank you, thAAAAnk you! You MUST see it when
it comes to Boston." Everyone assured Lionel that this
would happen. "You haven't LIVED until you've seen Pooh
in my costumes. And that's NOT all. There are going to be
PLENty of surprises when this show hits town, PLENty."

Uh-oh. Time to head off the runaway. I went to the cabinet and quickly put on a compact disc of the D Minor Toccata of Bach.

Lionel came running over. "What are you DOing," he cried. "Turn that DOWN! Do you want to turn this place into a FUneral parlor?"

I looked at my watch. "I thought this party was over at seven o'clock."

"Are you CRAZY? This party's just getting off the ground!"

"Lionel," I said, "You and Pooh are the only homosexuals in the house. There is no hope for this party getting off the ground."

Pooh came over to us. We three stood out in that skirted and suited crowd like a pimp and two whores at midnight Mass. "Ah doen't know 'bou thet music, princess. Soun's lahk some monstah movie."

"Jesus Christ, you two heathens! That's a masterpiece of organ literature!"

Hans Baumann came up behind me. "Soooo . . . you like Bach."

The man immediately shot up three hundred points on my score card. Perhaps he deserved a trip to Tanglewood after all. "That's right." I glared contemptuously at Lionel and Pooh. "Not everyone else does."

A strange couple, the first of many, thanked Lionel, Pooh, and me for a lovely evening; the organ music was driving them out, as I had hoped. The woman looked as if her entire life were devoted to looking ten years younger than she should; her husband looked as if he would rather spend his money on a woman who looked her age but sat on his face. "It was a pleasure to meet you," the woman said to Lionel, taking this opportunity to study his red, white, and blue hairdo at close range: she couldn't quite place the shrimp shells, either. "I'd be delighted to have a party for you when your show opens in Boston."

"That would be fanTAStic! And promise me yours won't end at seven o'clock!"

"Don't neglect to invite plenty of eligible bachelors," I recommended, smiling like an imposter. Where the hell was Martin when I needed him?

The toccata hit an enormous climax, cutting off further conversation. We bid adieu to this lovely couple and to twenty more shouting dumb shows. When the living room finally cleared, I flipped to another CD and switched on the speakers in the den, jacking up the volume.

The great C Minor Passacaglia wrested all but fifteen of the most determined malcontents from my house. Those remaining now were either hard-core alcoholics or people who would rather lose a leg than return to their own homes. Paloma and Jason were conferring with some glabrous lush in the corner, probably Dueser, whose wife, I noticed, had not accompanied him to Boston. Hans Baumann sat mesmerized on a leather couch listening with his eyes closed to the Passacaglia, no doubt imagining wondrous things. Edmund Weaver and Percival stood decimating the cheese board while Hayward Tolland eased Martin's collection of first-edition Dickens from the bookshelves as if he were performing heart transplants. The rest of the guests I had never met and had no intention of meeting: too rich and still too ravenous. Amid this fray circulated Pooh and Lionel, hovering over this then that byway conversation like two mammoth hummingbirds. If Lionel didn't quit stuffing his face with mini hotdogs, he'd soon burst.

Finally Martin and Ruth returned from their little walk. Martin's smiling face altered drastically when he realized that eighty people could not have gone to the toilet at once. He immediately walked into the living room and killed the Passacaglia, replacing it with some smooth polyester slop from a local radio station.

"*Ach!*" shouted Hans Baumann from the couch. "*Was ist los?*"

Martin returned to the den and found me. "Hello my pet," he said. "Who put that music on? Where is everyone?"

"I think they all had to go to Little League," I said, avoiding the first question. If Martin pressed the issue, I'd blame the Passacaglia on Lionel.

"I'm DYing of starvation," announced the scapegoat in question. "Where can a man EAT in this blasted state?"

"Try Provincetown," I suggested. Lionel glared at me. He was waiting for someone to invite him and Pooh out to dinner. In Boston, of course, and in those outfits, they'd have to wait until Halloween.

Jason Street, vice-president of Weaver, Inc., looked at his watch. "Martin, holy crow! The softball game! Get your mitt and let's go!"

I looked at my husband. "You're not serious." Now I'd have to meet the wives of the company jocks? Forget it!

"It's their last game, honey." Martin said. "I promised to go." He turned to the room. "Everyone's invited. We're playing at eight o'clock in Franklin Park. Weaver versus Raytheon."

Everyone in the room agreed that, inebriated or not, such a classic confrontation was not to be missed. They'd all have to go home and change, though, and maybe pick up a few spare baseball bats: even the squirrels get mugged in Franklin Park. Soon only the Weavers, Lionel and Pooh, and Percival remained.

"You weren't SERious about softball, were you, Martin," Lionel said, smoking the stub of a cigarette that he had picked from an ashtray. "You just wanted to clear the house." He puffed once. "Ehff! What putrid ROT!" Lionel plopped the butt into an abandoned Bloody Mary. I saw Ruth's eyebrows go to heaven.

"Of course I was serious," Martin replied. "We've got a great team."

"It won the championship last year," his mother added.

I started picking up glasses and coasters; whenever I sat still, Fox made me crazy. "Eva, relax," Martin said, "we'll call the service tomorrow."

"Ah sho' hope it's not thuh same suhvice yo' called befo'," said Pooh, rolling his eyes. "They retah'd."

"They retired, all right," corroborated Lionel. "And it's a wonder they didn't die of exhaustion! My GAWD! Slavery is NOT dead, Pooh, dear."

"Cut the crap, dildo, you had the time of your life," I said. Ruth's back arched like a wet cat's. The word *crap* had offended her; I don't think she knew what *dildo* meant.

Martin looked reproachfully at me but I ignored him. Five years was enough time for the in-laws to accustom themselves to the argot of the lower classes. For a moment we all sat listening to a symphony orchestra play "Allegheny Moon."

"Dr. Boyd," Ruth said pleasantly. turning to Lionel, "I understand that your psychiatric practice specializes in maternal relationships."

The star tattooed on Lionel's cheeks turned a lurid brown. He looked over at me. I stared intently at him; he got it. "That's right," Lionel replied, "I am in residence at the City Hospital of Lower Greenwich Village. We have some incredible cases down there—incest, murder, mutilation—all brought about by overbearing mothers."

A slow smile levitated the bottom half of my face; Lionel was the best pinch hitter in the business. I wondered what Ruth's next question would be.

Martin kiboshed that. "Please, Lionel, this is your vacation," he said, standing. "Don't even think about work." He glanced at his watch.

"Oh, but I LOVE to," Lionel insisted. "Overbearing mothers FAScinate me."

"Edmund, dear, I'm afraid we must be running along," Ruth said, detaching her husband from the cheese board. "James is holding dinner for us."

"Certainly, darling," Edmund responded. He knew as well as I did that this was the butler's night off.

Percival Noonan rose accordingly. "Where do you think you're going," I said. "We have a date, remember?"

Percival beamed. Martin did not. "Eva! No more dishes tonight!"

"Who's doing dishes?" I retorted. "Percival and I are going dancing."

"Ah love dancin', sugah," Pooh said. "Ah'm comin too."

"You are NOT going dancing," Lionel said crossly. "In this town you'll cause a riot."

"Okay." I said, "who's going where? Martin's going to the softball game."

"We'll go, too," said Ruth. "Come, Edmund."

"What about your dinner?" asked Dr. Boyd. "Wasn't someone waiting for you?"

Without responding, Ruth sailed to the lavatory, there to freshen her makeup. She glanced a most disapproving look off me on the way out. From the beginning, she had read Fox in my eyes; now I let her read as much as she liked. Sooner or later she should understand that her product did not enjoy a market monopoly.

"Martin, shouldn't you change into a sports shirt or something?" I said.

"Come upstairs with me, will you, Eva," he said.

The moment we got to the bedroom, Martin shut the door. "What the devil is going on here? I don't know who's worse, you or those two fairies of yours."

"What are you talking about? We're not doing anything unusual."

"That's what you think." Martin threw his tie onto the bed. "You and Lionel are a pair of bloody piranhas! My mother is horrified."

"At what? This isn't Wimbledon with Queen Elizabeth, Flappy."

"Can't you modify your behavior for one evening?"

"Shit, I'm sick of modifying my behavior! Why doesn't your mother modify hers?"

Martin stalked into the closet. He had never thought about that.

I plunked down on the bed, wondering why we had given this stupid cocktail party in the first place. Then I remembered: all because of a little fib for Fox. *The first of many,* Chuck opined. *And it wasn't a fib, it was a lie.* I laughed her off; that's because I am a fatalist. Lies, fibs, whatever, The Great Pilot had charted them all on course towards this party as surely as He had contrived my first class in self-defense. Always testing, testing: and I, always failing, failing. I laughed that one off, too. Let's face it, as far as my resistance to temptation is concerned, I was born with spiritual AIDS.

Martin emerged very apologetically from the closet wearing a new shirt. "Eva, I'm sorry," he said. "You've got a point about my mother."

"You mean you still want to stay married?"

He stopped buttoning his shirt. "Of course!"

"Nuts." I watched Martin calmly run a comb through his hair. I didn't understand the Weavers. They were incapable of a good clean fight. We went downstairs.

Ruth and Edmund were already waiting in their Mercedes. "Adios, Martino," cried Lionel. "You really MUST have a limbo stick at your next party."

"Right," said Martin as he flew out the door, minus his softball mitt.

I turned to the remaining three guests. "Okay, Percival and I will cover the den and the library. Pooh, you hit the kitchen. Dr. Boyd, the living room."

"Jesus CHRIST," Lionel screamed, "you're saTANic!"

"Figget Broa'way, Lahnell," said Pooh. "We'h on a plantation."

"Boys, boys," I orated, "what are a few cocktail glasses between friends?"

"I'll tell you what they are," Lionel screeched, "they're an insult to my human dignity and my constitutional rights." He marched upstairs. "Pooh! Come HERE! We are LEAVing this instant! I will NOT tolerate this!"

I shook my head; Lionel had been reading too much of the *Globule* lately. "Well, I guess it's up to us, Percival," I said. "Are you game?"

"I'd like nothing better, my dear," Percival replied. "Where is my apron?"

We finished about two hours later. Percival repeated his speech about children and appointed himself my guardian angel. I drove him home and cruised by Fox's. The apartment was dark; if he was inside, he was not reading the comics. I went home and for the first time in several weeks put in a productive evening with the pencils and erasers. I outlined a Mother's Day hymn and almost finished the funeral music; J. S. Bach had prodded my muddy imagination. Martin slid in around eleven. His team had won and it was apparent that he had forgiven and forgotten all.

Who should call a few days later but Orville my publisher, wondering if I had finally lost my mind, as I had been predicting for years. Never in our long association had I gone this long without sending him something. I informed Orville that my worst fears had been confirmed.

"Marvelous, Eva! When's the happy event?"

"What are you talking about?"

Orville saw that he had committed a major *faux pas* and switched immediately to a discussion of royalties. I instructed him to adopt me ten more children in Ecuador with part of the proceeds; the rest I needed for phone calls to gentleman friends three thousand miles away.

"Are you working on anything at all these days?" Orville asked anxiously. The thought of his most lucrative gusher drying up was as horrendous a catastrophe as the entire world converting to Hinduism.

"I'm in the middle of a Mother's Day hymn," I said, "and you'll soon be getting that funeral music you've been dying for."

"Ha ha! Good one, Eva!" If I made trite jokes, then I was still functioning. "One more thing I meant to tell you—the convention this year is in Boston."

"What? The Sacred Music Convention?"

"Yes, ma'am. I think I told you about it a few months ago."

I vaguely remembered a phone call somewhere along these lines the day of my first self-defense class. No wonder it had flown out the left ear. "Oh."

"You should be there to accept your Hymnist of the Year award."

"When is this?"

"The first week of December. Which of your pieces would you like them to perform?" That was part of the prize to prove they hadn't awarded it to some schlepp.

"I don't know. Which would you like to sell the most?"

"The Christmas oratorio."

"So we'll take sòmething from that, eh?"

"A fine idea." Orville loves it when I think Advert & Promo. He realizes that royalties have a direct bearing upon inspiration.

I went back to my study and worked some more on the Mother's Day hymn, trying very hard to block my own mother from my mind. It was impossible to write verses about bedtime Bible stories and getting sweetly tucked in whilst images of Chuck on a postprandial rampage tore through my mind. I wondered if perhaps, had I gotten tucked in once or twice, I might have turned out a little better. *While you're at it, wonder why you're not Chinese,*

Chuck pinched. In her honor, I composed a verse about happy childhoods being foretastes of heaven. It was pure fantasy.

I had been calling Fox steadily since Tuesday. He was not home.

Friday morning at nine, I picked up Dueser and Hans Baumann at the new Westin Hotel downtown. After considerable debate, my husband and I had agreed that since I did not have the time to personally chauffeur the pair around New England, it would be very sociable of me to drop them off at Tanglewood on my way to New Jersey. If things worked out, I could bring them back to Boston after having deposited my mother at the boozer clinic in Stockbridge.

Needless to say, sociability was not my outstanding characteristic these days. Irritability was. "Goot morning," waved Herr Baumann, "haff you eaten breakfast?" He was wearing his Alpine hat.

"Some time ago," I replied. "I hope you have."

"No, we haven't," his friend answered. This one wore reflecting sunglasses and Bermuda shorts. His knees should have been covered.

"Mr. Dueser, I presume." Taking his bag, I held open the rear door. "Alley oop."

"Vat doess zat mean?"

"It means get in the car pronto," I told him. "You get the front seat."

Instead of accessing directly onto the pike at the hotel, I shot out Mass Ave towards Cambridge. "Where are we going? Out to breakfast?" inquired Dueser from the back seat. In the rearview mirror I saw him about to light a cigarette.

I cut to the curb and jammed on the brakes. "Give me that," I ordered. The cigarette was snapped in half then chucked out the window. I shot back into traffic. "No smoking in the car," I pronounced, "and that includes pipes." Bau removed his hand from his little leather purse.

I pulled into Fox's street, slowed to a crawl, and stuck my head out the window. Aha! Singing! "I'll be right back," I told my guests. "Don't move." Dashing up Fox's stairs, I banged my fists against his door.

"Who's there?"

In reply I kicked his door. "Will you step on it, you moron? I don't have all day." Now my foot hurt.

"Sorry, no morons here," replied his voice from inside.

"Shit!" I ran back downstairs and jumped into the Bavaria. We went from zero to sixty to zero within ten seconds. Never in my life have I made the light at the end of Fox's block.

"Kaffee, *bitte?*" asked Hans.

"Come on, you guys! We're behind schedule!" However, mindful of my obligations as Mrs. Weaver, I pulled into a Dunkin' Donuts. Everyone in town calls it Drunken Donuts in reference to the steady clientele.

"Vat's ziss?"

"Fassnachts. How do you like your coffee? Black? Mr. Dueser?"

"I don't eat junk food," Dueser sniffed. "And I don't drink coffee or hard liquor."

That was a good one. Tuesday night he had personally put away one magnum of champagne and twenty Chesterfields. "He's from California," I told Bau. "We'll have to go somewhere else."

Fortunately, Cambridge abounds in health-food stores. You'd think with all this competition there'd be some price wars going on. No way; only the disgusting capitalists engaged in that. Five minutes later, I presented my guests with their breakfasts.

"Vat's ziss?"

I looked over at the brown mass in Bau's hand. "That's an organic fig bar. You've got some herb tea also."

Bau took a bite. "Ziss iss not zo goot."

"Neither is mine," lamented Dueser. I was beginning to understand why neither his wife nor Paloma had come along on this trip.

"Too late now, gang," I said, smiling at the toll collector. "We're on the pike."

With one hand on the steering wheel, I reached into the glove compartment and got the radar unit. The moment it was up and running, my foot depressed the accelerator to the floor; the Bavaria responded like a bitch in heat. "Welcome to the Massachusetts Autobahn," I told Hans. We started zipping past cars right and left. I turned the radio on: Telemann. It got turned right off again.

"Is there any good scenery around here?" asked Dueser.

"In ze front seat," laughed Bau. He had been staring at my legs since his arrival in the car.

I pretended not to have registered that. "The state is flat and the pike is straight," I said to Dueser, "So tell us about your great deal with Martin." For the next hour/ninety miles, papering his tale with innuendo and hyperbole, Dueser presented his account of last week in San Francisco. He made no mention of Paloma, vineyards, or upper decks; also, Dueser's selling price and Martin's buying price disagreed by eight million dollars.

"So I guess you're going to retire now," I said.

"Retire? Never. I'm going to set myself up in Malibu—start another company—get a beach house—a nice lady friend—"

Ah, such an original male fantasy. "What about your wife?" I asked.

In the rearview mirror I saw Dueser wince like a spectator at the boxing matches. Twisting in his seat, Bau looked askance at Dueser. "Vat, you are marriedt?"

"Separated," croaked Dueser, convincing no one.

"So amm I," echoed Bau. Ditto.

The early warning system started to whine, so I quickly cut to sixty-two miles per hour, breezing innocently past a speed trap while some Minnesotan in a brown Lynx bagged himself a fifty-buck souvenir of Massachusetts. "Ach, you Amerikens," Bau deprecated, shaking his head like Wyatt Earp after a shootout. Mark my words, he'd buy one of these devices the moment he returned to Boston.

The speedometer soon reindicated ninety-five: I dislike traveling with newly liberated husbands.

"Say, Hans," said Dueser mournfully after we had bypassed the fourth and last Howard Johnson's on the turnpike, "Do you know of any good places to eat in Vienna?"

My guests began exchanging information concerning the best restaurants and nightclubs in their respective quadrants of the world. If either had taken his wife to any of these places, I'd eat Bau's *Tarnhelm*. Swinging off the exit, I sighed. Was Martin the only straight arrow in this licentious bog? If so, it would be an extraordinary distinction. Perhaps I was deluding myself, come on, Paloma's veins didn't pulse with stamp-pad ink. Perhaps Martin behaved no differently on the road than these two schmucks. *You mean maybe Martin behaves no differently than his wife?* Chuck smirked.

Now I was really upset. That would be a disaster.

Ten minutes later I deposited my guests at the main gate of Tanglewood, shutting my door just as the cloud of dust generated by the Bavaria caught up with us. "If you don't hear from me tomorrow morning," I said through the closed window, neglecting to ask where they were staying, "you'll have to find some nice lady friends to drive you back to Boston."

Bau could have strangled the stupid Ameriken Dueser. At this rate, they'd be doing nothing here but going to concerts.

I sped down the Taconic to New Jersey thinking wild jumbled thoughts about Martin, Fox, Chuck, death, and my Christmas oratorio. What a junker! Every single component of my life operated in perfect disharmony! It couldn't be possible that Martin, the steadiest cog, was failing me. He was supposed to have a lifetime guarantee. I shot into an abandoned gas station on the median for a little warranty work.

Paloma answered the phone. "Mr. Weaver's office."

"Hey, wait a minute! Isn't this his private line?"

"No, I'm sorry. Is this Mrs. Weaver?"

"Of course it is! Where's Martin?"

"He's right here. One moment."

Martin came on the phone. "Hello, pet, what's up?"

"Flappy, are you having an affair with Paloma or anyone I don't know about?"

For a long while I heard nothing. Then Martin said, "Excuse me a moment please, Paloma." I suppose she walked out and shut the door during the next ten seconds. Martin waited another half minute, carefully choosing his words. "Eva, what are you trying to do? I was in the middle of dictation."

"Stop avoiding the question, Martin."

"No, I'm not having an affair with my secretary, for God's sake! Nor anyone else! I'm married to you! What's gotten into you? Weren't you supposed to drive out to Tanglewood with Hans and Dueser this morning?"

"I did already. Now I'm in Poughkeepsie."

Martin got very quiet. "Slow down, Eva. That's an order."

Neither of us said anything. That reminded me of Fox; it drove me insane with frustration. "You know, darling," Martin said finally, "maybe you should keep your mother company in Stockbridge for a few days."

"Are you kidding? Do you think I'm nuts or something?"

"You've been under a lot of stress lately."

"I HATE that word!" I screeched. "Don't use it!"

My husband didn't know what to make of all this; when I call him at the office, it's usually to ask where he hid the spare set of house keys. He thought it wise to switch to a lighter topic. "Did you have a nice trip?"

I burst into sarcastic laughter. "It was revolting! I don't want either of those shitheads in my car again."

"Now Eva, you don't mean that."

"Of course I mean it! I've got to go, Flappy, this conversation is getting me very upset." Before Martin could start patiently talking me out of any rash decisions, I hung up. Then I felt very bad. "Jesus Christ!" I shouted to the empty phone booth. Every time I hung up the phone now, no matter who was on the other end, I felt bad! Every time I talked to my husband, I felt bad! Every time I touched Fox, I felt bad! Every time I took a deep breath, I felt bad! *That's because you are bad*, said Chuck. I got into the car and floored the accelerator. Now even speeding made me feel bad.

Shit, I prayed for the first time in weeks, *this is one hell of a mess*. I drove intently another five miles. It was a little dangerous down here because of all the dead woodchucks in the road. *Okay! Happy now? You've proven Your point!* I spat, *So do something decisive, will You?* Lightning bolts and broken necks came to mind. So did car crashes. Bah, why did I bother? Good clean solutions only happened on TV! In real life, everyone stayed alive, festering hideously.

I got to New Jersey a little before one. "Hi, Chuck," I called, walking in the front door. "I'm here."

"Out back, Eva." I went to the patio, where my mother was sitting with a pitcher of extremely pale lemonade. She had lost around ten pounds but seemed to have gained it all in the face. You could nurture a kangaroo in the bags around her eyes. If she had been to the hairdresser in the last six weeks, she should take him to small claims court. And where did she get that horrendous housecoat? Not even Woolworth's would stock such an abomination.

"Hey, you look great," I said, kissing her cheek. She was reading a little devotional for daily clean living.

"You look a wreck," my mother said. "I hope you didn't pay much for that outfit."

I looked down at my dress, detecting nothing wrong with it. At the time, two hundred bucks had seemed a fair price for all those ruffles. "How about some lunch, Chuck? I'm starving."

"There are plenty of cold cuts in the refrigerator. I'll make you a sandwich."

"Don't get up! I'll make it!" Otherwise I'd get a few fingers with the tomatoes. "What would you like? Ham and cheese? Salami? Iced coffee? Hot coffee? Got any coffee ice cream?"

Chuck didn't reply. She was busy with her devotional. I went to the kitchen, called my father's office, and announced that I was taking Chuck to the clinic for a few days. He didn't like that very much; his wife was falling short of expectations once again. Like the Weavers, my father is a firm believer in silent example, only his emphasis is on silence rather than example. He should have married a deaf mute. Instead, Chuck ended up with the deaf mute. What the hell, it was too late now. I'm tired of analyzing where my parents went wrong.

I brought Chuck a turkey sandwich and some cole slaw. She had zero appetite; all she wanted to do was drink that lemonade and absorb two weeks of missed catechism. "Are you all packed?" I asked once. A stupid question:

my mother has kept a valise next to her bedtable ever since I can remember.

With a sigh, Chuck finished the booklet. "You should read these, Eva," she said, "they're very inspirational."

She had to be kidding. That little booklet was the Norman Rockwell of religious instruction. Each day it spoonfed its readers one half a legitimate Bible verse buried under two paragraphs of pasteurized anecdotes, topped with a quotation from some orotund nerd like Henry David Thoreau. Shit! Couldn't Christians take the real thing anymore?

I cleared the table. "Okay, all set? Let's hit the road."

"Where are we going? I have a bridge game with your father tomorrow night."

"Chuck, I told you at least four times that you've got a reservation in Stockbridge." She just didn't want to remember. "Dr. Chubb is looking forward to seeing you again."

"I can't leave your father alone for a week, Eva. He'll starve."

"He will not. The freezer is full of pot pies and Dilly Bars."

"We're invited to a big brunch on Sunday."

One thing has always puzzled me about my parents. People keep inviting them out. They must act totally different in public than they do at home. "Please, you've been going to brunches for thirty years. You can miss one. Tell Robert to say you're visiting Martin and me." Oh God! When I said Martin, I thought Fox!

"I should call your father."

"Forget him! He knows you're coming with me."

"And he never told me? That son of a bitch!"

"I just informed him ten minutes ago."

"Did he say I should stay home?" Chuck asked hopefully.

Actually, he said he didn't want her home again until she "shaped up." For Christmas, my father was going to get fifteen sessions with a lesbian marriage counsellor. "He said a change of scenery might do you good," I replied.

"That pompous louse! That does it!" Chuck spun into

the bedroom. "I'm leaving!" I heard her slamming her bureau drawers.

For no apparent reason, I opened the liquor cabinet. It contained two dozen bottles, all empty except for maybe an inch of the most sickening liqueurs. Chuck had remembered she was going, all right. I sat on the couch and waited for her; she was on the phone now expressing regrets to Mrs. Bridge and Mrs. Brunch. As always, Fox darted across my mind, disappearing into a dark cave but leaving behind a whirlwind of dry leaves. I wondered what his mother was like. Christ! Was I ready for a second set of in-laws? Sure I was. It's always easier to start off with a new ball of string than to untangle the knots already in your hand.

Now Chuck was phoning my sisters, telling them to invite my father over for dinner on alternate nights. I went to the bedroom. "Will you stop shooting yourself in the foot," I said. "Let Robert fend for himself for a few days." I grasped her suitcase. It weighed a ton. "What's in here, Chuck?" I said, unsnapping the hasps. "You know you can't take any snacks or drinks with you."

Ah, but she could take a hundred New Testaments and two thousand tracts. For a moment I stared at them as if they were cash. Then I shut the suitcase. Chuck's missionary zeal increased with her thirst.

"Think I'll be able to slip those in?" Chuck asked sarcastically.

"You did last time." Now I was getting seriously depressed.

Traffic was heavy going up to the Berkshires. Chuck chatted nonstop about my sisters and brothers, their marriages, their careers, and their children, each of whom had inspired a minimum of five precious anecdotes. I couldn't imagine what Chuck could be telling my siblings about Martin and me; we furnished her with no raw material whatsoever. With us, all she could do was broadcast forebodingly. But that was her specialty: Chuck had predicted one heart attack and three unwanted pregnancies while everyone else was still unpacking wedding presents. Let's face it, disaster and ruin were in her blood, and of all her children, I had inherited that most obviously. That's why

Chuck felt the closest to me. I was also the only one of six who wasn't a teetotaler.

By Newburgh, all this talk about nieces, nephews, and slipshod fathers had agitated my lust like an April monsoon. I didn't want to hear any more about my relatives. I wanted to get out of the car and lie down on a certain beat-up bed with a singer I missed dreadfully. Looking for relief, I switched on the radio and began scanning the dial.

"Hold it! That's a good station!" cried Chuck. An inept chorus was singing *The Old Rugged Cross*.

"Ladies and gentlemen," a hypnotic voice intoned, "we are living in the worst times in history. Sin is everywhere! What can we do to keep ourselves pure?"

"Is this necessary, Chuck?" I interrupted. "Can't we try for something a little more upbeat?"

"Shhh! You of all people should be listening to this!"

I gritted my teeth and passed four tractors in a row. "First, we must WANT to be pure! We must WANT to turn from evil! The Lord can do nothing if we don't open our hearts, our minds, to the power of the Almighty! The love of Jesus is enough to make us turn from ALL temptations! Our blessed—"

I turned the radio off. "Sorry, I can't take that."

Chuck sighed. "I just don't know where I went wrong with you, Eva."

"Care for a few clues?"

That registered like fingerprints on water. "I suppose it's too much to expect all of my children to turn out properly," Chuck continued. "I had a long discussion with Beatrice Boyd about this." That's Lionel's mother. "We went to see Lionel's show on Thursday."

"Oh! *Cloistrophobia?* How'd you like it?"

"Beatrice is in absolute shock. She had to be helped from the theater. I tell you, Eva, that son of hers has degenerated awfully. He's written the filthiest musical I've ever seen."

"Wait a moment," I said. "Lionel doesn't write anything. He just designs costumes."

"Whoever wrote this is going to roast in hell, believe me. I remember one number in particular. The black priest sings it. The lyrics I would not even want to repeat to you."

"That's not necessary. I wrote them."

Chuck put her face in her hands. "Oh Eva! How could you!"

Notice that my mother expressed no shock and no disbelief whatsoever. She'd believe I was the Antichrist if I gave her half a chance. "Come on, Chuck, where's your sense of humor? I was helping Lionel out of a jam."

"Oh! Poor Beatrice! I'll never tell her this! It would just kill her!"

"The black priest is Lionel's lover. Make sure you don't tell her that either."

Chuck searched her bag and pulled out a little book entitled *When Your Children Fail You*. I did not ask her to read aloud. Finally, around Hillsdale, the traffic thinned out. I turned the radar detector on. "What's that?" asked Chuck, putting her book away. She already knew it by heart.

"That's so I can make a little time," I answered, creeping up to eighty.

"Isn't that illegal? You should turn it off."

"The use of radar detectors is legal in the state of Massachusetts."

"What's the speed limit in the state of Massachusetts?"

"Come on, Chuck, it doesn't say fifty-five in the Ten Commandments!" I looked over at my mother. "That's one of the reasons you're so screwed up. You can't separate theory from practice." She also watched too much TV.

"You're trying to make excuses for breaking the law."

Of course I was. That was my life's work. Jesus Christ! Why wasn't I an atheist like Fox? He made up his own laws as he went! "Guess I'm just a hopeless criminal," I sighed, maintaining eighty miles per hour.

As the Bavaria flew by more and more cows, Chuck realized that she was approaching her destination. It was time for her parting speech. "Now Eva," Chuck began, "if I don't come out of this alive—"

"Will you stop it! I'm much more likely to die before you, believe me!" The moment I said it, I cringed. That sounded just like something Chuck would say.

"I want you to know that I've promised your sisters the

silver. You have enough already from Martin. I would like them to get my fur coats, too. What I really wanted to say was you should take care of your father. He's incapable of getting along without me. It will be very tough for him." Chuck began to cry, imagining the spastic widower she had created. "He's a good man and a good provider." Now she blew her nose. I didn't think I could tolerate much more of this. "Maybe we've let each other down here and there, but all in all, he's been the only man for me ever since I was sixteen." Tears now drenched the handkerchief. I'm sure Chuck was reliving an episode she had seen on "The Edge of Night." That didn't help my headache. "I'll be sorry to leave him. The best years should have been ahead of us. Never mind." She raised her face to the roof of the car. "We'll be together in Paradise."

That did it. "Jesus CHRIST, Chuck!" I screamed. "Any more of that and you're going to WALK to the lunatic asylum!" The woman needed a frontal lobotomy ten times worse than Charles Manson. "I don't want to hear ANY MORE of this garbage about Robert and you and heaven, do you hear? It makes me sick! And you're not going to die, for God's sake! People like you hang around until they're one HUNdred! And put that thing down!"

Chuck had slipped a little thermos of lemonade into the car without my knowledge. I tried to grab it away from her and succeeded in spilling sugary swill all over my dress, Chuck's pants, and the leather seats. The Bavaria narrowly missed a ditch. "You're turning into a devil," Chuck observed, "but I refuse to worry about this. I've done my best with you. Now it's all in the Lord's hands."

"And drop this Lord's hands business! Jesus, Mary, and Joseph! That is pure PAP!" Even as I shouted, the wisp of a hymn came to me. Altos and organ, title *Almighty Hands*. It was the missing link in the funeral music.

Chuck tissued her pants clean. Why the hell did lemonade come right off of polyester but never silk? I'd have to ask Martin this aggravating question.

"Your profanity disturbs me," Chuck said sadly, "and that *is* one of the Ten Commandments."

"It's not profanity," I replied, "it's direct address. Hey, here we are."

I crawled the car through the summer crowds milling the streets wondering what overpriced junk to buy next. They usually settled for the two-dollar ice cream cones. Chuck became very quiet as I pulled into the driveway of Nizor's Sanatorium. She had already been here four times and at each prior dismissal had declared herself fully cured.

"Now Chucky," I said, pulling into a parking space, "I want you to stay here as long as you need to. Just don't try to convert Dr. Chubb. He's Jewish."

I realized too late that I had just made Chubb a primary target. "Where's my lemonade?" my mother asked.

I reached between the seats. "There's one schluck left." I handed it over. "I should be talking you out of this," I said.

"That's Chubb's job," Chuck shrugged, upending the thermos. We went inside. The place looked just like the Red Lion Inn down the road except security was a little tighter. Chubb met us at the desk.

"Mrs. Hathaway! Welcome back!"

I said good-bye to them there; Chuck had delivered enough speeches for one day. "Call me any time," I reminded her, handing over the missionary suitcase. "Good luck," I said to Chubb. If he didn't salvage her this time, she had had it. I walked out quickly; each time I see my mother ascend a staircase on some doctor's arm, I think I might never see her again.

Instead of driving straight home, I went to the bar at the Red Lion Inn. "To my mother," I said to the bartender, raising my glass.

"That's an alcoholic's favorite toast, you know," he said.

"Is that so." I finished the martini neat and went to the phone booth. Fox answered after two rings. "Hey, windbag, where have you been?"

"Removing footprints from my front door."

"What are you doing tonight?"

"Got something in mind?"

I said nothing: Herr Hans Baumann plus Alpine hat had just walked into the bar. Shit, why did this only happen when I wore a bolt of primary colors?

"Eva? Are you there?"

"I've got to go right now. Can I see you?"

"I'll be here."

"You be there in two hours."

Bau had obviously ditched Dueser and was trying his luck as a solo husband in Stockbridge. He wore an ascot and smoked one of those pipes like the grandfather in *Heidi*. I stayed in the phone booth, gabbing with the dial tone as I observed Bau seat himself at the bar and order a beer. Pretty soon a woman in tennis clothes sat next to him and asked for a light; I knew from her eye makeup that Bau's cock had just found overnight lodging. As he pulled out his gold lighter and did the eyes-over-the-smoke routine, I slipped into the street. Another martini would have done wonders for my disposition.

At a gas station I called my husband. "Martin," I said, "I think I'll stay with Chuck tonight."

I could just see him looking at his watch. "Where are you?"

"In Stockbridge."

Now he was calculating my average speed since last speaking with me. "I don't want you driving any more today, Eva. Have yourself a nice dinner and go to bed."

"The refrigerator's full of cheese and little eggplants."

"I'll have them." He was lying. When I'm not home, Martin skips supper. "The carpenters are supposed to come tomorrow at seven to start on the greenhouse."

"Can you handle them until nine?"

"Of course."

"So I'll see you then."

"Goodbye, my pet. Sleep well."

I arrived ninety minutes later at Fox's. There were four speed traps on the pike, but all aimed at the traffic headed out to the Berkshires. The troopers probably figured that no one was in any rush to get into stinking hot Boston for the weekend.

I knocked like a losing pitcher on Fox's door. "Hi."

"Oh dear," he said. "You've had a hard day at the office."

"Mind if I take a bath?"

"Just a minute." He hugged me; at once my circulation

improved. I drooped out of his arms and went to the bathroom.

He came in a few minutes later, sat down on the floor, and leaned over the tub. Submerged to my chin, I regarded him with less animation than a periscope. Fox stuck a finger into the water, looking for me. "I missed you," he said after a while.

"Where were you?"

"In Chicago." I waited; he smiled. "You would have been proud of me. I did a *Rigoletto* on one day's notice."

"Was it good?"

"Real good. I'm invited back next season."

Now I smiled. "Way to go." I didn't much want to talk. As I sighed, my breath rippled the water.

"What's the matter?" Fox said. I shook my head: gettin' old, givin' up. "Tell me."

"I took my mother to a boozer farm today."

Fox fished under the water and found my hand. He kissed it. "I'm sorry."

"She thinks she's going to die there."

"Do you think so?"

"No." She had too many tracts to distribute. "But you never know." God damn it, why couldn't Chuck take a few hints from Ruth Weaver? My mother-in-law had no intention of dying before her husband. "I don't know why that woman still gets me depressed."

"She's your mother, honey."

That's right. And I was turning out just like her. It was horrifying.

My breasts broke the surface of the water like two dead perch. I was getting cold. "Would you mind leaving me alone awhile?" I said.

"Yes, madame, as a matter of fact, I would mind." He flipped the lid down and sat on the toilet. "Just pretend I'm not here."

I dragged the curtain shut and put the shower on. That way he couldn't tell if I was crying or not. I stood there a few minutes then pulled myself together. When I opened the curtain he was waiting with a towel and a Kleenex. My dress was neatly folded on the toilet seat.

"You," was all I could say. I was never going home again.

"That's right." I stepped out of the shower and Fox mummified me.

"Now I can't blow my nose."

"Here," he said, stifling me with the Kleenex. "Blow."

He hiked me like a Persian rug over his shoulder and walked to the bedroom. I was unraveled and placed under the covers. "Hungry?" he asked.

"Peking ravioli and a Mai Tai."

"How about pretzels and beer?"

I demolished half a bag of pretzels and two beers. That brought my lifetime consumption up to three bottles. Fox lay on top of the bed watching me get crumbs and salt all over his sheets. "Tell me your life story," I said. "Everything."

"Thought you'd never ask."

"Never thought I'd want to know." I belched loudly. "When's your birthday?"

"May thirteenth."

"How old are you?"

"Twenty-seven."

My mouth cannoned pretzels all over the sheets. "Jesus Christ! You're just a baby!" I had never associated with a younger man in my life. They reminded me of those sour little gherkins you put in tuna fish salad.

"I act older than my age." Fox swept up a few crumbs. He placed my empty beer bottle on the floor. "Don't worry, you'll get over it."

Not for a couple minutes, buddy. Shit, how could I have made such a gross miscalculation? He moved like a thirty-five-year-old, talked like one, sang like one—aha. He didn't screw like one. I chuckled. "And all this time I thought it was me."

"What does that mean?"

"That's a private joke. Continue your tale of woe."

"That's your life, baby, not mine," Fox said. "Where was I?"

"You just foisted yourself upon an unsuspecting world. Then you grew up in Brooklyn. You told me that already."

"I did? When?"

"Saint Patrick's Day. You had had a few drinks to bolster your courage."

"What else did I say?"

"Biographical or erotic?"

"Do you want me to go on with my life story?"

"Sure." I burrowed under the sheets and shut my eyes. "I'm listening."

"Open your eyes and listen. I don't want to talk to a corpse."

"You tenors always need an audience, don't you."

"Of course! This is a great story!"

"What kind of a mother did you have?"

"My mother ran away when I was five years old."

This man did nothing but puncture all my theories of evolution. It was beginning to undermine all my self-confidence. "How come?"

"She wasn't the domestic type."

"How many kids were there?"

"Just one."

"Gee, what did you do to her? Were you still wearing diapers or something?"

"No! She was just a frustrated violinist. She ran away to South America with some clarinet player."

"What did your father have to say about that?"

"He said it was the best thing that ever happened to us."

"Didn't you miss your mother?"

Fox shrugged. "There wasn't anything to miss. She was always in the dining room practicing the violin and forgetting to buy milk."

That was the last straw. "So how come you're not screwed up like everyone else?"

Fox smiled. "I have a great father."

This was getting too complicated for me now. I should not have had that second beer. "What's his name?"

"Rudy."

"What does he do?"

"He plays the violin, too."

"I see." A starving musician father; a runaway mother; no siblings; no girlfriends. I should count my blessings he was only an atheist and not a gay anarchist. "So why aren't you a violinist?"

"It was cheaper to sing."

I turned on my side, not wanting to hear any more of Fox's life story tonight: further episodes concerning Juilliard, the barbells, operas, Rudy, and Cambridge would only upset me. Fox and I had a basic and terminal problem, you see: despite the fact that I was rich and he was poor, although I was a lambkin of God and this guy was a fucking heathen, despite that I knew precisely where I was going and Fox could only sing in the dark, we were exactly alike. For Christ's sake! The last thing I wanted was another me! Why did I keep falling for different shadows of myself? This was an infinitely more warped quest for immortality than any excess of childbearing.

"What's the matter? Did I say something wrong?"

"No. I'm just feeling particularly mortal tonight."

"What can I do?"

"Sing a little."

"What would you like to hear?"

"Your voice."

As he walked out of the bedroom I cracked an eye: Fox from the rear was as striking as Fox from the front. Without him beside me, the bed tilted out of whack; it, too, was trying to dump me. Ah, what a great life. Fox hit a chord and began some Brahms lieder.

Music out of his mouth was the most excruciatingly sweet torment I had ever heard. That voice dogged my innermost thoughts: if anyone alive could unlock my rough little choruses, Fox could, and that frightened me, because I did not want my soul bared to an atheist. It was too close to the other side. *So don't show him your music*, Chuck growled. Shit, no wonder the woman was sleeping tonight in a loony bin. She had never shown a man anything.

Fox switched to Strauss and did one lullaby. Then the singing stopped. I heard his footsteps approach the bedroom and, as ever, my heart began to expand and contract a little more decisively than before. Fox leaned against the doorframe looking at me: my great and beautiful hope, my great despair. The two collided and a little spark ignited tinder that I had abandoned maybe thirty years ago, when

Chuck had torn down all the draperies, shouting that we could all expect a fifth sibling in seven months.

He sat on the bed, placing a hand on my forehead. Rudy had also raised a practical nurse. "Feeling better?"

"Lie down and I'll tell you."

10

"I'VE GOT TO GO," I said. It was almost nine o'clock.

Fox stared at a crack in the ceiling, waiting for it to move. Judging by his pallor, he had not slept all night. A little crease bisected his forehead and the sandman had left enough stock in his eyes for kitty litter. He breathed in tight shallow knots, like a sick owl. The poor devil looked as ancient as I. "Wait," he said, "we have something to talk about." His tone of voice implied an imminent trip to the woodshed: I lay very still.

He turned his head; I studied his face, memorizing curves and vents, and wanting him. "This is the last time you'll be leaving my bed for Martin's," Fox said. "Do you understand?"

"I hear you." My head filled with hot slag.

"I don't want to see you any more," he continued, "until you make up your mind. It can't be both of us."

"Bastard," I whispered as more, hotter, slag crowded my temples. Oh Jesus! An only son! A bachelor! A tenor! This man wouldn't recognize a gray area if a herd of elephants charged him! *Start laughing*, Chuck cued, *it's showdown time*. Nope, not yet; I would not laugh until Fox had bowed and departed, leaving me with an armful of dusty old ropes and, if I was lucky, a spare bouquet. I slid towards the side of the bed.

"Is that all you're going to say?" Fox asked.

I did not reply but looked at those big gray eyes of his

239

instead. It would have been much less revealing to shout until my eyeballs rose from their sockets; Fox sees too much. He doesn't realize, though, that my vision is as sharp as his. In his eyes I saw myself ten years ago, invincible with hope, living for the impossible, and loving so fiercely that there could be no possible solution but total defeat or total victory. This time the outcome depended on me and with each day I held Fox captive, he would despise me a little more, until finally he would understand the silences of a coward, and leave. For this unspoken catastrophic defeat, result of an undeclared war, Fox would never forgive me. Those gentle gray eyes would hate the sight of me as passionately as they loved the sight of me now. I could not bear it.

He joined me in the shower a few minutes later. Fox took a cloth and began soaping my back. We had never made love in the shower. For that matter, we still hadn't hit the kitchen table, the living room floor, or Walden Pond on a warm spring night. Now it looked as if we never would.

Fox put the soap back. "Up or down," he said.

"Up," I said. I put my arms around his neck and my ankles around his back. The first time I tried to kiss him I got a mouthful of water. The second time, I started down at his throat, out of firing range, working slowly as a barber around his chin. I kept one arm behind his neck and with the other felt his biceps as he held me close: hard. My hand slowly grappled down his arm, searching for the hidden weapon. He had already buried it, so I took his balls into custody. That was when Fox decided he had to sit down on the side of the bathtub. He finished me off just before the hot water ran out.

He reached across the tub and turned the water off. I sat draped over him, saying nothing, dripping, as he wilted inside of me. Finally I popped him out calmly as a chicken laying an egg. "I love you," I said, "more than anything or anyone."

He looked me straight in the eye; I wondered which of his parents had given him the long black eyelashes. "Stay with me."

My pulse dipped like a cattail in the breeze. I briefly

imagined myself living here, writing hymns and teaching Fox how to sing. It would not be a bad life once I redecorated the apartment. But not today. "At this very moment," I said, "ten carpenters are gouging a hole in the side of my house."

"Oh yeah? What about the hole you're gouging in me?"

"You'll have to fix that in Rome."

"Using the method that's worked so well for you, eh?" Fox lifted me off his lap and got out of the shower. I watched him dry himself; the thought of that penis anywhere but inside his pants or inside of me filled me with thick black pain. *Now imagine him married to someone else,* Chuck suggested, *sleeping with his wife ALL the time.* Jesus! Whose side was she on, anyhow?

"I'm on your side, pal," Fox said, "but it's getting tough." He left the bathroom.

I dressed and found him in the kitchen boiling water. He had washed out two coffee mugs. "Am I going to see you before you leave?" I asked.

"Not unless you're coming to Italy with me."

I wouldn't be seeing him for six weeks then. "Understand one thing, Fox," I said. "I don't want to hurt Martin any more than necessary."

"That warms my heart."

I was getting nowhere. Explaining divorce to a bachelor was tougher than getting a hobo to appreciate the national debt. "Your problem," I analyzed, "is that you can't understand how I could love two men at the same time."

"And your problem, my dear, is that you vastly underestimate your husband's ability to get along without you." He put down my coffee. "It's a subtle form of self-flattery."

"Is that so? I thought it was a blatant form of guilt."

"Same thing."

Fox had probably meandered through this Freudian labyrinth while he was alone in his loden chair thinking about me. I'd have plenty of time to do the same over the next two months. I put the mug to my lips; he made excellent coffee. "I'm genuinely fond of my husband," I told Fox. "I've been living quite peaceably with him for five years. Doesn't that count for anything?"

Fox did not argue with City Hall; the memories broke my heart. "Baby," I continued, "there are so many things out of my control, things that I can't change anymore."

"Don't give me that garbage. You damn well control your own life." This time I didn't answer. "Come on, Eva, you only live once! Are you going to be Mrs. Weaver until you die? Is that what you want?"

"Before I met you, it didn't seem such a bad idea."

"But you did meet me." Fox looked me in the eye; whenever he did that, the deserts bloomed and the Mississippi ran backward.

I put my head in my hands. "Why didn't I meet you six years ago," I moaned. *That would have been no fun at all,* Chuck laughed.

"Stop asking God futile questions," Fox said, running out of patience.

"I thought you were an atheist."

"Whatever I am, I believe in a lot more than you do." Fox left the kitchen; at once the room paled, near death. I followed him to the living room. "I want an answer when I get back," Fox said. "Yes or no. Not maybe, not I need more time. You're not going to take me down with you."

Ah! He's catching on! Chuck cried. *The lad's much smarter than you were.*

He never had a mother sending out two sets of signals, that's why. I glanced at my watch: time to return to my proper doghouse. "So you're going to be the toast of Rome?" I asked, lifting the car keys from my purse.

"I'm going to try."

With his looks, believe me, all he'd have to do was open his mouth and not sound like a pair of worn brake shoes. Before seeing me again, I estimated that he would go to bed with, say, four women, at least two of them singers; odds guaranteed that at least one of these creatures would make him moderately happy. That killed me. "I've got to go," I said.

"Okay."

He walked me to the car. This time I had two parking tickets: one for getting too friendly with a fire hydrant and one for not having a Cambridge resident sticker. "Why did you park there?" Fox asked.

"I was in a rush last night."

"You're lucky they didn't tow you."

As we spoke, a tow truck prowled up the street. "There you are," he said.

"I hate Cambridge, you know," I told him. "I could never live here."

"Oh? Where could you live?"

"New York. Maybe a nice apartment on Central Park."

Fox folded his arms and looked at me. "Prove it."

Jesus Christ, the boy was insistent! Life with him would be hell! "Are you going to write?" I asked, getting into the car.

"Maybe."

"Is there someplace I can call you?"

"I doubt it."

Liar! "Can I write, then?"

"They'll lose it."

Was I now supposed to throw myself at Fox's feet, begging for a lock of hair to stow between my parking tickets? Pfuiii! I almost started laughing at myself. *Too soon, Eva,* Chuck cautioned. *The circle is not complete.* "You are one fine bastard," I said, getting into the car. "Have a wonderful summer."

Fox stepped back, pleased with his little stratagem. Believe me, I sympathized with the guy: those running against the incumbent must fight with any toothpick available. "See you when I get back," he said.

"That's right." I started the engine; that made our farewell official. I looked at his beautiful face, trying not to think of the next six weeks without it. I had no pictures, no letters, not even a sock to keep next to the crowbar in my nightstand; now I wished I hadn't covered my trail quite so well. *Too late now,* shrugged Chuck.

"It's never too late," Fox said. I put the Bavaria into reverse; Schmo ahead of me had left three inches between his taillights and my front bumper.

"So long, pal," I said.

I didn't wait for a last minute outburst; Fox didn't seem about to deliver one anyhow. Instead I pulled away from the curb as if I were merely going to fetch some breakfast. Whatever Fox was thinking, it appeared to be humorous. I watched him in the rear view mirror until that bogus porcelain smile crumpled into the flat straight line it should have been all along. Breakfast, I muttered to myself, it's just breakfast. I rolled down all the windows and shot twice around Memorial Drive, drying my hair. Before going home I stopped at the bakery.

Two pickup trucks and Percival's slate Saab precluded me from entering my own driveway. I had to dislodge my neighbor's German shepherd from the parking space across the street; as I slammed the driver's door the beast eyed my car balefully, choosing the first of four tires upon which to urinate.

"Anyone home?" I called, breezing through the front door. Now I was beginning to feel a little giddy. It took all my concentration to remember details of the fiction I had told Martin last night. I was half an hour late.

A buzz saw replied from the kitchen. Before facing that carnage I decided to change into some fresh clothes; even if I had spent the night innocently slumbering in Stockbridge, a crumpled lemonade-stained dress would undermine my credibility. Plus I needed a little time to check the phone book for hotels in case Martin had tried to reach me at the Red Lion Inn.

Five minutes later I walked innocently into the kitchen. There stood my husband, Percival, and two carpenters with protuberant beer bellies. They were telling their slimmer colleagues outside where to pile all the wood, glass, and steel brackets.

"Hello," I said, "anyone interested in a *palmier?*"

"Eva," Percival greeted me with delight, "there you are, cute as a button!"

I detest the adjective "cute." It applies to four-foot-ten snub-nose cheerleaders and dachshund pups. "I'm here, all right."

"The lady of the house," Martin said, kissing me on the cheek. "My wife Eva." I shook hands with the armchair fullbacks before they left for a donut break. "Did you have a nice ride home, darling?"

"There's not much inbound traffic on a Saturday morning," I answered, searching the counters for coffee. I began to grind some beans.

"Eva," Percival said, "come see what we're going to build for you."

I looked suspiciously at Martin: he always unveils foolish and risqué plans in the company of a third wheel in the hope that this will inhibit me from too berserk a reaction. Alas, after five years and a few severe embarrassments in stodgy restaurants, Martin had still not abandoned this Weaveresque delusion. I noticed, however, that he had become much more discriminating in his choice of third wheels.

I leaned over the blueprints spread across the kitchen table. They depicted the same gargantuan greenhouse I remembered from before. "Okay," I said, "I give up."

Percival slid away the top sheet, revealing drawings for the new gym in the basement. I could probably buy the Y downtown for what this was going to cost Martin; we would have enough redwood here to incinerate the Sierra Club. There was only one problem with this Olympian's dream: I was not planning to be here to use it.

"Martin," I said quietly. "You can't build this, sweetheart."

His face fell. "Why not?"

Percival collapsed into a chair; I thought he was going to have heart failure. Now I felt truly awful: his blueprints were my hymns. What was I supposed to tell these two? *Try the truth,* Chuck said. At that, I had to laugh. What this woman had destroyed in the name of truth would make the Ayatollah gag.

"What is so amusing, Eva?" Martin asked with a trace of annoyance. He sounded exactly like his mother.

"I thought we were moving to California," I replied lamely.

"You're moving to California?" Percival whispered.

"Of course not, Gerald! Eva is being facetious! We have no intention of moving from Boston!"

I poured seething water over the coffee grounds. By affirming that he had no intention of moving from Boston, see, Martin really meant that he had no intention of moving to New York. After five years of marriage I had become quite habile at interpreting these nonverbal asterisks; they could be as devastating as Chuck's most explicit insults and in fact, were generally much more effective because their megatonnage amplified in direct proportion to the opponent's neurotic imagination. Many an argument could have been avoided in this house had Martin only said what he was thinking. Take this New York business, for instance. Why must Martin keep using the phrase "no intention"? This not only cast an inflexible and antagonistic hue upon all discussion, it also implied that anyone with any intention of moving to New York was bonkers. And this knee-jerk "we" business I found extremely irritating also. In my entire married life I have been very careful not to refer to my husband and myself as "we" except in the most limpid pronominal sense; shit, if I had a nickel for every time Chuck had used "we" when she had really meant "I" or "Robert," I could have bought my own penthouse on East Sixty-eighth Street by now.

"What happened to my penthouse, you two," I fumed. "I've had it with these gyms and laboratories." Percival and Martin exchanged questioning looks, as if one had withheld information from the other. *Are you crazy?* cried Chuck. *The last thing you want them to know about is this penthouse!* "I meant beach house," I said feebly, pouring half a cup of coffee down the side of Martin's mug. Jesus, I should go outside and join the carpenters. "I'm sorry, I'm a little tired today."

"Eva's had a rough week, Gerald," Martin explained. "She spent all yesterday in the car." He broke a *palmier* in half and leaned it against his cup. "Where did you stay last night, darling?"

Immediately my guard sprang to attention. For one hysterical moment I imagined that Martin had had me followed yesterday. Not possible, unless he had hired a Piper Cub. Then I imagined Fox in a fight with three thugs Martin had hired to kill him. Then I looked down at my dress, searching for a huge stain caused not by Chuck's lemonade, but by beer and related gushy materials. Whoever claimed that criminals all had a secret desire to be discovered was not a criminal. "Quincy Lodge," I said. "Why?"

Martin chuckled. "They never heard of you at the Red Lion Inn."

"Were you to the Berkshires?" asked Percival. "It's lovely out there this time of year. Did you go to Tanglewood?"

"Nope, I was depositing my mother at a lunatic asylum."

Were it not for Martin's dismayed face, Percival would have burst out laughing. Instead, he thought he heard the carpenters calling him.

"Eva, that was unnecessary," Martin chided when we were alone. "And please! Nizor's is a respected clinic. You make it sound like Bedlam."

"It's Bedlam now, believe me," I said. "You should have seen the suitcase Chuck brought in with her."

Martin refrained from pursuing this distasteful matter. "How are Hans and Dueser getting home? Should I send George out with the limousine?"

"Are you kidding? They're having the time of their lives trying to get laid!" I related what I had seen of Kraut Kasanova and the tennis player. Martin found that amusing rather than repugnant. Then again, he had met Bau's wife in Stuttgart.

"Where do you think Dueser parked for the night?" he asked.

Maybe he stayed at the Quincy Lodge, Chuck brayed. I had not thought of that; my ribcage embraced my lungs like a starving python. "No idea," I said, my voice wobbling oddly. Shit! Why did I have to pick a hotel in Lenox? Any halfbrained ass would have slept in Springfield! Various scenarios whipped through my head: Dueser had seen me drive away from the Red Lion Inn; Dueser had scanned the guest register at the Quincy Lodge while checking in with that tennis player's roommate; Dueser had spent the night in Cambridge with that woman in the bathing suit who lived next to Fox. He could have met her in the Tanglewood Book Store. Dueser had probably called Martin at eight o'clock this morning and told him everything. Now Martin was setting a trap, waiting for me to make one mistake. Then he'd carve me up with the kitchen knives.

Martin crunched his teeth into the *palmier*. "Now I understand that strange phone call from you yesterday," he said.

Panic overtook confusion and begot a brutal headache. I steepled my fingers over the bridge of my nose, searching for the tumor that was making me hallucinate. "What phone call?"

"I beg your pardon. You don't remember disrupting my dictation to ask if I were having an affair with my secretary or perhaps the cleaning lady?"

I had completely forgotten about that phone call. It was ancillary to the plot, rather like a terrorist sending out for pizza. "Oh! That! Sorry. Your friends were giving me ideas."

"Great ideas, Eva."

"Great friends, Flappy."

Martin reached for the newspaper. "Boys will be boys." And what was he? A hermaphrodite?

Hearing no screams or smashes from the kitchen, Percival Noonan cautiously stepped back inside: walking in on a silence could be equally fatal. He bobbed to life at the sight of two dummies plotzed neutrally over the *Globule*. "Ho! So! We're going to make great progress today on this greenhouse! This is a splendid crew!" Martin promptly excused himself to go to work. Now that he had paid for the greenhouse, he didn't want to see it until it was all done.

I looked once out the rear door at the splendid crew. Three of them were smoking cigars and the other two were eating meatball subs. All they had built since seven this morning was an impressive heap of empty doughnut bags. "This is your A team?" I asked Percival.

"They built your mother-in-law's gazebo."

"Say no more." I poured the rest of my coffee down the sink. Right now I could use a bit of Chuck's special lemonade. "Well, Percival, I've got a bit of work in the study. Can you manage here yourself for a while?"

"Certainly," Percival responded, gliding a Parcheesi board back into his briefcase. "I'll work on your gym."

"Forget the gym, I'm telling you."

"Please, Eva! What don't you like about it? Are there too many mirrors? Would you like a steam room instead of a sauna? Both?" Percival pointed to his plans. "We could put one here with no trouble at all."

I saw that this gym was going in the basement whether I liked it or not. What the hell, perhaps Martin's second wife would use it. "Never mind, Percival, your plans are wonderful. Don't change a thing." I stirred up a large quantity of lemonade. "Just go easy on the sunken bathtub."

En route to the study I picked up a small bottle of vodka; Chuck claimed it worked much better than aspirin for headaches. Lionel claimed it gave him brilliant ideas. Richard swore it steadied his hand. Bah. Vodka usually put me to sleep. That's why I wanted it now. It seemed the most economical method of passing six weeks without Fox and without writing. *What, now you're not going to write,* Chuck cried. *Don't ever talk to me about shooting myself in the foot.* That precipitated a generous shower of vodka upon my lemonade. My mother will never understand that she deliberately maims herself, whereas weapons I have never loaded habitually and mysteriously go off in my hand. There's a big difference.

I sat at my desk, dragging out three hymns that I had been assembling these last few weeks. The net result was mucilaginous horseshit that even a Baptist would not sing. I threw them away and searched for that funeral music that had so enamored me on previous occasions. I couldn't find it. That's another bonus of high-octane lemonade: it cleans your house for you. I pulled out a sheet of virgin staff paper and stared at the narrow parallel lines, comparing them with the random rills streaming down Fox's face in the shower this morning. That fascinating juxtaposition of plane geometry and hydrophysics hypnotized an hour of my life away before I snapped awake in surprise. In the meantime my pen had dried up so I uncapped another and drew a few treble clefs of sundry dimensions. My brain was clinically dead. *Come on, you lazy shit,* encouraged Chuck. *Write something.* "I can't think," I whimpered. All I could do was throb with misery. *Write, you tramp,* Chuck shouted. *Stop feeling sorry for yourself.* "I miss Fox," I burbled, rheumy with melancholy. "I want to go to sleep." *Write, damn you, gigolos are an expensive habit.*

That perked me up considerably; I always compose best when I'm a little pissed at something. I flipped open a

Bible and began scanning for suitable subject matter. As usual I got sidetracked in Revelation reading about the various plagues and holocausts that The Great Warden had in store for his charges. That gave me the idea for a hymn entitled *Bedlam's End*. Just as I was sketching in the introduction, the carpenters began hammering the sides of my house. I added timpani to the organ part. Then the drills started eating into the shingles. I had the sopranos drill a high G sharp for twenty measures. One of the carpenters dropped a plate of glass. I added cymbals.

The phone rang as I was still casting tenors into the lake of fire: Fox calling to apologize. "Hello."

"Hi, baby." It was Martin. Served me right.

"What's up?"

"When would you like to leave for California? Is Sunday or Monday better for you? Paloma's making reservations now."

"Are you kidding, Flappy? How can I go to California with these Flintstones destroying the house?"

"Gerald will keep an eye on them. That's his job."

Give up, Eva, said Chuck. *He's not going to call you.* "Sunday."

"Good, that way we can fly out with Dueser."

"Make that Monday."

"That way we can fly out with Paloma."

"For Christ's sake, Martin! I didn't know you were running a chaperone service!"

From the outburst Martin inferred that I had my heart set on a romantic San Francisco holiday. Nothing could be further from the truth, of course. The purpose of this journey was to prove to my husband that we were totally incompatible. If the man had any sense at all, he'd throw me out within the week, marry his secretary, and live happily ever after. "I have an idea," he said. "I'll put Paloma and Dueser together on Monday and we'll fly out Sunday."

"She's not going to like that," I said.

"Part of the job," Martin replied. "She'll do it."

My husband was either very callous or very naive. *Or a very fine actor,* Chuck added. Fine! Fine! The sooner this farce ended, the better!

"What farce, Eva?" Martin asked.

"I thought we were talking about airplanes."

Martin cleared his throat. He often does that instead of biting his tongue. "Are we agreed, then," he finally said, "we're flying to California from Boston, together, in an airplane, this Sunday afternoon at four? Tell me if I am confusing you."

An idiot cannot confuse a moron, Chuck said, pausing between words. "Uhhh-uhhh."

"Silly girl," my husband sighed. "What am I going to do with you." He hung up before I could offer any concrete suggestions.

Now that the prologue had backfired completely, I returned to *Bedlam's End.* It needed a bassoon part for some of the plagues. As I was working that in, Percival knocked on the door.

"Come in."

He was carrying the pitcher of lemonade, a bowl of grapes, and some leftover tortellini salad on one of Martin's rare sterling trays. "I thought you might be needing a little refreshment," Percival said. "You've been in here for hours." Martin's architect had also happened to bring along two glasses, two plates, and two forks.

"Have a seat," I said, pouring one and a half glasses of lemonade. "Where's the team?"

"Out to lunch. Eva! My God! What are you doing?!"

"Quiet, Percival, I'm treating a headache."

"My dear girl! That's quite a bomb! Have you been sitting in here by yourself drinking those all morning?"

"I have been composing grand and invigorating hymns all morning." I looked at my lemonade: this was about the color Chuck's had been. "To the greenhouse," I toasted.

Percival anxiously raised his glass. "To your health." He forked a tortellini. "Eat this! Right away! I insist!"

"I'm not hungry." I sloshed some more lemonade past my tonsils. It tasted like paint thinner. Perhaps a grape would remedy matters. I delicately plucked one from the crystal bowl, brought it to my mouth, then dropped it. Both Percival and I watched it roll under the leather armchair as if it were the clinching birdie of the Masters Tournament. My raw throat bleated for first aid but I didn't dare try another grape; those fuckers were alive. "On second thought, I might have one of those tortellini, Percival," I said.

Percival transported two to my mouth, shadowing his fork with a napkin as if the tortellini walked a flying trapeze. I managed to bite the fork.

"I'm so sorry!" he cried.

"Forget it," I said, running a finger along my front teeth. "It wasn't your fault." Time for another dose of lemonade. I wondered how much more I would have to gag down before life mended itself.

"Eva, I think you should go to bed," Percival said. "You don't look at all well."

"I just got out of bed," I replied. "I do NOT want to go back to bed." This infernal lemonade had stimulated the flammable oils of one gland too many; lying down would just ignite the whole trough. Damn! Had Fox had the breeding to keep his cock on ice, I would be discussing Charles Wesley, greenhouses, and the two hymns I had just completed that morning. Instead, here I sat with strep throat, a raucous headache, a *Bedlam's End* that would better serve humanity as a placemat, and a sharp curiosity concerning the existence, girth, and duration of Percival's erections.

"Let's take a walk, then," Percival suggested. " Enough of this stuffy room! Let's get some sunshine."

"I hate sunshine."

"Are you a vampire?"

"Of course I am." I sucked blood out of marriages.

"Then we'll go to the basement. I'll show you where your gym is going to go." Percival was determined to get me away from that lemonade.

Grasping my arm, he accompanied me to the kitchen, hesitating to let me anywhere near the deck. "I'm all right, Percival," I finally told him, disengaging my arm, "and I have health insurance."

I leaned out the hole in my kitchen wall. Suddenly the house lurched, nearly tossing me into a web of steel girders.

"Eva!" Percival squawked, grabbing my skirt. "Get

away from there! You are in no condition to go leaning out of windows!"

"This is not a window."

"Don't argue with me, my dear girl! Your husband would never forgive me if I let you fall out!"

"Martin is a very forgiving man." That's what drove me mad. I sat at the kitchen table; Percival had set up his Parcheesi board again. "Perce, would you mind getting me a roll or something that doesn't make a mess? I'm starving." He brought over a bag of pretzels. "That's what I had for dinner last night." I pushed the bag away.

"Pretzels? At the Red Lion Inn?"

I got up from the table. Certain strategic areas of my brain were no longer functioning; I could not remember where I had told Martin I had slept last night. It was not the Red Lion Inn, though. "Maybe I should take a nap," I said. *Maybe you should come to Nizor's Loony Bin*, beckoned Chuck, *Dr. Chubb could do great things for you*. "Fuck Dr. Chubb!" I shouted. "He's a lunatic himself!"

Percival was watching me very carefully. "I think I had better call Martin."

"Are you crazy? Don't you dare call Martin!" I wanted to crumple to the floor and cry and above all confess everything to Percival. I think he had been divorced once or twice. Then I remembered Ruth mentioning that both of Percival's wives had run off with other men. "Promise me you won't call Martin," I said calmly. "This is between you and me."

"I promise," Percival answered, "but I am most worried about you, Eva."

"Don't be silly." I went upstairs and put my blue kimono on. It was two in the afternoon of a beautiful summer day. I drew all the drapes and sat in a chaise longue looking at my legs. Three great hymn tunes bucked across my mind like wild turkeys; I had no ink with which to shoot them before they disappeared forever. I wondered if Chuck would turn Nizor's Boozer Clinic into a monastery before they excommunicated her. I wondered how many Italian women would run their slim manicured hands over Fox's back before I saw him again.

Damn it! Why wasn't I a man? Then I'd be at the Y

lambasting a punching bag or dictating furiously to a secretary or, most probably, trying to lay somebody else. But no, not me! I preferred to sit in a darkened bedroom and develop gangrene! *So get up and start fighting*, said Chuck. "In a minute," I replied. I had to let the poison advance a little more. Then my recovery would be more of a challenge.

How very ironic that I had learned nothing of the art of self-preservation in the ten years I had been immobilized. Somewhere between that first rape hold and this chaise longue, a weak link had let go, and I had better figure out right now what it was, else I'd be rotting in darkened bedrooms for the rest of my life. I returned to the first Saturday morning I had met Fox. I had sparred so well; he had gotten nowhere. Even the first time he had invaded my house, I had suffered no more than a few hunger pangs; Fox had departed with the black eye. But something had happened between that episode and Saint Patrick's Day . . . something very insidious and destructive that had eaten away all my armor so that the slightest pea could penetrate it and kill me. *Simple*, Chuck solved. *You allowed yourself to fall in love with the guy.* "Wait a moment," I challenged. "How about your Buddy allowing Fox to cross my path in the first place?"

All things work together for the good of those who love the Lord, intoned Chuck. *Although with you it's problematic.*

"Anything you say, Reverend Jim Jones," I cried angrily. "Maybe you can tell me what's so 'good' about writer's block."

You're trying to punish yourself.

"For what? Walking into an ambush?"

Chuck frowned. *You call a six-foot Hercules with a soft voice and a steel cock an ambush? Try the Maginot line!*

I tapped my fingers nervously against the armrest. "All right, what do you suggest?"

Get rid of Fox.

I see. And like magic the Muse would return, my husband would become Superman, and I would suddenly want to live to a ripe old age. "You misunderstand," I said, " Fox has changed the basic DNA."

Chuck hesitated; biochemistry was never her forte. *You*

can't have him, she sighed. *Therefore you want him. If you could have him tomorrow, you'd want Martin back again.*

"Why would I want Martin back? Shit! All he's ever done is leave me alone."

Precisely what you wanted.

As usual, Chuck had everything backward. Never in my life have I been able to have a serious discussion with the woman. What the hell, I'd debate one more point she had all wrong. "I do not punish myself," I began. A knock on my door cut me off before I could finish telling Chuck that her Buddy did plenty of that already. "Is that you, Percival?"

This time he came in with a tea tray. "Are you alone, Eva?"

I frowned. "Are you missing a carpenter?"

"I thought I heard voices."

"I was talking with my mother."

"Oh! How's she doing?"

"She's hopelessly insane and her illness is hereditary."

Percival poured two cups of tea. "Tell me what's really wrong."

If I knew that, dad, I'd be sitting on the throne of God writing how-to books. "In twenty years I have composed nothing but shit."

"I don't believe that."

"Why not? You've never heard any of the shit I wrote."

"But I know you."

"You don't know me at all, Percival!" I drank some tea. It contained nothing but lemon. "Agghpf! Where'd you learn to make tea? Westminster Abbey?" I opened my nightstand drawer and found a silver flask of whiskey behind the crowbar.

"You are not putting that in your tea, Eva!" He took the flask away.

"I told you my mother's illness was hereditary," I said. "Give that back."

Instead Percival put it in his pocket. "I have not been able to sleep since Tuesday night," he said, his eyes beseeching me. "You've done something to me, Eva. I find myself thinking of you all the time."

"I don't believe what I'm hearing." *So tell him to stop,* said Chuck. "What brought this on, Percival? Are you trying to divert my attention?"

"Ah, I love to hear you say my name! How should I know what brought it on? You brought it on! It's marvellous! I haven't felt this young in years!"

"You mean you feel great?"

"I do mean that, Eva, truthfully."

I leaned back in the chair and closed my eyes. "It must be hereditary," I sighed.

"What's that? Madness?"

"Happiness." Jesus, I was tired; fear of insanity burns up a tremendous amount of energy. "I think I'll take a nap." For an hour Percival read to me from *The Collected Sermons of Cotton Mather.* I did not go to sleep.

Martin somehow got Paloma to fly out to California with Dueser on Monday, freeing us to leave the afternoon before. Waiting for Fox to call, I delayed our departure until the last possible moment; George the chauffeur had to violate every traffic law in the book to get us to the flight on time. Even as we boarded the plane I expected to be paged. As we flew over Yellowstone Park, half dreaming, I saw the stewardess approach with a note from Fox: she delivered it to the man behind me. I did not know the fellow at my side. All he could talk about was apartments and what a great time we were going to have in San Francisco.

"Eva, are you listening to me?"

"Eva, pet, what are you thinking about?"

"Eva, wake up, we're here."

With great foreboding I opened my eyes. We didn't need any earthquakes for this trip to disintegrate into total disaster; I should not have let Martin bamboozle me behind this seat belt with talk of wine, the Pacific Ocean, and the unspoken but crushing onus of wifely duty. I knew exactly why he wanted me to accompany him on this trip: San Francisco was not the town for a heterosexual male to roam solo. Believe me, Martin was looking out for his own bunhole, not his wife's encroaching insanity. If he cared about that, he'd buy an opera company.

For dinner we went to a steak house near Symphony Hall. I found myself checking my watch continually, calculating what time it was in Rome. "Let's have the sirloin for two," Martin said. "They do that very well here."

"Who ate the other half?" I asked.

Martin deafly read the wine list. The host had a responsibility to keep dinnertime conversation genial and entertaining. "How about a Château Montrose?"

"Sure," I sighed, wondering how a more conniving woman would behave in my shoes. It seemed almost cruel to be nice to Martin; then when I told him I was leaving him, it would be a much worse shock. On the other hand, only a half-breed bully would deliberately go around looking for fights. Even Chuck had never resorted to open baiting unless she suspected my father was reading the sports page three times through instead of twice. What the hell, until I could think of a good way to alienate Martin, I'd act like a civilized dinner companion. "So Flappy, what kind of an apartment are you interested in?"

"A nice one where you'd like to stay for six months."

"Six months? Christmas is in six months!" I had to make up my mind in six weeks. "I thought you'd be through by September."

"I could use a little break from Boston, Eva, to tell the truth."

"But you're never there! How can you be tired of it?"

Martin ate a snail. I should have ordered that instead of this chichi vegetable purée. "Guess I must be hitting my midlife crisis."

"Come on, Flappy, you're not even forty." This was not possible. Martin didn't fall apart. "What's the problem? Are you overworked? Bored? Frustrated? Impotent?"

"I haven't checked lately."

"I just said that for a joke! Forget it! You don't have to check!" I put my hand over Martin's; at once I saw Fox's gray eyes staring calmly at me. God, this folly had to stop. I took my hand away. "I guess I'm not much help, am I."

"I don't know what you are lately. You've not been yourself for a long time."

"Maybe I'm having a midlife crisis of my own," I suggested. "Shall we trade symptoms?"

"Why not trade cures instead."

"That's no fun at all, Flaps."

"Try me."

Here was the perfect opportunity I had been searching for. "Why don't we get divorced," I said. "That would solve everything."

The snail on Martin's fork paused in midair, dripping garlic sauce like a cracked radiator. "You're not serious," he laughed, mashing the snail between his teeth. I don't think this solution had ever occurred to Martin; the Weavers did lack a certain flair for tergiversation.

"Don't tell me you weren't thinking the same thing."

"Actually, pet," said Martin, "I was thinking we should have a few children."

I felt the blood drain from my face and stream all the way to Rome. "You're not serious," I laughed, but not as convincingly as Martin had.

"We're not getting any younger, Eva."

No, indeed. Life was finite, and each day I passed without Fox was one day less I'd have with him in the end: The Great Landlord was not prone to extending leases. "Why drag children into your midlife crisis, Flappy? They make everything ten times worse. I know that from personal experience."

"Eva, someday you've got to outgrow that mother of yours."

The waiter placed a charred and bleeding steak between us. "Would you like me to carve this, sir?"

"Yes," I blurted, desperately needing a few seconds to examine how this conversation had divagated from divorce to children to Chuck and then had crash landed, as always, on me. Any other female would have settled on two lawyers by now. The waiter disappeared. "Flappy, just because your mother tells you she'd like a few grandchildren is no reason to inflict twenty years of anxiety on me."

"My mother said nothing. Neither did my father. Your mother's been the squeaky wheel, actually."

Whoops, time to tack. "But you don't even know how to make a TV dinner."

"What does that have to do with anything?"

"I have never seen you run a vacuum. In fact, all you do around the house is chuck socks under the bed. I'm the guy who has to dig them out and pick the woobies off them."

Martin did not like the drift of his little trial heir balloon. He silently masticated a blackened pyramid of steak, pondering where to send up his next. "That's what nannies are for, Eva. I've been telling you to hire a maid since the day we were married."

"I don't like people wandering all over the house. They kill my concentration. I'd always have to check they're not screwing in the wine cellar or something."

"That's ridiculous and you know it."

"Martin," I sighed, "you will never understand me. I must have absolute silence when I'm composing. I don't even like the mailman tramping on the porch. A baby would be screaming day and night. Then I'd have to check that the nanny wasn't sticking diapers pins in the kid's buns by mistake. Then I'd have to keep the house pristine for the daily visits of doting grandmothers. And then, after all that trouble, the kid would turn out to be a juvenile delinquent and go to hell."

"Just like you, eh?"

"Precisely."

We finished the steak in silence. "All right, darling," Martin said finally. "Promise me you'll think about it."

"Think about what? A divorce?"

"Nannies."

I'd think about it, all right. I knew a great nanny who was on his way to Rome. "Okay." Now I felt bad again. My husband had done nothing to deserve this. *Except marry you*, Chuck noted. "Martin," I despaired, "why did you marry me? That was a huge mistake."

Shaking his head, smiling, Martin pushed his plate aside. "That was the best thing I ever did," he corrected. "You're my Little Miss Sunshine."

I paid The Great Toll Collector every last token in my possession and still I was not allowed to pass. Jesus Christ! Was Fox ultimately going to cost me everything? *Get rid of Fox*, Chuck repeated for the millionth time. The woman was Satan. "But we don't even act married, Flappy," I said. "We never see each other, all we ever talk about is your company, we have no social life, we're never going to have any kids, and on top of everything, I'm not so sure I like you anymore."

Martin kissed my hand; the moment his lips touched my flesh, my pulse gelled: Fox. "Shit! I'm trying to be serious!" I snapped, pulling my hand away.

"Of course you are, darling," my husband said. "That's what's so charming."

Chuck cackled hideously. I swallowed half a glass of wine, wondering how I could boomerang Martin's words back at him and knock him out. Pfuii, impossible. "I still don't understand why you married me, Flappy," I insisted. "You need me like a hole in the head."

"I need you all right," Martin said. "I love you."

"That's riDICulous," I almost shouted.

For the first time in many months, Martin looked me in the eye. He knew everything, I swear it; but he was going to wait it out, like Job. I would eventually rebound, like a blue-chip stock temporarily mismanaged. "Why are you so unhappy, Eva? Am I doing something wrong? Are you sorry you married me?"

I stared at the tablecloth; all the gravy stains had spattered my side of the table, as usual. "No, baby. You're doing fine." It just wasn't enough anymore. God damn it! It used to be enough! I sighed, deathly tired. "Could you get along without me, Flappy?"

Martin's face had not looked this ashen since his favorite accountant had committed suicide. I felt sick; why was I planting these seeds of doubt in the poor man's brain? Why couldn't I just tell him the truth and get it over with? Oh God! I was the most deceitful scumbag of a wife in history!

"I would not even want to try," Martin said very quietly.

Forget Fox! He was just a passing meteorite! I rubbed my forehead. "I'll be all right, Martin," I choked, lunging clumsily for the Weaver Method. "It's just stress and perhaps overwork. Please bear with me."

My husband looked suspiciously at me; he was not used

to hearing me talk like his mother. "What's really the matter, Eva?" he asked. "Tell me."

Two suntanned yuppies walked past the table, halted and did a double-take. "What a fantastic surprise! Look who's here, Ivan."

At once my husband stood up, introduced me to Ivan and perhaps Lucinda, then invited them to stay for a drink. Instantly these chatterboxes completely shredded my meticulously crocheted web of marital intrigue and suspense. Martin prattled about Dueser, our great apartment search, lovely San Francisco, and the comparative degustation of Atlantic and Pacific salmon. Then he ordered another round, neutralizing our prior conversation for good. Shit, now I understood why Chuck and Robert maintained such a hectic social schedule.

"You're an absolute delight," Ivan said, turning to me. His hairdo would put a topiary shrub to shame. "Where have you been hiding your wife, Martin?"

"Oh, here and there," my husband replied, fondly tweaking my cheek. I almost bit his hand. "She's my best-kept secret."

"And all this time we thought you were the most eligible bachelor in California," said Ivan's eligible bachelorette. If the woman had once unglued her eyes from my jewelry, I might have taken her aside and told her to wait a while.

"I don't often have a chance to accompany my husband on his business trips," I said. Ruth Weaver herself could not have delivered these lines with more conviction.

"Is that so? What do you do?"

"I write hymns."

"Hymns!" An immediate pall smothered the table, as if I had a microphone stashed in my nose.

You've really made a great name for Yourself, haven't You, I prayed.

Martin leapt to the breach. "Eva composes all kinds of wonderful tunes," he said. "But she'll only admit to the hymns."

"Have you done any movie music?" asked Ivan. He felt safe enough to light a cigarette now.

"None that you would see." Orville had conned me into three proselytizing soundtracks for the Mormons.

"Porno?" Lucinda gushed.

"Enough questions," Martin interjected. "My wife is on vacation."

Now Ivan was inspecting my jewelry. "How long will you be staying?"

I looked at Martin. "Two days."

"My God! That's way too short!" Ivan said, then blushed. "Excuse me, Eva, I didn't mean to swear."

"Sure you did."

"Darling," Martin cautioned, signalling for the bill: his cronies had outlived their usefulness. After a few more insincere platitudes, Ivan & Co. departed.

"Where'd you meet those two?" I asked.

"Ivan works for Rodotron." Martin signed the check.

"She likes you."

Martin pulled back my chair. "She's got good taste."

And an empty jewelry box. We left the restaurant without running into any more women with good taste. Martin said not one word in the taxicab nor the elevator. He took a long hot shower, indicative of great mental concentration. I shut my light off, trying to fall asleep by the time Martin emerged from the bathroom. No chance: mattresses and showers haunted me these days.

Still saying nothing, Martin slid into bed and put his arms around me. Fox pirouetted across the sheets and was gone. My left leg screamed to stretch but I ignored it: one false move would precipitate further verbal dissection or, worse, sexual activity. *You louse,* Chuck cursed, *You shame me.* One cold tear rolled out of the corner of each eye and rapidly plopped to Martin's arm. Still I didn't move.

Martin let the tears roll onto the pillowcase. "Tell me what's wrong," he finally whispered.

I took a deep breath as many tears sluiced down my cheeks. "I'm sorry, Flappy," I said, "I just have to get away from you for a while."

"How long is that?" No questions asked: never any questions asked. My God! No wonder the Puritans could describe Hell so graphically!

"I don't know."

Martin said nothing. His gentle, even breath warmed the back of my neck; my tears still ran cold.

*   *   *

The next evening I was back in my own kitchen staring at the new door that led to the new greenhouse Percival had built for Martin. I had no desire to walk through it; in fact, its very existence depressed me. Field Marshall Noonan and a platoon of loutish carpenters would begin transmogrifying the basement into a gym the moment their greenhouse was finished. God alone knew how long they would be disrupting the dust down there; my murky presence above would certainly not spur Percival on to any speed records. Shit, I should not have returned to this arena. I should have sought sanctuary in New York, or the Everglades, or Pluto.

I called Richard Weintraub. When I don't hear from him for several weeks, that means he's found the love of his life again.

"Hello?"

"How is she, Romeo?"

"Eva!" Richard covered the phone with his hand and attempted to pacify a sleepy voice at his side. I shook my head; not one in fifty has ever believed that Richard was talking with his cousin. "How's everything?"

"Upside down, bambino."

"Is that unusual?"

"My life is ruined."

Richard paused, weighing his chances of matrimony with me against those of the female reclining next to him. "Hey! That's great news!"

"You stupid moron, if you can't talk, why didn't you just say I had a wrong number? I'll call you back tomorrow."

"Tomorrow, great! Good luck! Say hi to Aunt Lily for me."

"Blow Aunt Lily out your ass." I hung up. Christ! What did Richard see in these neurotic bitches? *His mother*, Chuck said.

I had half a mind to call Nizor's Insane Asylum and demand to speak with Chuck Hathaway. But it was almost midnight. I called Lionel instead.

"Hello, you gorgeous black bouquet, I know where you'd like to bury your nose."

"Hi, Thread."

"Who's this?! Eva? How DARE you!"

"Come on, Petunia, why don't you look before you shift into reverse."

"Why don't you call me at a decent hour like everyone else?" Lionel shrieked. "Only my lovers call me this late and you know it."

I said nothing. Lionel added two and two.

"What's the matter, sugar? Is that big bad karate chopper breaking your heart? Don't cry now. Uncle Lionel will solve everything. Tell me."

"I just left Martin in San Francisco," I sniffed.

"Did you have a fight?"

"We never have fights, we just have these little farts."

"So why'd you come home? Frisco is a GREAT town."

"Not without Fox."

"And where is this giant behemoth at the present moment?"

"I don't know. Don't call him that."

"Eva, baby, this man is ruining your life."

"I know he is! That's why I'm calling you!"

Lionel sighed. "My dear girl, there is something you must understand. Husbands are for one thing and lovers are for another. You must not mix them up."

"Why can't I have the same man for both?"

"Because that's not how it works! You want to throw Martin into the garbage, then find out this karate chopper doesn't know shit about municipal bonds? Be serious! How can you marry a foghorn who's done nothing but screw you blind? And who says he wants to marry you, anyway? Has he proposed on hand and knee?"

"Not exactly."

"Of course he hasn't! Why wreck a great romance?"

This was making me positively ill. "Now I can't write."

"Eva, darling, didn't I warn you about this MONTHS ago?"

"Stop gloating and help me."

"Go to the study and get a pencil. Forget about that stupid karate chopper. Forget about that nebbish of a husband. Think about the great hymns you're going to write and all the money you're going to make without either of them.''

"What do you mean, without either of them? You've just been trying to talk me into keeping both of them.''

"Will you stop these stupid semantics? I'm trying to help you.''

"I'm going to leave Martin.''

"Don't be an ass. You'd never write another hymn in your life.''

"I've written enough hymns.''

"You haven't made enough money.''

Shit, always back to economics. Lionel and I would have been much better off as the children of coal miners. "I'm going to bed.''

"No you're NOT, you bitch! You're going into your little room and start writing a hymn! I'm going to call you in two hours and it had better be done! Good-bye!''

What a stupid conversation. I went to the refrigerator, looking for wine. Not a drop. I went to the bar and found a bottle of port. The phone rang. I died and quickly resurrected in case it was Fox.

"Hello.''

"Where are you, you stupid ass, in the den pouring yourself a drink?''

I slammed the phone down and put the port back. Then I went to my study and pulled out some paper. Why was I getting so agitated about two men who never called me? Why hadn't I married Lionel, for Christ's sake? Incest, said Chuck. That gave me the idea for a hymn entitled *Other Brother*, tenors and bass only. It would be very popular around Thanksgiving and Christmas time, when distaff attendance at choir rehearsal declined drastically. Every time I felt Fox or Martin edging into my mind, I swept them out with a bold image of Lionel in his drum major's uniform; with each clearance *Other Brother* focused itself more sharply. My God, life would be easy without these two gentlemen yanking me in half! Why hadn't the thought occurred to me months before? *Too easy*, Chuck said disgustedly.

At two o'clock Lionel called. "It's just about finished,'' I reported, "and I'm dedicating it to you.''

"Thanks, doll. What's it called?"

"Other Brother."

"Does that mean something homosexual?"

"How should I know? I only scribble dots on the paper."

"I'm going to call you tomorrow," Lionel said. "Promise me you won't hit the bottle before noon."

"Why not?"

"Because I might not wake up before then."

Evidently the Black Bouquet was there. "I think I deserve a nightcap," I said.

"NO! You are OFF that poison! You already look forty years old! Take a bubble bath and go to sleep!" Lionel hung up.

After setting the alarm, I went upstairs and looked in the mirror. Forty? Pfuiii! Try fifty! I fished my little silver flask from its cubbyhole. Percival had emptied it. "Call me instead," instructed a little note. "Anytime, day or night." I soaked in the tub until three in the morning, and each time I thought about life without Martin who had wed then forgotten me, without Fox who had never even asked me to marry him but expected me to relinquish the man who had, a new tune scampered like a prairie dog across my sandy brain. I had not felt this free or this young in ten years.

Enough tolls? I asked, *May I pass?* There was no answer.

Percival Noonan dropped *Heart Ablaze* onto the kitchen table. "Eva, my dear girl! I thought I was seeing a ghost! What are you doing home?"

"I'm not sure." I peeped out the hole in the kitchen wall. All five carpenters were eating submarine sandwiches under the maple tree. "How's the greenhouse doing?"

"We should be finishing up today." Percival looked at me. "This is quite a surprise. Is everything all right?"

"Thank you for the delightful note on my flask upstairs," I responded. "That was certainly thoughtful of you."

"Oh dear," said Percival, "you are still under the weather."

"On the contrary," I corrected, tying my shoelaces,

"the weather is perfect. Hold the fort for me, will you?" I ran across the BU Bridge over to Cambridge and past Fox's house. All his windows were shut. I paused a moment on the sidewalk, hating every loose shingle and that creaky, sun-dulled porch. How dare the inhabitant of such a wreck give me an ultimatum! I chuckled and ran home.

"Hi, Richard," I called presently. "It's me again."

"Sorry I couldn't talk. It was our last night together for three weeks."

"I understand all too well, my dear boy. What's her name?"

"Brasilia."

"What's her first name?"

"Not funny, Eva. She's a lovely individual."

Ho hum. "Hey! How are my covers doing?"

"Come down and see for yourself. Or should I come to Boston? Is Martin home?"

"Why don't we swap houses for a month?"

Richard doesn't even like to swap pencils. "You're awfully snappy this morning."

"That's right. I'm turning over a new leaf. No more men. It's great."

"May I ask why you're calling me, then?"

The paper houses of three psychiatrists tottered precariously on the tip of my tongue. "Stop this, Richard! What are you doing for dinner tonight?"

"Against my better judgment, I guess I'm taking you out."

"Why, thank you. How about that Indian joint around the block?"

"That's too hot for me."

"How about the Dairy Queen?"

"You need a whipping."

"I just got a whipping, baby."

"Is that so? Who finally gave it to you? Martin?"

"Hoo!" I burst into manic laughter. "Not quite! Martin was just the whip."

"What does that mean?"

"Tell you at dinner."

"You sound strange. Where is he?"

"California." Percival knocked on the door of the study.

"Whoops, the architect's here. See you around seven? Good." I hung up. "Come in!" My throat didn't like that shouting. It began to molt.

Percival brought in a glass of iced tea. "Thirsty?"

"That's very nice of you," I said softly, downing the entire glass.

Percival sat in the green leather chair across from my desk and watched me sharpen a few pencils. It reminded me very much of the way Martin sometimes sat and looked at me. "I have a summer home on the Cape," he said. "You are welcome to use it any time."

I put the pencils down. "With or without you in it?"

"Either way."

Ah, why weren't all men sixty years old? I sharpened each of my pencils over again, trying to get hold of myself: one simple act of charity had crippled the great righteous anger which was supposed to sustain me for the rest of my life. "Thank you, Percival," I said slowly, "but I couldn't possibly."

"The offer stands nevertheless." Percival got up to leave. "Hope springs eternal."

"What makes you say that?"

"You're alive, aren't you?"

Percival had it all backwards. The only hope was that the other guy was dead, not alive. "I'm afraid so."

"Eva! Don't talk like that! I won't hear it!" Percival walked to the doorway, turned, and looked at me as I assiduously honed another inch off all my pencils. Then he left, shutting the door very quietly: the classic WASP exit.

At two, as I was beginning to explore the dowel potential of pencil stubs, Lionel called. "Are you working?" he said.

"Of course I'm working."

"It's about time! What's the title of this one?"

"Stubby Angel."

"Are you kidding? How disGUSTing!"

"I'm dedicating it to Pooh."

"Jesus Christ, is this the thanks we get for keeping you sober and productive?"

"What would you prefer? Royalties?"

"I'd love another cakewalk."

"Go back to bed." I hung up, looked at my watch: time to hit the road. I packed a suitcase and went to the kitchen. "Percival?" I called into the hole in the wall.

He emerged wearing a pith helmet. "Yes?"

"I'm going to New York for a few days."

Percival walked me to the car. "What should I tell Martin if he calls?"

"Tell him what a lovely greenhouse you're building him."

"And when he asks for you?"

"Tell him I'm out buying fertilizer." Come on, if Percival picked up the phone, then I wasn't at home and Martin would not ask for me. In a week, if curiosity began eroding his appetite, he'd have Paloma call. The divorce lawyers must understand that he was just trying to follow my instructions and stay away from me for a while.

Several hours later I rang Richard's doorbell. "Hi there, blondie, where'd you get that tan?"

"What's the matter with it?" Richard asked.

"Nothing! It's very sexy."

"Are you kidding?"

"Now I am."

He took my suitcase. "Come on upstairs."

I had never seen Richard's apartment so clean. He had acquired a new sofa and a huge rug from one of Hong Kong's lesser masters. Lo and behold, a portable dishwasher had displaced the garbage can in the corner of his kitchen. "Whoever she is," I said, taking a gin-and-tonic, "marry her."

"Why do you say that?" Richard asked.

"Who dynamited your apartment?"

"Brasilia. She runs a housecleaning service."

"Where did you meet her? Sunday morning at the Ethical Culture Society?"

"Someone sent me an anonymous gift certificate." Richard halved a cracker and applied an even tablespoon of liptauer cheese to its surface. "Was it you?"

"I only send gift certificates to the Christian book club." I fanned my face with a Bloomingdale's catalog. "It was probably your downstairs neighbor."

"Maybe it was my mother."

"Very doubtful." Richard's mother thinks her son's bellybutton lint should be bronzed. "Your rabbi? Your shrink? Not the fat one who told you to date Chinese girls, the other guy."

"Anyway." Richard continued, "then I bought the carpets. Brasilia's brother runs a furniture store in the Bronx."

"Does her father sell used cars?"

"Eva! You're jealous."

"I'm trying to save your life, peabrain." Of course I was jealous. Richard's entire artistic inspiration derived from his thwarted desire for me. Once that was rechanneled into dustbrooms and dingle balls, he'd have no current left for esoteric hymn covers. "What does she look like?"

"She's not you, if that's what you mean."

"What do you find so attractive about her?"

"She likes me. I find that extremely attractive."

"So what? I like you, too." Much better than I liked Martin or Fox, in fact.

"Let's not get started on this again, Eva." Richard finished his buttermilk. "Ready for dinner?"

"Are we going to work on covers now or later?"

"Later. How many covers are you talking about? Orville's sent me nothing for two months."

"That's because I haven't sent Orville anything for two months. I know you've got a few marches lying around, plus a kiddie hymn. I just did a gay offertory."

"And how am I supposed to illustrate that?"

"You'll think of something." I put my glass down. "Indian?"

"Italian."

At the restaurant Richard immediately ordered a large bottle of soave. "I feel like getting drunk tonight."

"What for?"

"There's a full moon and it's hot." Plus we were both playing hooky. This was more perilous than the A train after midnight. *Talk about the weather and Martin,* Chuck urged. "So tell me about this creature," I said. "Is she Jewish?"

"Catholic."

"What will your mother have to say about her son diluting the species?"

"What can she say? She's the one who keeps telling me to get married."

"That'll teach her." I finished my soup. "How old is your friend?"

"Your age."

"And she's never been married?" Richard was headed for catastrophe. "How is she in bed?"

He hesitated a bit too long. "She's learning."

Of course! You had to teach Catholics everything! This time I poured the wine. "Does she like your drawings?"

"She thinks they're cute."

"Cute?" The syllable hung like an icicle from my nose as the waiter slid a plate of Veal Piccata in front of me. "You'd better start telling me what's great about her, baby," I said. "Right now."

Richard sniffed his scallops. "She makes terrific lasagna." He picked up his fork. "She takes good care of me. I'm comfortable with her."

I think we had already had this conversation, with roles reversed, perhaps five years ago, in a Cuban restaurant. "You've given up, haven't you, you stupid schmuck."

"I've adjusted myself to certain facts of life."

"You are going to regret this."

"Hey! Don't tell me what I'm going to regret! I'm tired of cruising the lingerie counter at Bloomingdale's looking for Helen of Troy. This grand-passion shit is a figment of some scriptwriter's imagination." Richard ordered another bottle of wine. "Who the hell wants to marry a lover? I'd be dead in three months. What's so bad about marrying for companionship?"

"It's a rather drastic method of meeting Helen of Troy."

"I don't understand."

"You won't until you're married."

We ate glumly of magnificent food. "Wine?" Richard asked.

"No thanks." Why hadn't I married Richard? He was the only man who appreciated me for what I really was, a hymnist, not a wife, not a lover, none of this other crap rotten with emotions and impossible expectations. "How long have we known each other?" I asked.

"About ten years."

I imagined sitting ten years from now at a table with Fox, my friend. It was not possible. A sharp stone pierced my heart and was gone, transformed into a meteor. "How did we last so long?"

You didn't get married, Chuck scoffed.

Richard reached across the table and touched my hand, dragging his fingers slowly across my knuckles. The gesture aroused many memories. "Capricorns are stubborn bastards," he said. His thumb slid slowly into my palm; my mouth went dry. "Let's go." He got the bill, inspected it cursorily, and for once did not wait for change: for sixty cents, Richard would not risk the loss of a serendipitous fling down Memory Lane.

The night had turned damp and oppressive as a laundromat. Draping long Modigliani shadows on the orange-lit sidewalks, we walked three blocks back to Richard's apartment, edging carefully around a drunk dozing on his stoop. The downstairs neighbors, without air conditioning, screamed at each other as a Miller Lite Beer commercial regaled sixty million cooler Americans. Richard opened four separate locks and walked immediately to his air conditioner.

"Sit there," he said, "in two minutes you'll want a sweater."

"In two minutes I'll want a highball."

"How about a decaf?"

"A decaffeinated highball?"

Richard put a late Beethoven quartet on his stereo, turned all but one light in the corner off, and lay down on his couch looking at me. "Why don't you come over here?"

"You'll have to turn the music off."

Richard let the quartet finish. We sat in silence as another, different quartet, this one composed of two dogs and two drunks, sang the repertory of Manhattan in July. "You know, Eva—" Richard started.

"—Don't say it." I turned the air conditioner to its lowest setting and took a shower. When I came out,

Richard had cranked his bed out of the wall. It flips up and down like those old-time ironing boards. I lay down on the left side; Richard has always preferred to sleep closest to the bathroom.

He brushed his teeth, finished the crossword he had begun that morning on the toilet, and took a brief shower. As always, he gargled with some witches' brew his mother procured from her brother the pharmacist. By the time he leaned gently into the bed, I had almost forgotten about him.

"Are you asleep?" he asked, nestling into me. Living flesh at once perturbed the mists of several sinuous dreams.

"Boxer shorts?" I murmured, feeling behind me. Wait and see, Brasilia would have him in long johns and a sleeping cap by Christmas. The Pope had not yet outlawed these. "It feels odd to be here again."

Richard's hand followed the rise and fall of my hips as closely as an F-111 over the Scottish countryside. "Not to me."

"What would your dear Brasilia say about that?"

Richard's hand paused. "She's not quite my wife." His hand continued. "Did I give you this nightgown?"

"In Paris."

"Do you still wear it?"

"I wear it all the time."

"You mean Martin sees it?" Richard croaked. "That's treason."

"Stop it," I said. "The natives are not restless." I was very drowsy now.

"Don't go to sleep, Eva," Richard whispered in my ear. "God knows when I'm going to get you back in this bed again."

I whipped my last reserves into the field, instructing them to shoot anything that moved. "I'm not sure I should be here."

"Why not? Because you're married?"

"Something like that."

"Don't you miss me at all?"

"I miss you, Richard," I said. "I miss lots of things." Freedom, hope, the will to survive . . .

Four tires skidded to a halt on the street directly beneath

Richard's window. "Move, asshole!" someone yelled, then blasted off.

I finally turned towards him. The whites of Richard's eyes opalesced in the gloom; I wondered if gray irises were dominant or recessive. "Don't get married, Richard. It kills everything."

"You want me to die a bachelor? Childless? Forgotten?"

"Don't forget bald."

"Tsk." Richard rolled on his back and watched the reflection of passing headlights traverse his ceiling. "I'm tired of being single."

Ah, marriage, mighty fortress only to those who had never been inside! I was twice as single now as I had been five years ago! "Richard," I said, rolling on top of him, "go ahead and marry her. We'll continue this discussion on your first anniversary."

"With you on top of me?"

"Don't tell me she's never been on top."

"It makes her nervous. Perforated kidneys or something."

"Tell her you'll only go in halfway."

"I tell her that already and she's on the bottom."

Richard put two hands on my hips and shifted them an inch forward. Jesus Christ! Why were two half-crocked, half-naked, middle-aged morons talking about a prudish cleaning lady? "Hey," I said, spreading my fingers over his chest, "shut up." I bent over and kissed him; once again, as he would for the rest of my life, Fox lasered through me.

Richard has always had a most intense, oral way of making love. I'm not sure whether it's because he's Jewish, because he's the son of a dentist, or because he's afraid of straining his draftsman's hands on rough terrain. No complaints: it's a great mouth. Unfortunately, since last meeting mine, Richard's tongue had had fifty drill sergeants commandeering it into fifty different ditches; now it seemed to have lost all sense of direction. Two hundred subsequent visits to the psychiatrist had not turned up any compasses; hell, they hadn't even weaned him of that revolting mouthwash.

"What's the matter," I asked, "got an itch?" Richard was rubbing his balls against my kneecaps. Weimaraners with active bladders had done the same.

"Don't you like that?"

"Try another trick closer to home plate."

Richard reached under his pillow and got a feather. "Don't move."

"Don't you dare tickle me with that filthy thing."

"Come on, Eva, it's great."

"Put that away and screw like a man."

Richard tried first a back rub, then a front rub. It was no use. Neither of us could get very excited. "I suggest," I said after three unsuccessful rubbery assaults, "we go to sleep."

"I'm impotent," he moaned. "This is a catastrophe."

"Will you stop it. You're just not used to a straight shot." Neither was I, with men I didn't love.

"What do you think is the matter? I can't believe this! Dr. Augsburg and I have spent two years analyzing my sexual problems."

"Since when have you had sexual problems, Richard?"

"Since you left."

That was five years ago. I felt terrible. *You'll feel even worse when the same thing happens to you,* Chuck said. "Sorry," I said.

"It wasn't your fault." Richard pulled the sheet up to his chin. "Yes it was." He laughed a little. "It's finally happened! I can't believe it! With you, of all people!"

"Don't be ridiculous," I said. "You've been drinking lousy wine, you've had a lousy day, you're about to marry your putzfrau, and you're not used to operating without a traffic cop."

"Are you disappointed?"

I couldn't care less! "Of course not."

"We can try again in a few hours."

"Don't press your luck. Just joking! Go to sleep!"

For an hour or so, I collapsed like a drug addict; then an undefined street noise woke me. Richard's apartment was hot and he was snoring. I didn't want him touching me. *A little late for that now, isn't it,* Chuck observed. I sighed; if Richard woke up with the tiniest nodule of an erection, I would be obliged to restore his self-esteem. Shit, what were six inches between friends? I owed him anyway:

Richard had slowly and singlehandedly nursed me back to life after the first Mr. Catastrophe.

Richard rolled in his sleep; my abdomen tensed until his snores resumed. Very quietly I edged out of bed and got a glass of water from the kitchen. I was unnaturally awake. For a long time, I sat at that tiny kitchen table listening to the shifting soloists of the night, all restless, all craving a different theater. I crept over to Richard's drawing table, lifted some paper, and returned to the kitchen, there to lure a memento or two from my insomnia. For some time an organ postlude had been hibernating deep in the mud; I'd prod it, testing the season.

The first eight measures flew out of my pen. Then the pen inexplicably became allergic to paper. Shit! I started another piece, this one a duet for sopranos; every other choir loft in the country contains two prima donnas vying eternally for the utmost crag from which to obliterate the enemy. This time they would be singing about divine love as they let the fur fly. *You're cruel,* said Chuck. "Shut up," I said, scratching in another few lines above high G. "This is financing your vacation at the nuthouse." The duet shattered about halfway through, so I switched to a juvenile anthem with guitar accompaniment. *Why aren't you doing anything for tenors?* Chuck asked. "Don't like 'em," I replied. "Leave me alone."

"Eva," Richard said, "what are you doing?"

"Jesus Christ! You scared the shit out of me!"

Richard came into the kitchen. He had put Brasilia's boxer shorts back on. "It's five o'clock."

"Take that stupid underwear off and go back to bed."

Instead Richard padded behind my chair and looked at the mess I had made of his good drawing paper. "Do you always write hymns in the nude?" he asked.

"Do you mind? It's a hot night. You were the one who removed my nightgown, if I remember correctly."

"Whatcha got there?"

"This is an organ solo. You can draw a fancy cross for that one. Here's a duet for two sopranos. I'm thinking of lightning and two pigs or something. This here is a guitar number about chastity. Maybe you can do a cowboy in boxer shorts."

"Have you lost your mind?"

"What are you talking about? These are great ideas, Richard."

"For 'Looney Tunes,' maybe, not Orville."

"Will you go back to bed? You've disrupted my entire train of thought."

Richard went to the refrigerator. "How about some orange juice."

"I'd love a screwdriver."

"You're getting orange juice." Richard placed a glass on the soprano duet. "Come back to bed."

I glanced up. Richard's boxer shorts did not fit him very well now. "You sure know how to test a friendship, don't you?"

"What's the matter? Am I ugly? Dirty? Too hairy?"

I put the pen down; that guitar number shat anyway. "You really want to sleep with me, don't you."

"Of course I do, damn it!"

"Quiet, you'll startle your hard-on." It was running for cover already. I went to the bathroom, then back to bed; Richard had neatly folded down my corner of the sheets. I sat and looked at him; once upon a time that face had delighted me.

"No go, eh?" he said.

God, I needed a screwdriver! "Now is not a good time. Things are messed up."

"With Martin?"

"With everything."

"Sorry. Want to talk about it?"

"No." I lay down.

"Here, go to sleep. I won't bother you."

I closed my eyes and saw the Parthenon. Jesus Christ! How did one shut off these hellish faucets?

"Believe it or not," Richard murmured, "Martin is one of my heros."

What brought this masochism on? "That's absurd."

"But he is," Richard explained, quickening. "He's got class—you know? He could convince a toad that it needed a computer."

"But he really believes that."

"That's the point, Eva. He believes in something. Then he persuades everyone else and makes a fortune."

"He hasn't convinced me."

"Martin's no fool." Richard laughed obscurely.

"What is so amusing?"

"You women want everything. If the guy spends all day writing poetry, you want money instead. If he makes money. you want poetry. If he's in Califomia with computers, you want him home. If he's home, you want him back with his computers. That's why we two blew up, you know. You wanted everything."

"Wrong," I said. "I wanted nothing and you wanted me to want everything." Richard would repeat that verbatim to Dr. Augsburg, who would run ten thousand biopsies on it and finally recommend that his patient stop wearing boxer shorts to bed. "Plus your mother didn't want you hobnobbing with a *shiksa*."

"Don't sidetrack me," Richard continued, "I've spent a lot of time thinking about you and Martin, and particularly about what he's got that I haven't got."

"You've already mentioned class," I said disgustedly. "don't forget oyster forks."

"Are we having a serious discussion or are you going to be a brat? Cripes! If you weren't such a good composer I'd have nothing to do with you."

"You bought me dinner because I'm a good composer? Come on."

Richard's molars tested the laws of isometrics. "Can't you just shut up and listen instead of sabotaging every point I'm trying to make?"

"I'm trying to direct your meandering thought processes. And I don't want to talk about what a great guy Martin is. I don't want to talk about anything." I got out of bed and looked out the window. It was going to rain today.

"Have you ever sat down with Martin and a piece of paper and written out everything you'd like from each other?" Richard said after a while.

"Like a shopping list? That's obscene."

"How will you ever know why you're mad at him?"

Shit, I was mad at him for being born. "Who says I'm mad at him?"

"You're mad at something."

Yeah, I was irritated at a lifetime of hostility between a haughty brain and a mulish heart that had resulted in nothing but seven hundred hymns for the throats and ears of utter strangers. I was irritated at endlessly talking, talking, about the courses of rivers, as if they could be reversed by modulated speech. I was irritated at falling in love with powerful ghosts. "I'm mad at myself," I said, "and that is maddening." Across the street an old man was hanging his socks to dry on the fire escape. I stared at him until he looked at me, then I winked at him and came away from the window. I was also irritated with men of polite sensuality who could not stand in for one evening for their more hot-blooded kin.

I plopped on the bed. "Want to know why you can't screw anymore, you stupid schmuck? Because you prefer to exchange shopping lists with cleaning ladies and sit on little leather couches reciting your woes to hired ears. That's more sanitary than laying me, isn't it? After all, I'm married to your hero, you're hitching up with Mother Superior, and for one night, it's too dangerous dragging all those submarines out of the mothballs, right? Jesus, you're a coward, Richard. That's why we never got anywhere."

"I'm a coward, eh?" Richard retorted. "Let's talk about you flitting off into the countryside and getting married to your godfather, then moving into a monastery and illuminating manusripts for the rest of your life, then bitching that you miss bagels and Broadway. Why the hell should I screw you? You burned me once. You're not going to burn me twice. You call that cowardice? I call that intelligence."

"Where's my nightgown," I said. "I'm leaving."

Richard pulled me down and rolled on top of me in one deft move. "No you're not."

"Get off of me," I said. "I have no intention of sleeping with you."

"Like hell." Richard expertly shoehorned himself inside of me. Where had that erection come from? *Your imagination, maybe?* Chuck scoffed.

"Fox," I shouted, "God damn you!"

"Try wolf," Richard said, "and don't swear at me. This is supposed to be a pleasant experience."

"It's anything but, you disgusting shit! Fox!"

"Pipe down, will you? My neighbors are going to call the cops." Richard started to eat my right nipple.

"That does not belong to you," I screamed. "Spit it out."

Richard put his hand over my mouth. "You know," he said, speaking between waves, "you really kill me, Eva. I don't know why, but you came here with the express intention of getting laid, didn't you?" I shook my head. "Of course you did. Hey, keep doing that. It feels terrific." I stopped struggling and lay still. "Oh, now we're going to play dead, eh? You were always very bad at that. Know something? I'm very tempted to strangle you. Hey, great, you're moving again. You have no idea how good you feel. Let me tell you a few things now that I have your attention. You've ruined my life. I can't fuck anyone else without thinking of you. I can't draw a line without thinking of you. I've bankrupted myself on three psychiatrists and all they can say is See you next week. I think the thing to do is never see you again. I'll marry Brasilia and have ten kids. They'll make me forget about you. Ouch, I'm going to come any minute. See what you do to me? Why do I live for this torture? Hey! Ah! Oh! Eh! How impolite of me! Oy! Gaaaaah!" Mortally wounded, Richard fell to the side.

I ran my hand over his back and behind, thinking of departed backsides. "Great shopping list," I said gently. Richard was still, after all, a friend. "Are you going through with it?"

"First I'm going to die."

"Don't you dare." We still had seven covers to finish. Richard rolled over. "How was I?"

"Not bad for a big buffoon."

"Did you come?"

Of course not! "Of course." I got out of bed. "Well, now you can tell Dr. Augsburg all about it, forgetting no detail." That should take five minutes. "Coffee?"

"I'll make it."

I ran out for some rolls from the Italian bakery across the street. The man who had been hanging his socks on the fire escape was still staring fixedly into Richard's window.

"Okay, big boy." I said, heaving the bag onto the kitchen table, "are you in a drawing mood?"

"I'm in a great mood." We went to Richard's drafting table and banged out five covers in one hour. Then we got to the gay offertory.

Stubby Angel? What can I do with that?"

" How about a black acolyte with sort of a see-through gown?" I suggested.

"Why black?"

"Because I'm dedicating this to Pooh."

Richard drew a likeness of Lionel's lover. "How's this? Too recognizable?"

"It's great."

"Orville's never going to take this, Eva." Richard handed me the sketch. "Here, give it to Pooh for his dressing room. I'll do something else. Sing the opening again for me, will you?"

I hummed and mumbled half a verse. Richard drew a female nude seated at a table writing.

"What's that?"

"That's you this morning." Richard now drew himself standing behind me.

"Why aren't you wearing boxer shorts?"

"Please, Eva, this is art, not life."

"I'll say! You gave yourself more hair than Bozo the Clown!"

"Tut, tut," said Richard. "You might notice I'm being kind to you also." He drew the paper off the pad and gave it to me. "For your dressing room."

"Thanks."

"Shall I continue?"

"Come on, baby. we're supposed to be drawing hymn covers, not sex manuals!" Again I hummed the opening of *Stubby Angel*, waiting for comment.

Richard leaned back in his chair, appraising me. "You're one great lay. you know that?"

"Will you get OUT of here!" I shouted. "I'm trying to sing!"

"Is that what you call it?" Richard picked up his pen again. "Now I see why you're so frustrated. You can't sing yourself and nine choirs out of ten butcher your hymns. Then on top of that, the best singers are assholes.''

I got up and went to the window. "Hi, honey." called the man on the fire escape.

"Why don't we call it a day." I said. "I'm getting a headache.''

"It's only nine o'clock in the morning." Richard came over behind me.

"Don't touch me!"

He immediately stepped back. "What did I say?''

"Nothing, nothing.'' I combed ten fingers through my hair, amazed to find an unopened cranium beneath them, and tottered onto the couch. "Ah, Richard," I sighed, "I shouldn't have slept here last night.''

He sat next to me. "Why not?''

"It's beginning to make me feel bad.''

"What? Guilty?''

Chuck burst out laughing; I winced at the noise. "Just bad.'' I missed Fox; I sort of missed Martin. Adding Richard to that confused rubble of emotions only made my stomach churn. "I think I'd better leave.''

"Where are you going?''

"Back to Boston.''

'What are you going to do there?''

"Read junk romances.''

"You can do that here.''

Wrong. I could act in one here. "Won't work, baby." I loaded my suitcase. "Thanks for dinner.''

"You forgot something." Richard went to his drawing board and put his sketches into an envelope. "Here. Someday I'll figure you out.''

Why wreck the fun? I paused at the door. "Are we still friends?''

"Always." Richard walked me to the car. The man on the fire escape was now using binoculars. "Call me when you get home." He opened the driver's door. "Are you all right?''

"Yo.''

Trying to beat a huge raincloud, I drove very fast back to Boston, narrowly avoiding two radar traps before Hartford. When your body is tootling along at ninety-five miles an hour, you don't waste much concentration on wolves, foxes, and martins.

Moments after I stepped in the front door a barrage of hammering from the basement stopped me cold: I needed a drink. Mixing one, I went to the den and called Richard.

"I'm home," I said a little too cheerfully. "Thanks again for your hospitality."

"You're home already? What were you trying to do, kill yourself?"

"I hate slow death."

"Whatever's bothering you," Richard said, "you know you can always come here." He paused. "Thank you for last night. It meant a lot to me."

"Don't mention it." I drained my glass; the ice cubes smashed into my lips like huge dice against a gaming table. "Forget about me, Richard."

"What, and turn to stone?" Richard laughed. "Good-bye, you brat."

Ah, Capricorn, lifeblood of psychotherapists! I stood refilling my glass when Orville called.

" Hi sweetie, would you like to hear *I Hope Forever* this weekend?" That was my first platinum album, Chuck's first mink coat.

"Where and who?"

"St. Paul's in San Francisco."

"NO!" I began to cough. "Sorry, Orville, didn't mean to shout. I just got back from San Francisco. Anything closer?" Half a Tom Collins danced in my nose.

"How about the Unitarian Cathedral in Newark?"

"Why are they doing such a big piece in the middle of summer?"

"That sanctuary is the coolest place in town."

"I just got back from New York. Isn't anybody singing in Nova Scotia?"

"Sorry, not that I know of. How are your other pieces coming?"

"Richard Weintraub and I did five covers this morning."

"Terrific. By the way, we're going to do part of the Christmas oratorio at the convention in Boston. I'm bring-ing a thousand copies with me."

"Think you'll sell them?"

"No question."

"I'm working on a soprano duet and another guitar number."

"Look forward to them." I'd slip the gay offertory in with a deceptively prim cover. We sent each other's spouses our best regards and said good-bye.

"Percival," I called down the stairs to the basement.

"He ain't heah."

"When is he coming back?"

"Tamarrah."

"I see." I went to the study and called Nizor's Lunatic Asylum.

"Hi, Chuck, how's it going?"

"This is a fabulous place, Eva, you should be here."

"I'm thinking about it."

"What's the matter?"

"Nothing."

"Yes there is. I can tell it in your voice. Are you in California?"

"I'm home. Martin's in California."

Chuck mumbled something under her breath. I only heard the Amen. "I hope you're not writing more pornography."

"No, as a matter of fact I'm working on hymns."

"What blessed news. When is Martin coming home?"

"Six weeks."

"Oh dear. Excuse me." I heard footsteps, then pages turning.

"Chuck? Are you still there . . . Chuck?"

"Just a moment, Eva, I'm reading."

"Come on, you can read your Bible all day long! And quit talking like Grandma Moses! Robert will laugh you out of the house."

Chuck's newly acquired manners bled like mascara in the rain. "That son of a bitch! Dr. Chubb told me he's caused half my problems."

"Who caused the other half?"

"My children."

"Say, that's terrific! Now you can really get well!" I heard some more flapping of onion skin followed by monotonous gibberish. "Okay. Chuck, I'd better see what the carpenters are up to. I'll call you in a few days."

"There's something drastically wrong with you. I hope you haven't done anything to hurt Martin."

"I don't believe you said that to your own flesh and blood."

"We are all the children of God."

But only six lucky winners in all of history could be the children of Chuck. "You're in great form," I said. "Have you dispensed your entire suitcase yet?"

"I've started a prayer meeting in my room every night."

"Wait a moment, that's why you got kicked out last time! Why are you doing it again?"

"Eva, this clinic is full of lost sheep."

"And what are you, Mutton Chop?"

"I think it's time for me to get dressed for lunch. You're a big problem, Eva, but I can't worry about it. Everything is in the Lord's hands."

I sighed. "Of course."

"Give my love to Martin, poor fellow."

I leafed through the mail and received nothing from Rome. Therefore, too dull to compose, too blind to read, I took a brief nap that lasted until sundown. The carpenters had left. I ran to Lars Andersen Park, then back through Brookline to the Charles River, where huge crowds had gathered for a pop concert in the Hatch Shell. There I sat until ten, swatting at mosquitos and pretending to enjoy the fraternity of ten thousand heavy smokers. When the band trotted out its vocalists I ran home, locked up, and went to bed.

I did not comprehend why, instead of feeling carefree and rejuvenated, I had less poop than before. *Indecision compounded by guilt,* Chuck canted cheerily. *resulting in loss of will.* I could have smacked her. "Choose," I prayed, searching the dark bedroom for a signal. "I can't." Nothing, not even a ripple of the curtains; should have known. I went to the window and looked over Martin's rosebushes gleaming blackly in the moonlight. How had I allowed mere humans to deprive me of my will again? I must find it: it was the basic component of survival. Love, contentment, fulfillment . . . they were mere icing on the

cake: one hundred years from now, no one alive would
know or care whether I had led a happy existence. Only
the hymns would remain, bobbing placidly as lifebuoys
over a troubled lake.

"Fox," I whispered, too spent to even be angry anymore.
Now only the slightest twinge accompanied his name;
whatever great emotions he had conjured had vanished
along with him. "So what was the point." I prayed. Jesus
Christ, so few men made me feel like a woman! The Great
Librarian could have lent him out just a while longer as a
small token of gratitude for all those hymns.

I would have to replace him, that's all.

"Percival," I said the next morning, "the greenhouse
looks wonderful."

"Eva! You're home again!"

"Have a seat," I said, "I have a favor to ask." Percival
took the chair beside me. "Would you mind if I stayed in
your beach house for a while?"

"My dear girl, it's been waiting for you."

"It's not next door to Ruth's, is it?"

"Heavens, no! She's in Harwichport. We're in Hyannis."

"Would it be possible for me to stay there for a few
weeks?"

"You can stay there until Christmas if you like."

I took his arm. "I don't know how to thank you."

"You can let me come out weekends and just sit in my
rocking chair."

"It's a deal."

I went upstairs to pack. Before leaving I called information to get the number of Martin's apartment in San
Francisco.

"Hi, Flappy."

"Hello, baby." Martin yawned as if we had been separated for mere hours. "What time is it?"

"By you? About six o'clock. Sorry it's so early."

"No problem. I was just about to get up." If I caught
him at four, he was just about to get up, too. "How are
you feeling?"

"All right." No one said anything for a long time. "I'm
going away for a few weeks."

If I listened very hard, I could hear the echo of a more garrulous conversation between two women. Perhaps Martin was straining to hear the same thing. "Where are you going?" he finally asked.

"To a little beach cottage. By myself." I waited; nothing, damn him. "How's work?"

"Pretty good. I should be done in a few weeks."

"Are you taking care of yourself?"

"I think so."

"Okay, I've got to go. If anyone dies, tell Percival about it."

"Does he know where you're staying?"

"He's got the number." I sighed. "Bye."

"Good-bye, my love. I can hardly wait to see you again."

I hung up the phone. He had to be kidding.

Percival gave me keys and directions. His little beach house turned out to be a manor on the sea. I wondered how he had managed to prevent his wives from grabbing it; then I remembered that *they* had left *him*. They were fools. The neighbors left me alone to sit on the porch reading and writing all day. I listened to operas all night. One rainy spell I listened to the *Ring* straight from beginning to end, then couldn't pick up a pencil for a week afterward. Percival did, indeed, occupy his rocking chair on weekends. We completed four jigsaw puzzles. Several times I went fishing. After a month I ceased to worry about the carpenters, the electricity bills, watermelons in my front gate, burglars, and the postcards that I never received; the sun and salt air had evaporated them. Only that huge hollow remained, slowly bleaching. I talked to Martin about once a week, periodically checked the obituaries to see if anyone I should know about had died. Chuck departed Nizor's Loony Bin, five dozen redeemed souls under her belt, a new woman.

Towards the end of August I began to get restless as a horse sensing a far-off tornado. "Percival," I said one evening over a jigsaw, "what do you think of Martin?"

"He's a wonderful fellow and a brilliant businessman," Percival replied without hesitation. "I have the highest respect for him on both counts."

I sequestered the border pieces from the rest of the puzzle. "Do you think Martin could get along without me?"

Percival plucked a miniscule cow from my pile. "Martin loves you, Eva. There is no doubt in my mind about that."

I did not puff with pride and contentment; on the other hand, I did not wince. I just sat. If my husband still loved me, then I had to go home. There was no choice, really; Fox must understand that. *How well did you understand ten years ago,* Chuck asked disgustedly. Agh!

"What's the matter, darling?"

I went to the window and looked out over the still water; tonight I would like to walk into the Atlantic and swim forever eastward, towards Italy, until I quietly drowned. "I have to go home," I said. "It's time to start over again."

Percival said nothing.

I returned to Boston several days before my husband was scheduled to arrive. I dusted off his house and tested all the equipment in his new gym: Percival had done a splendid job. I trimmed all the rosebushes and made a huge batch of stuffed onions. I took the Bavaria in for a checkup and dropped in on the gynecologist. Every other woman in the waiting room was big as a whale.

We did the usual lump-and-Pap routine. "And how's your IUD doing, Mrs. Weaver?" he asked.

"Do me a favor," I said. "Take it out."

11

MY HAND SNAKED under the pillow and stealthily grasped the crowbar: I would tee off just behind my intruder's left ear. Had I left the front door open? Who had keys to this house besides Percival and Martin? Shit, I knew who it was: Fox coming to strangle me. In fact I had been dreaming just that as the squeaks from downstairs had peeled me gently from slumber and stuck me back on my own cold bed. Pity: Fox brightens up a subconscious landscape.

No, it had to be Martin. He thought he was coming home from San Francisco some time this week. But my husband always goes straight to the refrigerator, then the pile of mail, then softly announces himself as he climbs the stairs. Whoever was down there was still fumbling around with the locks on the front door. That narrowed the field to either Percival or Jack the Ripper, and Percival was in Washington at the groundbreaking of a new building. He had wanted me to go with him, but those ceremonies always reminded me of funerals.

No doubt about it, I was about to be murdered. For five weeks in Cape Cod I had seriously considered being consummately dead instead of this half-assed dead I was at present; now that only seconds separated me from the final ecstasy. however, I discovered that I really would prefer a rain check. Many loose ends had yet to be tied. *Typical,* taunted Chuck. "Sorry to disappoint you," I said, pressing the panic button behind my nightstand.

Immediately the house came alive, angry as a hornet's nest. Shit, I think Martin had installed a siren under every third shingle. He'd be very gratified to know that his system actually worked, albeit for a questionable cause. I didn't know about the Ripper, but the racket scared me shitless. I ran into the closet, threw a robe on, and crept into the hallway, poised to spring out the front door the moment I saw flashing blue lights.

Suddenly the din stopped. "Eva! Are you all right?"

"Martin? What are you doing home?"

"I live here, if you recall."

I jiggled helter-skelter down the stairs. Martin had atrophied at least fifteen pounds, and not via exercise; he had the eyes of a box turtle. If I put a fluffy gray wig on him, he'd put his mother out of business. "I thought it was a burglar," I explained, kissing his cheek. "It didn't sound like you."

"I forgot how to kill this damn alarm." He stepped back. "You're looking well. I don't think I've ever seen you with a tan."

"I was at Percival's place in Hyannis for a few weeks."

"I know."

"How do you know? Did Percival tell you?" I'd throttle him.

"No one told me. It was the logical place for you to go."

Gee, and all this time you thought you were keeping him in excruciating suspense, chortled Chuck. "Oh." Blue lights crept slowly up the street, reminding me of the patrol car that had interrupted our marriage in a frozen ditch. "The police are here."

"Not bad," Martin said, checking his watch. "Four minutes." Sure, that's because it was a false alarm. "I'll take care of them." I followed him out to the porch, watching him talk to the same two officers who had responded to Richard's panicky call some time ago. The younger policeman noticed me and waved. After a few moments, they drove away. Five or six disarrayed neighbors who were milling on their front steps returned to their houses.

"That's strange," Martin said, closing the door. "When

I told them my name, the old cop laughed and said, 'Sure, Jack.' ''

"What did the young cop do?"

"He was flirting with you."

"They must take a lot of shit this time of year." Undergraduate reunions and fraternity rushes annually caused fifty times more property damage than busing. "Come on, want to see what Percival's built for you?" I took him to the kitchen.

Martin peered into the greenhouse. I had been writing hymns in it early in the morning when it was still cool and quiet. "Don't worry, Flaps, I'll clear all that stuff out tomorrow. Then you can set up your batteries."

He walked to the cluttered table. Unless my eyes were playing tricks on me, Martin had gotten shorter, too. "How's work going?" He lifted a paper. "What's this?"

"A drawing of Pooh. Richard was fooling around." Jesus Christ, how had that gotten there? What had I done with the sitting nude of me? *It'll turn up,* Chuck said.

I took Martin's bony arm; was it because of me that he was emaciated like this? *No fair!* I prayed, steering towards the gym. "Percival has installed every weight machine known to man," I said. "I hope you're going to use a few of them." I squeezed Martin's biceps. "Tomorrow we start the Lard Boy diet."

Martin glanced noncommittally over the machines but spent a lot of time inspecting the seams in the redwood, the rubber floor, and the tile. "Nice work," he said. "Where's the sauna?"

"In the corner."

We came back upstairs. "How about a nightcap, Flappy?" I handed him a brandy. For several minutes we said nothing; believe me, the sudden advent of a spouse can be more disconcerting than the Second Coming.

"Paloma quit today." Martin said heavily. Aha, that's why he was so distraught.

"How come?"

"She wanted to stay in California."

"With you or without you? Go ahead, I can take it."

Martin still hesitated. "With me."

I looked over at him. "So what are you doing here?"

"I'm trying to save my marriage."

"Are you sure you want to talk about this now? Wouldn't we do much better after a night's sleep?"

Martin studied my face for a long time. Not my eyes, my face. He was probably wondering how all those diamonds and Bukharas had bought him nothing but a hag. "Do you love me?" he asked.

Something was drastically wrong. A Weaver would never ask such a personal question, particularly of a spouse: why instigate a shipwreck when you were already lost at sea? "Of course I do," I swelled. "You're my husband!"

He put his brandy down. Oh God! Fox had put his brandy down in exactly the same place, with exactly the same authority, when was it? Three lifetimes ago? *Cut the melodrama*, scoffed Chuck, *It was last March, right after your fifth anniversary.* "At least we've got something in common," Martin said. "There's hope yet."

That worried me. When men start talking about hope, that means they're about to lose it. I arose and pulled Martin's hands. How the hell had he gotten so thin? Screwing Paloma? "Come on," I said, "things will look much better in the morning, including me." I slung my arm around Martin and ushered him upstairs. While he stood still as a clothes tree I undressed him, then folded him into bed. The poor guy looked whipped and white. "Open up, Flappy," I said, administering from the silver flask.

"Eva," said Martin, "I missed you so much."

"I missed you, too. Now go to sleep." I went downstairs and turned the lights off. Bag the alarm, Martin was home. By the time I came back upstairs, he was snoring lightly maybe three tones above normal; when Martin loses weight, his pitch rises. I felt very protective of him; if I ever saw Paloma again, she'd get a piece of my mind she'd never forget. Gingerly, I lay down. The bed seemed overcrowded.

I woke up first in the morning and edged in a couple hours in the greenhouse before hearing Martin's footfall above. It was a beautiful day, herald of autumn and applesauce; when would Fox return to me? No matter. I did not really want to see him. It was unexpectedly pleasant to live without a typhoon raging in my gut and my head. Many schools of fish had returned to the becalmed sea; I was writing better than I had in months. About two weeks ago, I had started a little bauble for Lionel and Pooh to fart around with when they tired of bigamous monks. This one was a black western. While Martin was showering, I put the western away and tore the downstairs apart searching for Richard's second sketch. I had hidden it someplace very secure. That's all I remembered.

"Hey there, Big Boy," I said as Martin wandered into the kitchen, "sleep well?" I put a huge canister of granola in front of him.

"Yes." Martin's mouth brushed mine. He had forgotten that ritual last night.

"Hungry? How about eggs? Flapjacks? Hash? Want some cream puffs?"

"No thanks." Sipping orange juice, Martin scanned the headlines but did not touch the newspapers. That could wait until after he had saved his marriage.

I sat at the table and pushed the granola towards him. "Try this, Flappy, it was a pretty good recipe." Martin obligingly picked out an almond.

"Are you feeling better than you did a few weeks ago?" he asked. "I've been very worried about you."

Ah, the asking-if-I-was-feeling-better trick. "I'm doing better, thank you." If he picked up the newspapers now, I'd leave him for good.

"Can you tell me what the problem was?"

Fox splashed noisily across my imagination and was gone. "Me." *You stupid moron*, Chuck shrieked, *you just blockaded the exit!* She does not understand that if I had answered Another Man, Martin would remain an emotional cripple for the rest of his life. His family would never forgive him for being the first avowed Weaver cuckold since 1620. "It's hard to explain," I fumbled. " For a while I just didn't like you. You're not the world's most attentive husband, you know."

"I know I work too hard," Martin said, "but I'm doing this for us."

Come on, that was like saying I bought frilly ballgowns and sequined handbags for "us." "I'll be right back," I said, going into the greenhouse and returning with paper and pencil. "I think we should make a shopping list, Martin."

"A shopping list? Now?"

I ignored that petulant outburst. "Okay, tell me what you want from me and I'll write it down. Then I'll do the same thing to you."

"Is this necessary?" Martin asked, annoyed. Jesus Christ, you'd think I had asked him to sodomize the German shepherd across the street!

"Come on, Flappy. this is how all the intellectuals save their marriages." I started listing numbers and periods down the page. Martin watched me as if I were signing a warrant for his execution. I stopped at twenty-five. "Okay. shoot."

"Eva, I don't want anything from you."

I threw the pencil across the room. "Shit! How are we supposed to salvage this marriage if you don't want anything?"

Martin slowly chewed an apricot, procrastinating. "Why don't you go first? It might give me a few ideas," he suggested finally.

"No, Flappy. that's not how it works. You'd just copy all my ideas. You have to go first." That way, I could copy his ideas.

Martin cleared his throat as I retrieved the pencil and inspected its tip. "Number One," he said. "I would like Stuffed Onions tonight for dinner."

I slammed the pencil down. "Oh come on! That's not what I meant!"

"What did you mean, then? Am I supposed to say something like 'I want you to love me forever with all your heart'? That means nothing, my girl."

I frowned. Richard's paranoid lists were about as effective as his feathers.

"Wait," Martin said. "I just thought of something."

"This had better be good," I warned.

"It is good." Martin paused for grand effect, something his mother always did before divulging what she had received from Edmund for Christmas. "Number One: I want my wife to stay just the way she is now."

I lay the pencil down as if it contained nitroglycerine rather than lead. There was no point in pursuing this stupid list. "Okay. Flappy, you win," I sighed, pushing the paper aside. "Let's talk about something more constructive. You first."

Martin was eating more and more granola. "Have you been thinking about nannies?"

Under no circumstances was my husband to know that I was now operationally fertile. He'd be inseminating me every night. "Have you been thinking about vacuuming the house?" I parried.

"Sure! From top to bottom the minute we're done here."

"Flaps, that is not true and you know it."

"Darling, seriously. I'm going to spend the morning doing housework. I'm going to turn over a new leaf, watch."

"Are you crazy? I just sterilized the place before you got home."

"But I thought you wanted me to help more around the house."

For Christ's sake, Martin no more belonged behind a dustmop than I belonged behind the lectern at the annual stockholders' meeting. Why should I penalize him for the myopia of a woman who had waited on her son hand and foot from the moment he had departed her womb? What was to be gained by handcuffing a millionaire to a quart of Lestoil anyway? *Pure vengeance,* Chuck said. Bah, she should know. The highlight of her week is watching Robert take out the garbage.

"I'll make you a deal," I sighed. "You stop rolling your socks into balls and I'll take care of the rest."

"Wouldn't it be easier to just hire a maid? We'll get Percival to remodel the carriage house."

"Why don't you just stop balling up your socks instead of forcing maids and nannies on me? I don't want anybody here. I'm not going to tell you that again."

"I guess that takes care of my contribution to this discussion," Martin said. "Your serve, pet."

I started picking raisins out of the granola. Maybe the Weavers were on the right track after all: once you were married, you stopped asking questions and started going to country clubs. I was even beginning to understand the profound wisdom of separate beds. *After two kids*, Chuck ruled. *Not before*. I scowled. The woman collected grandchildren the way secretaries collected teddies in Filene's Basement.

"What happened to Paloma?" I asked. "Do you want to talk about it?"

Martin's face grayed for a moment, as if I had reminded him of a recently deceased uncle. He didn't realize that there were really four people involved in this discussion. "Eva," he asked, "would you give up a great job if you fell for the boss?"

"Of course."

"Why, though? Does it really interfere to the extent that you can't work?"

I had to be very careful here. Martin could be setting up a masterly trap. "Women are like that," I said. "Their heads take dictation from their hearts." *Ah, but not you, eh?* needled Chuck. Of course not me, I retorted.

"I wasn't thinking of you at all, darling," Martin said.

"Shit, why not?" I snapped. "Am I a fucking robot or something?" Martin invested a few moments nibbling his tongue. "Sorry," I said, "I misunderstood." I stared at the granola: not a raisin in sight. "Were you surprised? About Paloma, I mean."

"I guess I shouldn't have been," Martin said. "She had been acting very quiet for weeks. I thought it was overwork."

"Give her a little more credit than that, Flappy." What the hell, I could afford to be generous now that she was out of the running.

"You knew all along, didn't you?"

"So did you, pal." Come on, Martin playing dumb just didn't wash. "Did you at least kiss her good-bye? Never mind, you don't have to answer. Did she tell you she didn't want to see you again until you were a divorcé or a widower?"

Martin's face turned salmon. "Nothing of the sort!"

Poor Paloma. I excavated two apricots and lay one on Martin's placemat. I once had a cat who did the same with dead birds. "I guess you weren't sleeping with her then."

"I'm not going to ask by what roundabout logic you deduced that, but it's a little disappointing." Shit, it had been a trap and I had stomped into it like a suicidal poacher.

Time for the smoke bombs. "I'm sorry, Martin," I answered, "it's just that sometimes I wonder about that sex drive of yours."

"Excuse me? You aren't suggesting that I should have had an affair with my secretary?"

"First of all, she's not a secretary, she's a woman. Secondly, what the hell did you do out there for six weeks? Read *Good Housekeeping?*"

"I worked like a dog! What did you do?"

"I worked like a dog." That night spent with Richard was no exception.

Martin leaned back in his chair, openly gazing at the *Globule* now. "Ah, Eva," he said, "we're two peas in a pod."

"I don't know why you keep saying that."

"Did you miss me as much as I missed you?"

"Of course not. Percival kept me company."

Chuckling, Martin tweaked the tip of my nose. "My crazy little girl."

"Don't call me that."

"What, my love?"

"Girl, crazy, little, and my."

"But those are your special weapons," Martin said, reaching for the newspaper.

"Hey! Put that down! We're having an argument!"

"About what?" Martin said. "Paloma? Percival? My sex drive? I'm listening, Eva." He looked at me.

When will you ever learn, Chuck smirked, *That guilt is a boomerang?* Even as she spoke, it sheared the back of my head clean off. "Court adjourns until tomorrow," I pronounced, testily massaging my hairline. "I can't hack this." Without a word I picked every last raisin out of the granola as Martin read the worst page in the paper, the editorials. I skimmed through the obituaries, then went down to the gym.

For one week, Martin faithfully deposited his socks in the hamper rather than under the bed. We went to a few movies and a bogus rendition of *Hamlet* out in Marblehead. Around the middle of the month Ruth threw an end-of-season party on the Cape, so we spent a weekend there with the in-laws and Martin's sister Clarissa, who brought along her new boyfriend Peter, a criminal lawyer whom she had met at a malpractice suit. I don't think Ruth liked him. He kept talking about rapists.

Martin hired a new secretary, Pauline, a matronly Armenian whose previous boss, aged fifty-three, had just died of a heart attack. Within three days, she got her sea legs and started terrorizing the loiterers at the copy machine; Martin immediately gave her a raise. He was sure Pauline would never fall in love with him except as a mother; every day she brought him dolmades or baklava and refused to leave the office until he had eaten it. I asked Martin how much Pauline's previous boss had weighed when he died and he promised to check on it.

Meanwhile, Orville was getting all cranked up about this Sacred Music Convention in Boston. Apparently several media types from the Bible Belt were sending up television crews to cover the activities; they wanted to show the folks back home that for some, it paid to be a Christian. For days, Orville tried to get me to agree to an interview, but I finally convinced him that it would be fiscally ruinous to reveal to a loyal public that Fanny May Tingle was no Louisa May Alcott. As a sop, I promised Orville that he could accept the Hymnist of the Year award for me and get himself photographed with all kinds of evangelical types. Then he could invite them all over here for a reception; it was the perfect milieu in which to impress his clients. I had no idea what brought on this generous mood.

I worked on the black western for Pooh whenever I ran out of canonical steam. Martin returned each day from the office at seven and hit the sauna; Percival had installed an intercom phone for him on the nether bench. Afterward we ate on the deck. I don't remember what we did at night. Martin putzed in his greenhouse, testing solar batteries, and I read or listened to operas. Richard Weintraub passed through town once en route to Maine, minus Brasilia, who disliked insects. He lasted one night by himself in a pup tent and returned to New York with a bad back. We did not talk much because Martin had lately begun to stay in the same room as his wife's guests. Every once in a while I'd glance over and catch him looking at me. He'd smile and resume his reading.

We slept together once or twice, on my calculated safe days. Certain strangers from our last cocktail party invited us to reciprocal galas at their homes. I smiled and drank, complimented the hostess on her lovely rig, and then thought about Fox until Martin took me home again. I did not understand why I could not shake the fellow. If I woke up, Fox's lips were brushing my shoulder. If I drifted asleep, it was to rejoin him. I was back to where I could not write a note without hearing him sing it. I didn't polish one silver tray without seeing those rusty spoons clanking on Fox's porch. Day and night, the man gurgled in my blood, altering my vision, vanishing for hours only to surge into my throat at the sound of a telephone or a doorbell. But I was going to tell him no. It was one thing divorcing a husband whom you detested. It was another can of worms divorcing your friend.

Fox returned one crystalline morning in late September as the breeze was trying very hard to give the leaves a foretaste of diaspora while the leaves were all holding fast to their branches and laughing impudently. I had been working in the greenhouse since six in the morning and couldn't wait to get outside. As soon as Martin left for work, I ran to the Jamaica Pond, wearing shorts instead of sweat pants because I would run faster if I were a little cold. Today everyone on the track grinned at each other, exposing teeth to the wind, knowing there would not be many more days like this. Ducks honked robustly on the water.

He was sitting on a bench at the head of a long upward curve watching a fisherman retrieve his lure from an over-hanging limb; anglers here couldn't fish without a duck license. From a great distance I recognized that unmistak-able slouch and stopped dead. He hadn't seen me yet and there was still time to do a deft about-face. Whoops, the fisherman snapped his line. Fox returned his attention to the track and saw me. I suppose the best thing to do was jog nonchalantly forward as if chest seizures did not hurt.

I stopped at the park bench. Some Italian barber had clipped and waved Fox's hair like a best-in-show poodle's. He wore a black leather jacket and no-nonsense black pants. Nice black shoes, white shirt. Ah, whoever she was, the woman had taste. I looked at his face, measuring how far my memory had wandered in eight weeks: I did not recall that little line at the corner of his mouth, nor the elegant, almost plucked, curve of his eyebrow. But that was fallout from the hairdo. The mustache was new and superfluous; he had finally learned how to match socks. Otherwise, Fox was the same unkempt slob he had been before he left.

What the hell, I'd break the ice. "Hey there, moron."

"Ga'fuckin'dammit!" shouted the fisherman, casting once again into the trees. He flopped onto a tree stump and zipped open a beer.

Fox was looking at my thighs when I turned my head back to him. I think my knees were still covered with greenhouse mud. I had been putzing around in the basil and rosemary this morning. Last time I'd shaved my legs? Puberty!

"Remember me?" he asked.

"Name's Lazarus, isn't it?" An attractive jogger whom I saw every morning at the pond ran past. He took one look at Fox and me and became a wooden Indian. Shit, it would take days to get him to smile at me again.

"How've you been?" His voice sounded unfamiliar and rehearsed.

I stepped back: two men, jogging side by side behind wide-body baby carriages, bobbed by. "Not bad." *A lousy liar*, Chuck commented. I frowned. "Yourself?"

"Fine, thank you."

"You grew a mustache."

"You've got a tan."

Oh for Christ's sake, enough of this costive juvenility. "Look, what the hell are you doing here? Since when do you get all fluffed up and watch the ducks at eight o'clock in the morning? Where'd you get that gigolo jacket? And who talked you into that haircut? It makes you look like Mighty Joe Young."

"My, you're charming today."

"Go back to your Italian fan club." I cantered off. He would never come after me in those good shoes.

Damn it, he had wrecked another great morning. What was I supposed to do now? Go home and cry? Start making lemonade again? Call Martin and tell him he had to beat someone up for me? Skip past Fox's bench another three times and pretend he had only asked me for directions? Aha, I'd run around the pond until I almost got to Fox's bench, then I'd turn around and run until I almost got to the bench from the other direction, then I'd turn around again, ad infinitum.

The plan worked perfectly until I got one hundred feet from the last curve and those two idiots with the big fat baby carriages came up behind me. I thought I had left them far behind at the water fountain. In no way could I reverse direction now without infant mortality. Fox saw the whole thing and sat, arms lazily outspread, whistling "La Donna è Mobile" as the three of us pranced by. I didn't even look at him.

Just go home, advised Chuck. *Make Martin some nice Stuffed Onions and forget about this.* I burst out laughing; the woman had no idea how much voltage I had to work off before I'd even be able to sit down. At the boathouse, I cut off the track and ran along the Jamaicaway to the Arboretum, keeping my eyes pasted to the fractured asphalt: this sidewalk contained more tectonic faults than the entire South Pacific. Twenty school buses lined the driveway of the Arboretum. Within, hundreds of schoolchildren jostled around the three or four trees in the park which had begun to yellow, pulling each other's hats off and threatening to wee-wee as the biology teacher doggedly explained nature's seasonal miracles. This was obviously not the place for a wounded soul seeking sanctuary. I blazed home, went down to the gym, and turned on Percival's treadmill for inclement joggers. Without the wind and the sun, I could only smell myself thumping stupidly nowhere, so I shut the thing off and took a shower. *Why are you shaving your legs?* asked Chuck. "Pipe down," I answered, "Everything is in the Lord's hands." Chuck said nothing, not even Amen. What hypocrisy.

I went out to the front porch and opened *Oliver Twist;* if Martin felt compelled to spend a fortune on historic first editions, the least I could do was read them. I started the first page over ten times. Bah, it may as well have been Swahili; my tumultuous mind ate and disgorged words faster than a paper shredder. Moment by moment as it tilled the mounting evidence that Fox had another woman, my brain swelled alarmingly, until now it was much larger than its housing. If I didn't have a drink immediately, my eyeballs would pop into my lap.

With trembling hands, I went to the den and poured myself a half glass of Martin's best scotch. Good *Lord,* moaned Chuck, *It's not even ten in the morning.* Jesus Christ! The woman was more pedantic than a Pharisee! I swallowed heavily, twice, then returned to the porch with *Kansas Moon, Kansas Cornfield.* It had cost eight thousand bucks less than the Dickens and the stories turned out the same.

This time I only had to read the first page over twice before absorbing enough information to turn it over. *Put that slush down and get out of the house,* Chuck reprimanded. "Cool it," I said, "I'm waiting for some important mail." I returned to the paperback and slalomed over two more pages describing how the heroine, Dominique, had ended up in a Kansas pigsty and not the French royal court, where she belonged. I wondered if the author of this blowsy shit sat in a big empty house, just like me, and daily metamorphosed herself into a luscious milkmaid. Then I started thinking about cheese and the last time I had nibbled a decent Roquefort. I think it was in France with Richard. That had been a great trip until he had proposed to me under the Eiffel Tower. It was a humid afternoon and we were trying to walk off an attack of menstrual cramps. Why Richard chose such an inauspicious moment, I will never know; he has never quite forgiven me for dodging into a public bathroom instead of dissolving into joyful tears. I keep telling him he would have been more devastated had I answered him with a burst of diarrhea, but men don't understand these things. They prefer to believe that cramps, or indeed, any infirmities that daunt a woman's appetite for their stupendous penises, are psychosomatic.

I saw Fox sauntering down the street. He was carrying flowers; that terrified me. My heart started revving faster than a playboy's Lamborghini. *Will you calm down*, shouted Chuck. *He's just a man.* "You lie," I laughed at her. "He's the fork in the road." *Jesus Christ*, I prayed, *Do something*. Fox was getting closer and closer; I could see the rest of my life frisking within the bounds of a black leather jacket. Oh God, if I only knew whether or not he came here to say good-bye! *What does it matter?* exclaimed Chuck. *If he doesn't, you will.* "What does it matter?" I muttered. "Are you a woman?"

Fox opened the gate and walked to the front porch, stopping when he saw me. "It's me again," he bowed, presenting me with the flowers. "Your favorite moron."

That thawed my frostbitten guts somewhat; now if only I could break the lockjaw. I exhibited my most delphic smile and took the flowers to the kitchen. Fox followed me in.

"What have we here?" Fox asked, peeping beyond the new door. "Very nice."

"It's a greenhouse."

"You don't say."

"Look downstairs." I pointed to the basement door. By the time he came back, I might be able to handle compound sentences. Fox rattled around the machines while I located a vase for his flowers. Soon I heard his footsteps on the stairs.

"That's really something, Eva," he said, sitting at the table. Off came the jacket. My skin began to sizzle.

"Martin built it for me," I informed him. "How about something to drink? Have you had breakfast?" I backed towards the refrigerator, never letting Fox out of my sight; he was deadly proficient at attacks from the rear and we had several items on the agenda before anyone touched anything.

"Coffee would be fine."

I put some water on. "So tell me about your summer. It was a grand success, I take it." Operaphiles did not buy you black leather jackets for singing ineptly.

"I lucked out," Fox began. "The conductor was great, the cast was great, the audience loved me . . ."

"Before or after that haircut?"

"You really don't like it, do you?"

"Continue with the sack of Rome." We'd split hairs later. I warily presented Fox with a cup of coffee and sat at the opposite corner of the kitchen table. If he made one false move, I'd grab the rolling pin. "How was the Rossini?"

Fox sighed. "Eva, do we really have to talk about this now?"

"Of course we do!" I would not be sober enough to conduct an Other Woman interrogation for thirty minutes. "Did any managers hear you?" Forget Rossini; that mustache was beginning to wear me down. I wondered how it would feel between my legs.

"They had the good sense to show up on my best night," Fox said. "I've got a contract with one of them."

"Does that mean you're going to move to Italy?"

"No, New York. Strike while the iron's hot and all that."

"When are you moving?"

"I've moved already."

So he had come to say good-bye and sail off into the sunset. Damn! I should have known the moment I saw that haircut! The lights all went out. *Eva!* bulwarked Chuck, *Do NOT give yourself away again*. She caught me in the nick of time, particularly with the "again." This called for supreme self-control: I wondered how Ruth Weaver would react in such a situation. "How very thrilling," I said, spearing imaginary asparagus. "I'm so very happy for you."

Fox burst out laughing. "What was that all about, you little idiot?"

"I'm afraid I do not understand." Shit, this wasn't coming out correctly at all. I knew I should have worn a suit.

"What's the matter with you? You act as if I were a total stranger."

"You are, pal."

Fox's face paled; for a moment he looked like the crazed dingdong I once knew. "What makes you say that?" he asked very quietly.

Perhaps he had not come to say good-bye after all. My stomach suddenly levitated; with each word this interview was drifting more off course than a loose blimp. Why the hell did I drink that scotch? Two swallows had utterly swamped my logic in an ocean of lust. *Coffee*, Chuck directed. Before getting up I looked at Fox, then the rolling pin, then the coffee pot, judging distances. His legs seemed to be pretty far under the table.

I edged cautiously over to the counter. "My dear boy," I intoned as haughtily as possible. Would Ruth's hands be shaking like this? Of course not! I had to pull myself together. "A lot has happened since you left."

"Such as?"

Let me see now. I think I had caught two flounder on August sixteenth. I had bought three hats in Bonwit's, but only one of them fit. "If you had been in touch with me, you would have known," I said. "Now I am not at liberty to discuss it." A great line, one of the Weaver classics.

"Cut the crap, Eva," Fox warned. "Say what you want to say."

Go for it, Chuck screamed as if her life, not mine, were at stake.

"We're through," I said. Hey, that was easier than slitting wrists. I turned my back to Fox and poured some coffee. He should take this opportunity to slam a few doors in rage, and be gone.

Two seconds later one arm was on either side of me at the counter. I looked at those long slender fingers and started to bleed. "Turn around and tell me that," Fox said. I didn't stir; if he moved half an inch closer, he'd be touching me. That cushion of air between us already singed my back like an inferno. "Turn around, damn you."

I don't understand this, I prayed, *I have followed every single fucking rule to the letter. You and Chuck have some sort of sting going here, don't you?*

"Stop that mumbling and look at me," Fox snapped, spinning me around. Sorry, I couldn't face those lips at point-blank range, not now, not ten years from now, with or without husbands, and not pull them onto mine. I dodged under Fox's arm and ran into the den. There I could lock the doors and climb out a window.

With anyone else, of course, I would have made it. Against a nimble and powerful opponent who knew the layout of my house as well as my mind, however, I didn't have a chance. Chuck laughed uproariously as Fox caught me in a rear hold not ten feet from our original point of confrontation. She was laughing at her own joke, the bitch.

"We're going to have a little talk," Fox said into the back of my head. "Where would you like it to be? The den? Your office? The greenhouse? The deck? How about that fancy new gym?" Surely the fellow didn't expect a reply with that .44-magnum hard-on stuck in my breech. "You name it, Eva, I'm waiting." We stood there breathlessly posed in some idiot's frieze, one foot from the other side of the universe.

With my nose and teeth I nuzzled his shirt sleeve back and very slowly trawled my mouth along his forearm. "Don't do that," Fox whispered. Too late now, buddy; if he had wanted to talk, he should never have cornered me in the kitchen. His skin tasted like very hairy peaches. Whoops, make that cantaloupes: I had just given him goose bumps. My teeth gently lifted the skin over his wrist. Very ripe peaches.

"Ehhhhhf." Fox suddenly pushed me away and stomped into the den; instantly I reverted to the Other Woman theory. By the time I caught up with him, he was sprawled upon the leather couch, hands over his eyes. We two had a remarkable talent for giving each other splitting headaches. I glanced at the bar. Shit! How could I have forgotten to put the scotch back? Ruth Weaver would never have made such a stupid mistake. *Ruth Weaver would have looked the guy in the eye and told him to go home*, Chuck corrected. Bah, that's what they did fifty years ago. This was the emancipated generation.

Arms folded like a ruffled schoolmarm's, I walked over to the couch and looked down at Fox, imagining him slurping pasta from Contessa Giannina Fabrizia's finest silver as she begged him to stay the night. What the hell was he doing here? I had never begged him to do anything but leave and the closest he had gotten to my silver was the crowbar under my pillow. *Scrooge*, chastised Chuck.

I went to the office and pulled out a copy of my Christmas oratorio. It was already in its third printing and by the time this convention was over, Orville would be doing the hotcake salesman routine. Fox still lay massaging his eyes with those long slender fingers; if I rolled down on top of him, his arms would fall around me like heavy, beautiful ropes. *Then what,* scoffed Chuck. *You ask if he's had a vasectomy?* I dropped the score onto his stomach.

"What's this," Fox said.

"I wonder if you would do something for me for old time's sake."

"I don't quite like the sound of that."

The more he talked, the less I thought he had another woman. My confidence spit blood and tried to sit up. "How about for money?"

"Forget it."

What? Tenors would fart onstage if someone paid them for it! He had to have someone bankrolling him, no doubt about it. The Pasta Princess. I reached for the Christmas oratorio: Orville would have to find his own screamer for the convention.

Fox put his hand over the music. "Wait a minute, did you write this?"

"I would be obliged if you would please return my possessions to me," I said.

"Who's Fanny May Tingle?" Fox opened the cover.

"How should I know?" I barked. "Give me that music, please."

"You did write it, you little stinker." Fox looked over the first page. " 'A Christmas Oratorio. To Paul!' Hey! My name's Paul!"

"Shut UP! I know a million Pauls! If you're not going to sing it, you can't see it," I shouted, diving for the score. Before I knew it, I was pinned to Fox's stomach staring at the ceiling or, rather, at the Christmas oratorio, as he whistled and hummed through the opening chorus.

"Not bad," he said.

I did not reply. This was postintellectual rape. *If you didn't want people to read it, why'd you write it?* jeered

Chuck. "I wrote it for your Buddy. you stupid ass," I said, "but you would never understand that."

"What buddy?"

"Would you kindly unhand me?" Jesus, how did Ruth pull it off? It was ludicrous to talk like this to the ceiling.

"Later," said Fox. "I'm working." He skipped the next tune, a soprano and alto duet, and hummed through the following chorus. I distinctly remembered giving birth to that chorus, note by bloody note; now Fox sang it through as if the thing had bloomed upon the earth easily as a spring crocus. "Hey, that's good Eva," he said. "Did you write this all by yourself?"

"No, I stole it from the Mohawk Indians." Now we were coming to the parts I had written directly after Fox's self-defense class. I remembered sitting one snowy March afternoon at the kitchen table writing the next chorus, wondering who he was, fascinated, afraid, confident, and very coherent: Martin had just left for Stuttgart and I was going on safari.

Fox opened to the tenor solo and studied the page for some moments. By the time I wrote that number, I had made up my mind to call him, knowing that I would eventually end up exactly where I was right now, and not caring, because whatever he cost, that is what I would pay. All of that resignation, and trust, had infiltrated the tenor aria; I could have written that at no other time in my life.

When he had finished, Fox lay a few moments breathing into my hair. I could feel his pulse sedately rocking my shoulder blades and shut my eyes, all rhythms responding. "You wrote that for me, didn't you?" he said.

Adios, another secret. I had only one left. "Why do you say that?"

"I can tell." Still I said nothing. "It's good."

Good? It was great, the bastard. "Would you sing it at a convention for me?"

Fox rolled to the side. I slid down between him and the back of the sofa; now we were finally facing each other. "What convention?"

I took a moment to assess those wayfaring gray eyes; ha, he still loved me. "A hymnwriters' convention in Boston in December. If you're in the country, of course."

"Which week?"

"The first."

"I'll be back by then," Fox said. "Good, I can do it."

"Back from where?" I said, nearly wailing.

"Italy." Fox said. "That's one thing I wanted to talk to you about."

Shit! Not yet! "Would you kindly allow me to seat myself properly," I said. "I find it extremely difficult to converse with you in a recumbent attitude."

Fox scanned my face, this time without humor. "What have you been drinking?"

"I'm afraid I do not understand."

He sat up. "What's that on the bar?" He strode over and brought it back. "Recognize this?"

I sniffed the neck of the decanter. "I believe that is a bottle of fifteen-year-old scotch whiskey belonging to my husband. May I offer you a glass?"

"Are you going to make me slap that beautiful mouth or are you going to start talking like a human being?"

"My good fellow, you must stop maligning my mother-in-law or I shall have to ask you to leave the premises."

I got my mouth slapped. That did it, no more Ruth impersonations. Time to try Chuck's approach. *Bible verses?* my mother inquired with delight. "Thou art deluded," I replied, swallowing two inches of Scotland's finest. About five bucks' worth went down the wrong pipes. Sputtering and tearing, I stumbled back to the kitchen sink and stuck my palm under the faucet, splashing water into my mouth.

"All right?" Fox asked, coming up behind me.

"Since when did you start smacking women around?" I snapped, triply on fire now: booze and violence were great aphrodisiacs. My whole body quivered like a cauldron of water just under the boil.

"You're the first woman I've ever hit."

"Gee, does that mean we're going steady now?" I said sarcastically. In two minutes this man had shredded all the bunting I had so laboriously woven around myself these last eight weeks, leaving me to die of exposure to that lawless elemental love that blew houses down and husbands away. Jesus, why was I fighting this so damn hard? The man belonged to me! *And you belong to Martin,*

Chuck said. Ah, she was wrong. That was only on paper and over coffee.

Fox picked me up and set me on the counter. Once again he pegged a wooden arm on either side of me, fencing me in. We were just about at eye level. "Let's pick up where we left off," he suggested calmly. "You were telling me about the high points of your summer."

High points? What summer? That string of nights listening to the Atlantic sucking on moored boats? "Hell from beginning to end," I reported. "No high points."

"Where was Martin?"

"California."

"Where were you?"

"Cape Cod."

"Alone?"

"Yes." Percival would forgive me.

That hurt him: touché. "Why didn't you come to Rome?"

"The same reason you didn't write, baby." Now I knew why I didn't like that mustache. It hid the great beautymark above Fox's lip.

"So did it work?" he asked, and waited.

"No." I pulled his head in and kissed him; it was the only way to escape those gray eyes. "No." How did I live without that mouth? "No."

"Eva," Fox said, "listen. I want you to come to New York with me."

"What about the Pasta Princess?"

"Who?"

"Your Italian girlfriend."

"Small potatoes."

"How many small potatoes?"

"Four."

"Do you have VD or herpes now?"

"No, do you?" Shit, did Brasilia? I had forgotten to ask. "Who was it, Eva?"

"Small potatoes." I looked up. "Just one, and just once." Jesus, Richard would never speak to me again if he heard that. I suppose Martin would be pretty ticked off also. "Who gave you the jacket?"

"I bought the jacket." Fox sat down at the kitchen table

and looked at me for maybe five minutes, head to toe, inch by inch. "What do you think I've been doing all summer?"

He'd been attempting to beat me into surrender with his silence, that's what. "Singing."

"By that you mean furthering my career, don't you? Eh? Now why do you think I've done that?"

"Because you're a smart young fellow."

That brought him over to the counter again, minus half a temper. "Let's keep age out of this, shall we?"

"Sure, baby." I ran one finger in a little course over his mustache and lip: all debates were null and void within a three-foot radius. "What are we talking for?" I whispered. "I don't want to talk." *Cross your legs,* Chuck screamed, kicking me in the head.

That stupid bastard sat down at the kitchen table again. It was getting awfully hot in the kitchen. I took my cardigan off and he watched that. "Where was I?" he said. "Damn you, now I can't even think straight."

Welcome to the club, Ajax. "You were telling me how you busted your ass all summer, for my sake, of course, so that we could sneak away together with a minimum of financial discomfort."

"How elegantly put."

Fox was doing better than I had done ten years ago, believe me. When it came to the showdown, I was either sulking or screaming, drawing my enemy out or flattening him, trying anything to cut those immutable ties he felt to that insipid heifer back home. That was my fatal mistake, of course; the weaker I made his wife look, the less chance that my intended would ever leave her. It's the White Knight Complex. Fox was very wise to leave Martin out of this. I just wondered what line of argument he would use instead.

He knit his hands a few moments and several times seemed about to say something as I sat on the counter watching his deltoids undulate under that white shirt. Fox finally looked up at me. He didn't have to say anything; lightning zigzagged between four eyeballs. I wanted him so much I thought I'd faint.

Once more he came over to the counter, breathing lightly and rapidly, as if he wanted to surprise a burglar around the corner. "Would you mind if we went upstairs?" he asked. "I can't argue with those eyes of yours."

Stay in the kitchen, Chuck shrieked violently, *it's the middle of the month!* Bah, her Buddy knew it as well as I did. He could have postponed Fox's arrival. I wrapped my arms around Fox's neck. He hauled me to his chest, where I hung like a baby koala. "Step on it," I said.

He paused at the top of the stairs. "What's your answer? I want to know before I lose my mind completely."

I said nothing. After all, I was a Weaver now.

Fox tossed me on the bed, then tossed himself on top of me. "Do you know how I've dreamed of being here again?" He looked at my big fat mouth. "And those lips! Jesus! They drove me insane!" He kissed them. "You're in my blood, damn you, I knew it the minute I saw you strutting around those wrestling mats."

"Stop stealing my lines," I said, shifting under him. "That's plagiarism."

Fox sighed; I had just planted his cock on the bullseye. "No, that's love." He began to sway delicately. "You know why I moved to New York, don't you? And you know why I'm singing like this, don't you?" I held my tongue as little pulses of heat shimmied up my guts. "You don't think you're going to find another one of me, do you, Eva?"

"No," I croaked. "Take your clothes off." Chuck screamed bloody murder. Fox pushed up my sweater and ran his hands from my stomach to my neck, counting ribs. "Strip, damn you," I whispered.

"You break my heart, honey," he said. "You really think you're doing the right thing staying with Martin." The name rang no bell whatsoever. "You'll never be happy with that man, Eva. He's a nice guy but he'll never understand you. He's had five years and hasn't made a dent, has he? But you figure that's part of the deal, don't you?" Fox brushed some hair off my face and kissed my forehead. He had an erection the size of Lincoln Center. "Alone, tough as nails, slugging it out with that big Fu Manchu in the sky . . ." He pulled my skirt off, next his shoes. "I'm going to be a big success, you know, I can feel it in my bones. It feels a little like you. One is all wrapped up in the other and they're both going to happen.

You don't believe that, do you? You don't believe in anything, you cynical little tart. You made a big mistake and now you're covering your ass with a million rules and regulations." Fox stopped talking a moment to take his shirt off. Jesus Christ! How long was he going to prattle on like this? "Tell me, does Martin take your clothes off piece by piece like this?" I shut my eyes. "I didn't think so. He seems the type who just puts clothes on. But that's what you wanted, wasn't it?" Fox took my sweater off and leaned over. I nearly passed out this time. "Eh, you feel good." With one hand he pulled the covers back. "Slide under. You have the most delicious collection of underwear. Who bought it? Martin?"

"Make love to me," I begged. Did that erection hurt him as much as it was hurting me? God, I hoped so!

"Where was I? You have a habit of jamming my brain waves. I've thought for weeks about what I was going to say to you and now I've forgotten everything." Fox removed his pants. I love a challenge." His legs slithered down mine. "I adore your legs.

"Go to hell!

"Ah! That's where I left off! Olivia! The first woman I screwed, according to your instructions. A singer, stupid as a cow, huge tits, and she smelled like meat loaf. That lasted about four nights, until I heard her sing. Then I dropped her. The second one was a stage hand, about seventeen years old. She smelled better but she had no imagination. The third one was the best. What was her name? Francesca! She ran the opera festival. Loads of money and she knew how to spend it. She had a great face, like Nefertiti. She screamed in Rumanian when she came."

"Okay, okay!" I pulled a pillow over my ears. "And how did you enjoy yourself, you stupid bastard? Loads of laughs, wasn't it? Spilled guts and the Milky Way each time?"

Fox pulled the pillow off and brought his face in close to mine. He hated me. "Wrong," he spat, "forever wrong." He divested himself of a few odds and ends and got under the sheets. I pounced on him like a hungry cat and began eating his throat. Jesus, had the Pasta Princess been feeding him steroids? That hard-on would make an Amazon weep! "There's only one of you," Fox cursed, "and I've looked." I ran my hand over him and his whole body winced. "God, I've looked."

So stop looking, moron, you're home now and it was all a bad dream. I edged him inside of me: ah, there would never be another thrill as intimate, as dissolving, as this. "You," I whispered, kissing the salt in the corner of his eyes, "it's always been you." As Fox started slowly bobbing beneath me, I began to cry. When my tears hit his stomach, he reversed axes, saying nothing. I would never forget those gray eyes glinting at me as the wind blew through that bright morning, stirring up leaves, and smoke, and despair.

Fox suddenly upped the speed: he wanted to get it over with. "You break my heart," he said again. "But isn't that what you wanted?"

"No," I cried, shaking my head, "I only wanted you."

I got him and ten million more of him. "There you are," Fox said. "For the last time."

He rested a few minutes, then kissed my neck good-bye. I could not bear to watch him shroud that beautiful body, so I just lay in the bed watching the sun titillate the chandelier. That only reminded me of the spoons on Fox's porch, so I shut my eyes. After I didn't hear anything for a long time, I opened them. Fox stood at the foot of the bed looking at me.

"I have just one more question," he said. " Then I won't bother you again."

Oh boy, a great stab wound, sharp, deep, unexpected. I showed nothing. "What."

"If you love me, and I know you do, and if life without me is hell, and I know it is, then why are you staying with Martin?"

He leaned over the brass railing like a cowboy in a Death Valley saloon. I knew in my soul that man would belong to me as long as I lived. "Because he got here first."

Fox bowed and left. This time I heard a distant door slam; surely the wind had done it. *He's gone,* crowed Chuck. *And your suitcases are still here.*

"Take," I said to what was left of him, "take, damn you." The wind dashed through the trees.

* * *

Martin called around two that afternoon. I was working in the greenhouse on Pooh's western. "Hello, darling."

"What's up, Flappy?"

"I'm afraid I won't be home for dinner tonight. We're trying to finish up an emergency project for Tagahashi."

"Can't you finish that here? I'll make dinner." Shit, of all nights for Martin not to come home until three in the morning! *It's Your move,* I said. *You'd better make it.*

"We'll make it, pet, but all our papers are at the office. We wouldn't be able to enjoy your dinner anyway. Don't wait up. I have a feeling it's going to be late."

"Don't get too tired," I said. "You might miss the opportunity of a lifetime."

"Eh? Ah, Pauline is buzzing me like mad. Must go. Love you." Click.

I called Orville. "I got you a singer for the convention."

"Wonderful! This is going to be a great success, Eva. Half of North Carolina is going to be there."

"Doing what? Putting out contracts on Ted Kennedy?"

"Buying hymns, ma'am. And did you know there's a gospel literature convention right across the hallway?"

"Richard Weintraub told me about it."

"Would you mind if I invited a few of them to your reception?"

"Of course not," I replied, kicking myself for even suggesting it. "What have you got on the road this month? Anything I might like to hear?"

"How about your Thanksgiving pageant?"

"That thing's still in print?" I had written this ardent fudge when I was eighteen and thinking of becoming a missionary, four months before I met the first Mr. Catastrophe.

"My dear, we can't keep it in stock, especially this time of year."

"You don't say." Maybe it was better than I remembered. "Where's it playing?"

"Merlin, Ohio."

Where the hell was that? *Shut up and go,* said Chuck. *You haven't been to church in months.* "Merlin, Ohio. Got it. When?"

"November seventeenth." Orville rustled some papers on his desk. "I think it's a Methodist church."

Shit, Methodists never had enough altos. "I'll find it."

"I'm sure you will. What are you working on now?"

A hoedown for black sodomites. "Ah—a baptism hymn."

"Lovely." We signed off.

I went to three movies at the Nickelodeon Cinema, all breast-beating apocalypses attacking the Western democracies. Shit, no wonder outer space films were doing so well. I called Martin at the office around nine. "How's it going, Flappy?"

"It's going to be a long night, I'm sorry to say."

"What are you eating?"

"Pauline is stuffing everyone with moussaka."

"What? She brought that to the office? That's ridiculous!"

"No, sweetheart, we ordered it from a carry-out in Newton."

"Oh. Do you think you'll be getting home by midnight?"

"Ah—well—possibly—"

"Never mind, just wondering. Okay! Back to work!"

"What are you working on, pet?"

"Nothing. I'm at the movies."

"What's playing?"

"Attack of the Planetoids."

"Enjoy the show, my love. See you later." That's right, when I was sound asleep and Martin was less horny than a woman in labor. What the hell, I'd try to seduce him in the morning. *Giving the home team last ups, eh Eva*, Chuck smirked.

Around midnight I arrived home with a sore neck and slopped wearily into bed. I didn't even think about Fox. It had never happened; he had been gone for so long that today might have been a dream. *You'll wake up in nine months*, slapped Chuck. What for? Chuck snarled something satanic and I went to sleep.

Martin rolled in around five. As always, I was dreaming of Fox, nothing specific, just Fox. I could tell from the way my guts felt when I awoke.

"How did it go?"

"We're getting there." My husband removed the crowbar from his pillow and slid under the covers. "Baby, could you wake me at seven-thirty?"

"Martin, do you know what time it is?"

"Don't tell me, please. I might not wake up."

At seven o'clock, my hand inched across the sheets and located Martin's pendulous reproductive organs. "Hey. Flappy," I whispered, "got any energy?"

Madame Tussaud, cart it away. "Flaps," I continued stubbornly, getting two hands into the act now, "you are so sexy in the morning."

Martin groaned. "What time is it?"

I rolled on top of him. "I think I should wake you piece by piece."

"Eva," Martin said, patting my shoulder, "honey, I feel like lead." His hand plummeted back to the sheets and lay still.

"Try for a wet dream," I encouraged, "I'll take care of everything else." For five minutes I attempted, this time with my mouth, to raise the *Titanic*. I got nothing but jellyfish and seaweed.

So much for your grand plan, Chuck admonished. "Your Buddy put the bug in the hardware, not I," I reminded her. Shit! Not once in five years had Martin lost his ignition. *Very clever*, I prayed, *but he's not out of bed yet*.

Who says there is no God? The moment I finished, Martin peeled back the blankets and stumbled to his feet. "Hey, what do you think you're doing, Flappy?" I shouted. "You've got a few chores to do here!"

"Eva," my husband said, "I have an eight o'clock meeting."

"It is extremely important that you sleep with me this minute."

Chuckling to himself, Martin leaned over the bed and kissed me. His breath smelled like moussaka and dead pipes. "What brought this on, pet?"

Oh God, he knew. Now he was standing back to watch me hang myself. I had better guard my tongue. "I guess it was all the movies I saw yesterday." I faltered, following Martin into the shower. I started soaping him up and got a little courage back. "Hey! Look! There's a little hard-on, Flappy! Let's see if you can do anything with it."

"Eva, please, this is not the time. Tonight would be much better."

I did some rapid calculating. "No later than seven o'clock, okay?" Even that was stacking the deck. "You might never get another offer like this ever."

"Well, well, this is a change." Martin slid the shower door back and dried himself. God damn it, that erection would do fine! I gazed wistfully after it as Martin tucked everything into a pair of briefs. "What kind of movies were you watching, pet?"

"Porno." I went to make some coffee.

Martin called around four that afternoon. "Darling, how about coming out to dinner with Tagahashi and me?"

"Wait a moment, I thought we had a date at seven o'clock."

"Sweetheart, you weren't serious, were you?"

I know exactly what that meant: more lucubrations at Weaver, Inc. I let my silence do all the cursing.

Martin cleared his throat and progressed to sunnier altitudes. "Will you come here or shall we meet you downtown?"

What the hell, I'd give it one last shot. "Maybe you should come home for a nap before dinner."

"No time, love. I'll snooze here in the office for half an hour."

The three of us ate three lobsters, Martin and Tagahashi wrapped up their crisis two sunrises later, and by the end of the week, my husband took a few moments to fulfill his marital obligations. There was no doubt in my mind that the ship had sailed without him.

It was a strange and almost fairy tale month. I spent a lot of time in the gym downstairs. My relationship with Martin had never been better; after five years, certain shifting sands were finally turning to shale. He bought a solar battery company up in New Hampshire and a ski cabin nearby. Percival shared many lunches with me; I had finally found that girlfriend my mother had been bugging me to get for twenty years. Chuck embarked upon a teetotaler's reign of terror, clearing the house of all flammable liquids and forbidding my father to drink beer anywhere but the garage or the basement. He fervently hoped she would revert to the cranky old drunk he knew and loved before the snows came and he had no access to brandy. I finished the western for Pooh and cranked out eight sundry hymns. My brother married the twerp from Idaho.

Lionel jetted into town to lend his genius to the Boston production of *Cloistrophobia*. He had let his hair go red again and was experimenting with a fussy goatee. "Eva," he said, "you look terrific! What happened?"

"Good clean living."

"What? You? Don't tell me you dumped that karate chopper!"

"Haven't seen him in weeks."

"That's incredible. How does it feel?"

"It doesn't feel." That's what worried me. "Say, Lionel, I'm going to ask you a big favor."

"Of course, lamb, anything."

"Fox said he'd sing at the hymnist convention in December. Would you play piano for him? The Park Plaza's just a block away from the theater district."

"Well! I guess it's safe for me to meet the fellow now that you're through with him. How are we supposed to rehearse, though? I don't have a spare minute. This production is giving me MASSive headaches."

"Orville wrote him a letter last week. He's coming to Boston the day of the convention. You just run through the number once before you go onstage. Fox will know his part. Then we have a big party afterwards."

"What am I supposed to wear for this? Not a three-piece suit, I hope."

"Why not, baby? You're going to be on TV. And please keep your hairdo one color until this is over."

Lionel did not like that. "I MUST wear a choir robe. I have not owned a three-piece suit in ten years. It is the most barbaric costume ever invented."

"Fine! Wear a choir robe!" I gave him the music. "Here, it's easy. I made you a special idiot's reduction of the piano part."

"How thoughtful," he said sarcastically.

I dropped the western into his lap. "Here's a little something for you and Pooh. Composed in my spare time."

Lionel leafed through a few pages. "My GAWD! You've done it again!"

"It's nothing, really." I said. "Just for fun."

Lionel leapt to his feet. "You've got your balls back! That's WONderful, Eva. You had us very worried there."

"A momentary derangement." I got up. "So you'll do it? Thanks."

Shortly before Thanksgiving, when my period was several weeks late, I flew out to Merlin, Ohio to hear my Thanksgiving pageant. Over the years I have tried to attend as many performances of my works as possible, just to make sure that I'm keeping within the realm of middle-American possibility. It does no good, artistically or economically, for me to compose lovely hymns that no one but a Metropolitan Opera hippopotamus can nail correctly. Believe me, it's much more difficult to restrict myself to simple melodies and words and yet produce something that does not sound offensively abecedarian, like Gregorian chant.

I rented a car and drove south from Cleveland on a wintry Sunday afternoon. Isolated flakes of snow blackmailed the gray air, terrifying motorists. Thank God I had brought four unfinished hymns along with me; I might be marooned here until Thanksgiving. Shortly after dark I checked into a funereal inn not far from the main event. Jesus, what did people do in this town besides watch TV and buy gas?

Evidently, they went to church. Folk of all ages and sizes jammed the pews; to insure a larger congregation than usual, the minister had promised not to deliver a sermon. I picked up that tidbit from the woman sitting next to me. She was knitting bookmarks for the Africans and looked very happy. In fact, everyone in this church looked happy. I stuck out like a sore thumb, and it wasn't only the hat. The knitter asked if I were a lawyer from Cleveland coming to settle the Barrow estate. That sounded likely enough, so I said yes. Never in my life have I told people the real reason I haunted their church; it would contaminate their reactions to my hymns.

The choir director had graduated from Oberlin Conservatory up the road and was determined to make practical use of his doctorate while he waited for a real job to come along. He had been choir director for fifteen years, town librarian for ten. The organist, a plump and vestal figure destined for voluminous robes, emerged from a small door and primed the darkened sanctuary with *We Gather Together* That great hymn brought tears to my eyes. When the organist had finished, the choir shuffled in. I pegged the soprano soloist immediately; she was the only female onstage with a bouffant hairdo, golf-ball-sized earrings, and enough lipstick to paint the entire choir red. The tenor and alto soloists were a little harder to pick out; I guessed the mousy blond with the big nose and the skittish fellow wearing a toupee in the back row. The bass soloist was always the Goliath on the extreme rear left. Out came the choragus after a suspenseful silence.

I had not heard my Thanksgiving oratorio since a bunch of Texas Lutherans had butchered it in 1980. I held my breath, waiting for the organist to blast away. If she screwed up the scales in the introduction, no choir on earth could come in correctly. In fifteen years I had heard exactly three choirs, all in New Jersey, hit the opening chord square on the head; each of those three organists had been a moonlighting Liberace. Needless to say, I had never written another introduction that contained bold and dramatic scales for two hands simultaneously.

Whoops, nerves and too many doughnuts before curtain time: the organist smashed through the introduction with less panache than an aardvark on water skis. The choir director looked over at her for a nod or some indication of the beat; he was pissing in the wind, please, you couldn't locate the side of a barn in that hodgepodge. At his desperate signal, the choir opened their mouths and emitted a loud noise, particularly that soprano. Too bad; that's a great introduction when it's done right.

I glanced around me at the churchpeople. They didn't notice anything wrong. In fact, they were sitting there enrapt as if this were the greatest choir on earth. Each time I see this reaction, and it is each time I go to hear my hymns, I cannot believe it. Doesn't that caterwauling irritate them? Shouldn't that organist be stockaded? Shit, aren't they listening to the music at all? *Sure they're listening to the music,* Chuck said. *You're the jackass listening to the notes.* Of course I was listening to the notes! For Christ's sake, I was the guy who wrote them! What I was hearing now was such a pathetic shadow of what my mind heard when I wrote this piece that it drove me insane. It was like baking a cake with the costliest, most precisely measured ingredients, only to have it flop each and every time. Bah, the story of my life.

My heart in knots, I looked over at the choir. They were getting warmed up now; their conductor was regaining confidence with each flourish of his baton. That stupid organist was finally beginning to distinguish between the white and the black keys in front of her. Up stepped the soprano soloist and unleashed a volcanic aria. She was supposed to be the first Pilgrim. Ha, that vibrato could have sunk the *Mayflower*.

"Isn't she great," nudged the knitter. "We're so proud of Lou Anne."

"Tremendous," I obliged.

Lou Anne and Co. shot through a few intermediate scenes, then the fellow with the toupee stood up: the tenor, as I had guessed. He was the chief Puritan. The fellow had an excellent voice. It reminded me very much of Fox's on an off day.

"Isn't he wonderful," I was told. "He used to sing professionally in New York."

Didn't they all. "Terrific." A great melancholy stole over me quickly as a winter night. Fox, prince of my blood, gone? I stared at the choir and wished to God I had been born in Merlin, Ohio. By this time I would have married the gas station owner, had four kids, gained fifty asexual pounds, and I would be up there tonight singing in that choir for all I was worth. Jesus, where had I gone wrong? How had these people managed to figure it out? They couldn't all be stupid, or naive, or hypocritical. Was there some hidden wisdom in the soil out here that would forever elude me? Had, as Fox once said, my possessions destroyed me? No: diamonds, gyms, and ski cabins were fun, but I could always do without them. What had ruined me was my mind, and that possession had been congenital.

You always were a devil, Chuck averred. *Very unlike your sisters.* Great! How the hell was I supposed to change my spots now? My first memory is one of flinging sand in my brother's eye; it was a very natural thing to do. There was plenty of sand in Merlin, Ohio, and I would have thrown it here, too, I know it. *You know nothing,* Chuck scoffed. She was right. I knew nothing. Else I would not have ended up with a jolly minstrel's baby inside of me instead of my husband's. It was the ultimate evolution of the sand routine.

The church lights came up for a slight intermission/ offertory. As the choir seated themselves, the organist started an insipid chime arrangement written by J. Phelps McTuttle, one of my friendly rivals. This fellow wrote the liturgical equivalent of romance paperbacks; I had heard this particular offertory dozens of times and it never failed to catapult me into insulin shock. Why didn't that fat bitch play my Thanksgiving Medley or something else decent?

"Do you like that sort of music?" I asked the knitter next to me.

"It's lovely." she said. "Very inspiring."

"Not the offertory," I nearly snapped, "the Thanksgiving pageant."

"Oh! Very, very exciting. It reminds me of *The Messiah.* You know? The one they sing at Christmas?"

"I'm afraid I don't," I said coldly, returning eyes front. Jesus Christ, what did a Merlin illiterate know? The lights went down.

Up jerked the choir, moving on to the Indians now and the first Thanksgiving in Massachusetts. The bass portrayed the Indian chief, the alto Pocahontas. Moment by moment, I felt a tremendous itch creep along my entire epidermis; I had to get out of here and maybe run ten miles to neutralize it. The mousy alto started her solo and I'll be damned if that whole thing didn't sound like *Comfort Ye, My People.* How could I have written such derivative twaddle? How could Orville sell it? How could people buy it, then sing it? I'd die of mortification if anyone in Merlin figured out I had written this stinking pageant.

Smiling into the rafters, the alto sat down: Pocahontas had just converted to Christianity. My God! What abysmal mush! Once again I taxed my peripheral vision to its limits, spying on the churchfolk. "Amen," muttered someone's grandfather, probably Pocahontas's. Focused in deepest concentration upon the stage, no one moved. Cripes! Was I the only discriminating musician in the house? My mind was playing tricks on me. Maybe this *was* a masterpiece. Oh come on! No! Maybe these people were all drugged, or deaf. Here came the soprano again, bugling how everyone had so much to be thankful for. A tom turkey would have sung that better.

"She's gorgeous," whispered the woman ahead of me to her husband, who agreed. I could have rapped him one. *Will you sit still,* shouted Chuck, *it's almost over* I cleared my throat and froze. Why had I come out here? What had I possibly expected to hear? The choir turned to the last chorus, a huge Thanksgiving rouser, surely the worst piece I had ever written. My face turned redder than cranberry compote; that piece was the output of a religious fanatic.

The organist floored it until I thought the pipes would rumble off the walls. Meanwhile the choir maniacally screeched themselves blue in the face. Look at that, even their last words were "Hallelujah." This was a *Messiah* clone, all right. What a fucking dilettante I was! I should never have written a hymn in my life!

After a short silence, as if they couldn't believe this was over, the congregation burst into applause; two hundred years after Plymouth Rock, human beings were finally allowed to express emotion in the House of the Lord. "Great, Lou Anne," shouted the fellow ahead of me. Amens resounded through the hall like multiphonic mantras. "Encore!" shouted one particularly energetic fellow.

"That's Pastor Coyle," said the knitter. "He gets mighty worked up."

"They're not going to do an encore, are they?" I asked. If I didn't get an immediate lungful of November night, I'd keel over. Apparently the choir director thought the same; he bowed and flew offstage, hem fluttering at his heels. The organist launched into my *Thanksgiving Medley* again, gesturing with her head for the choir to file out before the crowd went mad.

Pastor Coyle jumped onstage. "Praise the Lord and

goodnight,'' he blessed. ''We thank you for coming and we'll see you at midweek prayer meeting!''

Now where was everyone going? ''Coffee and cookies downstairs,'' invited the knitter, putting her wool balls away. ''We'd love you to join us.''

''Oh! Thank you! Perhaps some other time,'' I answered. ''I'm expected back at the hotel, I'm afraid.'' Bucking an enormous tide rushing the other way, I squeezed to the front doors of the church, running down the stairs and back to the inn as if Lucifer himself were after me. Whipping my hat on the bed, I pulled on a sweatsuit and tore into the night. The clouds had blown away and the air was bitter cold. Agh! Is any creature in the universe more pathetic than a defrocked fanatic? I passed the choir director coming and going on the deserted Main Street. That wretch would not sleep tonight, either.

For two days, I hardly spoke to Martin. He could not understand why those Merlin pageanteers had so severely depressed me; after all, he didn't get depressed when people bought and used his computers. I broke out laughing when Orville informed me that over three hundred churches were performing that disgusting drivel this week. My publisher attributed this odd reaction to preconvention jitters, which made no sense whatever: to all intents and purposes, Fanny May Tingle was not even attending the ceremonies. She wasn't even throwing the reception. Mrs. Martin Weaver was.

Lately I had been feeling a little sick in the morning, a problem caused less by impending maternity than by the thought of eventually telling someone about it. Perhaps this had not been such a wise idea after all. Suppose the kid looked exactly like its father? Suppose that family had a history of mongolism? Suppose Fox ran into me five years from now and did a little backpedaling? The thought of diaper trucks, nursery school, and particularly PTA meetings made me extremely irritable. *Why didn't you think about this before?* Chuck asked. That was a fine display of hindsight from a woman who had conceived four children unintentionally. She knows very well that none of this baby business would have started had she not browbeat me into abandoning Fox.

"Darling, are you ready to go?" Martin called from downstairs.

I jumped away from the full-length mirror in our bedroom, where I had been inspecting my torso for telltale convexity. "What time is it?" I screeched back. Shit, you'd think we were going to a moon launch or something. It was just Thanksgiving dinner at the Weavers'.

"Three-thirty. I'll warm up the car."

"Be my guest! Burn a gallon of gas!" At that moment half the men in America were probably sitting in their cars, glancing alternately at their watches and the horn, wondering whether to toot or to just sit quietly as their wives made them late for the football games.

I selected the most tailored dress in my closet, added pearls and rouge, and entered the Bavaria momentarily. It was hotter than Nice in July. Martin backed swiftly out of the driveway; dinner began promptly at four. "Hold it, Flappy." I said, "have you got the wine and chocolates?"

"Oh! Sorry!" Martin did a three-point turn in the nearest alley.

"What were you doing in the car for ten minutes, may I ask?"

Martin frowned. "Picking M&Ms off the floor."

"The bag broke." I had been tearing it open with my teeth when some ass sideswiped me behind Copley Plaza last week. Pfuii, some thanks I got for saving two halogen headlights. "Got any left?"

"Eva, you're not serious! We're going to have a huge dinner." Martin pulled up to the front gate. "Where is everything?"

"On the kitchen table, exactly where I showed you." I watched him unlock the door, wondering why all husbands automatically became idiots between Thanksgiving and Christmas. Perhaps Lionel Trains had severe side effects after all.

We appeared at the Weavers' exactly at four, the first arrivals. Even Edmund was still upstairs swearing at his cuff links. "My son!" Ruth cried, enveloping Martin in her arms. I tried not to look. "You're still so thin!"

"Happy Thanksgiving," I said, handing James the but-

ler my coat and a small fortune in chocolate. Where was
the nearest bedroom? I could use a nap.

The doorbell rang as Edmund stepped down the staircase. "Hello, Eva," he said, kissing me. "You're looking
lovely today."

I think he meant it; that's the secret of Edmund's success. He opened the front door. "Gerald! Come in."

It was Percival. "Happy Thanksgiving!" he announced,
handing Ed booze and Ruth a huge spray of flowers. Arms
now free, he came directly over and hugged me. "How's
my sweetheart?"

"Kicking." I kissed him. Ruth was watching us like a
hawk. She didn't know the details but she knew everything; all you had to do was look at Percival's face.

"Follow me to the library, everyone," she said, grip-
ping Percival's arm like a truant officer. "Clarissa will be
here any minute."

James had just finished pouring champagne. We toasted
each other's health and swallowed daintily since belching
was forbidden under this roof. *You can't drink*, Chuck
screamed. *It'll wreck the baby*. Was she kidding? I was
born with bourbon in my veins, thanks to her.

"James," I whispered, "would you have some ginger
ale handy?"

"Ginger ale?" Ruth inquired from across the room. She
had been deep in conversation, so I had thought, with
Percival.

"I am parched," I said, dropping onto the couch. "Forgive me." Fox swooped across my imagination and disappeared behind the cliffs.

The doorbell rang: Clarissa and that crypto-preppie boyfriend with the bowtie, Peter, who presented Ruth with a
smoked ham and a framed print of the *Mayflower*. This guy
was shooting for the whole pie.

Percival slid beside me on the couch. "How was Ohio?"
he asked.

"A fiasco."

"Gerald!" Ruth called. "Would you mind carving the
turkey? Edmund refuses to touch it!"

Percival patted my hand. "Of course, Ruthie." James
led him to his banishment.

Peter sat on the opposite side of the coffee table, eyeing my legs for a few moments before remembering that he was here to earn points, not to enjoy himself. "Eva," he began, tossing a macadamia into his mouth, "what have you been up to since we saw you at that terrific clambake?"

"Nothing new or exciting." Chuck's strident laughter nearly split my temples.

"Not true," interrupted Martin, seating himself on the other side of the nuts. "Eva's become an expert herbalist."

You call that exciting? "Martin and Percival built a greenhouse," I explained.

"Eva means Gerald," Ruth interrupted with a smile.

Peter had already swallowed two glasses of champagne and was not keeping up. "Greenhouse?" he said, fixing on a word he knew. "That's interesting."

Martin saved us all from further embarrassment by explaining in precise detail exactly how he and Percival had designed this monstrosity. He hadn't even gotten to the solar batteries before James announced dinner.

Ruth clutched her son's arm in admiration. "I had no idea greenhouses were so complicated, dear."

"They're a snap," I said. "Ask Percival." We trooped into the dining room. The table looked exquisite, as always; Ruth has few peers when it comes to the art of entertaining. I would miss that if I ran away with Fox. *Forget Fox,* Chuck said, *You're a Weaver now.* I stood behind my name card, rubbing elbows with Martin and the upstart Peter. Percival sat at Ruth's hyperimmediate right.

In came the celery-and-oyster bisque; out went my appetite. Edmund said grace and James poured a pale yellowish wine.

"This is delightful," raved Peter. "Nothing on earth surpasses a fine oyster."

Either Peter had not met enough women, or he would eat anything to marry an heiress. I glanced at Percival, who winked at me with the eye farther from Ruth.

"Martin," his mother said, "I understand that San Francisco was a tremendous success." She turned to Percival. "Martin and Eva were out there all summer."

"How nice," Percival replied, his face cherubic. "It's a beautiful city."

I looked quizzically at Martin. He had never seen such

fascinating soup in his life. What the hell, I'd cover for him. "It certainly is."

"Is Rodotron all wrapped up now, dear?" Ruth asked. I'm sure Martin had told his mother ten times that Rodotron was all wrapped up. This exhibition was strictly for Peter's edification.

James collected the plates as Martin, with assists from Edmund, explained the ins and outs of corporate takeovers to Peter, who counterweighed valiantly with as much as he could remember of California business law. I was the only one at the table not to have finished my soup, a lapse not unnoticed by my hostess.

Clarissa got to tell everyone about her latest eyeball operations as James passed around the turkey. I wondered what sort of bird Paul and Rudy Fox were demolishing today, and with whom, where. I hoped that Fox was in better shape than I had been at this stage of the game ten years ago. *The hell you do,* scoffed Chuck, *You hope he's traumatized.* Why should I hope that, for Christ's sake? Meeting me was punishment enough.

"Eva," called Percival, "I understand your awards ceremony is next week."

"That's right." I'd see Fox next week. My guts flooded and the riptide whooshed up my neck.

"Which award is this, Eva dear?" asked Edmund. "How splendid."

"Hymnist of the Year," I said.

"That is like the Pulitzer or Nobel Prize of sacred composition," Ruth informed Peter. "Eva's won it three years in a row." I nearly burst out laughing. The last time I remember Ruth congratulating me was when I asked for her Stuffed Onions recipe.

"Is there a cash prize for that?" Peter asked. The table hushed.

"I forget." Orville was sending it all to the First Methodist Church in Merlin, Ohio: organ lessons for that bimbo.

"It's a large sum, believe me," Ruth said, assuring him of the value of this prize. "Not that Eva needs it, of course."

Martin stepped into the ring. "More stuffing, anyone?" That swabbed the decks until salad, when Clarissa mentioned that she had not seen a decent movie or play in months.

"Ho! Eva!" said Edmund, spearing a walnut. "That reminds me! Your friend Lionel Boyd sent us two tickets to his play next week."

"Dr. Boyd?" I croaked. "He did?"

"You don't want to see that play, Dad," Martin said. "I think it got very bad reviews."

I whirled in my chair. "Come on, Flaps! It got great reviews!"

"What's the name of this play?" Peter asked. "I love the theater."

"*Cloistrophobia*," I told him. "It's about a black monk who gets going with a lesbian nun in a strange monastery. It's a musical comedy. The costumes are great."

"I've heard of that," Clarissa said. "If you're not using your tickets, Mother, Peter and I would love to go."

That did it. "I'm sorry dear, we must attend or Dr. Boyd will be crushed. He sent me an extravagant bouquet of roses with the tickets."

"What'd he do that for?" I asked, shit, that joker had a plot up his sleeve, I knew it, and I was going to be the punchline.

"Darling," Martin soothed, "Lionel is a very impulsive fellow."

"Eva has many extraordinary friends involved with Broadway productions," Ruth told Peter. "Dr. Boyd wrote me a fine note."

"What was in this note?" I asked suspiciously. "Lionel usually telephones."

"Really, Mother," Martin said, not liking this any more than I, "it must have been a prank."

"Nonsense, darling," Ruth responded. "Mr. Boyd invited us to the show and to an exclusive party afterward."

"What day," I demanded, "and where's this party?"

"Friday the fifth of December, I believe." God damn it! Awards day! "Dr. Boyd was not sure of the whereabouts of the party."

Sure he was, the conniving weasel. He just wasn't sure how he was going to pull this off without getting beaten to death.

"He sounds very intriguing," Clarissa said. "What sort of doctor is Mr. Boyd?"

A fucking zombie witch doctor, that's what! Martin shot me a warning look. I picked up my wine. *Put that down,* shouted Chuck, *The last thing you need is a shrivelled mutant!* I stonily replaced the glass and counted to ten: one Fox, two Fox, three Fox, inhaling and exhaling slowly on each count. It reminded me of childbirth school. I'd kill that son of a bitch.

"A psychotherapist," Ruth said, remembering. She did not remember, however, that overbearing mothers were Lionel's specialty. "James, I believe we're finished." Ruth looked at her next gopher on the agenda, Percival. "Tell us, Gerald, what have you been doing lately?"

He'd been meeting me for lunch six times a week, of course, chronicling the family history since he and Edmund first met at Harvard. "Well, as you know, your chalet has been occupying my attention for some time," Percival began. He winked at me. I think even Martin saw that. Percival didn't care; he knew a Weaver would never get up and hit him, particularly at the dinner table.

"Have you spent any time at your summer home?"

"No, none at all," Percival answered after a slight hesitation.

Fortunately. Edmund picked up his friend's SOS. "So how far along are you with that chalet, Gerald? Will we be staying in it this winter?"

That got us through the pumpkin pie, thanks to Peter, who had spent a lot of time in ski lodges throughout the globe. Whether he knew it or not, the fellow had single-handedly saved this meal from drowning in its own otiosity. I doubted Clarissa was going to marry him, though; twice I caught her looking into the gravy boat, holding her breath, and distinctly thinking of someone else, probably the new orderly at Mass Eye and Ear. If it were another doctor, Peter would not be here.

Everyone filed into the library for cordials. This time Percival planted himself next to me on the couch before Ruth could assign him a chair twenty feet away. "Are you feeling all right, sweetie?" he asked. "You didn't eat a thing."

Ten thousand fingertips, all of them Fox's, scuttled lasciviously over me. They were all trying to rescue his baby, but that would never be. The baby was my consolation prize and I would never turn it over to Fox, nor to Martin, and particularly not to Ruth or Chuck. No more Ruths, and no more Chucks; this critter would become the first successful human being in fifteen generations of hell fodder. *Good luck,* laughed Chuck, *You'll need it.* I tossed my head. "I ate plenty," I said.

Percival poured me a cup of coffee. *Put that down,* shrieked Chuck. No *caffeine until July.* God damn it! How else was I supposed to stay awake? I carefully replaced the cup onto its venerable gold-tinged saucer. Now I was beginning to understand why my mother became a monster during gestation.

Peter was looking at my legs again. I think he was dying to ask a few questions about Lionel but dared not wipe out his lead with Clarissa's parents. Jesus Christ! Where were all the fearless men? Fox! Those gray eyes watched me always now, waiting. Jesus, it drove me mad! My tongue burned to taste his throat! What use were my arms if they couldn't encircle his back? I'd give every hymn I had to have that reckless body sunk into mine NOW! Did these people have any idea of that exquisite dangerous life beyond this library? By God, they did not! Every neat gilt corner reeked of death! Mine!

I got up. "Excuse me," I said directly to Ruth, "I need to take a walk."

Martin caught up with me in the hallway. "I'll come along."

"Don't you dare," I half muttered, half laughed. "I'll kill you. Martin stood still and I didn't look back.

James retrieved my coat from the closet. "Which direction are you walking, Eva?" he asked. "In case someone asks."

"North for Percival, south for anyone else."

"Very good." He held open the front door and I headed into the night. In three months this gorgeous warm coat would not fit me anymore. Nothing would fit me. Fox, keeper of the keys, where are you? This baby had already backfired completely. Instead of making me forget its father, it reminded me with every dart of nausea, with every swollen joint, that its father was alive, and away from me. Would those long slim fingers never run over my round belly? Would those gray eyes not watch me deliver this baby? Then I didn't want it! I had never wanted it! I only wanted its father! *Oh Jesus*, I prayed, *I think I made a huge mistake*.

I walked swiftly down Beacon Street. How could people live in these monstrosities, accumulating china and children, mowing lawns, driving station wagons, for years on end? My soul cried for a twentieth-floor cave in Manhattan where I could turn the lights off at night and stare out the window at glistening concrete, neon, and rude raw men driving themselves as far as they could go, as fast as possible, soaring or crashing spectacularly according to the luck of the draw. Fox was thrashing in that black ocean now, without me. How could a baby possibly assist him? For that matter, how could I possibly assist him? In six months the chemistry would fizzle and he'd have nothing but a cantankerous old biddy screeching at him to take out the garbage. *Not true*, said Chuck, *He's much different than your father* Big deal! Was I much different from Chuck? It was just a matter of time before the garbage, the coffee grounds, and the toilet tissue became the compelling issues of our existence.

"Eva," called Percival, some steps behind, "wait." He caught up with me, the epitome of a gentleman in a cashmere coat and black hat. His wives had been fools to leave him. "Care for some company?"

"Sure." We covered another three blocks without speaking.

"You stand that family on its head," Percival said, smiling. He looked over at me; I buried my chin in some slain beast's fur as we walked past another five or ten Thanksgiving banquets. "It's just what they need."

"Is that so?" I laughed sarcastically.

"Don't be so hard on them, honey," Percival said. "They love you."

Perhaps they did, but I loved Fox more. "I'm leaving Martin," I said.

Percival was not expecting that, not after all those jigsaws in Cape Cod. "You're not serious . . ." I kept walking. "But why. Eva? He's a wonderful man."

"I agree completely."

That silenced him for a few moments. Percival took my arm. Finally he sighed. "There's someone else, isn't there?"

A small sad smile rumpled my lips. "Yes." Yes, always yes, yes as long as I had insides to spare and a longing elusive and gigantic as Halley's comet. "It's all my fault."

"I've heard that before."

"But it's true, Percival. Martin is kind and generous and everything a woman would want." How fatuous that sounded. *Sure does, you shit,* Chuck agreed.

"Who is this other man? Is he a real improvement, Eva? Think carefully."

Think? That was the problem! With Martin, I thought; with Fox, I felt. Which was the truer measure of love or improvement? Perhaps the scales should be read backward in a mirror; perhaps I should imagine both Martin and Fox gone and see whose absence hurt more. Bah, that was ridiculously obvious. I would miss Martin softly and constantly in my head and in a fond corner of my heart. But I would not miss him in every atom and hot tingling nerve that made me very much alive and, above all, a woman. Improvement? Fox was not an improvement over Martin. But with Fox, I was an improvement over myself. "He's everything," I said finally.

Percival sighed; one did not utter such lines before crossing a private Rubicon. The conversation was upsetting him. "Let's go back," I said, "before they start playing rummy without us."

"How long has this been going on?" Percival asked.

"Eight months."

"Oh dear. I rather suspected it all summer."

"I didn't see him all summer. I've been fighting this, Percival."

"I know you have." He kissed my gloved hand.

"Have you ever been in this situation?"

"No, my dear, unfortunately not. My wives quite contented me. It was a brutal shock to discover the feeling was not mutual."

"Stop punishing yourself, Percival. Your wives should be shot."

Percival smiled; the idea had never occurred to him. "Am I going to meet this fellow?" he asked. "No! I don't want to meet him. Yes, I do. Ah, this news has startled me.''

Hey man, this was mother's milk compared to the other half of the news. I felt a little twinge deep inside: alive, and mine; grow, baby. grow. "He's singing a piece of mine at the convention next week. If you can't hack that, there will be a party afterward at home. Ruth and Edmund will be there pretending they never saw *Cloistrophobia*.''

"Is Lionel going to tell them you wrote that number?" Percival had seen the show this summer after I had told him about the cakewalk. He thought it was the most wicked, funny thing he had ever seen. Then again, he knew who wrote it.

"Of course not," I snapped. "That shithead is hoping they'll find out all by themselves and disown me. He thinks he's doing everyone a favor.''

"I'll be there with my saber," Percival said. "Have no fear.''

The night had turned very cold; it was the season for two people to stay in bed under six inches of down. I looked up at the stars and thought I saw Fox.

We turned into the Weavers' front walk. "Tell me something, Percival, how did you get over your wives?''

Percival lifted the brass knocker and hesitated. The porch light coppered his brown eyes as a crescent of white breath floated out of his mouth. "I met you," he said, rapping against the front door.

12

I WOKE UP SICK. My stomach had been lying in ambush for seven hours, concocting new disguises, waiting for the moment I would half open my eyes and stop dreaming of Fox, at which point it would transform itself into a galloping steed, then a rock, then perhaps a blizzard. Every morning for weeks now it had been trying like hell to dislodge the new arrival flourishing inches below it, to no avail. Fox's microscopic barnacle intended to stay.

For several minutes I lay still, watching the chandelier over my bed entice the sun. My nose felt cold; winter had finally claimed the nights. Martin was in California this week, reviewing the troops. He had left the day after Thanksgiving and would not be back until Friday, in time for the Hymnist of the Year awards, weather and/or Paloma permitting. She lived in San Francisco now, working for that knothole Dueser. Although my husband swore up and down that he would not be seeing his former secretary, I could hardly believe him; they had launched too many raids together over the last eight years. Yesterday I had driven him to the airport with hardly a word, just about delivering him into Paloma's arms. Martin had asked for that, though: ever since that awful Thanksgiving dinner, he had been gabbling incessantly of Nizor's Insane Asylum in Stockbridge, and of how I should perhaps deposit myself there before Christmas, recovering from exhaustion. If the bin had no openings, his mother knew of three mentalists who would be delighted to treat me at any time here in Boston. I wondered if Ruth suspected that it was not I but this marriage that was exhausted, and that if I needed three specialists, they were an abortionist, a chaplain, and a travel agent, in that order. *You forgot the lawyer,* Chuck prodded. Instead of replying, I went to the bathroom and leaned my head against the toilet, waiting.

This baby had me all screwed up. I wanted it ferociously. then I hated it; it made me abominably proud, then ashamed; it made me unable to look at Martin, and at the same time, it made me love him more than I ever had, until I realized that Fox was inside me twenty-four hours a day now, a living fire. That made me crazy. *Just wait until your waistline goes,* Chuck carped. *We'll see what gets burned and crazy then.* The woman had been screaming at me ceaselessly, exhibiting none of the Christlike magnanimity she so loved to read about. I don't understand. If I had murdered Lionel, say, or burned Weaver, Inc. to the ground, that was forgivable; once semen got into the act, however, I had lashed myself onto a bobsled express to hell. Jesus Christ! How had the Puritans ever propagated themselves?

The phone rang as my stomach did its bursting-antigravity-dam routine. "Hello," I croaked, swallowing acridly. Perhaps it was Fox.

"Are you sick?" Chuck asked.

"I had to run to the phone." I'd be running straight back to the bathroom in two minutes. There was no time to spare. "What's new? How are you feeling?"

"I'm in excellent shape. The Lord has cured me."

"He should be getting pretty good at that by now." Chuck sighed. I heard some moving liquid in the background. "What's that noise? Are you washing dishes?"

"I'm making fruitcakes for Christmas."

Rum was Chuck's downfall. In four decades perhaps one fruitcake in ten had made it to the holiday table properly marinated; I'd better not ruffle her feathers. "Praise the Lord."

The pouring stopped. "What made you say that?"

My stomach did a perfect jackknife, then a belly flop. "Chuck, could I call you back in a few minutes? I'm feeling a little ill. Promise me you won't drink any rum in the meantime."

Chuck hung up on me. I hobbled to the bathroom, barfed nothing but lye, and dialed my mother as quickly as possible. "How're the fruitcakes?"

"Why are you sick? Are you pregnant?"

"God damn it! I told you not to drink that rum!"

"I didn't drink anything." Again I heard that pouring. "Who's the father?"

I laughed a little too hysterically. "Is this some sort of joke? Why did you call me? It's eight o'clock in the morning!"

"Where's Martin? I have something to tell him before he goes to work."

She was trying to disorient me with these unrelated questions. They did the same thing in all the junk romances. "He's in California on business until Friday. May I perhaps take a message?"

"Stop talking like the Weavers, Eva. You sound ridiculous."

"Will you tell me the bloody message and leave me in peace," I screamed. "Jesus Christ! Can't you tell I'm not feeling well? What is the purpose of this call?"

"First, I want to tell Martin that I found his birthday card and I'll send it right up to him."

"That's terrific! His birthday was six months ago! Never mind! Send it! He needs a good laugh! What else did you want to say?" This migraine would shatter my cranium.

"My plane's getting into Boston Friday morning." Chuck paused. "You are still getting that Hymnist of the Year award, aren't you? I've told all my friends about it."

"Save your plane fare, Chuck. Orville's accepting the award again. You won't get any pictures. It's going to be very boring, just like the last times." At the convention last year in Houston, Chuck had created a major disturbance trying to take pictures with a suggestion box.

I heard enough pouring for fifty fruitcakes. "Don't you want me to come up?" Chuck asked, thirty-four years of disillusionment in her voice.

"Of course I want you to come up!" I lied. "Just

promise me you'll sit quietly! No more going around telling people you're Mrs. Tingle!''

''Eva, please,'' Chuck pooh-poohed, ''I would never do such a thing.''

Not when sober, perhaps. Thank God no one had believed her. ''When's the plane? I don't think I can pick you up before one or so.''

''Why not?''

''Big party, Chuck. Go buy yourself a new dress with the Bonwit's card I gave you. Something frilly.''

''Oh, I couldn't do that.''

''Why the hell not? You're a good-looking woman! The Lord will forgive you! No more brown jumpers or I'm taking the card back!'' Chuck said nothing. Something was bothering her above and beyond six weeks on the wagon. Those fruitcakes were fizzing sticks of dynamite. ''Are you okay? Is Robert not talking to you again?''

''I've been having very strange dreams about you.''

My gut didn't like that. ''Really.'' I quavered, violently rubbing my stomach. Chuck's worst dreams have always come true.

''They're so bad I'm not going to tell you.''

''I've got to go. I think I ate a bad shrimp last night.''

Chuck didn't believe that. ''I'll take the trolley to your house. Don't drive a car in your condition.''

''Would you put that booze away?'' I shouted. ''That loony bin cost me four thousand bucks! The least you could do is stay sober until Christmas!''

Chuck placated her soul with a morose recitation of the Nicene Creed. I hung up wondering whether I should have told her everything.

''Jesus CHRIST, Eva! Did you read the reviews?''

''Of course not.''

Lionel had been partying at the Hampshire House for two days and was not at the peak of his powers. Neither was I, shit, it was six A.M. and snowing heavily. '' 'This travesty of the Catholic religion is going to infuriate many theatergoers.' Can you believe that? Who said anything about Catholics? And what travesty? This is a musical! CRIMiny! The critics up here are ASSholes!''

Surprise. ''Keep reading.''

"Pooh, sit DOWN, Sugar Buns. I've already read this to you five times, you know what it says." Lionel cleared his throat. "'Pooh Excelsior, the Broadway star playing Friar Moe for a very limited engagement in Boston, mortifies the flesh in ways we have never seen before.' Now what the HELL does that mean?"

"That means if Pooh were white he would have been panned. Did they like your costumes? Make it quick." My stomach was waking up now.

"Of course! They're terRIFic costumes! And the cakewalk drove the audience NUTS! Wait a minute! Listen! 'Never was excommunication so titillating.' What awful language."

"So it was basically a good review," I yawned. "Great."

"Don't you DARE hang up, you bitch! Are you coming to the show tomorrow night? Pooh misses you."

"Aren't you forgetting something, sweetheart? Like sacred music conventions at the Park Plaza?"

Lionel gasped. "My GAWD! It's that karate chopper again!"

I exhaled thick soot, which curled slowly as a cat's tail above my bed. "Yep."

"I completely forGOT about that."

"The hell you did," I retorted. "You invited my mother-in-law to the party here afterward."

"Who told you such FILTH?" Lionel shrieked, a perfect castrato. The higher his voice gets, the more he's trying to cover up.

"The recipient of a lovely bouquet," I said acridly, "who will never believe I wrote that cakewalk."

"Jesus, Mary, and Joseph! I do everyone a HUGE favor and I get screwed! No, not you, Cuddles! Never you!" Lionel muzzled the phone, trumpeting his devotion to Pooh. Anyone within one hundred yards heard every word. "Eva, we've got to get some sleep. A reporter is interviewing us in three hours and we'd better be sharp." Once again Lionel stifled the phone to confer with his beloved. "Pooh wants to know if you can come to the Friday matinee."

"Chuck will be here. Should I bring her along?"

"SpAAAAAre me!" Chuck terrifies Lionel. He knows she

tells Beatrice his mother everything. "Is she going to be preaching at the party? You want your karate chopper to hear THAT?"

Why not? I was already floating a thousand miles downstream. "She claims to be completely cured."

"Come here, Cocoa Buns," Lionel said loudly into the mouthpiece. "See this one-hundred-dollar bill? That says that Eva's mother is going to drink five vodka martinis, then try to give you a Bible."

"Ah'm not so shore thassa good bet, Lahnell," Pooh said doubtfully. Chuck was a living legend amongst the cast of *Cloistrophobia*.

My stomach suddenly twirled like a loose quarter. "Are you all set up with Fox on your rehearsal?" I asked, writhing. Pregnancy was crucifixion.

"Relax, Mom! It's etched in stone here in my appointment book!"

Pain stabbed through my side; soon I'd be sick again. Fox! I wanted him to rock me a little, crooning into my ear that he loved me, until I quietly died. "Don't miss it," I said, "and you'd better know your part."

"Threats will get you nowhere, gorgeous! Toodle-ooo!"

I let the handset drop onto the bed and turned my head towards the window. Snow was so romantic . . . I remembered one Saturday afternoon several years ago when Martin had lit the fire in the bedroom, brought up two snifters and his finest brandy, and had helped me get over a cold. If the snow did that to Martin, I wondered what it would do to Fox. *The usual, of course*, Chuck snapped. *Men are all alike*. That was a mature, well-researched piece of philosophy from a woman who had only slept with one man in her life, and my father at that; shit, no wonder the poor thing believed all those bogus platitudes. She had to.

Today I didn't want this baby at all. The moment the creature tired of bullfighting with my stomach, it started cabling headaches hot and fast to my brain, which threw them all in a heap behind my eyes. If I thought about telling Martin I was pregnant, the whole heap ignited and gave me a fever. I had about two weeks before he figured it out for himself; Martin knows I have an unnatural hatred of pot bellies.

A plow chugged by, walling in everyone's driveway behind three feet of densely packed snow. When Richard arrived, I'd have him dig us out; Martin had a fancy new shovel that was supposed to relieve back tension. Whee, my head hurt. *This isn't going to keep up until June, is it,* I prayed, rubbing my temples. If so, they could do a caesarean on my skull. Big Buddy said nothing, as usual. I turned on my side, listening to the hushed earth; today would be a great day to be buried behind Old North Church. The critter didn't like that and let my stomach know it. Ten minutes later I left the bathroom and slowly dressed myself: enough rotting in bed, praying to The Deaf Puppeteer for departed gentlemen. If no replies were forthcoming in either case, I might as well make myself a little spare change.

I went to the study and worked for a while on a bombastic hymn designed for evangelical pep rallies in Yankee Stadium. The thing leaked onto the paper just about as fast as I could move my pen; why is it that the less optimistic I feel, the more optimistically I write? *Masks are your specialty,* Chuck told me, as if this were somehow undesirable.

The phone rang. "Hello, my sweet."

"Hi, Martin," I said. " Having fun?"

"This is not quite what I'd call fun."

Of course it was fun. It was work. "When are you getting home, Flappy? You haven't forgotten about the hymn convention tomorrow night, have you?"

"No, my girl, I'm looking forward to that. Just a moment. Here. The plane's due in at 12:45."

"So I can pick you and Chuck up at the same time."

"Your mother's coming to town?" Martin cleared his throat. "That's nice." He was lying. Last time Chuck had visited, she had insisted on mowing the lawn. Before I could stop her, she had run over three of Martin's rose bushes.

"Don't worry, I'll put her to work shovelling."

"It's snowing?"

"Yes, Flappy, it snows in Boston during the winter," I

said, getting annoyed. As usual, here I'd be saddled with snow, Chuck, and a party, while Martin merely cruised in at the last moment, ready to pull into his neatly plowed driveway and enjoy himself. Then I thought about Martin watching Fox's baby grow up, thinking it was his, and guilt clamped my head like a bear trap. I would never be able to make this up to him. *Sure you can*, said Chuck. *Have two children*. The woman was kidding herself. Two wrongs did not make one right.

"Two wrongs, pet?"

"Flaps, you have a bad connection. Have you seen Paloma?"

"No, I haven't."

"Why not?"

"Eva, there is no reason I should see her."

I had to think about that for a moment. Reason had never stopped me; if anything, it had without fail spun me in the opposite direction and given me a good healthy shove. "Do you think reason is hereditary, Martin?"

Martin started to chuckle, then decided he'd better clear his throat in case I was serious. "Why do you ask?" he replied evasively.

"I was wondering why you always do the right thing."

"I try but I don't always succeed."

Could have fooled me, pal. "Would you still love me if I didn't always do the right thing?"

"That depends on what you did." Martin smiled as he said it, but I knew he was deadly serious. People who always did the right thing allowed very little latitude for those who did not. I sighed.

"Okay, I'll get you at the airport. Try to comb your hair before you get off the plane. Chuck's going to be with me."

I could hear that brain spinning three thousand miles away. "Wouldn't it be easier for you if I just had George meet me, pet? My meeting might run late."

"No way, Flaps! We've got a lunch date at Jimmy's!" My mother has never left Boston without attempting to consume her weight in fried clams. "Chuck's taking us out."

Then Martin knew he was licked. "That's very sweet,"

he said evenly. I had to admire the cunning Weaver reflexes, which had once again left the opposition impotently punching thin air.

"Sure, sure!" I said furiously, hanging up. *Very crude, Eva,* Chuck reprimanded, *first you force the man on his secretary, then you force him on his mother-in-law.* "Jesus Christ, Chuck," I shouted, "where did you learn boxing?"

Now the doorbell rang. Fox! My insides flapped like undershirts on a clothesline. I ran to the foyer and opened the door.

Percival stood outside stomping snow off his rubbers. "Hello, my dear, I was just driving through and wondered if you needed anything."

I quickly flipped three switches so that a hidden siren would not go off inches from Percival's head and give him a heart attack. "Got a snowplow in your back pocket?" I asked, waving to Harry my neighbor, who was leaning against his shovel observing us with disapproval. I pulled Percival inside. "Like pea soup?"

"I adore pea soup." Percival sat at the kitchen table with a cup of tea as I put the fire under a massive green lump in an orange pot. For three days I had been hacking away at it piece by piece. "I am so looking forward to tomorrow, Eva," Percival said. "I can hardly wait to hear your hymn."

My skin started heating up a little, anticipating Fox. "It's not much," I replied, freeing a smoked pork hock from a mushy green wall. My fingers ran over those pale strawberry lips, trying to separate them. My stomach began to sink slowly, like a just-dead pickerel. I sat down.

"You are much too modest, my dear," Percival said, stirring the soup. "Awards are great fun."

Who wanted awards? I only wanted Fox. I got a loaf of pumpernickel from the breadbox and started slicing it. Percival watched me from the range. "What are you looking at?" I asked.

"You," he said, meaning my stomach. Percival knew. "You've changed."

I took a deep breath. It was not obvious. Was it? Was I hallucinating? Someone had to tell me. "Percival," I began. *Don't you dare!* screamed Chuck, splitting my eardrums. I bit my tongue until the ringing stopped.

"Yes?"

"Would you mind getting the butter?" I finished. We sat down. One look at that pea soup and my stomach dove for cover. "How's work?" I asked, replacing my spoon on its napkin.

Percival described three of his latest projects to me. He was at that stage in his career when all he had to do was draw a few pictures, boss three hundred people around, collect thousands of dollars from enthralled clients, and scoop up every architectural award in sight. Shit, what would I be collecting in forty years? *Chins and alimony checks,* Chuck said matter-of-factly. *You peaked too soon.* That was quite a joke coming from my mother. She had peaked at the moment of her birth.

"I'm so glad to see you're not drinking," Percival interrupted.

I looked out the window at the swirling snow; the moment Percival left I would curl up in front of the fire with a huge junk romance. Wine? I'd donate my life for a glass of Moselle. "Percival," I said, "stick to me like glue tomorrow, would you?"

"My pleasure," he replied. "Who's frightening you?"

"The singer."

Spoon nary pausing in midair, Percival said, "I see." Which held his tongue, cowardice or supreme bravery? Supreme indifference? Shit, it was easier to read microfilm than a blueblood WASP.

"Can you come out to lunch with us beforehand?"

"Unfortunately, I already have an appointment" Percival said.

"Oh." The thought of lunching singlehandedly with Chuck and Martin dismayed me. "Then we'll meet you at the Park Plaza at three."

Percival stayed for another hour, helping me call the caterers: the less I had to do with this party, the greater the chance I'd squeak through it. Orville had invited another four dozen influential Baptists, Richard was dragging over his most important Christian booksellers, and Chuck would try to convert them all a second time. "Jesus, Percival, this is going to be a disaster," I said, hanging up the phone. "I can feel it in my bones."

"Nonsense, Eva," he replied. "We'll have a terrific time."

"Doing what? Swapping parables?" I rubbed my forehead. "How did this thing get so out of hand? All I did was invite Orville over to dinner." A pox on southern gentlemen! They could talk yams out of a nose!

"It will be very interesting to mix with a different crowd," Percival continued, "wouldn't you agree?"

"No!" I shouted. "They're going to be exactly like my mother!" Alarmed, the kid hopscotched ten inches up my throat, wanting out. Instead I soaked it with tepid tea. "I'm never writing another hymn as long as I live," I muttered, brains on the half shell. "It's ruined me."

"Never say such a thing, darling!" Percival came over to my side of the table and stroked my hair. Bah, easy for him to say. He wasn't born straddling a picket fence. "I will not let you out of my sight tomorrow, I promise."

"That's a help," I said, feebly raising my head. "Do you know any karate?"

"None whatever."

"Do you still have your saber from the Harvard fencing team?"

"Eva, what are you trying to tell me?"

I looked at him. "I have no idea."

Percival sat down and contemplated his pumpernickel. "Are you going to eat that soup?"

"I hate pea soup." Actually I loved it. The kid hated it.

"I haven't seen you eat in weeks."

"Haven't been hungry in weeks."

Percival sighed. "What does Martin say about all this?"

I laughed sarcastically. "My husband is blind, deaf, and dumb." Percival blinked slowly as a doll made in Taiwan. *You've just insulted the man's tribe,* Chuck said. *Nice going.* I reached across the table, taking his hand. "Just kidding, Percival. Martin's been away." If Martin sewed himself to my skin and stuck there for one hundred years, he'd still be just beyond the horizon. Again I hooted at nothing, like a dazed owl.

Percival stared at me for several moments. Love had

pulled his glance a little off-center; it reminded me of Fox.
"Maybe I should stay here this afternoon," he said.

"That won't be necessary," I nearly screamed. "I'm
not going anywhere."

"I think you should go to bed. You look green."

Funny. I felt red. *Black*, corrected Chuck. She meant
yellow. "You've eaten too much pea soup, Percival," I
breezed, getting up. Two strokes of lightning slashed my
knees but I remained on my feet: no shirkers on this barge.
I escorted Percival to the front door and slipped his coat
back on.

Percival put a hand on my shoulder. Again I thought of
what fools his wives had been. "Things are much worse,
aren't they?" he asked.

"Much worse," I agreed. I did not identify the new
monkey wrench. Instead I opened the door and got a
faceful of snow.

"If I can be of any help, you must tell me." He pulled
on his gloves. "I have a winter home too, Eva."

"Got anything in Ecuador?" I asked. It was about time
those thirty kids found out who sent them the erector sets
and dollhouses every Christmas.

"Would you settle for Peru?" Percival kissed my mouth.
Funny how everything he did now reminded me of Fox.
"Peru, Vermont."

"With you on weekends?"

"Of course."

I wondered how many more weekends remained before
everyone in the world knew that Fox's stock had split.
"I'll think about that." As Percival slowly drove his Saab
away, two juveniles pelted it with snowballs.

For half an hour, rising every five minutes to prod the
fire, I tried to read *Queen of Slaves*, redundant drivel
about life in ancient Ethiopia. The more I read, the more
my insides wandered; I kept thinking about Fox's two fine
testicles and how I used to take them in my mouth like two
coddled eggs, softly gargling with them before my tongue
pushed them out and headed north, above the timber line,
to that mouthwatering soft rock that always wept to feel
my lips again. I remembered how first it would cry sugar,
then salt, both when it was homesick, and how it began to

boil after three minutes inside of me. Then I smelled honey and vinegar and that drove me nuts, because next I would start tasting it again. Once I tasted it, the kid would taste it and go berserk: I was swallowing its tail.

I threw the book down and lurched to my front window. The wind was obstinately sneezing snow off the houses, off the streets, off my neighbor Harry's Cadillac: it was allergic to shovels and plows. I'd go outside and irritate it a little.

"Hi, Harry," I called shortly. scraping Martin's finest shovel along the front steps. "Good exercise we're getting here." I attacked the snow as if Fox were buried beneath it, waiting for me.

"This Gahd damn shit," Harry replied, lovingly wiping a new drift from the windshield of his Cadillac. "What happened to kids with snow shovels?"

They were all clearing their drug dealers' sidewalks, of course. "You got me."

"Say, doesn't Mahtin have a snow blowah?" Harry wanted to know.

"It's busted." Chuck had mistaken it for the lawn mower last spring.

We each returned to our driveways; Harry gave up ten minutes later and drove to a bar, where he would spend the rest of his impromptu holiday toasting his hardier comrades at City Hall. I finished the front steps and progressed to the sidewalk, shoveling faster and faster the more the wind tried to obliterate my work. I wanted to see how violently I could get my heart to pump before it split in half. *Give up,* scoffed Chuck, *That thing's built like Brünnhilde.* Well, I guess I'd just have to shovel a little harder then! I hung my cap, then my jacket, on the picket fence; the wind flash-froze them. I started down the other half of the sidewalk. Now the wind hit me in the face. I didn't care. I wasn't really shoveling snow.

The streetlights came on and the wind sloppily powdered their noses. Soon after I had started on the driveway. a cab pulled up to the house. Richard emerged carting three stupid little valises behind him. He refuses to buy one large suitcase because he thinks the airlines will lose it. "Eva!" he shouted. "I've been calling you for hours!"

"You have not." I heaved a load of snow over my shoulder. In midflight the wind blasted it straight at Richard's face. Choking exaggeratedly, he dropped all three valises into the snow. The cab skidded off, looking for better fares.

"Will you cut it out," I yelled. "It's only water." I was suddenly seized with the idea that Fox was going to visit me tonight. I wanted to see what he looked like with snowflakes in his eyelashes.

Richard stumbled around the curb retrieving his luggage. He could make a snowman with what got shoved under his pants. "I thought you were picking me up downtown," he said irritably, swatting at his cuffs.

"Hey! You already got a free hotel! Stop whining for the limousine!"

"Is the front door open?"

"No, you've got to break a window."

Cursing, Richard mushed vigorously up the walk. Whatever snow I had displaced two hours ago had blown smoothly back; now it twinkled at me, daring me to try that trick again. My arms were too fagged to take it on, so I trotted up and down the front walk, say, thirty times, kicking that frozen dust out of my way. I whisked the new snow off the front step with my mittens.

Suddenly the porch light went on. Dressed in long johns and Martin's smoking jacket, Richard appeared behind the storm door. "Eva! What are you doing out there?" he shouted. " Burying yourself?"

"I'm waiting for a friend."

"Who? Get back in here! Your friend will ring the doorbell!"

No he wouldn't. I stood out at the gate a few minutes more waiting for Fox. Five solitary figures walked by, this evening's survivors of the Orange Line. Each passed me as if I might suddenly leap out and mug them.

"Eva!" Richard called. "Get in the house, you maniac! Now what are you doing?"

"Just a moment, I'm looking for my hat." Ten years ago Chuck had knit it for me with all the leftover yarn in her possession. It was quite an unusual piece. Aha! I yanked a fuchsia pompom from the drifts and walked to the front door.

"Your lips are blue!" Richard screamed. "I'm calling a doctor?"

"Will you shut up, you paranoid idiot," I said, stepping inside. "I'm not even shivering." The house felt like a steambath. I whipped off my sweater; underneath, my blouse was soaked. I sniffed the air. "What's for dinner, honey?"

"Dinner?" Richard shrieked. "I've been watching you out the window for forty-five minutes!"

"Richard," I sighed, "at least you could have made yourself useful."

"I had to know when to call the ambulance. You should have seen yourself out there! It was frightening!"

"What, an honest woman getting a little exercise?" I retorted. Chuck took a swat at me and connected. "I've got to take a bath." After three steps I had to hold on to the bannister. My guts belched murkily: diarrhea.

After half an hour Richard knocked on the bathroom door. "Dinner's ready," he said. "Are you about done in there?"

"Yeah, yeah." I had been trying to drown myself in the bathtub for twenty minutes. Chuck kept pulling my head out of the water. I wrapped myself in my warmest flannels. Richard was standing outside the bathroom door with a cup of pea soup. "Is that what you made for supper?" I asked.

"What's the matter? Don't you like pea soup?"

"It's great." We went to the kitchen. Richard had set the table using all the wrong silverware.

"What's this?" Richard asked.

"That's a soup spoon. You put down a bouillon spoon."

Richard looked at me as if I had erroneously called him out on strikes. "How many spoons do you WASPs need to eat pea soup?"

"Just one, dear, the soup spoon. Ah! Bagels." I chomped into one. "Where's Brasilia?"

"Working."

"When am I ever going to meet this divinity?"

"You're not." The doorbell rang. Fox! I knew it! "Who's that?" Richard asked, startled. "Martin?" He looked very guilty. That's because he still harbored notions of sleeping with me again.

"I'm not expecting anyone." *Come on, Eva,* Chuck snorted, kicking me. "Will you see who it is, Rich?" I asked. "My legs have had it." My forehead started to smolder.

"I'm not really dressed," Richard dithered, looking down at his thermal underwear and Martin's smoking jacket.

"And I am?" I shouted. "Shit, just answer the door! Unless you're expecting Brasilia!" Now my ribs were beginning to riot.

Richard walked uncertainly out of the kitchen. As he opened the front door, a ball of fire billowed in my throat; my skin crackled. I ran to the foyer.

There stood Percival, speechless. "Eva, my dear," he said. "I thought I'd check in on you before going home." His challenge flew right over Richard's head.

"Ho, Percy," I said, kissing his cheek. "This is Richard Weintraub." Percival extended his hand with the coldest benediction I had ever heard. I looked him directly in the eye. "Richard is not a singer."

"No, not me! Never! I design Eva's hymn covers," Richard explained way too glibly, as if he were talking to Sergeant Preston of the Yukon. "Sorry about my outfit! I fell into the snow. Eva just finished shoveling. We had nothing else to wear."

I shook my head; if this was the Chosen Race, we were in for a real barbecue. "Have you eaten, Percival?"

"Yes, thank you, my dear." That meant Percival had eaten pea soup in my kitchen seven hours ago and had intended to take me out to dinner tonight. He held my hand. "I just wanted to make sure you were feeling better."

"Feeling better?" Richard yipped at me. "You mean you felt sick?" He looked perplexedly at Percival. "She was out playing in the snow for an hour after I got here. God knows what she was doing before that!"

"I was shoveling the driveway, you moron!" I shouted. "There's a big party here tomorrow night, remember?" At once my blood halted, then gushed through my veins like a swollen river. I nearly fell over. The hell with it! I don't care if the kid gagged, I needed a drink!

"I'm going to finish a little pea soup," Richard said forebodingly, returning to the kitchen. "Excuse me."

"Eva," cried Percival, following me to the den, "let me help you!"

"Pour me a brandy," I said, slapping onto the couch where Fox had first seized me. "A big fat one." Oh God, I couldn't lie down here. The leather was alive. I paced the rug as Percival tried to find the smallest balloons in the cupboard. Fox had always wanted to make love on this rug but it scratched like hell, plus it smelled like Mesopotamian lice. *So he should have been on the bottom,* Chuck said. Jesus Christ! The woman was a triple agent! "Step on it, Percival," I said, "I'm going to die!"

He handed me a glass containing the merest thimbleful of brandy. I swallowed that as if it were Fox's cock. "More," I said. My hand shook.

"I think you should go to bed," Percival said softly.

Pfuiii, I was never going back to bed in my life! I locked myself into the study, went to the file cabinet, and pulled out every hymn I had ever written since the age of sixteen. I started banging out the tunes, singing various verses, and every single one was pure shit! The worse they got, the louder I sang. Fox never knew that my greatest ambition was to be a heldentenor: Siegfried, Tristan, ah, there were great roles. These two thousand hymns were flimsily veiled salvage, period.

I threw the Christmas oratorio in front of me and began pounding on the aria which Fox would sing tomorrow. My face turned borscht-red as I pictured him chuckling over the music, wondering how the hell such slop could have won the most prestigious hymn award in the country. God knows what Lionel would blabber to him at their rehearsal tomorrow; he and Pooh contained enough secrets to kill me a hundred times over. Bah, what the hell did it matter? Soon I'd be moving to Peru—the real Peru, not the one in Vermont.

Quietly, I opened the door of the study and listened. The house was silent. I tiptoed to the kitchen. There sat

Richard and Percival playing cards. "What the hell are you two doing?" I fumed.

"Babysitting," Richard replied, carefully laying the ten of clubs on the table.

"Gin," said Percival, displaying his hand. Richard should have known better than to play games of skill and bluff with a Boston Brahmin. Percival looked up. "A fine game, Richard. Now I should be going."

"You're going nowhere!" I snapped. "Look at it outside! It's a blizzard!" Richard looked fiercely at me; he did not want to be chaperoned tonight. That was tough shit. I belonged to Fox. "What's there to eat?" I said. "I'm starving."

"Pea soup," Richard muttered.

I opened the freezer. "Pizza. Corn. Ice cream? Pot pies? Hey! Flemish stew!"

Percival came over to me. "Why don't I make you a sandwich," he said, putting the casserole back.

No! Only Fox made me sandwiches! "Forget it! I'm not hungry!"

"Don't tell me that lovely recital didn't work up an appetite?" Richard said. "You screamed louder than ten Rodolfos."

It did not tax Percival's imaginative powers to see that Richard and I had been many places together. "Excuse me," he said. "I think I should be off."

"Will you stop it, Percival! You're staying here, in the pink bedroom."

"I'm in the pink bedroom," Richard snapped. "Sorry." He looked malignantly at Percival: Richard knows my predilection for older men.

"Okay! Perce, you're in the green bedroom."

"Fine." Fine, my ass. Martin kept his bug collection from Milton Academy in that bedroom.

"I assume one of you knows how to lock up the house," I said, leaving them. "I'm going to bed." Following a quick detour through the library, of course.

I secured myself in my bedroom, sipping a few spoonfuls of scotch as I watched the snow blitz the backyard. Why didn't Martin ever call me? Was I that boring? That ugly? Was he really that busy? *Why don't you ever call him?* Chuck parroted. Because he didn't need me to call him, that's why. The sound of my voice? He responded more gallantly to a dial tone! Oh, great father material, just great! The two of us would be lucky to keep this kid out of the electric chair before Installment Number One of the trust fund! *This sounds very familiar,* Chuck observed. *Could history be repeating itself?* "Nope," I said, "I'm going to be a better mother than you." Chuck laughed harshly. *Then why'd you marry your father?* she guffawed.

My whole body ached; it knew the blizzard had won. My gullet? Scorched earth. I slipped under the covers and stared at the chandelier above my bed as if it were the Archangel come to bring me good tidings of great joy. *You?* Chuck hooted. "Listen, Pal," I prayed. "You've got to muzzle that bitch. She's outlived her usefulness." Chuck laughed fifty times more loudly, waking the kid up. Fox! Martin! Arms! Any arms! Take it away! I didn't want it! It would be just another dud in a galaxy of duds!

A key turned in the lock. The rapist again, and I still wasn't ready to die: Fox breathed. I threw the crowbar at the noise, less to maim the intruder than to get that god-damn stick of metal out of my bed. I had slept with it since the age of thirteen.

"Oow," a familiar voice groaned in the dark. "Eva! What was that?"

I switched on the reading light. "Percival! Why didn't you knock? Where'd you get a key?"

"Architect's privilege," he responded, rubbing his shins. "I wanted to see that you were tucked in."

I ran to the door, gasped, and returned to the bed.

"What's the matter?"

"I think I might be sick. Excuse me." Shit, none of my sisters ever had morning sickness, afternoon sickness, or any sickness! Why me? *You started way too late,* Chuck said, *With the wrong father* I threw up pea soup and Martin's superb scotch.

Percival, having followed me into the bathroom, flushed the toilet. "My dear," he whispered, rubbing the back of my head. Fox used to pull my hair in that very spot when he was about to come. "You're making yourself sick."

I turned my face from the toilet and looked at him. "I'm pregnant."

Percival never stopped rubbing my head. I threw up gallons more pea soup than I had ever swallowed. After flushing again, Percival brought over a facecloth and cleaned me up. "Is that good news?" he asked.

"No." That answered both his questions. I went to bed and Percival stayed on the chaise longue reading. I think I had hurt his shins.

The phone rang at seven the next morning. It was Chuck. "Forget meeting me at the airport, Eva. No airplanes are going anywhere."

My heart looped perilously through a figure eight. Would Fox not make it up to Boston either? "That's a shame, Chuck."

"What's a shame? I'm taking the bus."

"Aha."

"Can you speak a little louder?"

"Nope." Percival was still sleeping on the chaise longue.

"What's the matter? Is Martin sleeping?"

"He'd better be." It was four A.M. in California.

"The bus arrives in Boston at one-twenty. What an awful trip this will be, traffic, hoods with those loud radios, people smoking . . ."

Chuck would be parading up and down the aisle in her pajamas giving away Bibles. They usually tried to evict her around Hartford. "The bus station's one block from the Park Plaza. You can walk. Don't stop in any bars on the way. Did you buy yourself a new dress?"

"I sent three hundred dollars to the Shepherds of Eternal Jesus in your name."

Damn it, I was already on the mailing list of every two-bit mission in the country! "Alleluia. Great. Swell."

"That's not Martin sleeping in your room, is it?"

"No, it's his godfather. Hey, showtime's at four. Look presentable, will you?" I hung up.

Percival stirred in his chair. His red silk tie hung loosely to the side; I bet his skin was warm and dry, like the south of France in July. I heard some water running in the kitchen and tottered downstairs to mend fences with Richard.

"Hi," I said anemically. "Sleep well?" Fifteen steps ago the kid had awakened. Now it was doing laps in some regurgitated pea soup.

Richard harpooned a bagel stuck in the toaster. "Who is that old fart?" he asked, roughly dredging cinders free. "Your lover?"

"No, no, no," I said, "never." I held my stomach: the pea soup spattered inside. "He's a friend of Martin's family. We're like father and daughter."

"That's what you think! Do you see the way he looks at you?"

I slid my head into my arms. Perhaps I should go back to bed. "I don't see anything," I said, but I wasn't looking anymore. My tonsils felt like Mount Everest in a hailstorm. "Any tea there?"

Richard pushed a cup in front of my nose. "He slept in your room."

"He slept on my chair." The tea nauseated me. "I was sick."

Richard touched my forehead. "You're hot. I knew I should have called a doctor yesterday."

"Forget it! I'm fine!" I swallowed some orange juice. "So are you going to sell a lot of stationery today?"

"Stationery? You can talk about stationery at a time like this?"

"Richard," I said, "give up, will you."

"You've got a fever."

"You've got the fever, buddy!" I shouted. "Forget about me! You're worse than a mastiff with lockjaw!" I bit into a banana. It was about the size of Fox.

Another burning bagel caught Richard's eye. He leapt to the toaster. "You're going to run away with that WASP banker upstairs, aren't you."

"That's inSANE." Cripes! Had I really told him that? I didn't remember. "He's an architect." Whap! The kid started swinging at the banana. That did it: the moment Richard and Percival left, I was going to call an abortion clinic. There were dozens of them within yards of the

Harvard/Radcliffe dormitories. *The hell you are*, Chuck jeered. *This is Fox's baby, not Martin's*. A sublime shot, one of Chuck's most perfect; I bent over the table, mortally wounded.

The phone rang. I didn't move.

"Hello?" Richard said. "Who? I'm fine, thanks. Sure, just a minute." He held the phone out. "It's your husband," he enunciated sarcastically.

"Uuuhgf."

"Eva? What are you two doing?"

"Eating breakfast." I dropped the phone.

"Your wife is sick, you louse," Richard snapped. "I'm putting her to bed." He slammed the phone down. What the hell, if I was going to run away with the architect after all this futile limbo, he may as well let Martin know what he really thought of him.

"I'm going to work," I said, getting up.

"Hey! What are you talking about? You're supposed to come with me to the card convention! Remember all those hymn covers you've got to autograph?"

"I'm sick," I said. "Very sick. You said so yourself."

"What the hell is going on here? You're not really sick! Who is that guy upstairs?"

"My travel agent." I locked myself into the study and played through a pile of unfinished hymns for an hour. Most of them hung dead on the vine. I wondered if The Great Vintner felt as bad about throwing rotten fruit into the trash as I did. Bah, probably not.

A key turned in the lock. "Architect's privilege again?" I asked, not looking up.

"Of course." Freshly showered, Percival carried a tray in with him. It was impossible to tell that he had slept in his clothes. "How are you feeling?."

"Too good to be true." The kid had been comatose for the first morning in weeks. Perhaps I should switch to a diet of burnt bagels and bananas.

"You look a little white." Percival felt my forehead. "You have a fever."

"I do not. Where's Richard?"

"I lent him my car. He drove to the Park Plaza." Ah,

Percival was a wily old tar. He knew Richard would stop at nothing to save three bucks in cab fare.

"And what are you going to do all day? Stay here and watch me get sick? What about your lunch date?"

"Cancelled it. Snow can come in very handy. you know."

"I've got to work today."

"And so must I, my dear." Percival left the study and returned shortly with his briefcase. "Pretend I'm not here," he said. "Unless you get sick."

The phone rang: terror pinched my stomach. The kid roared as I flashed to the bathroom.

"That was Martin," Percival said when I returned, minus bagel, banana, and fifty percent of my stomach lining.

I snorted. "Oh?"

"He seemed quite upset."

"Is that so? How could you tell? Didn't he cross his *T*s?"

"Eva." I blinked stupidly at Percival: just that once, he had leaned on the first syllable of my name exactly like Fox. "His plane's going to be delayed until six o'clock tonight."

I burst out laughing. El Gran Buddito had done it again. Whoops, there went the kid, trampolining up to my eyeballs. I grabbed my head; if the kid got away from me, I had nothing. "I'm going down to your gym," I said. "Take the phone off the hook." Headaches usually drowned during a heavy workout.

Percival and I arrived late at the Park Plaza for the awards ceremony. Until three we had been coaching the rented butlers in evangelical catering etiquette. Then I had gotten sick in the shower. It was a mess, all Percival's fault. He had insisted on making mushroom omelettes for lunch. Then we got stuck behind a dead trolley on the Green Line. By the time we hit the Park Plaza, they had already shut the doors to the Grand Ballroom. As we slipped inside, someone was on the podium praying fervently.

"Fanny," hissed a loud voice fifty feet away in the

dark: Chuck, bombed. I pretended not to have heard. "FANny," she called more loudly.

I yanked Percival over to the right, spying a few empty chairs. The moment we sat down, I heard a huge crash in the vicinity of Chuck's voice. "Watch it," she said too loudly, "don't you know I'm Mrs. Tingle?"

"Jesus Christ," I whispered to Percival, "bow your head! Maybe she'll walk by!"

No way. Chuck headed straight for the biggest hat in the Park Plaza ballroom. "You look terrible!" she exclaimed.

"Pipe down, Chuck, the man's praying," I whispered.

Percival arose. "I'm very honored and pleas—"

"Will you shut UP," I hissed, yanking him back into the chair. "Everyone is looking at us."

"Amen," crowed the supplicant. "Amen! Lights!"

Chuck was wearing one of her fur coats over a pair of orange ski pants and a flannel pajama top. "I don't know you," I said, looking straight ahead.

"They tried to throw me off the bus," Chuck said as if we were at the Hotel Sacher eating kirschtorte. "Can you imagine that?"

"How long have you been here?" I demanded, searching desperately for Orville. Ah, there he was up front, pointing something out to the TV crews from North Carolina. I followed his hand to an upright piano in the corner of the stage. What a shitbox! Fox would be better off accompanied by an accordion! *

"An hour," Chuck said. "They started at two."

"TWO?" How had I gotten that screwed up? Why hadn't Orville called me? "Did anybody sing yet?"

"Sure," nodded Chuck. "See that guy over there?"

My heart scattered like buckshot against my ribs. "Where? What guy?"

Percival put his hand over mine. "Eva," he whispered. "Shhhh." Now he sounded exactly like Martin.

I stood up. That wasn't Fox at all. It was Packard Parker. He had sung "The Star Spangled Banner" at every convention since the Crusades. He was also president of the National Hymnists Association. "What else happened?" I asked Chuck. "Did Orville say anything? Have you seen Lionel?"

"Lionel? Beatrice's Lionel? What could that SICK boy be doing here?"

Several people ahead of us turned around. "Am I bothering you?" Chuck asked sweetly. "So sorry! This is such an exciting day for me! I'm Mrs. Tingle!"

That did it. I made Percival sit between us.

"Edmund, what a surprise," Chuck said, extending her hand. "You've lost all your hair."

"Shhh!"

"Who said that?" challenged Chuck, standing up. "I demand an apology."

Percival took her arm. "Charlotte, dear, let's take a little walk, shall we? It's positively stifling in here." He looked down at me. "Coming, Eva?"

"I'll be all right." This hat was inciting a high fever. I took it off but my head continued to char. I guess I was getting nervous. Ten minutes choked by as some woman from Texas explained to the convention how well the treasury had done since last December. She talked as if she had a dead lobster up her ass. Then everyone voted to keep Packard Parker president for another year. He made a speech about the resurgence of Godfearing Christians in the United States and the beneficial effect this had had on choir lofts.

The television lights switched on. I looked around: where had Percival taken her? He was supposed to be protecting ME, not my mother, for Christ's sake! Packard Parker took the microphone and talked about how hard it was to choose a Hymnist of the Year from such a stunningly talented bullpen of composers. That was pure baloney; ask Orville's accounting team. "It is with great pleasure," Pack finally announced, "that we once again honor Miss Fanny May Tingle as our Hymnist of the Year."

Applause rolled through the auditorium. Orville approached the podium, note cards in hand.

"Ah ayum once aggin acceptin' this awahd foh Miz Tingle," Orville read humbly to the TV crews from North Carolina. "She wishes teh hayev no publick recognisshin foh heh mahvellous hymns an inspraytional endeavahs." Shit, that drawl would just about coat the Hancock Building. It thickened in direct proportion to the stack of sheet music Orville wished to unload upon the conventioneers. "We hayev chosin' a selecshin from heh Chrismiss orhatohria foh you teh heah this aftehnoon. At theh pianna is Mistah Lahnell Boyd an' singin' is Mistah Poll Fox. In theh lobby Ah hayev brott a few extreh copies of thiz stunnin' music in theh case yeh maht want teh pehchase it."

I pushed my palms as hard as possible against my chest: my heart was expanding like some mutant Godzilla, straining to break loose. My forehead sweat more ardently than a sterling julep glass. Alone before the mirror! God damn it! *Congratulations*, I prayed. Believe me, that was pure adoration: Buddha, Mohammet, or Confucius could never have pulled this off in a million years.

Out strode Fox, king, always king. The kid flapjacked; I shut my eyes, willing it still. Pfuii, no chance: onstage stood the center of gravity, and when it moved, the kid moved. I had to stand up, holding my gut.

Fox waited at the piano for his accompanist, who had not trailed him to that miserable noisebox. I saw that he had grown his hair, shaved off his mustache, and bought himself a new suit. My fingertips began inching imperceptibly towards him, spreading out slowly as a forest fire. He knew I was there, all right, I could tell by the faintly arrogant tilt of his nose. My mouth watered.

In stumbled Chuck and Percival. "There she is," Chuck hissed into the dim ballroom, pulling her reticent companion by the elbow over towards me. Seating myself between the two of them, scowling, I turned my face back onstage. Christ! What was Lionel wearing? A cross between Empress Eugenie's coronation robes and the Christmas tree in Rockefeller Center? A dense flock of sequins glimmered snazzily at the TV lights. Underneath that multimedia event I knew he was wearing nothing but a purple condom.

The conventioneers were still murmuring to themselves as Lionel raised his hands high into the air and crashed them down on the keyboard. "What is he doing?" I croaked. "That isn't the introduction I wrote." Against my will I felt myself going crosseyed.

"I just had a long talk with Lionel about that choir robe," Chuck said. "It's a disgrace."

"You did WHAT?" I leaned over to Percival. "How did this happen?"

"I'm afraid Charlotte got away from me," he replied miserably. "She happened to see Lionel in the lobby and bolted like a wild horse."

"What about the singer?" I gagged. "Did she nail him, too?"

"Pssssst!" Chuck elbowed me. The kid quadrupled. I bent over just as Fox began to sing. He had wisely decided to abandon the carnival next to him.

The sound of that beautiful voice floored me. I put my head on Percival's shoulder and wept for all the things I never was, things I'd never have.

"Eva," Chuck said when Fox hit the second verse, "sit up, will you? This isn't nursery school."

"Charlotte!" Percival whispered sharply. "Leave her alone! She's not feeling well!"

Fortunately this piece of news didn't register with Chuck; she started to hum a little bit, trying to find the tune Fox had woven in the air. She sounded like the Amtrak north of Albany.

"Shhh! For the last time!" someone hissed at us.

"I think we should leave, darling," Percival whispered to me. "This is not doing anyone any good."

"Leave?" Chuck cried, "what about the awards?"

"You missed them," I told her, resigned that now and always, this was my mother. Fox held on to a soft high F. He sang the way he made love to me, suspended in the ether forever. I sat up and put my hat back on. Percival gave me his handkerchief. "Let's go," I said, "before the lights come up."

"Wait a moment!" Chuck nearly shouted. "I didn't ride six hours in a bus to leave in the middle of this!" She stood up, cursing my father. He had put her on the bus.

Fox hit his third and final verse as his accompanist continued to muddle disjointedly at the piano. Lionel would never recover before Fox crossed the finish line; Chuck had totally unmanned him. I saw Orville beaming proudly at both performers as the TV crew panned between him, Lionel's robe, and Fox's mouth, milking these precious items of human interest for all they were worth. The conventioneers sat mesmerized by Lionel's robes. I don't think they heard one note he played or Fox sang.

But I did. The more he sang the more the notes became his. The man was not content to steal my heart, now he had my music, too. I got up and steered Chuck rapidly towards the exit. "Will you let GO, Fanny," she said loudly. "I'm trying to listen to your hymn."

"It's that crazy woman from last year," I heard someone say as we passed by.

"I'm Mrs. Tingle, you idiot," Chuck broadcast. "Lies like that will land you in hell, mark my words." Her fur coat hit one of the metal folding chairs, emitting a loud clank.

"Good Lord," said Percival. "What was that?"

"A silver flask," I muttered, "like the one in my nightstand, only bigger." I wondered if Fox noticed this bedraggled little parade in the rear of the auditorium.

"Excuse us," Percival said for maybe the hundredth time. "Thank you." I leaned heavily on his arm; the suds were creeping up my throat.

We were not five paces from the exit when who should slip into the ballroom but Martin. For a moment we gaped at each other. "What the hell are you doing here?" I said. Fox's voice spun my blood into mad little eddies.

"Where's that secretary, Martin?" Chuck asked. "Did you get my birthday card?"

"Hello," Percival greeted stonily. Were he not Edmund Weaver's best friend, I think he would have belted Martin. "What a surprise."

"I caught an earlier flight out of San Francisco." My husband addressed the source of his least uncivil reception, namely, Percival. "Where's everyone going?"

No one replied. That's because Chuck thought we were going to a bar, I thought we'd drop in on Richard's Christian card convention across the hall, and Percival intended to put me to bed again. Martin felt the wind blowing against him and peered exaggeratedly beyond us. "My God! Is that Lionel Boyd up there?"

"Please watch your language, Martin," Chuck said, then erupted a force-five belch. It was precisely at the end of Fox's aria, the quietest moment of the piece, the part I had written with my pen caressing his throat. All eyeballs within earshot burned at us with hatred. I'm sure Fox heard it.

"Pardon me," Chuck said as I shoved her roughly out of the ballroom. "I knew I shouldn't have eaten that Big Mac." As the door closed behind me, Fox finished singing my aria. His last words were "Come to me"; I had written that on purpose for him, ten months ago. *He came, all right,* Chuck said. *Look what happened.*

"Help," I wailed to Percival, clinging to his arm, never Martin's. I disliked Martin. He couldn't sing.

"I think we should go out and celebrate," said Chuck euphorically. "This is a happy day, Fanny." She turned around. "Congratulations. Say! You look awful! What have you been doing with yourself while Martin was with his secretary?"

Martin took a look at me and got a little upset: my face matched my hat. "George is waiting outside," he directed, shepherding us to the street. "We're going home." He tried to take my arm but I shook him away; I was engaged to Percival now.

My husband helped Chuck into the front seat of the limousine, where she pumped the defenseless George for his life story as he rolled us home. Meanwhile Martin, Percival, and I perched woodenly in the rear seat like dummies in a test crash. It was classic WASP battle formation, all eyes pointed forward, mouths clamped shut. Martin and Percival exchanged some violent *ahems*. My brain started to fricassee.

George braked in front of the driveway: once again, the Boston sanitation team had plowed a wall of snow between it and the street. By morning, we'd need a Sherman tank to blast a path through it. "Let me leave you a little reading material, George," Chuck offered in parting. "Oh NO! I've left my suitcase at the convention! All my things are in it! Eva, this is what happens when you rush people out."

"George," said Martin before I could rebut, "please drive Mrs. Hathaway back to the Park Plaza and try to locate her suitcase."

The chauffeur's Adam's apple dribbled four inches up and down; he would rather cruise through the heart of Roxbury with the roof down. "Yes, sir."

"Take your time," Martin added before slamming his door. We kicked through the snow to the house; all of my shoveling had come to nought, ah, the story of my life. Ten years ago I would have gone to my room and cried about it to Big Buddy. Tonight I'd just change my clothes and start shoveling again.

"Who's here?" Martin asked, noticing the lights on. I felt very sorry for him. He never had any idea what treachery lurked behind his front door.

"The caterers, Martin," Percival replied. "There's a reception tonight. Various people from the hymn convention are coming over."

"I see," Martin said, turning the doorknob. Shit! Had I forgotten to tell him? I glanced over at the corner of the porch where Fox had once nibbled my shins. Only a shovel lay there now.

"Sugah! Sugah honey!" cried Pooh, swaddling me like the Christ child. Tonight he wore a white jumpsuit three sizes too small and no underwear.

"Hi, babe," Richard said as he emerged tipsily from the den; he hadn't yet relinquished Martin's favorite smoking jacket.

"A reception, eh?" Martin said, squinting at me.

A butler type turned the bend into the foyer. "Let me take your coats," he said. "Praise the Lord!"

"A little stiff, but not bad," I said. "Tell us where you've hidden the booze."

"Eva, what's going on here?" Martin said.

"Percival," I sighed, mounting the stairs. "Please explain to my dear husband what's going on here." Percival looked worriedly after me, thinking I was heading for the bathroom. "I'm all right."

I got my dress off but did not get into shoveling clothes. Instead I sank to the floor, wondering what the kid was up to. I was very, very tired: the sight of Fox, even from several hundred feet away, had paralyzed me. Every atom in my body screamed for him, bleeding. He was larger than my life, larger than my death: he went beyond time at both ends, right up to the edges of the universe, right up to the very nose of The Grand Mystery, leaving me no maneuvering room at all between the eternal questions and their ultimate answers. *Sentimental peat,* Chuck said. *No basis in reality, as usual.* Wrong. I was the only one around with any basis in reality. Everyone else was finger-painting. Fox! My mouth burned to run down his spine, round the sweetest bend in all of creation, and swallow that magic mushroom that grew only on him! Would I never see his eyes when he came inside me ever again? What about those infallible hands? Those legs? Jesus Christ! This was so physical it was spiritual!

Laughing, the kid bit me; I rolled in torment half under the bed. What had I done but perpetuate my longing? Every day for the rest of my life I would see Fox now, in the flesh, growing before my very eyes, calling me Mom, and no amount of hymns, or gracious gentle evenings with my husband, or mere hours, would ever blur my sight. Fox! I whispered his name, clawing the darkness: separation was slow death.

"Eva?" The bedroom light flicked on. "Where are you, honey?" I held my heart, trembling like a sparrow. Martin walked into the bathroom, came back into the hallway. "Eva?" His footsteps circled the bed. "EVA! What are you doing down there?"

"I think I lost a shoe."

Kneeling, Martin trawled his arms under the bed, coming up with nothing but petrified Kleenex. Then he noticed that I was already wearing two shoes. "Are you all right?" he asked.

"No."

He cradled my face in his arms. "I'm sorry I missed the convention, darling."

Convention? Try life! *Eva,* Chuck berated, *be fair.* I had forgotten. It was his mother's fault. "Forget it." I sat up, grunting femininely. "Where's Chuck?"

"She hasn't come back yet. There are already a few people downstairs."

"Where's Percival?"

"In the greenhouse. He's very concerned about you."

"He's been very good to me." Martin flushed; either his ability to read between the lines had improved tremendously, or I was now block-printing between the lines. I couldn't tell and didn't care. Fox had stolen my erasers.

"Put some clothes on, love, you'll catch a chill on the floor like that."

Chill? I was burning up. "Would you mind getting me a glass of water, Flaps?"

"Sure." When he returned from the bathroom, I already had my sweatshirt on; Martin would notice at once that my breasts were swollen. He stopped. "Why are you wearing that?"

"Someone's got to shovel the front walk," I reminded him. "If anyone falls down, they'll sue the shit out of us."

"Baby. it's all taken care of," Martin explained. "One of the caterers is doing it right now."

That aggravated me. Instead of slipping some butler twenty bucks, Martin should be out there sweating himself. Nothing less would satisfy me. "Flappy, have you ever picked up a shovel in your life?"

"What does that have to do with anything?"

Oh ho, now I was going to get the patient argument, which always made such eminent sense, why Martin should pay the butler to shovel the sidewalk instead of doing it himself: money bought time, money bought freedom. Bah! I'd rather shovel! *You would, you stupid moron,* Chuck sighed. "Shut UP!" I screamed in a fit, choked with frustration.

Martin froze, then put the glass of water down on the night table. "I'll be downstairs," he said, leaving the bedroom. "It's your party." He had to be having an affair with Paloma. Any other man would have socked me.

I squeezed my eyes shut, trying to leap back five years to when Martin had first taken me out to dinner and closed some secret stopcock through which I had been leaking all my life. What had opened it again? Or was it still sealed and another, larger, pipe burst now? Ah, destiny, ancient plumbing laid before I was even born! I controlled nothing! I only watched the floods rise! *Jesus Christ,* I prayed, *I'm losing my mind.* Jesus kept His trap shut. That's one reason I never could relate to Him. The other is that He never got married.

I put on a red velvet dress and combed the worst of the pinwheels out of my hair: time for a drink and congenial laughter amongst people destined for heaven. The kid got squished behind a thick black leather belt.

Percival met me halfway down the stairs. "Hey there, handsome," I said shakily. "I understand there's some great scenery in the greenhouse." A half dozen strangers, all in brown leisure suits, milled about the foyer waiting for the next butler to emerge from the kitchen with a new platter of shrimp. "Where's Martin?"

"I think he's in the library showing someone a computer."

Pooh stood in the greenhouse drinking openly from a waterer labeled Plant Food that Percival and I had laboriously filled that afternoon. That was the vodka. Richard Weintraub held another plastic jug marked Distilled Water. That was gin, for Chuck. "Hello, boys," I said. "Any Leaf Cleaner left?" That was the scotch.

"Open up, princess," said Pooh, aiming a nozzle at my mouth. His balls looked like some huge smashed tadpole under his jumpsuit.

"That's enough," Percival said, cutting Pooh off in midstream. "Miss Tingle is tired tonight."

"How was your convention, Eva?" Richard asked. I had forbidden him to go.

"Lahnell got a new choir robe fo' tha show," Pooh said. "Izz senSAYshinnel."

"Indeed," I said. "And where might Lionel be now?"

"He should be heah any minute," Pooh said, "te help us celebrate."

"God help us all," I muttered, leaving the greenhouse with Percival. "Shall we check the galley slaves?"

A thundering doorslam turned our heads. "Praise the Lord," shouted a butler.

The kid did a cannonball into my lower intestine. I

heard Lionel's voice, and Chuck's, and then Fox's. "Percival," I said, "you don't happen to know of any hidden staircases in this house, do you?"

"Unfortunately not." My whole body began to chime; I could only stand stock still as the peals shook me. "Sweetheart! What's the matter?"

"The singer's here," I whispered, my voice trembling like a cornered mouse.

"EEEEEva," Lionel yelled above the din. "Where AAAAAre you?!"

I stared at Percival. "Help," I whimpered.

He folded my arm over his. "Charge," he said, striding into the foyer.

Lionel twirled around in circles, flourishing his cape as a group of Christian booksellers stood clear in amazement. Chuck had changed into a dress. Fox had not shed his new suit. His eyes found me. The clappers inside my head tolled the end of the world; had Percival not been holding my arm, I would have fallen down.

"Hello, Charlotte," Percival said as if this were a post-symphony dinner party. "I see you found your evening clothes." Chuck had opened her suitcase and was searching for tracts.

"This is what I was talking about in the limousine," she continued, handing one to Fox. "Read it very carefully and call me if you have any questions."

"Thanks," Fox said, still looking at me.

"POOH! Pooh Bear!" Lionel called into the greenhouse. "You owe me one hundred dollars!" Pooh lolled into the foyer holding a squeeze bottle marked Aphid Spray. "Eskimo! How was your matinee? Did you KILL them with that cakewalk by A.P. Tingle Fanny Edgewater?"

"Sho' did."

"Praise the Lord!" announced two butlers, emerging from the kitchen and proceeding to the living room, trays of hors d'oeuvres held high overhead. The crowd in the hall traipsed after them as if they carried the Ark of the Covenant.

Chuck glanced around the hall. "Where are the Christmas decorations, Eva?" she asked, throwing her fur coat over the bannister. "Are you going to be serving dinner?

I'm famished." My mother cut into line behind the butler.
"You have no idea what a mess that hotel was. Thank
heaven Lionel was still signing autographs backstage. I
insisted that he come over with this gentleman and sing
your hymn for me. I have to take pictures."

Lionel waited until Chuck had disappeared into the living room. "That woman gave me the shock of my LIFE,"
he snapped.

"Come on, I told you she'd be in town."

"Do you know what she did to me? Right backstage?
She tried to crawl UNDER my choir robe! To change
clothes, she said." Lionel shuddered. "It was huMILiating!"

Bah, only because she was a female. I looked at Percival.
"I think I should sit down." I dropped into a loveseat that
Martin had inherited from a virgin aunt who had not
known how to use it. Fox's eyes never left my face: what
in Christ's name had Chuck been telling him? The kid
hammered against my belt, calling for its father.

A load of conventioneers burst through the front door.
Martin, as usual, was missing when he was needed most.
Orville came over to me, filling the void. "Mizziz Weavah,"
he said, kissing my hand. "You look luhvly tehnight." I
hadn't seen my publisher in months; all that cornpone was
catching up with him. It seemed unbelievable that I had
slept with him, just once, ten years ago in Atlanta. We had
been celebrating the millionth copy of *I Whisper to Jesus*.

"Orville," I said. "Take over. This is your party. I
don't live here."

"Mah pleashah," he replied: eight hours in bed followed by ten thousand hours on the telephone had bred a
certain understanding. "Mistah Boyd," Orville began, in-
troducing himself to Lionel. "You weh a great boon to
this aftahnoon's proceedins."

"Why thank you," bowed Lionel, sweeping his cape
back and forth. "I'd do anything to serve the great cause."

I guffawed sharply. Orville pretended he had not heard.
Three people surrounded Fox, complimenting him on his
superb artistry. "Thank you," he said. "It was a fine
hymn." Now Lionel tried to outguffaw me.

Ruth and Edmund Weaver stepped into the house with
grand plaster smiles. "Look who's here!" screamed Lio-

nel in delight, embracing my mother-in-law's ranch mink coat as if it lived for him alone. "Ruthie! How did you like the show? Wasn't it FABulous? What about that cakewalk?"

"Very entertaining," dismissed Ruth curtly, scanning the room for Martin. She spied Percival with me on the love seat, registered us with momentary shock, and kept her eyes moving as if we were two copulating dogs.

"Praise the Lord!" cried a butler, relieving them of their coats.

"Hi," I uttered weakly as Edmund came towards us. Fox's eyes remained fixed on my face. Soon I would have to look at him. "Nice to see you."

"Martin's in the library," Percival called. That flushed the bushes of Ruth. Percival stood up and shook hands with Edmund, murmuring something close to his ear. Edmund asked Pooh to show him the greenhouse.

"What the hell BUG does that woman have up her ass NOW," Lionel commented loudly. "Some people have NO sense of humor."

Chuck wandered into the foyer with a plateful of chicken curry. "Eva," she said, "you've changed the den around." That meant she had looked in the liquor cabinet and found nothing but dried flowers.

I wobbled to my feet. The kid was giving me the worst cramps of my life. "I think I'm going to lie down for a moment," I announced. "Excuse me." Percival got up with me.

"You do look terrible," Chuck said as she dug into that nauseating chicken slop. "I would swear you're pregnant, Eva. Whew! This curry's hot! Where's the soda?"

"In the greenhouse, Charlotte," Percival replied angrily, escorting me upstairs. I edged around Fox as if he would electrocute me.

"Keep Martin down here, would you?" I told Lionel in passing. He nodded. My red velvet dress and I just made it to the toilet.

"Sweetie, you're sick," Percival said. "I'm calling a doctor."

"NO! I feel fine now!"

"I don't believe that," Percival wiped my mouth with a face cloth. "Your mother needs a good whipping."

She needed a man, that's all. "I told you she was a raving lunatic."

Someone rapped on the bathroom door; sixty years of good breeding drained all the color from Percival's face. I nipped his nose between two fingers. "Don't worry, it's not Martin." Martin always knocked softly twice, then waited.

"It's your singer?"

"He wouldn't dare come up here."

Fox strode into the bathroom. Shit, how did I always end up on the floor at his feet? "I'd like a word with Eva," he commanded.

"Come on! Can't you see I'm busy?" I stared into the toilet, waiting.

Percival slowly stood up; the bathroom could not contain a mule, a mare, and a stallion all at once. "I'll be downstairs if you need me," he said, patting my shoulder.

Fox stared at me for a minute. "How dare you," he whispered finally.

I didn't answer. Fox squatted onto the floor next to me and roughly pulled my face out of the toilet bowl. "Did you hear me," he said. "Look at me, you little thief."

I shut my eyes: when love turns to hate, it's forever. I prayed the man would strangle me. His hands rested only inches from my throat. "Why should I strangle you," he cursed. "That baby is mine."

No, no. All wrong. "Mine," I croaked.

Fox grabbed my hand and put it smack on his balls. My guts rocketed to Albania. "That's where it came from," he said. "Me. Us." So what? That was two minutes six weeks ago. I had been alone ever since. I spat into the toilet. "I'm having a problem getting through to you," Fox continued. "Let me start over again."

"Forget it," I said, getting up. Shit, the last thing I needed was a biology lecture.

Fox pulled my red dress, with me inside, back down to the floor. The kid unloaded a barrage of cramps. "You've done the worst possible thing you could ever have done to me," he said. "Do you understand that?"

"No." I was doing the guy the favor of a lifetime: paternity, no strings attached. Any man on earth would cut off his thumbs to trade places with him.

"Why did you do it?"

"It was an accident."

"You're a liar." Fox shook me. "You did it on purpose, didn't you?"

"You waltzed in at the wrong time of the month."

"You could have told me."

"You could have abstained." That was the problem with modern men. They figured that every woman alive either swallowed birth control pills or played tennis with the local abortionist.

"I'll NEVER abstain!" Fox shouted. "Not with you!" He put his face in his hands. "You knew it, too. Damn you, I'll never forgive you for this."

I remembered saying that myself once . . . when I was just a kid, like Fox. He'd survive. *Aren't you forgetting something?* Chuck said. *The other guy didn't have your baby.* At once a terrible swift pain hit me, and it wasn't the kid. It was enlightenment: I had passed on my hatred times ten, polluting Fox. *Another you,* sighed Chuck. *So much for eugenics.* I began to cry, swallowing a silent boiling ocean.

Fox cloaked me with his warm chest. "Let's leave," he whispered. "Now. Tonight. We'll be together." He kissed my ear. "Happy."

For a moment I believed that hypnotic voice and its sugarplum forecast; a wave of rarest triumph rippled over me, as if I had been dealt a full house riding on the jackpot of a lifetime. It was all so simple once you knew what made you happy. Then the kid rammed its heels into my guts, reminding me that what made me happy and what made other people happy were two extremely different things. Who was I? Who was Fox? Martin? Who stood at the head of the line, eh? I drew back. "Don't taunt me, Fox," I begged. "I've made my decision."

"Martin doesn't need you," Fox insisted. "Don't you understand that?"

I woozily shook my head. I was about to get sick.

"Martin can get along without you. He's been doing it for years."

"Shall we throw him overboard just to make sure?" The green walls compressed and expanded like a huge tiled accordion.

"Let's cut the jokes just one time, Eva. That's my baby inside of you—"

Out, out, gallons of despair, blood brother of death. "Leave this bathroom," I said, cutting him off. "I never want to see you again." Fox unglued a wisp of hair from the corner of my mouth. I would feel those cool fingers no more. "OUT!" I pushed him so hard that he banged his head on the towel rack.

Fox got to his feet. "You are," he breathed, pausing between adjectives, "the most vicious, hopeless, useless *moron* I have ever met." He slammed the bathroom door, then, moments later, the front door.

I waited for the relief, the absolution, to come. It did not. That upset me. *Tilt*, I protested. Big Buddy was playing dead. Therefore I washed my face, combed my hair, and rejoined the celebration. There were hundreds of believers downstairs now laughing, talking, and stoking their mouths with enough chocolate cake to significantly advance the date of their admission to heaven.

In the library I found Martin and Lionel playing some sort of computer game as Ruth cheered and clucked rapturously from an antique bench.

"EEEEEEva!" Lionel welcomed me into the fold. "Thank GAWD! I thought you'd NEVer come back!" He toped deeply from a plastic bottle.

Martin looked up. "Hi, sweetheart. We were just getting started."

"STARTed?" Lionel corrected, standing up. "Pooh! Get me some chocolate cake! I'm seeing TRIPle!"

Pooh was nosing along the library shelves, reading book spines. If my crotch seam pinched my ass like that, I'd be blue with pain. "Thiz'z quatt a collecshin heah, princess."

"These are very old and valuable volumes, Mr. Excelsior," Ruth hastened to inform him. "The great minds of all the ages lie upon those shelves."

"Izzet a fac'." Pooh did not like Ruth anymore, I could

tell. That's because she had pretended she had not gone to today's matinee. As Pooh withdrew *Wuthering Heights* from its neighbors, something scratched the back of my mind and was gone. Someone was pounding belligerently on the front door; I went to check it out.

Junior and his sidekick Alphonse, the two policemen who had dropped in on me before, stood in the hallway talking to a butler. "Sorry to disturb you, ma'am," Junior said. "Someone called in a rape."

"Here? This house is stuffed with Southern Baptists." A small crowd of leisure suits had gathered behind me. "You must have the wrong address."

"Do you know a Mrs. Tingle?"

I felt my cheeks enflame. "Could we continue this outside?" I asked, stepping onto the porch. "There is no Mrs. Tingle here."

Orville stuck his head out; evidently Lionel had put him onto the refreshments in the greenhouse. "Oh! Lahnell's lookin fo' yeh, Fanneh May!"

"Fanny May who?" Alphonse inquired.

"Fanneh May Tingle, officeh," Orville answered. "Come in an' hayve yahself some chocklut cayuk."

"Orville, get back inside," I said, pushing him. "Your guests need you." I quickly shut the door.

"I thought you said there was no Mrs. Tingle here," said Junior.

"There isn't," I shouted exasperatedly. "I'm MISS Tingle."

"Wait a minute," Junior said. "The mailbox says Weaver."

"Of course it does! My husband's name is Weaver. I'm Miss Eva Hathaway."

"You just said you were Miss Tingle," the older cop reminded me.

Lionel now came outside. "Hey! What happened to your karate chopper? He's got to sing!" Lionel eyed the policemen distrustfully. "What's going ON out here?"

For a few moments the cops gaped at Lionel's sparkling cape, then exchanged swift looks. "Perhaps you could help me," Junior said.

"I don't have to tell you ANYthing," Lionel huffed. "I know my rights."

"Would you mind telling us your friend's name?" Alphonse asked, pulling out a pad. "She seems a little bit confused."

"That's NOT true," Lionel shouted. "You must be harassing her."

"Just tell him my name, Thread," I sighed. "Then we'll go inside."

Lionel cleared his throat. "Her name is A. P. Edgewater," he said, "and that's a HUGE secret, so don't tell ANyone." Lionel slammed the door in our faces.

"God damn it," I cried. "No one's supposed to know that."

"What kind of operation do you run here anyway?" Junior said, staring pointedly at my red velvet dress.

The doorknob rattled. Martin, followed by Ruth, came out to the porch. "What seems to be the problem, officer?"

"We're trying to determine the name of this woman here," Alphonse said, pointing his pencil at me. "She may have given us a phony rape call."

"That's quite ridiculous," Martin said. He looked at me. "Isn't it?"

"What, you're asking ME?" I screamed. "I haven't seen a prick in YEARS!"

Ruth put a hand to her mouth, careful not to smear her lipstick. "Mother, go inside," Martin said. "I'll take care of this." For the first time in her life Ruth ignored Martin.

"Good luck, Flappy." I muttered.

Junior wrote something in his pad. "So you're Mr. Flappy?"

"My name is Martin Weaver," my husband said. "Flappy is a nickname."

"Sure, sure," Junior said, turning to Ruth. "Could you please tell us this lady's name, ma'am?"

"Of course," my mother-in-law said. "That is Eva Weaver."

"The HELL it is," I snapped. "How many times have I told you NEVER to call me Weaver?"

"Okay, we've got enough names for now," the cop said. "Do you live here?"

"Of course," I shouted. "What does it look like?"

"My wife is a composer," Martin explained.

"She's artistic," Ruth added from the sidelines as if this would clarify everything.

Pooh came out onto the porch. "Princess! We've lost yo karate choppah!" Pooh leaned in the door. "Negg'tiv, Lahnell! He ain't out heah!" he called. "Say, princess! Look whad Ah foun' in one a yoah books." Withdrawing a paper from a pocket in his jumpsuit, Pooh displayed to all the picture Richard had drawn of me at his kitchen table. "Iz'z jest lak th' one yo gave me! Who's ziz gennleman behahnd yo wi' no clo's on?"

"How artistic," Junior observed sarcastically.

I snatched the sketch from Pooh's hand and crumpled it up. "Jesus CHRIST! Couldn't you wait two MINutes to show me that? Get back inside, you moron!"

"Eva, please curb your tongue," Chuck said, joining us. "Where's that fellow who sang with Lionel? Everyone wants him to sing."

"And who are you?" the older officer wanted to know. He had a definite knack for dragging incriminating evidence out of helpless women.

"Chuck."

"That's it? Just Chuck?"

"My mother-in-law's name is Charlotte Hathaway," Martin said.

"Today I'm Mrs. Tingle," Chuck said proudly.

"You are NOT!" I shouted. "Not today, not tomorrow!" I spun on Junior. "She's AWOL from the insane asylum."

"Mrs. Tingle," the older officer cooed, "did you perhaps telephone the police this evening?"

"Of course I did," Chuck said. "There were strange men going upstairs into Fanny's bedroom."

The officers exchanged knowing looks. "Men?" said Junior. "Is that so, Fanny?"

"You will please call my wife Eva," Martin said.

"Look buddy, maybe there are some things about your wife you don't know," the officer replied.

I saw Ruth look pointedly at her son: obviously she had been telling him the same thing for over five years. Martin's eyes kept returning to the crumpled ball of paper which I had thrown into the corner of the porch. He said nothing now.

Percival joined the festivities. "There you are!" He stood anxiously next to me. "Should you be downstairs, sweetie?"

"Why not?" said Junior. "What's going on upstairs? What's your name? John Doe?"

"I'm Gerald Noonan, a friend of the family." Percival informed the man as if he were speaking to a malamute. "This lady should not be standing outside. She's quite ill."

"We're responding to a rape call," the older officer explained.

"Eva!" Percival gasped. "My God! Did that fellow rape you?"

"What fellow?" said Martin coldly, looking at me.

My brains swam. "I'm going to faint," I said. "Take care of this mess, will you, Percival?"

"Percival? Now that's very interesting," expostulated Dick Tracy the Elder. "You told me it was Gerald."

"Can't you two tell a false alarm when you see one?" I shouted. "We'll send you engraved invitations if anyone gets raped here, I promise!"

I stomped inside, collapsing onto Martin's loveseat. Richard passed with the Aphid Spray. "Give me that." I grabbed it, swallowing the nozzle.

"Hey. where is everybody?" he asked.

I shut my eyes. "Looking for the singer," I whispered. As I said it the million tiny gears locked into place at last. I went to my bedroom and started very neatly packing a suitcase, something I should have done one Saturday morning ten months ago. As I was zipping up my cosmetic bag, my husband came in and shut the door.

"Okay. Eva, what's going on?"

"Martin," I said, "I'm leaving you." I didn't think I'd ever utter those words to the kindest man I had ever met.

Martin watched me toss some knee socks into the suitcase. "So I see."

Which invidious variation of the Weaver Method was this? I had expected a comment like "You can't be serious," followed by a patient and bulletproof supporting argument. "I've known it for a long time," Martin said. "I just didn't know what to do about it." His quiet and familiar voice cracked me in half.

"There was nothing you could do about it," I tried to explain, my voice tattering like an ancient deed. "Nothing at all, believe me." I unhitched a few blouses from their hangers and began folding them.

"Are you leaving me for someone else?" Martin asked.

I began to say no, then didn't: that would be stabbing Martin in the back. "Yes." Fox's breath whispered over me, warm, alive as the tropics. It could not salve the pain. "I don't know why this happened," I said, "but it did."

"I don't believe what is happening," Martin said, sagging into the chaise longue. He said nothing for a few moments. "What did I do wrong? Did I leave you alone too much? I thought that was what you wanted."

"That *was* what I wanted," I whimpered. "Maybe you shouldn't have given it to me." I threw some skirts into the suitcase. "I was a lousy risk, Martin. You should have married a more law-abiding citizen, maybe one from Radcliffe."

Now Martin came over to the bed and took my arm; had I never met Fox, that touch would have quite contented me. Was I out of my mind? "Don't go. I love you, Eva. You're my wife."

"Don't say that," I trembled. "It's too late now." Jesus Christ! I loved Martin, too! Why was I leaving him? *You love Fox more*, Chuck said. Fox? Who in shit was Fox? Some stevedore I had met on a wrestling mat?

"It's not too late," Martin whispered. "We have so much going for us, Eva."

The kid turned into a can opener and started gouging up my insides. I sat on the bed, pressing my fist into my stomach. "I cannot be your wife anymore, Flappy." I said. "You should find someone else who would love you better than I. Paloma, maybe."

"Don't be an ass!" Martin said sharply. "I don't want anyone else!"

Ah, but I did, and love had finally overtaken the guilt. I

shut the suitcase and dragged it off the bed. "I have to go."

"I don't understand this at all." Martin sat in bewilderment on the bed, close to tears. I thought about all the times I had made love to him there, and how beautifully simple it had been. Oh! If I loved a man with everything that was in me and he left me for another woman, I would not understand either. Would Fox do the same to me five years down the road? Perhaps I should ask Martin for a leave of absence, with all goods and services returned with a smile if Fox did not work out. *You fucking coward*, Chuck slapped. *Go to hell*. The kid bolted. I ran to the bathroom and threw up.

Martin came in after me. "You're not well, Eva," he said. "We have to talk about this when you're feeling better."

Half of me agreed completely. The other half slept in Fox's warm arms, home at last. It was time to cash in my chips, twice in one lifetime. "I've got to go, Martin," I said. "Don't try to talk me out of it."

"Where are you going?"

"I'm not sure." My God, if I had known leaving Martin would be this excruciating, I never would have touched Fox. *That's baloney*, Chuck said, *You would have touched Fox if he were radioactive*. I looked at my husband sitting utterly forlorn on the bed and finally understood why Percival's wives had not taken his cottages in Cape Cod or Peru or anything else belonging to him. I wondered where they were now, and if they were happier. "Forgive me," I said, and left.

I don't remember how I got out of the house unnoticed; things were getting sloppy up in Overhead Accounting. Lionel was at the piano pawing some of my unfinished hymns for everyone's entertainment. I heard Ruth in the kitchen forbidding the caterers to say "Praise the Lord" any more that evening. Chuck? In the greenhouse, killing the plants. Percival must have been showing the policemen the gymnasium. I got to the garage, fired up the Bavaria, and backed out of my freshly shoveled driveway: Martin's clean crisp dollars had been instrumental in his wife's escape.

Three hours later I pulled into Nizor's Lunatic Asylum in Stockbridge. The snow had slowed me down. "Is Dr. Chubb around?" I asked the nurse at the desk.

"Was he expecting you?" she asked. "What is your name, please?"

My real name? How the hell should I know? I hesitated for so long that she had to ask me again. "Uh—Hathaway." I had awful cramps. "You're not booked up, are you? I'll go to the Red Lion Inn."

"No, no," she said. "Just one moment." She dialed a number. "Hello, Dr. Chubb? Were you expecting a Miss Hathaway? I see. Yes. Certainly." She hung up and peered at me. "Are you any relation to Charlotte Hathaway?"

"I'm her daughter. Insanity runs in the family."

She took me up to a room on the second floor. "I suggest you get a good night's sleep. Dr. Chubb will be in in the morning."

"Thank you." I removed my coat.

The nurse stared down at my dress.

"My Lord! Are you all right?"

I looked down for a very long moment. A large stain covered the front of my dress. I looked at the nurse and looked down at my dress again. "This is a surprise," I said. "A great surprise. A real surprise." My heart started to pound like the surf against the Asbury Park pier. I could hardly swallow. "Would you mind leaving? I should take a shower. What a surprise."

"Should I bring you some tampons?"

"This is quite a surprise."

I turned the shower on full force and sank to the floor of the tub, watching red turn pink, then clear, then run down the drain. I didn't believe it; the circle was complete, but there was nothing inside it. "You don't understand," I shouted. "I wanted that baby!" Chuck pulled my ears. *Don't ever use that expression,* she said. *It's quite offensive.* "Wrong!" I shouted. "The whole circle's offensive!" I started to laugh at myself. What the hell else could I do? I was back to Square One, with wrinkles this time! "Buddy."

I hooted, "do what You want! Shit! I surRENder!" If I shouted *surrender* with just the correct loudness and sharpness, it lingered deliciously against the tile walls before falling dead to the floor. Aha! What a hymn! *Shout Surrender!* I practiced the closing cadence.

The nurse stormed into the bathroom. "Miss Hathaway. I'm going to have to ask you to be more quiet."

"Who gave you permission to come in here?" I snapped. "What a shitty hotel."

"Take this sedative." She felt my forehead. "You have a high fever."

"I want a pregnancy test."

The nurse took one look at the rose in which I was bathing and smiled very patiently. "Of course, Miss Hathaway. First thing in the morning." She helped me dry off, then got me into my pajamas. "What is that?"

"A crowbar," I replied. " I can't sleep without it." I pulled open the bedtable drawer. There lay a tract, *When Your Children Fail You.* I balled it up, threw it away, and replaced it with the crowbar. The kid was still kicking me, I could swear it. "Don't worry," I said, patting my stomach. "We'll get you all fixed up."

Chuck sighed.

Dr. Chubb smiled at me. "Two weeks have done you a world of good," he said. "You're a much more receptive patient than your mother."

"I've only been here once," I replied, getting into the Bavaria.

"Don't feel bad about that baby. Eva," Chubb said. "You can always try again."

I laughed. "We'll see."

"Are you going to tell your husband about it?"

"About what? My coming here or the baby?"

"Both."

"Depends on the husband." I hit the ignition.

"Where are you going?"

"Home for Christmas."

I drove south to New York, never west to Boston again. As always, my metabolism surged a notch as the skyline of Manhattan jagged into view. I took a spin down Fifth

Avenue, smiling at the jaywalkers chugging blindly under mounds of disgusting, superfluous, hedonistic Christmas gifts. Ah, life! I was going to hang on to a ripe old age, bugging the shit out of Fox.

I parked the car in a garage two blocks from his apartment. "How long, miss?" the attendant asked.

"Ten minutes." That way, if he threw me out, I could make a quick getaway to Peru, Vermont.

I gave the doorman some song-and-dance about a surprise visit, adjusted my red hat in the lobby mirror, snuck up the elevator to Fox's apartment, and stood outside his door listening to him butcher Mozart. The kid needed a lot of work, with me. His voice had regressed atrociously. I pushed his buzzer, swallowing the imps caroming like loose toads in my throat. My blood began to slowly stir, this time for good.

"Who's there?" he called. I didn't answer.

I rapped again two minutes later. This time he opened the door.

Surprise your opponent. "Is this the Moron Rehabilitation School of New York?" I asked. *No, no, NO! Don't cry now, you idiot!* shouted Chuck. I disobeyed.

Fox eyed me a moment then bowed effulgently: a tenor, an encore. "At your service."

ABOUT THE AUTHOR

Janice Weber is, in fact, a successfully married concert pianist who makes her home in Boston. Her first novel, she says, "is not autobiographical, and you may quote me on that to my mother-in-law."